HOT CA$H,

COLD CLEWS

Hot Ca$h, Cold Clews

By Erle Stanley Gardner

Crippen & Landru Publishers
Cincinnati, Ohio

For information contact:
Crippen & Landru, Publishers
P. O. Box 532057 Cincinnati, OH 45253 USA

Web: www.crippenlandru.com
E-mail: info@crippenlandru.com

ISBN (softcover): 978-1-936363-46-9
ISBN (clothbound): 978-1-936363-45-2

First Edition: July 2020
10 9 8 7 6 5 4 3 2 1

CONTENTS

Introduction

Erle Stanley Gardner was one of the most prolific American authors of the twentieth-century. Best known as the creator of Perry Mason in the eighty works about the feisty lawyer, Gardner was also dubbed the King of the Pulps long before Perry and Della appeared. Loyal Crippen & Landru customers will know about Gardner's pulp career from the three previous volumes of Gardner's works edited by Bill Pronzini.

Born in 1889, Gardner came from a Boston family who moved to California when Erle was still young. The wilderness appealed to him. Gardner's father was an engineer who took his son to the rough country in Alaska and California. Gardner became fascinated by the deserts and barren, uncharted land in these areas, and many of his works featured them. Gardner wanted to live free enough to enjoy the land.

A human dynamo, Gardner struggled to stay focused long enough to complete a formal education. He opted to study the law in an office rather than sit in a law school classroom. His boundless energy served him well in the courtroom, but he soon chafed at life at a desk. He longed to be free of the confines of society and to that end, he chose to be a writer.

In the 1920s, Gardner began to write a novelette (defined as a story of 7,500 to 17,500 words) every three days. He came home from the law office and wrote until the wee hours of the morning. Using this regimen, he produced more than 600 short works of fiction before he finalized the switch to novel writing.

While many stories were hard-boiled, Gardner wrote about a variety of characters from lawyers to con-men. In the days of the Depression, even Gardner's con-men worked for the greater good. Lester Leith, the anti-hero of this volume, was a modern-day Robin Hood with panache. He gave his ill-gotten gains to the poor after taking a well-earned commission.

Leith lived alone in a luxurious apartment served by his butler Scuttle, who was, in fact, a police officer by the name of Edward Beaver. The faux butler had been placed in Leith's home to catch him in the act of robbing the rich. Leith was open about his ways, even sending Scuttle out for the odd assortment of gear that he needed to complete each robbery. The fun of the stories, which matched Gardner's own sly humor, was missing in so many of his other works. Leith accumulated the oddest variety of items for each theft and prided himself on the slippery ways in which he continued to avoid capture. Sixty-five stories from February 1929 to July 1943 appeared in all, making Leith one of Gardner's most enduring pulp characters along with Ed Jenkins. [Note: A complete bibliography is included at the end of this volume.]

Most of the stories appeared before the advent of Perry Mason in novel form and ran almost monthly in *Flynn's Detective Fiction Weekly* from 1929-1931. The pulp magazine asked for a new Leith story ever three weeks, and three of the stories appeared in the first month of the character's appearance.

By the early 1940s, Gardner had all but abandoned pulp writing for his more lucrative novels. By the time of his death Gardner had written more than 125 books, 80 of which belonged to the Perry Mason series, the character for whom Gardner is most remembered.

The Leith stories have languished, gathering dusts in a few anthologies and the collections of pulp magazine aficionados. The major difficulty in getting copies of the stories is price and availability. Single issues run between $40 to $100 apiece. If a collector could find all those issues, the cost would run into the high four-figures. The stories in this collection came from Gardner's own records at the Harry Ransom Center at the University of Texas in Austin. The collection there includes almost all of the 650 short works that Gardner wrote for the pulps.

In the early 1950s, Fred Dannay ran a series of Leith stories in *Ellery Queen's Mystery Magazine*. Dannay published five novelettes from *Detective Fiction Weekly* for the magazine, most likely from Dannay's own collection. The stories were met with such applause that the stories were later collected into *The Amazing Adventures of Lester Leith*, published in 1980. Gardner's estate made a few collections of Gardner's short works in the months after his death in 1970, which provided a few more stories. Since the anthologized stories could be collected with ease, readers have only been able to see the character from the vantage point of this handful of stories. Any appearance of the dapper detective since then has come from a previously anthologized story. This new collection nearly doubles the readily available stories regarding the charming Mr. Leith. We hope to produce more Gardner collections in the near future.

Jeffrey Marks
Cincinnati, OH
May 2020

Hot Cash

CHAPTER I

Harry Burr had a platform presence, a booming voice, and glassy eyes. He became a "reformer." His activities netted him fifty thousand dollars a month. The newspapers referred to him as "the great crusader. "

Sticky Hume was a gangster.

Sam Milne was a watery-eyed lawyer who knew which side of the bread held the butter. He handled the payoff which passed between Sticky Hume and the great crusader. No one else knew Burr could be reached. Sam Milne alone contacted the gangs.

Harry Burr was a crusader and a doer. Sam Milne was a crook and a thinker. Sticky Hume furnished the funds. Hume got them from various underworld activities. They called him "Sticky" because things had a habit of sticking to his fingers.

Sticky's tailor was the best in the city. The nails which had once been broken from manual labor, were now manicured, polished, carefully shaped.

Every month Sticky Hume levied rich tribute on those under him. The money dribbled in from various and sundry sources. Speakeasies dipped into cash registers. Mysterious trucking concerns wrote checks to "cash." These various sums trickled through numerous hands, the flood of cash growing in volume as the stream concentrated higher up.

How much money Sticky made in return for protection, no one actually knew. Harry Burr got fifty grand a month. Sam Milne paid it to him, taking the money from Sticky, seeing that it was delivered to Burr.

Milne was crooked and because he was crooked, he had sold himself too early in the game and too cheaply. Sticky Hume owned him body and soul. Sam Milne was avaricious, but he made piking money compared with Harry Burr.

"Blinky" Bings wanted to be a gangster. He had done an occasional stick-up job, playing a lone hand. A blonde spotted him for easy sugar and told him she loved him. Blinky took her into his confidence. The blonde fell for another sugar, and Blinky, feeling tough, made threats. The threats frightened the new sugar, who was a salesman. He blabbed his fears to the blonde. The blonde stepped into a pay station, called police headquarters, and talked.

An hour and fifteen minutes later, Blinky regarded the handcuffs on his wrists with a dazed expression, and asked the officers what they had against him.

The officers told him.

The charges covered every job Blinky had confided to the blonde.

Blinky went to jail. A runner steered him to Sam Milne, the lawyer who had a pull. Blinky had some two thousand dollars the blonde hadn't taken. Sam Milne took that Blinky got off on a technicality and a split with an assistant district attorney. He owned the clothes he stood in and had a horror of blondes. He thought Sam Milne was the smartest man in the world.

Sam Milne cultivated him, watched him through narrowed lids, studied him over glass rims, stared speculatively at him over cigarette smoke. After three months of this grooming, Sam Milne was ready.

Blinky was a new gangster. He wanted to be tough. He was credulous. His expressionless eyes blinked at the world in perpetual wonderment. He could be hard with a gun or quick with a sling shot, but his mental processes were always groping in a fog.

Sam Milne kicked the black bag.

"If you had what's in there, Blinky, you could be a big shot."

Blinky blinked at the lawyer. "How?" he asked.

"Fifty grand," explained Sam. "It's a pay-off."

"Who?" said Blinky.

Sam Milne got tip and walked to the scarred door of his office. He tried the lock. Then he went to the window and lowered the shade. The precautions were utterly senseless, but they convinced Blinky.

Sam returned, lowered his voice.

"Harry Burr," he whispered. "And if anybody knew I'd spilled it to you we'd both be put on the spot."

Blinky's eyes blinked.

"I thought he was the big reformer!" he said. "Everybody does," replied Sam.

"But," protested Blinky, "he was elected to office on the solemn promise he'd clean up the underworld."

"Yeah," said Sam. "He's cleanin' it all right."

He lit a cigarette and studied Blinky's face. He had taken a big chance with the giving of that information. Blinky couldn't be trusted with it. No one could be trusted with it. Sam Milne would have to keep tabs on Blinky now, from the time he left the office until he hit a marble slab at the morgue. Sam didn't intend the interval should be great.

"Huh!" said Blinky.

Sam waited until Blinky's eyes were on his face. Then he suddenly let a smile twist his countenance, the smile of one who has thought a great thought.

"Blinky," he said, slowly, impressively, "there's no reason why we should sit back and let that stuffed shirt take all the gravy. You and me could be splitting fifty grand by midnight if you wanted to show some nerve."

Blinky let his mouth sag half open.

"I got the nerve," he said. "I ain't much good on thinkin' things out."

Sam Milne smacked his palm against the thigh of his right leg. "It's simple, too!"

Blinky blinked attentively.

"Sure," said Sam, and lowered his voice to a hissing whisper. "The money comes from Sticky Hume. He pays it to me. I contact Burr. I'm the only contact he has. No one's in the know except us.

"Now I'm taking that bag out there to-night. Suppose you should follow and use a gun? See?"

Blinky looked at his friend with puzzled eyes.

"Stick him up?" he asked.

"Hell, no. There's a car follows me until I turn in to Burr's driveway," lied Sam Milne. "They'd smear you. No. What you do is stick up Burr after he gets the bag."

Blinky let his forehead look like a washboard.

"Huh?" he asked.

"Cinch," said Sam, and chuckled. "Burr can't make a squawk. How in hell could he explain having fifty grand in a black bag in his house? He couldn't. He was elected on a reform ticket. He tells every time he gets in public about having sacrificed his private business interests in order to execute a public trust. Burr couldn't even make a squawk, I tell you! You'd only have to walk in, lift the bag and walk out. You might have to croak one of the servants, but what's a croaking compared with twenty-five grand? And I could get you off."

"You could get me off?"

"Sure. I could guarantee it. The witnesses wouldn't dare to testify. I could get you off if you got caught, but you wouldn't get caught."

Blinky heaved a sigh and relaxed.

"How do I work it?" he asked.

"Simple. I'm leaving for Burr's house in ten minutes. You drive out there and park your car on the slope, so it's downhill. Keep the motor running. When you see me go in the driveway, you go to the front door carrying a black bag. You ring the bell. A butler will answer. You say that you have a bag to deliver to Mr. Burr from Mr. Sam Milne. The butler will let you in. About that time I'll be coming in the side door with the real bag that's got the money. You drop your bag. Start for the big room that's to the right and pretty far back. That's where Burr always receives the take.

"It's a study. There'll be a man with Burr that's tough. His name is Dumoe. He's supposed to be a secretary. He's really a gunman, and acts as a bodyguard. Don't take any chances with Dumoe. Sock him on the bean or plug him. Make a good job of it. Take the bag and go to 6478 Milpas Street. There's a furnished house there, and a garage. Here's a key to the house. I keep it for parties now and then. Hole up there until I come for you. Put the car in the garage."

Blinky let his jaw sag.

"It's sure complicated," he said. "Where do I get the car?"

"It's down here, parked in front of the office—a car I use once in a while for an undercover job."

Blinky started checking things off on his fingers. "Listen," said Sam, "you've only got to do three things, and then you'll get—" He crossed to the black bag, flung back the straps, slipped the catch, opened it up. "Half of this."

He looked back and up over his shoulder.

Blinky's eyes were staring.

"A cinch," said Sam Milne, the crooked lawyer.

Ten minutes later he escorted Blinky to the door of his office building, pointed across the street.

"There's the car. The keys are in it. Go to it." Blinky crossed the street.

The car was a new one, yellow, of distinctive lines. It had been in a smash recently and the left headlight was dented. The right rear fender was crumpled flat. The body had a long scrape of paint removed from it. A red tag dangled from the steering wheel. The car had been parked in front of a fire plug.

Blinky crossed to it.

Sam Milne stood watching him.

Blinky crawled in back of the wheel, regarded the red tag on the steering wheel, looked at Sam. Sam made a motion with his hands, as though to tear up the red tag.

Blinky tore up the tag.

Sam Milne went back to his office and picked up the black bag. He was smiling.

CHAPTER II

A Man With Brains

The residence of Harry Burr sat well up on a hill. The lights of the city showed as a twinkling sea of brilliance. The residence itself was like its owner, pretentious, blatant in its loud respectability.

Sam Milne swung his car into the private driveway.

He noticed that the car with the crumpled fender, the dented headlight and the scratched finish on the body was parked just where he had told Blinky to park it, under the street light, against the curb, headed downhill.

Sam Milne took his time about crawling from his own sedan, picking up the black bag and climbing the three steps to the side door.

Charles Dumoe, the big bodyguard, swung open the door. "'Lo, Sammy."

'"Lo, Gnick."

"Got the stuff?"

"Sure."

A huge form stepped forward, making something portentously impressive of the mere advance. A voice boomed forth a greeting. "Ah, Samuel Milne! Counsellor, good evening."

Harry Burr was a tall man who bulged importantly. He wore spectacles on a black ribbon and had a habit of thrusting his right hand into his waistcoat. When he spoke, even upon the most trivial subjects, he used a platform manner that made his presence dominate the surroundings. Loud voiced piety exuded from every pore.

"Good even'n'," said Sam Milne. He was jealous of Harry Burr's greater success in crookedness. Milne had sold out cheaply. He felt that he had brains. Harry Burr had nothing but a front.

"Ah," said the personage, glancing at the bag through his glasses, the black ribbon cutting against the impressive jowls of the man as a dignified color contrast, "you have brought something?"

It was always his manner. Always he acted upon the assumption that both of his hearers would believe the synthetic surprise with which he received the "small campaign contribution "which Sam Milne delivered.

The man had avoided sincerity for so long that he refused to be sincere, even with himself. He always went through the same deep-toned formula, as though his hypocrisy would convince his own credulity.

"Yeah," said Sam Milne. "I got a little campaign contribution, an'—"

He broke off, staring at the curtains which led into the alcove behind which was a door. An arm and a gun protruded through those curtains. Just above the gun was the glitter of an eye showing through a mask which had been carefully adjusted.

"Stick'm up," said the voice of the newcomer.

There was something grimly ferocious in the tone. Blinky Bings had nerve if no brains.

The great crusader collapsed into a jellyfish. Charles Dumoe narrowed his eyes, estimated his chances as being less than ten to one, faced death with a smile.

His hand went to the left armpit. He had the gun half drawn when Blinky's bullet crashed into his chest. Blinky was handy with a gun.

Burr's eyeglasses dropped to the end of the black cord and dangled. His pudgy hands covered his glassy eyeballs.

"Oh, my God!"

Sam Milne held his hands high in the air.

Blinky took the bag, vanished through the door. Charles Dumoe rolled over on the floor, groaned. "He got me," he said.

Blood frothed from his lips. Sam Milne regarded him with disinterested speculation. Harry Burr moaned inanely, "My God, my reputation! Ruined! Murder in my own house! There'll be an investigation. The one man I can't control will batter my reputation to tatters! I can't—"

Sam Milne grabbed him by the arm. "Quick. Let's see where he goes."

He pushed the great crusader through the curtains, through the doorway. The butler was running toward them. "Something the matter—"

Sam pushed the butler to one side, piloted Harry Burr to the front room. They stared out of the window. Blinky Bings was just climbing into the yellow car. In the light of the big street lamp the defects of the car showed clearly—the battered headlamp, the crumpled fender, the long body scratch.

Blinky Bings jerked off the emergency brake, gave the car the gas, and went down the hill.

"Hell," said Sam Milne, "I know that car. I seen it only this afternoon. Quick, let's get back to Dumoe!"

They went back to the wounded bodyguard. He was sitting up. His face was the color of putty.

"Bye, boys!" said Dumoe

"You can't die here—you can't die-here—you can't die here!" exclaimed Burr. "Drag him out, Sam, take him away. He'll ruin my reputation. There'll be an investigation—"

Sam Milne jabbed a rigid forefinger into the flabby waistcoat. "Shut up," he said, "and listen to brains talk."

Burr shut up.

On the floor, the wounded guard tried to smile. It was a feeble attempt.

"Listen," explained Sam Milne, the crooked lawyer. "This is once when you've got to use brains. Dumoe's going to cash in. If he's found dead here there'll be hell to pay, because you've got enemies who will insist on an investigation. You can't complain about what was taken. But I could. If they'd held me up I could have made a legitimate squawk.

"Now here's what we'll do. I'll load Dumoe into my car. I'll go far enough away to be out of the neighborhood. Then I'll raise a yell we were held up and robbed. I'll say Dumoe got shot in the robbery. See?"

"There won't be any shots," protested Burr.

"The hell there won't," said Sam, and picked up the telephone. He dialed an emergency number.

Sticky Hume answered in person.

"Lis'n, Sticky, this is Sam. I delivered the bag. A stickup followed me in and got the bag. Dumoe got the works when he went for his rod. He's cashing in. Now I don't know the guy that pulled the job, but I do know the car. It's a yellow car and it's easy to identify because it's been in a smash. There's one headlight cocked up and one fender gone. There's a big scratch along one side where the paint's gone. It's driven by a wise guy. He followed me around some this afternoon, making sure I got the gravy, I guess.

"But here's the point. He had the car parked in front of my office building while he was working up that end of it. And it was parked in front of a fire plug, see? Well, the traffic officer on duty, Pete Delano, tagged the car. I saw the red tag on the steering wheel when I came out. Just happened to notice the crate because it was new and bad been smashed. See?

"Now Pete Delano's got the record of that tag, the license numbers and the registration. See? It may be phony, but it may give us a lead.

"You start some of the boys running down that end. But get this straight and fast. I'm loading Dumoe into my car and I'm going to drive straight to the corner of Bradley and Washington Boulevard. I'll park the car there. You load some of the boys in a big sedan and send 'em there to meet me. When I drive up let them cut loose with their rods and smoke up the neighborhood. And I want to be nicked in the shoulder. For God's sake tell 'em to be careful about that.

"Then they make a get-away, see? The neighbors will come out on the run, and then I'll describe the stick-up, what happened and all that. It'll give Burr an out on the murder and on the stick-up."

There was one good thing about Sticky Hume. He thought fast and he reached quick decisions.

"Get started, Sam," he said. "It's a good idea. Thank God you got brains."

Sam hung up the telephone.

The glassy eyes of Harry Burr had lost their alarm and were beaming approval.

"Most excellently done, Samuel! Most excellently done, indeed! I feel that I am greatly indebted to you for your quick handling of a most unfortunate—"

"Shut up," said Sam, "and help get Chuck in my car." The crusader stepped back, frowning.

"You forget, counsellor, that I might get blood on my clothes. That would be hard to explain. James will assist you."

The butler bent down to Dumoe. "Take it fast," said Sam. "He won't last long."

They loaded him into the sedan, propped him in the front seat. Sam slid in behind the wheel.

Dumoe tried to make some comment, but the only sound was a choked gasp.

Sam sent the car back to the road, lurched forward. Dumoe lunged against the windshield, put out a feeble hand to straighten himself, mustered his strength to grin at Sam. Sam concentrated upon driving. The gangster's car was at the appointed place before Sam Milne drove up. Sam saw the glint of light on weapons and was worried.

It would be a fine chance for Sticky to rub him out if Sticky wanted to take advantage of the opportunity. But Sam had been valuable to Sticky. He couldn't figure where Sticky would gain.

Chunky Henderson got out of the gangster's car. He had a rifle. Chunky was a dead shot. He motioned to Sam to swing a little more to one side. Sam swung, leaving his left shoulder exposed.

Chunky fired.

Sam felt the impact of the slug, the stabbing pain. He was hurled back against the cushions of the seat. His left arm was numb. Great pains were tearing his shoulder.

Dumoe slumped forward, and spoke clearly, above the noise of the bursting bubbles.

"Good work, Sam. Glad I lasted. Bye." He collapsed forward like a sack of meal.

The gangsters fired twice into his body just to make sure it wouldn't look fishy.

Adjoining houses flamed into light as doors were opened, window shades raised. Men shouted. Someone blew a police whistle. Women screamed. The gangsters shot out a couple of windows, and then drove away.

A police siren wailed before the first of the householders had summoned sufficient courage to approach the riddled sedan where Sam Milne nursed his wounded shoulder, where Charles Dumoe sagged limply in a lifeless heap.

Sam Milne babbled out the facts.

"I had a cash fee—fifty grand in a bag. I picked up Dumoe uptown and asked him to ride with me, just in case. A masked guy with a yellow car slid up alongside and shot Dumoe before he had a chance. I tried to swing the car and he smashed me with a bullet in the shoulder.

"He jumped out, grabbed the bag and beat it. I don't know if he had anybody else in the car or not. The car had a crumpled fender, a dented headlight. There was a big scratch along the body.

"I saw that same car parked in front of my office this afternoon. It had been tagged for parking in front of a fire plug. The owner must have known I was to get this fee, and followed me to hold me up.

"The license numbers may be phony. But you should be able to trace the car. The man looked sort of familiar —the clothes, I mean.

"He wore a pin-striped blue suit with a red necktie. There was one button off on the left cuff. He had on a brown velour hat and wore a mask."

When Sam Milne had said all of that he slumped down behind the wheel and professed that he was too weak to answer any more questions.

The clanging bell of the ambulance scattered the crowd. The officers jumped into the police machine, started out with roaring motor and spinning wheels.

White-garbed attendants examined the two men in the car. "One of 'em's okay except for a shoulder shot. The other's for the coroner."

Stretchers were slid along the ground. The white-clad men opened the door of the sedan and eased Sam from the seat to the stretcher.

CHAPTER III

"He Isn't to Talk!"

Sticky Hume worked fast and to some purpose.

"Get Sam Milne where he don't have to talk." he instructed one of his henchman. "Have a doctor put him in a private hospital and clamp on the lid. Keep him there until the whole thing blows over.

"Get Sergeant Crothers to handle the chase for the stickup guy in person. Tell Crothers I said the stick-up isn't to talk. Get the bag of coin back, and see that the stick-up goes bye-bye.

"Now get started." The men got started.

Samuel Milne was rushed to a private hospital. A beetle-browed doctor who had sufficient pull with the hospital to get exactly what he wanted, had Sam Milne "buried "where he could not be interviewed even by the most persistent reporter.

Charles Dumoe went to the morgue.

Sergeant Crothers assumed personal charge of the picked men who went hurtling out to the address disclosed by the registration of the yellow car that had been tagged in front of the fire plug.

For the traffic officer had remembered the car perfectly. His record showed that the license were probably genuine, since the registration was for just such a make and model of car.

The registration numbers were taken from the officer's record of tags for traffic violations. The numbers were looked up on the register of machines and found to belong to one Ned Bings, who had given his residence as 6478 Milpas Street.

Doubtless Blinky Bings would have been astounded to have known that the car he was driving had been purchased and registered in his name. But many things would have astounded Blinky, had he but known them.

The police detail slipped quietly through the darkness as they surrounded the house at 6478 Milpas Street. Sergeant Crothers himself was the one to slip into the garage and point to the car with the dented headlight, the crumpled tender, the scratch along the smooth finish of the yellow body.

"Boys," he whispered, "this man is a killer. Don't take any chances."

The officers took their stations. A low whistle signified that everything was in readiness. Sergeant Crothers himself marched to the front door, pounded upon the panels, rang the bell, and then stepped well to one side, against the wall of the place.

Blinky Bings would have given them a fight in any event. He had too much nerve and too little brains to have submitted to arrest.

But Blinky never had a chance to determine what he was going to do.

He came to the door, opened it. "You, Sam?" he asked.

Sergeant Crothers kicked the door open with his foot. Blinky staggered backward. He was reaching for his gun as the lights glinted from the shield of the sergeant.

Crothers gave him just enough of a chance to get his hand on his weapon. Then the sergeant fired. He continued to fire until his gun was empty. Then he stood aside so that his men could press into the hallway behind him.

"There he is, on the floor," said Crothers. "He cut down on me with his rod."

By all the rules of the game, Blinky should have been dead. But Blinky Bings had great vitality, as is frequently the case with those who have limited mentalities. He gasped out a dying statement, despite the efforts of Sergeant Crothers to speed up the demise by jerking the body about, clamping handcuffs on the bleeding wrists.

"Try and find the bag," gloated Blinky. "I checked it and mailed the check to the only girl in the world — a brunette."

The voice of Sergeant Crothers drowned out the half whisper of the sobbing statement.

"You're under arrest. Anything you say can be used against you. Come on. Get in the wagon!"

He jerked the bullet-riddled form, heaved it up.

"Get on your feet!" he yelled, and kicked.

Blinky blinked twice, grinned foolishly. His head slumped back.

"Hell," said the sergeant, "he's dead."

And he relaxed his grip, let the limp form thud back to the

floor.

After that the newspaper reporters came.

CHAPTER IV

The Steps of a Dead Man

Lester Leith sprawled at his silken ease in a gaudy lounging robe. A spiral of blue smoke eddied up from the tip of his cigarette. Crumpled newspapers were piled about him on the floor.

A huge figure, over six feet of ponderous bone and heavy muscle, regarded him speculatively through shoe button eyes.

"Scuttle," said Lester Leith, "another cigarette." He flipped the short stub into the fireplace.

The ponderous man bowed.

"Yes, sir," he said, and extended a carved ivory cigarette case. Lester Leith took a cigarette. The big man held a match. There was a ponderous deference in his manner which was utterly lacking in sincerity.

Nor was this to be wondered at. The big man who posed as valet was, in reality, no valet at all, but a police undercover man set to spy upon Lester Leith; and a police officer does not readily nor convincingly assume the role of valet. Somewhere in the city was a super-crook who could read newspaper accounts of crime, beat the police to a solution and rob the robber. The police suspected that Lester Leith was this person. A dozen times they had almost caught him, and a dozen times Lester Leith had eluded them.

In the meantime, Leith very frankly took a keen interest in the newspaper accounts of crime. His finances grew apace. A trust fund, for the benefit of the unfortunate, also grew apace. The undercover valet wrinkled his brows in perplexity. The police laid careful traps. The traps were never sprung, but the bait was always stolen.

"Scuttle."

"Yes, sir?"

"I am interested in this remarkable robbery of Samuel Milne."

"Yes, sir, so I gathered, sir."

Lester Leith regarded the pile of crumpled newspapers on the floor.

"Do you make anything out of those newspaper accounts, Scuttle?"

The valet-spy became cautiously noncommittal.

"Mr. Milne was robbed, sir. The bag had fifty thousand in cash.

Mr. Milne's companion, Mr. Dumoe, was killed. The bandit was captured and died from gunshot wounds. He had driven to the depot, checked the bag containing the loot, and mailed the claim check to a girl. The police are trying to trace the bag."

Lester Leith grinned.

"Tut, tut, Scuttle! Is that all you have gathered from the newspapers?"

The valet's caution became the more pronounced.

"Yes, sir. Except, sir, that the chances of recovering the loot are very remote. There were literally hundreds of bags and trunks sent out from the depot. Unless the police can find the destination of the bag with the money they can't expect to locate it."

Lester Leith grinned.

"And they don't even know it was a bag, Scuttle. It may have been a trunk."

"Yes, sir. That's true, sir."

"And do the police know that this, gangster, Blinky Bings, actually shipped the bag as he said? He might have been lying, you know."

The valet nodded. His caution dropped from him. He spoke rapidly, eagerly.

"Yes, sir. They've traced him. You see, the car he drove was particularly distinctive, sir. It had a crumpled fender, a scratch along the body, a broken headlight."

Lester Leith nodded.

"Rather unusual, that," he commented.

"Perhaps, sir; but it was a big help lo the police, sir. They found that one of the red cap porters remembered having seen such a car drive up to the depot."

Lester Leith regarded the smoldering end of his cigarette. "This man who was killed—Charles Dumoe, I believe his name is—what does he do?"

"He acts as secretary for Mr. Harry Burr, sir."

Lester Leith's eyes narrowed slightly. The great crusader, Scuttle?"

"Yes, sir, the same."

"And how did it happen he was riding with Mr. Samuel Milne?"

"I don't know, sir. No one does. Mr. Milne said he picked Mr. Dumoe up. But Mr. Milne cannot be interviewed. His doctor has stated that complications are threatened. Mr. Milne cannot be disturbed."

Lester Leith drummed with the tips of his fingers. "Who is Milne's doctor, Scuttle?"

The valet-spy frowned, then consulted one of the newspapers.

"Dr. Paul Gromley, sir."

"The time of the holdup is given in the papers, Scuttle?"

"Yes, sir. It was eight thirty-two, sir."

"It happened at the corner of Bradley and Washington Boulevard, Scuttle?"

"Yes, sir. The papers give all that, sir."

Lester Leith blew a smoke ring, watched it twist and writhe upon itself.

"Yes," he said, almost dreamily. "Yes, indeed, Scuttle. The papers also mention that the criminal was dead within an hour, do they not, Scuttle?"

"Yes, sir."

"Yes, Scuttle. I wonder if you could find out for me precisely when the criminal died."

The valet's mouth sagged open.

"You mean—just when he died— that is—"

Lester Leith smiled, nodded.

"Yes, Scuttle, the exact hour of his death. I want to verify some astrological predictions. By the way, Scuttle, did you ever become interested in astrology?"

"No, sir. Of course not."

"Why do you say 'of course not,' Scuttle?"

"Because it's a lot of hooey, sir. If you don't mind my saying so, sir."

Lester Leith's smile faded. He frowned.

"But I do mind your saying so, Scuttle. Astrology is believed in by a large number of people, Scuttle. No belief which is shared in by so great a number can possibly be what you describe as a lot of hooey. Even if it is nothing else, it is a reflection of the inner thoughts of a great number of people. In other words, Scuttle, it would become an index of human credulity."

The spy sighed, a ponderous heave of the awkward shoulders.

"Very good, sir. I can't follow you, sir, so I shan't try. You wished the exact hour of Blinky Bings's death, sir?"

"Yes, Scuttle. The exact hour and minute. The very second, if possible. And, by the way, Scuttle, I wish you would get me a list of the astrologers in the city. I want only the best. Those who cast a horoscope and tell the past, present, and future for a small stipend do not interest me. I want someone who charges large sums.

"You can get me that list within the next hour, also find out what time the robber cashed in his checks. I'm going out for a while. Get me my clothes, Scuttle. I must leave here by five minutes past eight at the latest."

The valet's brows knitted. "I didn't know you had an appointment to-night, sir."

He waited, hoping that information as to the nature of the appointment would be forthcoming.

Lester Leith smiled blandly.

"I have an appointment, Scuttle, to follow in the footsteps of a dead man."

The valet's surprise showed itself in a single explosive: "Huh!"

Lester Leith arose, flexed his muscles, smiled tantalizingly.

"I see that you understand, Scuttle. Now my evening clothes, my hat, coat and stick."

And the valet, recognizing that Lester Leith was not going to give out any further information, realizing also that he was in most deadly earnest about going out to follow in the footsteps of a dead man fetched the hat and coat and stick.

By eight five on the dot Lester Leith, faultlessly attired in evening clothes, swinging a stick in careless hand, waved good-by to his valet.

"Ta-ta, Scuttle. I'll be back within an hour or so, and you can have the information I wanted at that time."

Lester Leith slammed the door.

The spy glided to the window, raised and lowered the shade twice, a signal to those who waited outside, ready to shadow Lester Leith wherever he might go.

CHAPTER V

Eight Fifty-Six

Nor did the police shadows go to any great trouble to conceal their presence. Lester Leith emerged from his garage in his powerful roadster. The shadows started the police car fell in behind.

Meanwhile, Scuttle, the spy, went to the telephone and reported to Sergeant Ackley. "He's got something up his sleeve on this Milne robbery, sergeant."

There was a grunt at the other end of the wire.

"If he has, he's got more than anybody else has. We can't trace that bag from the time it hit the depot. We can't even find out where the bills came from, or what kind of bills they were. They may have been in thousands, or hundreds or ten thousands."

The undercover man muttered an assent.

"And he wants to get a list of astrologers and find out exactly what time Blinky cashed in," he said.

"He what?" yelled Sergeant Ackley.

"Yes, sir. He's dabbling around with something or other, sir. You know how he is. He's got the astrology bug now, and he wants to get the exact time Blinky passed out."

Sergeant Ackley sighed.

"All right. I'll get a list of astrologers, and I'll look up the reports and find out just when Blinky went west — that is, if it's noted. It probably ain't. G'-bye."

He hung up the telephone. The spy walked over to a humidor, helped himself to a fifty-cent perfecto, sprawled out in Lester Leith's favorite chair, and gave himself up to meditation.

He was interrupted by the frantic ringing of the telephone. Arousing himself from his half sleep, the spy shook the ashes from the perfecto, now down to its last inch, and lazily removed the receiver.

"Yeah," he said. "h'lo."

Sergeant Ackley's voice smote his ear with explosive force.

"Lis'n. Beaver, you're on a hot trail. Leith's working on this Milne case a'right and he's getting somewhere. I've just had a report from the men that shadowed him. He drove out to the corner of Bradley and Washington, stopped his car and waited. He looked at his watch once or twice, seemed to be waiting for just the right time, so the shadows noted the exact time.

"Promptly at eight thirty-two, he jumped in his car and started smashing speed records. He went up Washington Boulevard fifty miles an hour. He drove like a crazy guy, went to the Union Depot, jumped out, took a bag from the back end of his roadster, rushed to the ticket window, bought a ticket for Centerville and checked the bag. Then he put the bag check in an envelope, dropped the envelope in the mail box, sprinted for his car, and burned up the roads to the place where Blinky Bings got his—6478 Milpas Street.

"Just as soon as he reached there he seemed like a changed man.. He quit speedin', stopped his car, lit a cigarette, and drove away, just as though he had nothing to do an' all night to do it in.

"Of course we telephoned the baggage man and had the bag held. Then we had the depot police go through it. It didn't have a damned thing in it except some old newspapers and a couple of magazines.

"Now I've gone into the time that Blinky Bings was killed. He got bumped sometime around ten minutes to nine, maybe a little sooner than that. You can figure right around five or ten minutes to nine. If he wants an exact time tell him eight fifty-six. Sergeant

Crothers figures he got out there about ten minutes to nine. It took him a few minutes to look the ground over. Then he and Blinky smoked it out, and Crothers telephoned in for the ambulance at five minutes after nine.

"I'm sending one of the boys around with a list of the astrologers. Don't pay much attention to that stuff. Looks like a blind. But he may have something up his sleeve. Don't overlook nothin', an' try and get him to tell you what he was rushing around for. G'-by."

And Ackley, having given his instructions, terminated the conversation with that calm superiority which was so irritating to his men.

Beaver, the undercover man, called "Scuttle "by Lester Leith because of a fancied resemblance to a reincarnated pirate, took a knife from his pocket, impaled the tip of the cigar, and smacked his lips over the aroma. By using the knife blade he was able to smoke the weed to the very last, long after the burning tip would have made any other form of handling impossible,

A knock at the door, in the code used by the police, announced the arrival of a list of the astrologers doing business in the city. The undercover man took that list, folded it in his pocket, contemplated the humidor longingly while he debated whether or not he could count upon sufficient time to smoke another cigar.

Lester Leith solved his indecision by fitting his key to the outer door of the bachelor apartment. The valet had assumed a deferential attitude by the time Leith had swung open the door.

Lester Leith was chuckling as he handed the spy his hat and coat. He dropped into the easy chair, took a cigarette from a pocket case, struck a match.

The spy watched him warily.

Leith lit the cigarette, took a deep drag, extinguished the match, and grinned at his valet.

"You've got the information I wanted, Scuttle?"

"Yes, sir."

"At exactly what time did Blinky Bings die?"

"I don't know, sir. The police arrived at the house where he was hiding at about ten minutes to nine. They took a few minutes to look over the ground. Then they arrested Bings. He fought it out with them. Crothers telephoned for the dead wagon at five minutes past nine. The best guess any one can make as to the exact time of death is eight fifty-six."

Lester Leith frowned, regarded the curling smoke from the cigarette with slitted eyes.

"Eight fifty-six," he repeated, half musingly.

For a long moment he remained in that attitude of thoughtful concentration. Then he turned to the valet. "You have the list of astrologers, Scuttle?"

"Yes, sir."

The valet handed over a typewritten list. Leith scrutinized it with speculative eyes.

"Tut, tut, Scuttle," he remarked.

"Sir?" asked the valet-spy, hurt in his tone.

"I was rebuking you for mentioning that astrology was a lot of hooey, Scuttle. Yet you will notice the number of people who have made it a life work."

The spy grunted.

"The number of grafters who live from it, you mean, sir."

Lester Leith smiled urbanely. "Even so, Scuttle, it would not be hooey. Any profession that can support such a number of people is worthy of profound investigation…Ah, Scuttle, notice this name. Mme. Zaz-zah! What could be better? Zazzah! The very sound of the name has a subtle fascination. Can't you see a dimly lit room, smelling of incense, a lighted crystal, a chart of the various zodiacal signs, a woman with mystic brown eyes?"

"No, sir!" grunted the valet, speaking from his police experience. "I can't see nothing of the sort. I can see a dirty room packed with cheap furniture, a lot of imitation foreign tapestries, a blob of glass, a kitchenette in the back, an atmosphere that reeks of garlic, booze, and incense, and a fat woman with three chins. She'll have rough hands and dirty finger nails. She'll have eyes like a hawk. She'll—"

Lester Leith held up his hand. "Enough, Scuttle! You are ruining my dreams with your damned practicality. Have you no sense of the romantic? Have you no desire to be lifted above the mundane humdrum of everyday life? A plague on you, Scuttle, I shall go and see Mme. Zazzah at once. I shall consult with her professionally.

"And, do you know, Scuttle, I rather fancy I shall ask the madame if she can solve crimes by the use of astrology. After all, Scuttle, if an astrologer could know the exact horoscope of a criminal she should be able to tell much."

The spy blinked his shoe button eyes in sudden thought. "Such as?" he prompted.

Lester Leith smiled.

"Well, let us suppose a certain criminal managed to rob a man of fifty thousand dollars in cash and, in a burst of generosity, sent the cash to a girl friend? Don't you suppose that a good astrologer could tell the sort of a girlfriend he would have? Don't you suppose she could consult the planets and tell just when this girl friend was born? Don't you suppose—"

The spy interrupted.

"No," he snapped, forgetting his role of servility for the moment, "I don't suppose nothing of the sort."

Leith's smile was patronizing, maddening.

"Quite right, Scuttle," he said. "I didn't think you could. My hat, Scuttle. My coat, Scuttle. My stick, Scuttle."

The valet regarded him with that impotent fury which always possessed him when Lester Leith adopted that tone of superiority.

Lester Leith turned at the door.

"Good night, Scuttle."

The spy gulped. His great hands were clenched into fists.

"Good night," he snapped, then added after an interval, "sir." Lester Leith gently closed the door.

CHAPTER VI

The Time of the Crime

Sergeant Arthur Ackley, seated at a battered desk charred in deep grooves by many a careless cigarette, scrutinized the report of the police shadows who had been delegated to tail Lester Leith.

So complete were those reports that Sergeant Ackley could account for the whereabouts of the man he suspected of being the master crook of the century at any given moment.

For instance, the sergeant knew that Leith was at this very moment at the office of Mme. Zazaah. He knew that he had previously made a quick run from the scene of the Milne holdup to the house where the robber had been killed.

The reports in the hands of the officer had been rushed to him following a telephoned report from the shadows. They faithfully chronicled every move Leith had made.

Sergeant Ackley studied those reports, his feet on a corner of the desk, a soggy cigar in his thick lips, his left thumbnail scraping the bristling stubble along the angle of his jaw.

One moment he was a hulking figure going through the routine. The next instant his feet left the desk and came to the floor with a bang. The cigar sagged from his parted lips.

His forefinger jabbed a button. An officer thrust his head in the door.

"Get Beaver," snapped Sergeant Ackley.

The officer took one look at the expression on Sergeant Ackley's countenance and flashed into swift motion.

Sergeant Ackley paced the floor, his hands behind his back. From time to time he muttered to himself, low rumbling grunts. He flung away his soggy cigar, groped for another in his vest pocket, tore the end off with his huge horse-like teeth, spat explosively, scraped a match.

Beaver, the undercover man who acted as valet to Lester Leith, arrived within twenty minutes, but Sergeant Ackley glared accusingly at him.

"Say," he bawled, "when I send for you it's important!" The undercover man nodded. He was breathless.

"I came here as quick as I could—"

"All right, all right, never mind!" yelled the sergeant. "You're a damned fool. No, no, don't get mad. I'm a damned fool. We're all fools, all except that supercilious, snooty Lester Leith!"

The undercover man widened his boiled lobster eyes until they looked like shoe buttons protruding from the sockets.

"What is it?" he asked.

"The time, you fool!" Beaver looked at his watch.

"No, no," groaned the sergeant, "not the time it is now, but the time of the crime!"

Beaver's forehead washboarded with perplexity. "I don't see—"

"The time, the time, the time! Blinky Bings couldn't have done it. Leith didn't do it. He missed it by fifteen minutes. Bings couldn't have done it. That was what Leith was testing—the time. He spotted it from the newspaper accounts. No one could have done it—"

Beaver's jaw sagged.

"For Heaven's sake, sir, are you crazy? What are you talking about?"

Sergeant Ackley heaved a deep sigh, sat himself in the swivel chair, glared at the undercover man.

"Just this," he said, slowly, speaking with an evident effort to control himself. "The holdup of Milne took place at exactly 8.32 p.m. The officers cornered Bings by ten minutes to nine. Now Bings couldn't have driven to the depot, checked a bag, and got back to the house on Milpas Street by ten minutes to nine. He couldn't possibly have done it. That's what Leith was testing out. He wanted to make the run at a time when the traffic conditions were exactly the same as when Bings was supposed to have made the trip. So he waited until exactly eight thirty-two, and then he burned up the roads. And still he couldn't make the run within the time limit. The reports of the shadows show that Leith arrived at Milpas Street around two minutes after nine o'clock."

Sergeant Ackley glared at his undercover man as though that individual was responsible.

Beaver sat down, said, "Huh!" and lapsed into thought. "Then Bings didn't go to the depot," he said at length.

Sergeant Ackley grunted. "The car was seen there."

"Then he wasn't at the holdup."

"Milne described the car."

"And he must have been at the house on Milpas Street."

"Sure," agreed Sergeant Ackley with heavy sarcasm, "he was there, all right. He got killed there."

Beaver blinked.

Sergeant Ackley took the cigar from his mouth, made jabbing motions with it to emphasize his words.

"This thing ain't on the up and up, see? This here bag of money ain't where they said it was. Maybe Bings had two cars that looked just alike. Maybe he went to the depot before he pulled the crime. The red cap porter ain't so sure of the time.

"Anyhow, there's something fishy about it and that damned Lester Leith is going to whisk the cash right out from under our noses unless we look alive. Now this is important, Beaver, you go back and report every single move that dude makes. You tell me everything he does, remember everything he says.

"In the meantime, I'm going to have so damned many shadows trailing that man that he won't be able to move without a shadow dogging every step. You get me?"

Beaver nodded. "Yes, sir." Ackley frowned.

"You wouldn't think a crook could solve a crime under our noses, hi-jack the swag, and leave us without any evidence to warrant an arrest, much less a conviction, not when we had him shadowed every minute, would you?"

The question was asked impersonally, more after the manner of one who thinks aloud, but Beaver answered it.

"He does it all the time," he said.

Sergeant Ackley glared at his subordinate.

"Well, he won't do it this time. Get the hell outa here and get to work."

And Beaver heaved his big bulk to catlike feet and oozed through the door.

CHAPTER VII

Within the Sign of Cancer

It was nearing midnight when Lester Leith slipped his key into the front door of his bachelor apartment. The spy was waiting for him as a cat might wait for a mouse.

"You saw her, sir?" he asked.

"Saw whom?" asked Lester Leith.

"The astrologer, sir."

Lester Leith divested himself of his coat and hat, dropped into his favorite chair, lit a cigarette. "Yes, Scuttle, I saw her, the great Mme. Zazzah, herself."

"Was she fat?" asked the spy.

Lester Leith's nod was gloomy. "Yes, Scuttle, she was fat."

"And did the room stink of garlic and incense, sir?"

"Yes, Scuttle, the room stunk of garlic and incense."

The spy fairly beamed. "I told you so, sir."

"Yes, Scuttle, you told me so." Lester Leith's face was a mask of utter gloom.

"And she was a fake. She didn't tell you anything!" gloated the valet-spy.

Lester Leith's expression continued to be filled with utter melancholy, but he shook his head.

"On the contrary, Scuttle, she told me everything."

The valet jumped as though he had been pricked with a pin. "Everything, sir?"

"Everything, Scuttle."

The valet squirmed in curiosity. "I don't see how she could have, sir," he said tentatively.

Lester Leith gave his head a dubious shake. "Neither do I, Scuttle, but she did."

The valet took advantage of what seemed most unusual preoccupation. He lowered his voice.

"Told you what?" he asked, soothingly, invitingly.

"Everything."

There was silence in the room for the space of several minutes. Then the valet tried again.

"You mean?" He waited.

Lester Leith began to speak in a spiritless tone, the tone of a man who has been condemned and knows there can be no appeal from the sentence.

"I am to become very ill, Scuttle. The illness will start as a pain in my side. A doctor will make the wrong diagnosis and insist upon an operation. If I have that operation it will prove fatal."

The spy regarded the arch-crook with incredulous eyes.

"Why, sir?"

"Because," said Leith in lugubrious tones, "Mars is in the ascendancy and the influence of Uranus is entirely blotted out, or perhaps it is vice versa, Scuttle. I couldn't remember the technical side of it."

"Surely, sir, you don't believe all that bosh?"

Lester Leith fastened mournful eyes upon the spy. "What makes you think it is bosh, Scuttle?"

The valet-spy resorted to something he had said earlier in the evening. "It's a lot of hooey," he said.

Lester Leith shrugged his shoulders.

"Many important events have been predicted by astrologers the world over," he said. "It is a science that has been developed everywhere by every civilization. You can't pass that off as a lot of hooey, Scuttle."

"When are you to have this sickness, sir?"

"Tomorrow afternoon I am to notice the first symptoms, Scuttle."

The valet thought for a few moments in silence. "Suppose the doctor doesn't operate, sir. Then what will happen?"

"Then, Scuttle, the illness will prove fatal in any event— unless..." Lester Leith let his voice trail off into impressive silence.

"Unless what, sir?"

"Unless I can get a nurse who has astrological influences which are the exact complement of mine and make her fees contingent upon my recovery. That will give her an interest in my recovery. If her horoscope shows that she will be financially successful upon that day and hour, and I can make her financial success depend upon my recovery, then, Scuttle, I will recover!" And a new note of buoyant hope crept into Lester Leith's voice.

The valet blinked as he digested this information.

"But, sir," he said, at length, interested despite his initial unbelief, "how can you tell about this nurse?"

"Ah, yes, Scuttle. There's the point. We must get a nurse who was born on seventeenth day of July, 1907. That will bring her within the sign of Cancer—I believe it's Cancer, Scuttle—and there will be certain planets in the ascendancy that will neutralize my unfortunate planetary influences."

The valet grunted. "What a bunch of hooey!" he said.

Lester Leith got to his feet with a bound.

"It's not too late to make the late morning newspapers, Scuttle.

Get me a big display ad in the want-ad section. 'Wanted, a trained nurse who was born on the seventeenth of July, 1907. One is preferred who was born near five o'clock in the afternoon of that day. Should be good looking.' Run that ad in the papers, Scuttle. Get it in a big display box. Tell the nurse to apply by personal call and give her this address. Insert also, 'handsome wages will be paid and a big bonus.'"

Lester Leith's face was now animated. His eyes were sparkling.

"But, sir," protested the valet.

Lester Leith jumped to his feet, waving his arms in impatience. "Get that ad in, Scuttle. Get it in, get it in!"

The startled valet moved toward the telephone. "Yes, sir," he said.

The telephone was in a soundproof closet, and the valet ponderously explained the details of the advertisement to the want-ad departments. It took him some time. When he returned, Lester Leith had vanished, gone without any word, without any sound. The spy searched the apartment, confirmed his suspicion that Leith had sneaked out into the night.

A smile twisted the features of the spy.

Sergeant Ackley had seen to it that Lester Leith's ruse would do him no good. Wherever Leith went, whatever he did, he would be trailed by the skilled shadows.

Beaver helped himself to another of Leith's expensive perfectos, and dropped into the reclining chair, determined to wait up if it was all night.

Hours passed. The spy was startled from a dozing sleep by the ringing of the telephone.

Sergeant Ackley's tired tones came over the wire. "You're a hell of an undercover agent," he said.

The spy grunted a confused question. "Why — what — how?"

"Why didn't you signal the men when Leith slipped out?"

"I couldn't. He had me at the telephone, and he sneaked out while I was telephoning."

Sergeant Ackley grunted. "Did, eh ? Lucky thing I had my men watching for that very thing. He tried to make a sneak."

"What," asked the spy, in tone quivering with eagerness, "did he do?"

"Went out to the scene of the holdup. This time he tried a new stunt. He had a bunch of bags checked at different checking stations. He'd start from the scene of the holdup, rush to the checking station, pick up a bag, go to the depot and check it, mail the check, and then rush to the house on Milpas Street. He did it four times.

"Once he made it within thirty seconds of the time limit. That was when the streets were deserted. Blinky Bings never made it. He had traffic to fight, lots of traffic."

The police spy grunted his surprise. "You've looked into the bags?"

"Not after the second time. There's no use. They're all empty. He ain't interested in the bags. He's interested in the time element. He's on his way back to the apartment. Thought I'd tip you off."

"Yes, sergeant. Thanks. He's consulted an astrologer and learns he's going to be ill. He wants a nurse who was born on the 17th of July, 1907."

Sergeant Ackley's tone lost some of its fatigue.

"He's going to be sick all right!" he promised. "I'm covering him in this job so there won't be any chance of a slipup. Better get to bed, Beaver."

"Okay, sergeant, but I'm not so sure about the bags. What was it that was taken, fifty grand in cold cash?"

Sergeant Ackley grunted.

"Don't be too sure about its being cold cash. It may have been hot cash. This chap, Milne, is keeping awfully quiet, just for a hole in his shoulder. I'm going to talk with him. You go to bed."

"Yes, sir."

And Beaver slipped into bed a full ten minutes before Lester Leith clicked back the latch on his door. But the spy heard the arch-criminal come into the room, heard him chuckle as he prepared for bed, and the spy corrugated his brows in thought. Why that chuckle?

It was a triumphant chuckle, the chuckle of one who has mastered the solution of an intricate puzzle. It was the sort of chuckle which Beaver had heard before, and it always presaged a perfect coup for Lester Leith.

CHAPTER VIII

Nine Thousand for Diamonds

The want-ads brought results. Three young women, each professing to have been born on the 17th of July, 1907, were waiting for Lester Leith when that individual opened his eyes in response to an apologetic cough from the police spy. "I'm sorry, sir. There are three applicants for the position of nurse, sir. I've had them waiting as long as I dared, sir."

Lester Leith rubbed his eyes. "What's the time, Scuttle?"

"Two-thirty in the afternoon, sir."

Lester Leith yawned again. "My tub, Scuttle?"

"Ready, sir."

"And the nurses?"

"What of them, sir?"

"Which one is the best looking, Scuttle?"

The valet consulted a list of names. "A Miss Quinn, sir."

"Which one was born nearest to five o'clock in the afternoon, Scuttle?"

The valet-spy consulted the paper once more. "Miss Quinn, sir."

Lester Leith reached for a cigarette. "Which of the young women looks like the best sport, Scuttle? That is, which one has a twinkle in her eye, an appreciation of life, a verve, a vivacity for living?"

The valet had no need to consult his list. "Miss Quinn, sir. She's a knockout!"

Lester Leith gathered his bathrobe about him. "Tell Miss Quinn she's hired, Scuttle. Tell her she will receive her customary wages and a bonus of five hundred dollars if I recover from the illness I am about to have."

The valet's eyes widened. "Good heavens, sir! You don't mean to say you are going to hire a nurse before you even get sick!"

Lester Leith's eyes were cold.

"You will please convey my message to Miss Quinn, Scuttle. Let the others go. Tell Miss Quinn to wait. Give the others each one day's wages to compensate them for their time. I'll be out as soon as I tub and shave."

And Lester Leith vanished in the direction of the bathroom, from which, presently, there emerged the sounds of splashing water, the sound of a cheerful whistle.

The valet-spy moved ponderously and with dignity to the reception room, where three very keen-eyed young women regarded him anxiously.

Twenty minutes later Lester Leith entered the room. He was freshly shaven, well dressed, courtly, deferential.

Miss Quinn arose to meet him.

"Miss Quinn," said Lester Leith, and bowed, "I trust I haven't inconvenienced you, and that the terms of your employment are satisfactory."

She was a well-formed young woman with deep, hazel eyes. Her face was more that of a picture actress than a nurse, but back of the twinkle in her eyes was a shrewd glitter of common sense.

"You don't look like a sick man," she commented.

Lester Leith let his eye run appraisingly over the contours of her perfect figure.

"I feel remarkably well, thank you," he said.

The suggestion of a flush colored her cheek. "I am afraid you will have to engage another nurse," she said. "My profession is to minister to the sick, not to furnish companionship to the well!"

Lester Leith became humble. "I am sorry. But you see I am *going* to be sick. The illness will prove fatal unless I have the best of nursing."

The hazel eyes clouded with suspicion. "When is this sickness to come on?" she asked.

"At fifteen minutes past five o'clock this afternoon," said Lester Leith.

The girl raised her eyes questioningly to the spy, tapped her forehead significantly.

Lester Leith caught the motion. "No, no, my dear Miss Quinn !" exclaimed Lester Leith, "I am not laboring under any mental derangement whatever. I am merely forewarned of what will happen, and forewarned is forearmed."

The valet blurted out the solution. "He's consulted an astrologer, ma'am!"

The girl's eyes snapped. "I see," she said. "And let me tell you something, Mr. Leith, speaking professionally, you hold the thought over yourself that you're going to be ill at five o'clock, and you will be ill. Don't forget that!"

Lester Leith shook his head.

"Not at five," he said. "At five-fifteen."

The nurse sighed. "I guess you need me, after all," she said. "I'll go and get my things and be back here within an hour, ready to go on the case."

Lester Leith's good feelings seemed to melt from him. "Hurry," he said. "I'm going to need you badly. You're the only astrological antidote for the condition of my planets."

"Humph," snorted the young woman. "I'm the only mental antidote for a case of self-hypnosis!"

And she was gone.

Lester Leith turned to his valet.

"Scuttle, I want you to take this check and get it cashed."

The spy took the oblong of tinted paper from Lester Leith's hand.

"Good heavens, sir! It's for fifteen thousand dollars!"

"Yes, Scuttle. It's for fifteen thousand dollars. You will keep six thousand in cash. The remaining nine thousand you will spend for diamonds. I want some very fine diamonds, a scarf pin, a finger ring, perhaps a watch fob. Get them at Nathan's. Mr. Nathan is a friend of mine. He will sell you sound values. Return as soon as possible with the money and the jewelry."

The valet's eyes were wide in astonishment. "But I don't understand, sir!"

Lester Leith beamed at him.

"You wouldn't, Scuttle. I knew you wouldn't. And, oh yes, by the way, Scuttle, get half a dozen hand bags and place them in the back of my roadster. I shall want to conduct some experiments."

The valet's face lit with understanding. "Oh, yes, sir," he said, "experiments in crime, sir?"

Lester Leith shrugged his shoulders.

"Experiments in psychology, Scuttle," he said. "And the sooner you start, the sooner you'll return, and the sooner you return the more you'll see of the beautiful nurse. You should have a chance to get quite well acquainted with her before—"

"Before what, sir?"

"Before I go to the hospital, of course," said Lester Leith.

"Yes, sir," said the spy, and oozed to the door, the check clutched tightly in his hand.

CHAPTER IX

According to Schedule

By the time he returned, Lester Leith was engaged in conversation with Miss Quinn. That young lady had donned a nurse's cap and apron, and looked very efficient, sternly so. She was talking in low tones to Leith, and Leith, in turn, seemed more dejected than at any time the spy could remember.

"Now," said the nurse, when the spy entered the room, "you must sleep."

Lester Leith shook his head gloomily. "I can't sleep."

"Well, you can lie down, in any event. I'll read aloud to you if you can't get to sleep. But you try."

"Very well," said Lester Leith with the docility of a child. "I'll try."

He stretched himself on the couch. The nurse tiptoed about. Already the atmosphere of a sick room permeated the place.

The nurse caught the spy's eye, beckoned to him, tiptoed into an adjoining room, beckoned again.

The spy followed her eagerly.

"Listen, Scuttle—"

"Beg your pardon, ma'am, but the name's Beaver."

The hazel eyes glinted over him in humorous appraisal, and the valet-spy shifted uncomfortably under the girl's cool regard.

"All right then, Beaver. Your master's going to build up a dangerous complex if we don't do something for him. The first thing to do is humor him, treat him as a potential invalid. Then, as five o'clock approaches, we'll gradually liven things up until, first thing he knows, he'll find there was nothing to his absurd fancy."

The valet nodded ponderously.

"Have you got any whisky in the house?" she asked.

The valet flushed. "Yes. ma'am."

"Lots of it?"

"A gallon or two, of the best case goods."

"That will be fine. I'll prescribe an eggnog. See that it's loaded to a fare-you-well. And get that look of gloom off your face. What was it you gave him when you came in?"

"Some personal things he sent me for, diamonds and money."

"Diamonds and money! Are you crazy?"

The spy's head rotated upon his massive neck. "No, ma'am. I ain't. He is."

She sighed, regarded the hulking figure once more. "Then it's contagious," she remarked, and started from the room.

The big hand of the spy dropped upon her shoulder in a gesture that was half a caress.

"Just a moment. I wanted to say—er—that is—"

She turned. Her eyes were cold. She gave the impression of being a young woman who could take care of herself under any circumstances.

"Yes?" she said, and something in her tone made Scuttle's hand drop from her shoulder to his side.

"I just wanted to mention that if you'd watch and listen quite carefully, it might come in handy later on when you're called to give your testimony."

"Testimony!"

"Yes, ma'am, but don't say anything about it."

She gave a sniff that showed contempt. "You're a poor actor," she said.

"Meaning?" asked Beaver.

"That you might fool Mr. Leith, but you won't fool me," she said, and flounced from the room, leaving the spy gaping at his reflection in a mirror.

Fifteen minutes later he was summoned to bring the patient an eggnog. He followed instructions to the letter. It was loaded with whisky until the reek of it permeated the room. Lester Leith held it with quivering hand, drained it, sank back on the couch. The nurse winked at the valet, began to read aloud.

"This is the bunk!" she said at length. "Haven't we got something more interesting than this book?"

Lester Leith shook his head wanly. "I don't want anything more interesting. I want to think," he said.

The girl looked at Beaver.

"There are some French novels— er—ahem—"

"That's fine!" exclaimed the nurse. "Get me some of those."

The valet moved away and returned with some deluxe editions. The nurse started to read, and the eyes of Lester Leith glittered to a new interest in life.

"Another eggnog," the nurse called over her shoulder.

The valet knew what that meant. He loaded the second one a little heavier than he had loaded the first. As he brought it into the room, he noticed that the young nurse had, indeed, found something that was highly interesting in the books, for Lester Leith was showing a decided animation as he propped himself up on the couch.

The late afternoon passed. Five o'clock sounded. Lester Leith's eyes were bright. His cheeks were flushed. The young woman was laughing with him now, joking, chaffing him in a manner which was well calculated to make Lester Leith forget that any evil impended.

The spy glanced anxiously at the clock. The young woman frowned savagely at him. The shoe button eyes darted elsewhere. Lester Leith seemed oblivious of the time. He laughed and chatted. The minute hand of the clock hovered on the quarter hour.

"That," said Lester Leith, his cheeks flushed, eyes sparkling, "reminds me of a story which Don Kimball used to tell. Kimball is one of the greatest salesmen in the world. He's the type that can get thrown up in the air and light on his feet anywhere. Well, one time Kimball had been staying at a hotel, San Mateo, I think it was, and—"

Lester Leith broke off, a slight twinge of pain distorted his features.

"As I was saying, the clerk at this hotel was a—"

Once more the pain distorted his features. He clapped his hand to his side.

"Funny, that's a sharp, shooting pain...Good heavens! It's

quarter past five on the fifteenth day of July, 1931, the exact day and the hour that the astrologer mentioned—"

The nurse placed a firm, cool hand upon his wrist. "That's all nonsense," she said firmly. "You have allowed yourself to become hypnotized. You were telling about a Mr. Kimball, I believe. Go on with the story."

But Lester Leith doubled up in agony. He placed his hand upon his right side. "Quick, Scuttle, a doctor!" The spy looked helplessly from master to nurse.

"Nonsense," said the nurse, "it's just mental, a bit of hysteria."

Lester Leith shook an agonized head. "A doctor, Scuttle. Do as I say. Get a doctor. Call Dr. Paul Gromley. He's as good as any. I remember hearing of him somewhere—at the club perhaps. Make it snappy! I'm dying! Something I've eaten. Maybe that last batch of whisky you used in the eggnog was bad."

The nurse got to her feet. "Now let's be sensible—"

"Scuttle, do you hear me?"

"Yes, sir."

"Very well then. Get the doctor at once."

"But the nurse, sir. She says—"

"Never mind the nurse. She can argue with the doctor about the diagnosis. I don't think Miss Quinn will want to take the responsibility of diagnosing a poisoning case—will you, Miss Quinn?"

That put the matter in a different light. The nurse clamped her lips together. "Get the doctor," she said.

The spy dived into the soundproof closet, telephoned. The nurse regarded Lester Leith with a cynical eye. She took his pulse, his temperature, looked at the pupils of his eyes, snorted.

The doctor arrived twenty minutes later. Lester Leith was writhing in agony.

Dr. Paul Gromley was a squat, spidery sort of man who wore massive spectacles rimmed with horn. He regarded the patient with that degree of satisfaction which he reserved for patients of wealth who might prove to be surgical possibilities.

"Where is the pain?" he asked.

"Right here," groaned Lester Leith, pressing his hand over his right abdomen, then howling with pain from the mere pressure.

Dr. Gromley rubbed his hands. "Vermiform appendix!" he said gloatingly.

Miss Quinn eyed the doctor with cool, hazel eyes. "He hasn't any temperature," she said.

The doctor stared at her.

"Not necessary in the early stages!" he snapped.

"And he has a perfectly normal pulse and respiration," continued the nurse.

"Thank you!" gritted the doctor in tones of icy disdain, "I will make my own diagnosis, Miss—er—"

"Miss Quinn," said the nurse.

"Ah, yes," said the doctor. "This is a hospital case, Miss Quinn, and that will relieve you of any further responsibility."

Lester Leith moaned and twisted.

"No, no. She stays. She's my special nurse. I won't have any other. But I want to go to the hospital right away. I've got my room reserved. It's five twenty-six in the Bethel Foundation Clinic."

Dr. Gromley started up with surprise.

"A hospital I control," he said. "How does it happen you have reserved your room?"

"I knew this was coming, I knew it, I knew it!" groaned Lester Leith.

The nurse touched the doctor's arm. "Doctor, a word with you. It's important." The doctor glared at her.

"Minutes may mean life and death to this man," he said. "You, sir, I take it you're the valet. Telephone the hospital and tell them to get the operating room right away."

Miss Quinn continued to stare meaningly at the doctor. "You had better hear what I have to say. It's important." The doctor glowered at her, muttered something under his breath, followed her to the other end of the room. The nurse whispered to him. Scuttle telephoned the hospital.

The form of Lester Leith twitched and writhed.

From the other end of the room came Dr. Gromley's impatient voice, raised until it roared through the confines of the room.

"Madam, I don't care if he's consulted a dozen astrologers. The man has an acute attack of appendicitis. He goes on the operating table within the next thirty minutes. Call an ambulance!"

And Dr. Gromley, turning upon his heel, strode back to the side, of his patient.

Lester Leith pushed his hand into his pocket, pulled out a sheaf of bills. The greedy eyes of Dr. Gromley feasted upon those bank notes.

"Can I keep these with me?" asked Lester Leith.

"Certainly. There's a safe in the hospital."

Lester Leith groaned, sank back upon the couch, thrust the bills loosely into his trousers pocket. The diamond ring upon his finger caught the afternoon light and glittered. The tie pin coruscated blue fires. Dr. Gromley noted these things and rubbed his hands together.

CHAPTER X

The Private Guard

There followed minutes of bustle. An ambulance came clanging to the door. Stretcher bearers came up the stairs and Lester Leith was trundled on a stretcher to the elevators, down the short flight of stairs to the street, into the ambulance.

And the police shadows, watching with puzzled faces, saw Beaver, the undercover man, carrying two grips in his big hands, sprinting for Lester Leith's roadster, saw a beautiful girl in the uniform of a trained nurse climb into the ambulance. They saw Dr. Gromley jump into a powerful coupe.

Gongs clanged, a siren wailed. Motors barked and the procession tore out into the boulevard, flashed across the intersection and headed for the hospital at terrific speed.

The police shadows gawked, decided to follow, opened up their own siren and tore through the afternoon traffic.

Lester Leith was rushed from the ambulance to the room he had reserved. Busy nurses prepared him for the operation.

Lester Leith beckoned to Miss Quinn.

"See that my things are put in the safe, will you?"

The hazel eyes smiled cool efficiency. "I have already done so." Lester Leith squeezed her hand. Dr. Gromley, clad in white from head to foot, his enormous rimmed glasses looking like owl's eyes of wisdom, thrust a head into the room.

"I'll make myself ready and then we'll proceed." Miss Quinn bent low.

"Didn't the astrologer say the first doctor would make a wrong diagnosis?" she whispered.

Lester Leith's eyes widened. "My lord! Yes! She did!"

"Get Dr. Kaye," she whispered.

Lester Leith sat up in bed.

"Dr. Gromley!" he bellowed, and there was that in the imperative resonance of the volte which ill became an invalid. The white-clothed doctor, halfway down the corridor, heard that call and paused.

"Dr. Gromley!"

He came back to the room.

"A hypodermic," he suggested to the nurse.

Lester Leith waved his arms. "Hypodermic, hell! I want a consultation."

Dr. Gromley's irritation was manifest in his manner, his tone and his glance.

"My friend, you have no time for consultations. I am certain of my diagnosis. Minutes count. Seconds are precious. A matter of ten minutes may mean your life."

Lester Leith met the glowering eyes. "Have it your own way, doctor. Either I have Dr. Kaye called in in consultation, or I fire you."

The doctor's face grew the color of a broiled lobster. "Sir!"

Lester Leith grinned. "You said it. I feel better already."

Dr. Gromley turned on his heel.

"Call Dr. Kaye," he gritted. "Let me know when he arrives."

And the physician strode from the room, swishing his operating robes behind him.

Fifteen minutes later Dr. Kaye bent over Lester Leith. The patient was strangely quiet now. In a weak voice he recited the interview with the astrologer. Dr. Kaye glanced at the nurse.

"You saw him develop the—er— symptoms, Miss Quinn?"

"Yes, doctor."

"Were they similar to hysteria?"

The nurse shrugged. "They came on at the stroke of the clock, at once and violently."

Dr. Kaye glanced at Dr. Gromley, who was standing a little to one side, his chin up, his foot tapping the floor.

"Perhaps," suggested Dr. Kaye, "we had better consult."

Gromley cleared his throat.

"Seconds," he said, "are precious—"

Lester Leith propped himself up on one elbow. "Dr. Kaye," he muttered, "please take exclusive control of the case. I feel so—sleepy—Dr. Gromley—you're fired— the astrologer—said— you'd— try to kill me."

And Lester Leith gave a deep sigh and became strangely quiet.

Dr. Kaye laughed.

"Plain case of suggestion," he said. "Pulse normal, respiration normal, temperature normal—"

Dr. Gromley strode from the room.

Dr. Kaye glanced at Miss Quinn. There was the barest flicker of a smile passed between them. Lester Leith gave a gentle snore.

Two hours later he awoke, apparently his normal self, but weak, nervous, fidgety. "Nurse!"

Miss Quinn arose from the shadows and glided to his bedside.

"It's so restful here. My nerves feel as though I'd been through hell. I want to rest—rest—I want to stay here for a week. Will you see I can stay here as long as I want?"

"Certainly," she said. "Go to sleep now."

"But doesn't Dr. Gromley control the hospital? He won't have me thrown out?" '

"Certainly not. Go to sleep. You'll have a nice rest. Here's some medicine Dr. Kaye left for you."

She handed him a goblet filled with a cool, sweetly bitter fluid. Lester Leith drained it, fell back upon the pillows. A smile tilted the corners of his mouth, and he sank off to sleep.

Through the long hours of the night his special nurse dozed upon a cot. The hospital attendants moved with noiseless efficiency through the hushed corridors with their smell of antiseptics. And the puzzled police guards patrolled every exit of the hospital, under strict orders to see to it that Lester Leith was not spirited away.

But Lester Leith slept peacefully, awoke with the rising of the sun, was shaved, breakfasted, and following a call from Dr. Kaye, allowed to rise.

"You'll be all right now," smiled the doctor.

"Just nerves?" asked Lester Leith. "Just nerves and auto suggestion." Lester Leith sighed. "Can I stay here for a week?"

"If you wish. It might be beneficial, regular hours, proper food and all that sort of thing, you know."

Lester Leith nodded. "That." he proclaimed, "is fine."

And by afternoon Lester Leith was his urbane self. He distributed gifts to the hospital attendants with a lavish hand. He started a bridge game in his room, and the nurses who were off duty were hired at a fabulous price per hour to come and play with him.

He strolled out to the sun parlor, chatted with convalescents, beamed upon one and all, and by nightfall was easily the most popular man in the hospital.

But he refused to crawl between the sheets at a decent hour. He insisted that he had been accustomed to sitting up until after midnight, and won his point. Ten o'clock found him anxious to get some money from his store of ready cash.

Miss Quinn piloted him to the office on the fifth floor where there was a safe divided into compartments, each compartment numbered with the corresponding number of a room. She took a key from the girl in charge and signed a receipt. Then they opened the drawer numbered five hundred and twenty-six, and Lester Leith removed some of the bills from the large store.

On his way back to his room, he motioned to a shadowy figure sitting just inside a half opened door.

"Who's that?"

"Private guard. Mr. Samuel Milne, the one who was shot in the holdup, is in there. He fears an attack, and the doctor doesn't want any reporters to interview him. They've got a guard there day and night."

Lester Leith grunted.

They returned to Leith's room. Leith grinned at the nurse. "Tomorrow," he said, "is your birthday."

She started with surprise.

"So it is."

Lester Leith handed her a hundred-dollar bill.

"Get yourself a little present," he said.

She shook her head, pushed the bill back. "No, thank you."

The voice was cool. Leith grinned at her.

"Don't be foolish. You saved my life. Gromley would have sliced me up like a butcher slicing bologna. Go get yourself something and don't think I'll have an idea I've got a ninety-nine-year lease because I handed you a birthday present."

The hazel eyes studied Leith's for a few moments, then she smiled her thanks and took the money.

"Tomorrow," promised Lester Leith, "we'll stage a party, a whale of a celebration. We'll smuggle in a birthday cake and have candles and all the trimmings!"

And then he went to sleep, and once more he smiled in his sleep. The nurse studied him for some minutes before she retired. Her hazel eyes were puzzled, maternal, and there was a glint of tenderness in them.

CHAPTER XI

A Piece of Pasteboard

Dr. Kaye called when the birthday party was in full swing. It was, of course, handled in a silent and surreptitious manner, and the physician received quite a surprise when he walked into the room filled with tittering nurses, shades pulled down, cake with candles on the table. But the shrewd-eyed doctor oriented himself without visible change of expression.

"I dropped in for a piece of the cake," he said.

And Lester Leith, once more his genial, urbane self, bowed the doctor to a chair, made a little speech of welcome, saw that a plate contained a generous slice of cake.

"My heavens!" exclaimed Lester Leith, a look of consternation upon his features. "We've forgotten something!"

The nurses looked at him. Dr. Kaye continued to munch his cake.

"The nurse on duty at the office— a good scout! I must get her. I have some little favors to distribute, and I want her to be here."

He took from his pocket a sheaf of bank notes, each in the denomination of one hundred dollars. Gravely, he handed one to each of the nurses.

"Compliments of Miss Quinn," he said, "and in recognition of perfect hospital service."

The nurses took their presents with astonished eyes. "I'll get the nurse in the office to step in for a second," said Lester Leith. "Perhaps one of you girls had better telephone her and tell her to come; sort of add weight to my entreaties."

And he slipped out into the hall, walked swiftly to the office where the nurse on duty regarded him with a smile. "You're wanted at once in room five twenty-six," said Lester Leith.

She shook her head. "I can't leave the office."

"I'll watch it for you. You'll be surprised at what's going on in the room." Lester Leith smiled, his winning smile.

The red light on the telephone switchboard showed a call from room five twenty-six. The nurse plugged in, listened. Her eyes grew wide. She flashed Lester Leith one grateful glance.

"Oh, you're wonderful! I'll be back. You watch the place!" And she was gone.

Lester Leith moved with a swiftness of precision which was a marvel of graceful efficiency. His delicate fingers did things to the safe. A certain drawer popped open, disclosing some currency, a wallet, some papers, a watch, and a diamond stickpin.

Lester Leith opened the wallet, ran through it rapidly. There was an oblong of pasteboard with some printing and a number on it. Lester Leith slipped that bit of pasteboard into his pocket, replaced the wallet, closed the drawer.

The nurse came back, cake crumbs on the corners of her mouth, a happy smile in her eyes. She was folding a hundred-dollar bill in her hands.

"You may not know it," she said, "but you've just about saved my life!"

Lester Leith bowed. "A slight token of perfect service," he said.

The nurse patted his hand. "The doctor wants you," she said.

Lester Leith returned to his room. Dr. Kaye regarded him with twinkling eyes.

"You have a habit of discharging doctors," he said, "so I thought I'd discharge you as a patient before you discharged me as a doctor. You can stay on here if you want to, but you're completely cured. If you want to leave you can. But stay away from fortune tellers and astrologers. Don't ever let anyone predict any misfortune for you. You're too impressionable. Don't ever let anyone hypnotize you."

Lester Leith grinned, shook hands.

"Well, anyway, you showed up in time to keep my innards in place. Otherwise I'd probably have been minus a stomach or something."

Dr. Kaye departed, looked at Miss Quinn.

"A good idea. I'm a well man again. Let's check out. You have a bonus coming for saving my life." He smiled, reached into his pocket, lookout a check book, scribbled a check.

The nurse regarded it with color mounting her cheeks. "I can't accept that!"

Lester Leith shrugged his shoulders. "Call my valet. Let's get packed up."

The girl still regarded the check.

*I don't know what you're trying to do, but—"

Lester Leith grinned at her.

"Don't be finicky. You're going out of here with me. After that I'll probably never see you again and you'll never see me. There are no strings on that check. You saved my life and you went dangerously close to being blacklisted for insubordination. That's compensation. It's a business valuation on my part of the value of what you saved me."

And he suddenly became frosty in his cold reserve, treating the girl merely as an employee.

She smiled at him, her eyes misty.

"And you're being so damned impersonal just so I'll accept the money!" she said.

Her hand sought his, gave it a squeeze. Her eyes were starry. But Lester Leith still retained his air of impersonal formality.

"My valet, please."

She sighed, looked as though she intended to kiss him, then folded the check and walked to the telephone.

Thirty minutes later Lester Leith left the hospital. Within an hour he was driving the police shadows frantic by rushing his car from the scene of the holdup to the depot, checking bags, mailing himself the checks, then rushing to the house on Milpas Street. Occasionally he would stop at a checking stand to leave a bag, stopping later to pick it up. The shadows came to regard the entire matter as one of routine. They tagged along, spiritless, making notes of the time.

Traffic was heavy, and Lester Leith was unable to make the trip within forty-five minutes of the time Blinky Bings must have made it in, provided he had clone as the police claimed.

Sergeant Ackley, getting reports from his men, compared the growing list of time schedules and frowned.

Then, abruptly, Lester Leith ceased making his trips and resumed the even tenor of his ways.

CHAPTER XII

Scuttle Will Be Damned

It was ten days later. The newspapers had featured the mysterious killing of Samuel Milne. Undoubtedly the attorney had been "taken for a ride." He had been discharged from the hospital, gone to the country to recuperate. He had tried to make the trip in secrecy.

But the bullet-riddled body of the attorney had been found by the side of the road. There were no clews to the killers.

Sergeant Ackley scanned the reports with puzzled brows, started checking certain records. He chewed cigar after cigar, ran his fingers through his coarse hair, scraped his thumb nail along the angle of his jaw.

Suddenly an idea struck him.

He gave vent to an exclamation, a curse, sat himself down in his office chair after the manner of a man who had received a sudden and violent blow in the solar plexus.

"Great guns!" he yelled, and started on a clumsy run for the door.

He broke all speed limits getting to the apartment of Lester Leith. Nor did he stand on ceremony as he banged his fists upon the door. As soon as Beaver opened it, Ackley burst into the room.

Lester Leith, attired in silken dressing gown and pyjamas, was smoking lazily, indolently.

"Ah, good morning, sergeant. Or is it afternoon?"

Sergeant Ackley wasted no time in greetings. He stood in the middle of the floor,' his feet apart, his eyes glittering.

"I should have seen it all from the start!" he yelled.

"Seen what, sergeant ?"

"What you did, you damned hijacker! You figured out that Blinky Bings couldn't have done the holdup, then gone to the depot and checked the bag, got the car out to Milpas Street, and been there when the police arrived.

"Therefore something had to be wrong. Either the time element, or where he had been. But the time of the shots was fixed, and the time of his death was fixed. There was only one other solution. Those shots were not the shots that accompanied the taking of the bag. That meant the bag had already been lifted and they didn't dare to report it as having been stolen—not from the place it was taken.

"That bag didn't contain fifty-grand in cold cash. It contained fifty grand in hot cash, and it was red hot, pay-off money to some higher up.

"But Blinky Bings knew Sam Milne. Milne had defended Bings. It's in the court records. I just got 'em today. And it looks as though Sam Milne planted the whole car business. A crook wouldn't have taken such a distinctive car to pull a robbery.

"And there was a parcel-checking station in the lower floor of the office building where Milne has his office. And you went there twice, got a bag and took it to the depot.

"Here's what happened. Milne had the hot cash. He wanted to cop it without being taken for a ride. So he checked the bag in the checking station, picked up another bag he'd planted there before. And he'd staged things so Blinky would hold him up, take that bag and beat it. And he'd planned to double cross Blinky, leaving a plain trail to Bings, knowing Bings would cash in his chips trying to smoke his way out.

"Bings went to the depot with the bag all right, but it was a bag that had been taken before the shooting at Bradley and Washington Boulevard. And the bag was a frame up. It was filled with junk, maybe a layer of money on top, probably not.

"After Blinky took it, Sam Milne didn't care whether he found out the double cross or not. Milne had it fixed so the law would take care of Blinky. Blinky was just the goat.

"You figured it all out. You managed to get taken to the hospital where Milne was holed up. Somehow or other you lifted the claim check for the bag Sam Milne had checked, and you took it to the depot and checked it, right under our noses. But you'd been doing the same thing so long that we got tired of trying to check up on those bags. We figured you were just experimenting with the time element.

"Damn it, I'm going to pinch you for this. I can show there was nothing the matter with you when you went to the hospital—"

Lester Leith held up a well-manicured hand.

"On the contrary, my dear sergeant, a most reputable surgeon diagnosed my case as appendicitis. He rushed me to the hospital. He was the one who insisted that I go there without a second's delay. No, no, my dear sergeant, you're barking up a wrong tree again.

"But your deductions are most interesting. Of course, you've hardly followed them to their logical conclusion. If the fifty grand was hot cash for a pay-off, as you term it, then Dumoe must have been mixed in it, and—"

The telephone bell had been ringing frantically. Beaver, the spy, reluctantly answered, came into the room waving his hands.

"For you, sergeant. The chief calling. He wants you on the wire right away."

Sergeant Ackley grunted, stepped into the soundproof closet. Five minutes later he returned. His eyes were sullen, his forehead beaded with perspiration.

"Well," he grunted, "you're in luck. The chief says to lay off that Milne case. As far as the department is concerned the case is closed—and he didn't mean maybe, either!"

Lester Leith laughed.

"Perhaps it was hot cash, after all, sergeant. Wouldn't it be discouraging if you had really worked out a perfect solution, only to have the higher-ups call you off?"

Sergeant Ackley fairly danced in an agony of exasperation. "Shut up!" he bellowed.

Lester Leith smiled, aggravatingly. "Tut, tut, sergeant—your blood pressure, you know! But you interest me. Tell me more of your theory."

Sergeant Ackley clenched his fists, took a deep breath, regained control of himself.

"You've got some sort of a rabbit's foot," he said, slowly, impressively. "You manage to pull off crimes right under a police guard, yet never leave any proof. But one of these days I'm going to get you!"

Lester Leith blew a couple of smoke rings, watched one go through the other. He smiled.

"Tut, tut, sergeant. You can never convict me when I can prove that police shadows have been on my trail all the time. A jury wouldn't believe your wild theories. I wish you'd put on a couple of additional men. They give me such perfect alibis. If you find your allotment of funds short I'd even pay for them myself. I just made rather a handsome clean-up in a—er—business matter."

Sergeant Ackley started to say something, choked on the words, whirled on his heel, banged the door.

Lester Leith beamed upon the spy, who was staring with wide eyes and open mouth.

"Most irascible, Scuttle. Can you imagine such a wild theory?" Lester Leith let his eyes cloud in thought. "And yet, Scuttle, if that holdup had been of hot cash, if Sam Milne had planned to make a goat of Blinky Bings, if Milne had ditched the bag of currency...well, there's just a chance, Scuttle, and, mind you, I say just a bare chance that someone who had been shrewd enough to think out the proper solution could have done what Sergeant Ackley suggests."

And Lester Leith blew another smoke ring, traced its perimeter with a well manicured forefinger.

A reminiscent smile played about the corners of his sensitive mouth.

The spy still stared, open mouthed, incredulous, dazed.

His shoe button eyes glinted with unwilling admiration. "I," he said, dropping his manner of synthetic servility, "will be damned!"

Lester Leith nodded.

"I wouldn't be at all surprised, Scuttle," he agreed.

The valet-spy continued to talk, after the manner of a man who is thinking aloud.

"You insisted on a nurse who was born on the 17th of July so you could disrupt the hospital routine with a birthday party. You had me get those diamonds and the cash so you'd have so much of value in the safe the girl in charge would never think of you as a crook. You consulted the astrologer just so you would have a chance to get sick and go to the hospital in an ambulance—"

"Scuttle!" Lester Leith roared.

The valet gulped, dropped back into character. "Yes, sir."

"Scuttle, do you believe all that, or were you merely thinking as Sergeant Ackley was thinking?"

The valet squirmed. "Beg your pardon, sir. I was just saying some of the things that Sergeant Ackley must have been thinking about." Lester Leith smiled.

"Of course, Scuttle, you wouldn't believe such things?"

"Oh, no, sir."

Lester Leith's smile broadened. "And I think you're quite right, Scuttle." The valet's face flushed eagerly.

"About the crime, sir?"

"No, Scuttle. About the fact that you will be damned."

And Lester Leith's smile became a chuckle as he watched the discomfited spy try to preserve his veneer of deferential servility.

A Tip from Scuttle

Lester Leith let himself into his bachelor apartment, handed hat, coat, and gloves to his valet, and sank into the deep chair by the fire. "Coffee, sir?"

"Yes, Scuttle. Rather strong. Ho—ho—hum!"

Leith stretched his arms high above his head. His valet watched him with a hard intensity, eyes like gleaming coals above the sweep of dark mustache. Leith had nicknamed him "Scuttle" because of his resemblance to a pirate's picture. Now, with the firelight catching the hard lines of the valet's face, the nickname seemed peculiarly apropos.

"Fat women should never give formal dinners," remarked Lester Leith.

"Yes, sir," agreed Scuttle.

Leith half turned his slim body, surveyed the valet with twinkling eyes.

"You know, Scuttle, there's something flattering about you. It's very reassuring to see a man of such ferocious appearance so ready to acquiesce in any statement I make."

"Yes, sir."

"And you know, Scuttle, Mrs. Ponsonboy is fat. In the privacy of my apartment I can call it that. To her friends I said she was looking 'well.' Perhaps I might have said she was 'pleasingly plump.' But to you, Scuttle, I'll confide, she was fat."

"Yes, sir."

"And the dinner was a dreadful bore. She has a daughter who sings. Now, Scuttle, a parent can never judge a daughter's voice, particularly a fat parent. Do you think so, Scuttle?"

"Yes, sir—er—that is, no, sir."

"No, indeed, Scuttle. And fat women, who get past forty and try to act kittenish, are rather cumbersome. How's the coffee, Scuttle?"

"Coming, sir."

"Ah—It's good to be in one's own home where one may yawn and stretch, and not bother to place conventional ringers over one's lips, Scuttle, why should convention decree that the hand be placed over a yawning mouth? It doesn't conceal the yawn. And, now that everyone has his tonsils removed, there'd seem to be no good reason—But we digress, Scuttle. My mind is merely running off at random. Come, this will never do. I'm losing interest in life, I'm afraid. I must put in more time considering subjects that interest me. Crime, for instance. Have you clipped me the crime news of the day, Scuttle?"

"Yes, sir."

"Good! I see the coffee's ready. Pour me a cup and sit down here, Scuttle. Read me the crime news. Better yet, tell me the most interesting bit of criminal activity."

There was the clink of cup on saucer, the dropping of sugar, the rasp of a spoon, the rustling of paper, and then Scuttle's voice came in a monotone.

"The Fancher murder, sir. The woman was found nude, two shots in her head, sir. Fancher was last seen with her—"

Lester Leith's drawling voice interrupted. "Anything taken, Scuttle? Any loot?"

"No, sir."

"Dear me, Scuttle. I'm afraid your crime tastes need to be cultivated. You're getting a tabloid mind, Scuttle. Mere nudity and violence cannot make an artistic crime. Skip the Fancher murder, Scuttle. What else have you?"

Scuttle's thumb and finger turned the clippings, selected from various papers. "The Follingsby diamonds, sir."

Lester Leith paused, the coffee cup half raised to his lips. His eyes suddenly snapped into hard attention. "Not the necklace that the newspapers made such a fuss about a year ago?"

"Yes, sir. It was stolen, sir."

Lester Leith abandoned himself to the luxury of soft mirth. "How proud of it they were! It was a typical gesture of the newly rich! Reporters were called in to see Follingsby present it to his wife. They had pictures of the check that paid for the stones, and a lot of blah about the multi-millionaire owners.

"Bah. Follingsby made his money profiteering on war contracts. He should have gone to jail. I'm glad they've lost the necklace. Any clews, Scuttle?"

"No clews, sir. That is, sir, they have the criminal. But they haven't found the stones as yet."

The mirth slipped from Leith's face as hot sirup glides from a mount of ice cream.

"Ah-h-h-h! Give me a summary of the facts, Scuttle."

"Mr. Follingsby was away, sir. Mrs. Follingsby had been wearing the diamonds, and she was nervous, sir. She had her social secretary occupy Mr. Follingsby's room for the night. The two rooms adjoined, with a connecting bath. Both the doors and windows were locked from the inside.

"Mrs. Follingsby left the diamonds on the top of her dressing table while she disrobed. The secretary was in and out of the room. Then Mrs. Follingsby started to put the gems in the safe, noticed that they seemed to have lost their fire, and made a more careful inspection. That inspection showed that a paste imitation had been substituted for the original string.

"She noticed also that the secretary's purse was lying on her dressing table, near where the diamonds lay. The assumption is that the secretary had been awaiting her chance, had been carrying the paste imitation, watching for an opportunity to substitute it.

"But she became alarmed, took the paste imitation from her handbag, grabbed the gems, rushed away and forgot her handbag. Of course, if Mrs. Follingsby hadn't stopped to make a careful examination it might have been days before the theft was discovered. That seems to be about all of the facts, sir."

"Humph!" commented Leith, his eyes as hard as twin flints, the untouched coffee still held in his hand. "And Mrs. Follingsby summoned the police, had the secretary arrested?"

"Yes, sir. The girl, Miss Dixie Stagud, a young Norwegian, was arrested. The police found a single diamond in the pocket of her fur coat. It was a diamond clipped from the necklace. It is the only one of the missing gems found, sir."

Lester Leith shook his head sadly.

"It's a trait of the newly rich to make rash accusations against servants. Let me see, what time is it? I broke away from that dreadful dinner early. Ah, ten-fifteen. Rather late for a call, but nevertheless, Scuttle, I wish you'd telephone Mr. Follingsby, give him my compliments, and tell him that I would like to see him in about an hour upon a matter of the gravest importance. Tell him that it concerns his diamond necklace. And now, my coat, hat, and gloves, Scuttle."

Lester Leith set down his untouched coffee, slipped to his feet with a motion of lithe grace, and became instantly transformed. The ennui of the social butterfly dropped from him. His motions were swiftly efficient. Within a matter of seconds he had emerged from the apartment.

Scuttle, in turn, became active. He first placed a call to Mr. Follingsby as requested. When that had been done he called an unlisted number and obtained a wire direct to police headquarters, a wire that was only used by half a dozen detectives on matters of the greatest importance.

"He's gone out again," breathed Scuttle. "It's the Follingsby diamonds this time. I've made an appointment for an hour later at Follingsby's residence. I haven't the faintest inkling of what he has in mind."

The voice that replied was carried from the receiver to every corner of the still room. It was a gruff voice, and its accents were impatient.

"All right, let's not slip on this. We know Leith has been hijacking stolen jewels. We can't get the proof—yet. Most of the time he slips out when we don't know when or where he goes. Tonight we've got him nailed at both ends. You stick on the job at your end. I'll take care of the other. We can't afford to pull any boners on those Follingsby diamonds. Report in again in an hour and a half. I'll keep you posted. You've let him slip through your fingers half a dozen times before. Let's get the proof this time."

Scuttle's hand that held the receiver grew white where the tension of the skin over the knuckles betrayed his emotion, but his voice was steady as he replied.

"Yes, sir," and hung up the telephone.

II

The desk sergeant regarded Lester Leith's immaculate figure with narrow-eyed suspicion. "Bail for Miss Dixie Stagud has been fixed in the sum of ten thousand dollars. She's held on suspicion of grand theft. You can't see her unless you're her lawyer."

With a bored gesture Lester Leith flipped his hand to his pocket. "If one puts up bail for a prisoner he has the opportunity of getting a return of his bail by delivering the prisoner back into custody."

"Yes, that's right. Why?"

"Because I desire to bail Miss Stagud out of jail."

"You'd have to get your bond approved by—"

Lester Leith's withdrawn hand interrupted the speech. Two packages of treasury certificates thudded on the desk. "United States currency, sergeant. You'll find it correct in amount. I trust it will not be necessary to approve that, because I have an important appointment in thirty minutes."

The sergeant gasped, sputtered, then started in motion the necessary machinery that unwound the red tape and released Miss Dixie Stagud to the custody of Lester Leith.

"We'll have to hurry to keep my appointment," announced Lester Leith, making a deep bow to the startled eyed young blonde who appeared on the arm of a matron.

"But I don't understand—" began the girl, eying him with puzzled approval. "They tell me you've put up bail— Oh, but I don't know you!"

Lester Leith extended his card. "Permit me, my dear young lady, Lester Leith, at your service. And only too pleased to be of some temporary aid to you in your unfortunate predicament. I read of your case in the newspaper, realized at once you were innocent. If you'll accompany me I think I can demonstrate to all concerned that you had no connection with the crime."

The girl sighed, took his arm, and flashed him a tired smile. "It's a pleasure to meet a real gentleman—after enjoying the society of my employers."

"Thank you. My roadster's this way."

The sergeant took down his telephone as the couple left the jail. In short, rapid sentences he conveyed to higher-ups an exact account of what had transpired.

Thereafter, several machines purred through the night in the direction of the Follingsby residence. One of them was the red road-ster of Lester Leith. Three of the others were police cars, filled with detectives and uniformed officers. Another car, a light runabout, contained Lieutenant Silvey, the head of the gem squad. His lips were tight with determination, and he personally saw to the distri-bution of his forces.

Within ten minutes after Leith had been received at the Follings-by residence, Lieutenant Silvey had completed his plans. He rang the Follingsby doorbell.

Hearing the sounds of loud conversation from the drawing-room, the officer brushed past the servant who opened the door, and entered.

Lester Leith, himself, arose with a smile of welcome. "This is, indeed, a pleasure, lieutenant. Perhaps you may be of some assis-tance. I have dropped in to explain to Mr. Follingsby the grievous error he has made in accusing this young lady of grand theft. He adopts the position that I have brought a thief to his house, and refuses to listen."

Lieutenant Silvey swept his eyes over the occupants of the room, opened his mouth to speak, but closed it as Follingsby bellowed forth a torrent of words.

"Damned outrage! The police can't make me stand for it. This damned social dude can't make me stand for it. I won't stand for it. Bring a brazenfaced hussy back into my house like this! Preposter-ous! My wife signed a complaint that was to put her in jail. Why isn't she there now? I'll prosecute her to the limit. If the officers of the law can't do it, I'll hire officers of my own! The idea—"

He was a short, stout man, his eyes glassy, his face florid. His head was held far back to minimize the double chin and make him ap-pear taller. His chest stuck out like a drum major's. What might oth-erwise have been an erect figure was somewhat impaired by a most excessive waistline.

Lieutenant Silvey managed to catch his eye.

"A word with you," he said, clamped a thumb and forefinger about the man's forearm and firmly escorted him to the far corner of the room.

"That man's suspected of being one of the cleverest thieves in the state." he whispered. "He makes a practice of studying crimes and beating the police to it. He's uncanny when it comes to running down clews, making keen deductions, and getting the boodle. We're laying a trap for him on this case. Just keep quiet and follow his lead. The place is surrounded."

Follingsby snorted. "Well, I'm not supposed to act as decoy for any incompetent police—"

Of a sudden cold lightning played from the officer's eyes. "We've been trying to get this bird for two years. Either you play ball with us or you'll wish you had. Get that?"

The thunder died away to rumblings.

"All right, all right. I was just going to mention that I didn't see what right the police had to call upon me, but I'm willing to do anything to get those diamonds back. I'm a heavy taxpayer—"

"Forget it and come on. Play into his hand and follow my lead."

The two men moved back to the center of the room and encountered Lester Leith's amused, supercilious smile.

"He may have the cooperation of the police department, I'd like to make a few demonstrations concerning the theft of the necklace and the innocence of this young lady," drawled Leith. "To do so, however, I must have all of the occupants of the house assemble at the scene of the crime. When I say all, I mean all."

Lieutenant Silvey flashed a warning glance at Follingsby, dropped his left eyelid slowly and emphatically. "'Certainly," blustered Follingsby. "I'll attend to that. But, understand this, I don't give a damn about a lot of theorizing. I want those diamonds."

There followed the hasty shuffle of assembling steps, whispers rustled through the corridors, preceded white-faced servants as they trooped up the stairs. Within a matter of minutes a motley assemblage was grouped in Mrs. Follingsby's room.

"Aw, who are these vulgah persons, George? Ah, yes, the police! Such a bothah, y'know. I presume we have to put up with it Yes? Real-l-ly!"

A decade before she had been a cashier in a motion picture palace. The meteoric rise to wealth of her husband had been accompanied by a veneer of synthetic culture on the part of his wife.

"Howevah, one must put up with certain inconveniences when one associates with the common herd."

Lieutenant Silvey could not forego his revenge. "Mr. Lester Leith is *the* Mr. Lester Leith," he said. "Perhaps you've heard of him. Clubman, sportsman, social leader. You've probably read of him in the papers."

The glassy eyes of the woman goggled to her husband. "Why my *deah* sir! Why didn't you say so. Do come in, my dear Mr. Leith. I've barely missed meeting you a numbah of times. It's so strange that we should move in the same circles so long without having met. Do be seated. It's a pleasuah!"

Suave as ever, Lester Leith bowed.

"I thank you, madame. And I trust it will not be impertinent for me to remark that I hope it will be a mutual pleasure in the near future. I have just agreed to finance Miss Stagud in her action for defamation of character. We are to split the damage recovery. I think it will be high.

"But that is a mere matter which does not need intrude upon the present discussion. Probably you will wish to settle the case out of court, anyhow. What I wished to point out tonight was the facts establishing the innocence of my—ah—client.

"I've been talking a bit with some of the servants while the little group was gathering. What I've heard confirms the suspicion that formed as soon as I read of the crime in the paper.

"Had you found the diamond in the pocket of this young lady's coat, *or* had you found her handbag left near the paste necklace, you might have suspected her. But the finding of both was too much to expect. And why should she have sneaked from her room, gone downstairs, taken the trouble to clip one of the diamonds from the necklace, and left it in a separate place from the others?"

Mrs. Follingsby sputtered her wrath, dropped her acquired accent.

"How should I know all of the moves of a crook. The little hussy imposed on me. Swiped my rocks as soon as my back was turned. I know she did it. The doors were locked, from the inside. There couldn't have been any one come in through the doors or windows—"

Lester Leith intruded upon her angry discourse. "Your pardon, Mrs. Follingsby. But if you'll arrange the room just as it was the night of the crime I believe I can demonstrate how the crime was committed."

Lieutenant Silvey glanced meaningly at Follingsby. That individual placed his flushed face next to the fat neck of his wife and whispered rumblingly. The woman arose with sneering lips.

"Perhaps you know more of the habits of crooks than I do," she sneered.

Leith smiled affably. "Crime is divided into many branches, my dear Mrs. Follingsby. It is no slight upon the ability of your husband that he has not been able to perfect himself in all of them. It happens I've made a study of certain forms of direct crime."

With which the smiling, debonair Leith withdrew.

III

The police officer took occasion to rumble a swift warning. "Lead him on. He's up to something. Play into his hand. The place is watched. Remember, this may discover your jewels!"

Her face mottled with indignation. Mrs. Follingsby went about the room arranging furniture, placing the paste imitation upon her dressing table.

"Ready!" she snapped.

Leith opened the door, smiled. "Ah, yes, and your handbag, Miss Stagud? Where was it the last time you remember having it?"

"In the adjoining room," she said, her eyes hopeful but puzzled.

"Be so good as to place it there, please." The girl hastened to obey.

"Now, if you'll lock the doors and windows," suggested Lester

Leith, and stepped into the hall.

Lieutenant Silvey, his features wearing an air of puzzled abstraction, took charge of locking the rooms. "Ready," he called.

Instantly, noiselessly, Lester Leith's face appeared at a crack in the half open transom above the door. His startled observers saw that in his hand he held the handbag which, but a moment before, had been left on the dressing table in the adjoining room.

Then they laughed, a laugh of sheer tension and relief. For the manner in which Lester Leith had obtained possession of that handbag became immediately apparent. A jointed fishing pole was in his hand. The bag dangled from a half straightened, barb-less hook.

But Lester Leith's face was grave.

Noiselessly, he thrust the stiff pole through the crack above the transom, held it dangling over the dressing table on which reposed the paste imitation.

Then the oiled reel silently unwound the silken line. The purse dropped noiselessly into position. The hook shifted to the paste imitation, caught it. The reel spun the fine line and the paste imitation disappeared through the transom.

Lieutenant Silvey was at the door, shooting the lock. It seemed that he did not trust Leith even with the paste replica of the necklace.

"Simple," smiled Leith.

"Too damn simple!" growled Silvey.

Leith indicated a member of the group. White-faced, lips trembling, eyes watering, a liveried servant strove to keep his eyes from the floor—and failed.

"You see, it was a very amateurish crime all round. And that means some professional criminal bribed a trusted servant, a servant who wasn't very expert. I found the things in your room, Roberts. While you were arranging things in here I slipped down to Roberts's room. I heard he was on duty on the night of the crime. The jointed fishing pole was under his mattress.

"After all, Lieutenant Silvey and I know that you didn't think this thing up. Somewhere in the city some fence desired those stones. He was the one who made up the paste replica. He was the one who got you in debt to him, finally sprung his idea—"

But there was no need of going farther. The guilt of the man was apparent. His face switching, tears streaming from his eyes blurted his story.

"I'd have confessed anyway. I'd never have stolen for an innocent girl being convicted of crime. He's a pawnbroker. He got people coming to him for money. I was playing the races, and he encouraged me, took my notes, got me in deeper and deeper. Finally I stole a little money to make a payment, just a little. That I stole a small article or two, finally he became ugly, threatened to expose me. An' what was I to do? He blocked out the plan, told me how to work it.

"I was the one that suggested to Mrs. Follingsby should better have someone sleep in the adjoining room. I'd been watching my chance for six months."

Lieutenant Silvey stared at Leith. "And you deduced this from a newspaper account?'

Leith smiled. "In part. But, you see, I'd heard, in a roundabout way, a very roundabout way, my dear lieutenant, that a certain fence had made a bid for the Follingsby diamonds. I couldn't get his name.

"Now one clew might be all right, but two such made-to-order clews, two such perfectly ridiculous slips were too much. And why should the girl have left the bedroom, and gone downstairs to put a single incriminating gem in her coat pocket, then come back to await discovery of the substitution?

"And while the papers played up the shrewdness of Mrs. Follingsby in noticing the substitution, you'll see that the replica wasn't made to really fool her. It's almost nothing but glass and tin. Anyone would notice it. No, manifestly, the idea was to have her notice it almost at once.

"The newspaper photographs and diagrams showed that there were transoms over each door. And I noticed that the dressing tables had been placed directly opposite each transom. It was all very clear."

Lieutenant Silvey turned fiercely upon the sobbing servant.

"Who was the man? Where are the gems?"

"Silverstein—Moe Silverstein, he calls himself—on the corner."

But Silvey had exploded into action.

"There's only one man in the city we'd rather get than Moe Silverstein. The dirty fence! We've been laying for him for more than a year!"

He flung up a window, blew three short, sharp blasts on his police whistle.

Almost instantly scurring shadows flitted across the dim street. Heavy steps sounded upon the porches. Doors were thrown open. Grim faced men came trooping into the house.

Lester Leith smiled suavely at the officer. "You seem to have your reception committee well trained, lieutenant."

But Silvey did not reply. He was busy, and he was mad. There was a certain irritating superciliousness about Lester Leith that caused the dark blood to mantle the officer's temples.

"Handcuff this man. He's confessed to the theft of the necklace. Two of you men stay here and search the house. He may be lying. The rest of you come with me. Allow no one to leave the house or get to a telephone.

"Leith, I think I'll ask you to come with me. You're too damnably clever to be left here. I want you where I can watch you."

"You flatter me," drawled Leith. "I like to drive my own car. Perhaps you'd allow the young lady and myself to drive immediately ahead of your car?"

The request was made in drawling insolence, and was vetoed in hot wrath.

"You'll ride beside me in a police car, and the young lady will remain here, under guard!"

Leith bowed. The tilt of his head concealed a flash of swift triumph that twisted the corners of his mouth. "As you wish, my dear lieutenant."

IV

The cars roared through the night with speed that made the tires screech a protest on the turns. For the first few blocks they used the sirens to clear the traffic. After that they trusted entirely to driving skill. They dared not alarm their quarry.

Lieutenant Silvey directed the disposition of his forces. Men dropped from slowing cars, took up stations at doorways, alleys, corners. Silvey's car and one other drew up directly before the office of Moe Silverstein.

It was a little cubbyhole, cobwebby, squalid. The door bore no legend. A pale-yellow light showed through dust incrusted glass. Moe Silverstein did business with a very few, very select clients. And the nature of his business was such that he kept open until the first streaks of dawn came to pale his dim lamp.

Silvey gave a cautious knock at the door, then banged his nightstick. "Open in the name of the law!"

There was the sound of shooting bolts. The door swung back on silent hinges. A stooped little buzzard of a man stood in the doorway.

His nose hooked downward. His chin hooked upward. Somewhere between was a thin, cruel mouth, much like the beak of a bird, hard, powerful.

The eyes were great pools of lambent fire, masked from time to time, at other times reflecting emotion with strange fidelity.

Just now the eyes depicted injured innocence, hurt incredulity. The dark skin, glistening with a coat of natural oil, had the appearance of cobwebbed dirt. The thin, claw-like fingers twisted and twined, one over the other, perpetually rubbing the harsh, rustling skin.

"What's the trouble? What's the trouble? A great time it is to come disturbing an honest man in the keeping of his books. But don't stand there gawking, come in.

"Come in and wreck the business of an honest man. Day and night I labor, trying to make a living for my family. I build up the reputation of being an honest man and then come the police! Not in twos or threes do they come. I might explain such a coming. But, no! They come in carloads and droves. The neighbors crane necks from windows, see Moe Silverstein getting raked over the coals. They whisper and whisper.

"Come in, come in. You've ruined the reputation of an honest man. It isn't enough. You probably want to turn everything upside down. But come and have it over with. I am a busy man. The sooner you come the sooner you go. The sooner you go, the sooner I can get to work. And it will take work to build up my reputation again. After this, people will be afraid to do business with Moe Silverstein." But Silvey paid no attention to the patter. He pushed the little man aside, held him against the wall, jerked his head to the squad outside.

"Make a good job of it, boys."

They came trooping in. The dirty floor gritted with the shuffle of many feet. The door slammed shut again.

"Start with the safe!" snapped Silvey.

The safe was as ancient and old-fashioned as the rest of the office. It was a massive affair of iron—heavy, cumbersome. The walls were nearly eighteen inches thick. Upon the grimy doors appeared a dirty, checkered landscape. The paint had long since cracked and peeled in places, leaving only glimpses of grimy color.

The hinges had once been nickeled. Now they were rusted and tarnished. Great bolts held the hinges to the body. Above the door appeared in dirty gilt paint the name of Moe Silverstein. The knob of the combination was so begrimed that it was hard to distinguish the various figures.

"Open it!" snapped Lieutenant Silvey.

"You have a warrant?" asked the bent little man, his large, mournful eyes appraising Silvey in unwinking humility and hurt amazement, much as a wounded deer regards the approaching hunter.

Silvey cursed.

"I've got a red hot tip that you've got the Follingsby diamonds. I've got no time to monkey. Either you show us around here of your own accord or you go to jail as a suspect, and we get a process of court to-morrow. Which'll it be?"

"Such goings on!" exclaimed the little man, but he bent to the safe. "And you all see the combination as I turn it!" he muttered.

Silvey snorted.

"Open it up. We'll see what's in it."

The bony fingers turned the dial. Because of its grimy condition, the fingers moved it very slowly. The eyes of the officers were on the bony hands with the large blue veins. The eyes of Lester Leith were on the ancient safe, the turning dial, the tarnished figures.

The clicking of the bolts preceded the opening of the huge door. Lieutenant Silvey's hand grasped Silverstein's collar, jerked him back.

"Don't touch anything, Moe."

"What?" wailed the bent man. "My private documents? My books? My own profit and loss? The police have no business with them. Surely—"

He became quiet as Silvey's hands darted about the interior of the safe.

It was as the man had said. Books, trinkets, odds and ends, filled the grimy interior of the safe, smaller than one would have judged from the outside. But the massive walls left room for only one shallow compartment, sharply different from the modern cabinet with only an inch or two of thickness.

While the lieutenant went through the safe, his men went through the room. Not a thing was left untouched. They even covered the wall, the ceiling, the floor. When they had finished, they were no better off than when they started.

Disappointed eye met disappointed eye, turned to the large, placid eyes of Moe Silverstein.

"Such an outrage! Now you are finished. I hope you leave me alone for another two weeks."

Silvey's hand caught the man's coat. A nod enlisted the aid of the other officers. They combed every fold of his garments, and that search, also, was fruitless. A money belt disclosed a large sum of money. But there was absolutely nothing in the line of jewelry, much less the Follingsby diamonds.

"Do we hold 'm?"

The little man sputtered into a volcano of protest at the question.

"Hold me? Hold *me*! Because some crook says he gave me a necklace you hold me without a warrant, without evidence? In the night time? What an outrage! You have made your search. You have found nothing. You will put shadows on my trail again. For a week, two weeks, everywhere I go I will be trailed. But that I cannot help!"

"Aw, shut your mouth, Moe!"

"But try and arrest me! Try to take me from my place of business without a warrant! Just try it. I will have it such a judgment that my lawyer will rub his hands. I will bring a suit against the police, against the rich millionaire who claims to have lost his diamond necklace. Ah, what a nice suit it will be!"

Lieutenant Silvey made a peculiar, tasting grimace with his lips, like one who has bit into a persimmon and found it green. His eyes rested in cold dislike upon the bent form of the fence, then flicked over Lester Leith's smiling countenance.

"That's all," he snapped.

"I'll drive around to Mrs. Follinsby's and get Miss Stagud, lieutenant, if you don't mind."

Silvey strode from the place. He dared not make any charges against this man who was prominent socially, reputed to be immensely wealthy. The police suspected what they suspected, but they dared make no direct accusation without evidence. Nor did he dare to arrest Moe Silverstein—yet. Roberts could tell his story. If the Follingsbys wanted to swear out a warrant the police would gladly serve it. But Moe Silverstein was clever, damnably clever.

The disgruntled lieutenant barked an order. Men withdrew from the place.

Of the entire crowd, Lester Leith was the only one whose face did not show savage disappointment.

He stopped to light a cigarette, and the wind blew out the match. With no trace of hurry in his leisurely motions, he reached for another match.

"Come on, if you're going back with us," snapped Silvey.

"Presently. I must have my smoke, lieutenant."

Another match flickered out. Leith reached in his pocket. Silvey leaned forward, spoke softly to the driver.

"Get a taxi then!" roared the lieutenant, and the car whisked away from the curb, leaving Leith standing there, an expression of almost comic bewilderment on his face.

"Hey! Wait!" he called.

But Lieutenant Silvey was having his first pleasant experience of the evening. "Go like hell," he told the driver.

The red car screamed around the corner, and, with its disappearance, Lester Leith rippled into swift activity. Like the shadow leaf he darted back to the dingy door.

V

Open up! We're coming back!" he bellowed.

The door swung open.

"Such an old trick! Do you think I make necklaces from thin air? That I would produce—"

Moe Silverstein broke off in surprise as he saw the lone figure at the door.

Lester Leith strode across the threshold, entered the room, slammed the door.

The safe still remained open, the books taken from it and piled on the floor. The entire place was just as the police had left it. It was as though the fence had awaited their return.

"Just be seated," ordered Leith, and pushed the stooped figure into a chair. His hands made swift motions that seemed like the fluttering gestures of a hypnotist. But each of those motions was deadly efficient.

His silk scarf was thrust into the mouth of the fence. Short lengths of cord bound the hands and feet to the chair. And then Lester Leith turned to the safe.

The large, soulful eyes of the fence followed his every motion.

"Rather unusual to have the hinges bolted on in just this manner—eh, Moe?"

Leith's voice was pleasant, purring, but, at the words, the color drained from the face of the bound figure. He struggled frantically against his bonds.

Leith laughed outright, picked up a small wrench that had been in the safe.

"And the wrench should have given the police their clew. One doesn't ordinarily keep small wrenches in one's safe, eh, Moe?"

Leith's swift fingers fitted the wrench to the small, nickeled heads of the bolts, gave a few turns until the bolts twisted freely in his fingers.

Then a startling thing developed. The bolts were not merely short bits of metal holding the door to the safe.

Instead, they went the entire length of the safe, proving to be long rods with a few threads at the extreme end.

As the rods were removed from the safe, the entire left wall of the massive box dropped forward on the inside. What had been thick metal, supposedly stuffed with asbestos, became merely a hollow shell, and the white that caught the faint rays of the light was the top of a tuft of cotton.

The interior wall was hinged at the bottom. It dropped forward and down. Had the bolt been removed while the safe was closed no clew would have been given as to the secret compartment.

Lester Leith's gloved hand darted into the compartment, groped for a moment and then pulled a glittering string of gems into the light. Again the hand made a swift trip. This time loose gems of the finest water came to view. Again and again, the hand slipped into the compartment. When it had made its last trip Lester Leith sighed with sheer delight.

The figure on the chair was throwing itself against the pressure of the cords like a fish flopping on the floor of a boat.

Leith closed the compartment, replaced the bolts, smiled at the bound and struggling figure, caught the glare of agonized rage in the large eyes.

"Tut, tut, Moe, you shouldn't take it so hard. It's all stolen, you know. And you inspired most of the thefts. Take the Follingsby affair, for instance. You led an honest servant to crime, arranged things so an innocent girl would probably have been convicted, sent to the penitentiary. And Lord knows how many other crimes have been hatched in that maggoty brain of yours.

"I'll loosen the cords a bit so you can get yourself free in five minutes or so. I'm not in the least afraid of you making a report to the police, or shouting for help. I am a little afraid you might find a knife or a gun somewhere.

"I'll take the gag, if you don't mind. I like that scarf very much. Hereafter it'll have most pleasant associations. I wouldn't have gagged you at all, only you might have acted on impulse and made a noise before you thought of the effect.

"Good night, Moe, good night!"

And Lester Leith stepped to the door, shot back the bolts and slipped out into the night. Two blocks later he found a cruising cab. He arrived at the Follingsby residence shortly after the police had left with their prisoner.

In his red roadster he found a shadow, huddled down upon the cushions.

"Oh, it's you. I waited to thank you. Lieutenant Silvey said you were coming in a cab."

Miss Dixie Stagud's voice was vibrant with gratitude. "No thanks necessary. I assure you it's been a most pleasant and profitable evening. I'll drop you at your hotel on my way home."

"I—I haven't any hotel. I haven't even any money."

There was a swift motion. Leith's hand closed over the girl's cold fingers, pressed something into them.

"Merely an advance on the settlement Follingsby will make on our suit for false imprisonment. He won't want the notoriety of a lawsuit over the thing—And the Rossmore is an excellent hotel. We'll drive by there."

The girl fingered the crisp bills.

"You're so good—so wonderful—and I feel you don't even intend to start a suit against the Follingsbys. You're just trying to give me this money—I can't take it."

But Leith's reassuring laugh mingled with the purring throb of the motor.

"I'm not given to lying as a rule, my dear young lady, please believe me when I assure you that this is purely a matter of business with me. I might almost say that it's the riding of a hobby, the practising of a profession."

And there was that in his tone that carried conviction. "But you put up bail, came to my rescue—"

Two arms clasped around his neck. The car swerved as a warm kiss was implanted full upon his lips.

Lester Leith gave a low laugh of sheer pleasure, a laugh that echoed his enjoyment of life. One hand left the steering wheel, patted her shoulder. She snuggled close to him, squeezing his arm, stopping from time to time to wipe tears of relief from her eyes.

At the door of the hotel he sprang to the ground, assisted her to alight.

"How did you know I was innocent?" she asked, anxious to get his opinion of her.

He laughed. "Your name. It's pronounced Staygood. No girl with such a name could steal gems."

She joined in his laughter, but there was a note of unappeased curiosity in her voice. She would have asked more, but Lester Leith escorted her to the desk, saw that the clerk understood her lack of baggage, raised his hat, bowed formally, and returned to his roadster. Around the corner, he drove into an alley, jumped from the car and went to the rear where two spare tires were mounted. His swift fingers unscrewed the tire cap in the innermost tire, which turned out not to be a tire at all, but a carefully designed receptacle for such things as might be dropped into it through the small opening.

He stuffed the gems through this opening, replaced the cap, and drove through the other end of the alley, swung to the boulevard and back to his apartments.

With the car safely locked in his garage, he came up on the elevator, opened his door, and met Scuttle's questioning look with a smile.

"And now, we'll have that coffee, Scuttle."

The valet nodded, turned, then paused as there came a pounding on the door. Without waiting for his master's permission, he swung the door open.

Lieutenant Silvey and two uniformed policemen stepped into the room.

"Sorry, Leith. We've followed you up from the garage. We'll have to search you."

"Search me?"

"Yep. We stuck a shadow on Moe Silverstein's. The shadow reports that he saw you come out. Five minutes afterward Moe came running to the sidewalk waving his hands like a crazy man. He yelled that he'd been robbed, and then, when the officer wanted more information, dried up like a clam.

"What did you go back there for?"

"To get more matches," smiled Lester Leith. "You'll remember I was trying to light a cigarette? The wind whipped out three matches, and I didn't have any more. You drove away and left me standing there, and I *did* want a smoke.

"So I remembered Moe and stepped back. The door was unlocked. There was a box of matches on top of the safe, I remembered, and so I took a few out. Naturally, I didn't pay Moe for them. Isn't it just like his avaricious nature to think he should have been paid—robbed of a handful of matches, eh? Ha. Ha."

Silvey's eyes glinted from those of the valet, took on a dangerous gleam. "You object to being searched?"

"No, no. Not in the slightest. I was merely thinking what a comedy it all was, all over a match."

Silvey snorted.

"We've already searched your car. They're not there. They must be on you. Personally, I feel we're hot on the trail of the Follingsby diamonds."

Leith drew himself to his full height.

"That, gentlemen, comes dangerously near being an accusation. Please make haste and then leave me, Scuttle, get that coffee ready. I'll have my cup as soon as these well-meaning but blundering minions of the law leave."

"Maybe you'll go with us," growled Silvey.

The search netted them one handful of matches, a very well filled wallet, a cigarette case, pen and pencil, a small notebook, and a supercilious smile.

"Really, gentlemen," drawled Lester Leith when they had finished, "I wouldn't want to seem to make light of your profession; but that search was so meaningless a gesture, such a foolish move! And you think you're hot on the trail of the Follingsby diamonds, eh?

"You know I'm minded of a slang expression. 'Not so hot.' Really, gentlemen, I feel it will be quite a long time before you ever see any of those diamonds. Of course, that's merely my personal opinion. I may be wrong."

Lieutenant Silvey's face darkened with wrath, for a moment he glared into the eyes of Lester Leith. Then his gaze flashed to Scuttle, gave him a meaning glance, and the officer turned to the door.

"Come on, boys," he said.

The door slammed. Lester Leith sank into his deep chair. "The coffee, Scuttle?"

"In a moment, sir."

Leith stretched, sighed, yawned. "After all, Scuttle, it's an interesting field of thought those gentlemen from headquarters have opened up. Suppose Moe Silverstein *did* have those gems secreted? He'd probably have a great deal more of stolen property hidden in the same place.

"Then suppose, now, mind you, Scuttle, I'm just supposing; suppose I should have detected that hiding place, returned and robbed the man?

"You see, he'd hardly dare to complain. A complaint would have necessitated a description of the loot and he'd have to point out the place from which it had been taken. You see, the very thorough police search of the office made but a few moments before, would have precluded the idea of any jewels being there—unless they were in a most secret place.

"It's rather an interesting thought, Scuttle. Particularly so when one considers that Moe Silverstein is a criminal of the highest intelligence, but the lowest morals. He conspires to commit crimes, gets others to betray the confidences of their employers. It would hardly be a crime to rob him, rather a public benefaction.

"Yes, Scuttle, the idea has much to commend it. If you should ever contemplate a criminal career, my dear Scuttle, I would suggest that you limit your activities to robbing robbers. Not only is there less moral stigma attached to the operation, but there is virtually no risk. The victims dare not complain."

Scuttle's lips clenched tightly. Color flooded his face. Almost it seemed that Lester Leith was mocking him. "Nevertheless." he said with forceful tone, "Lieutenant Silvey will get that necklace. He's a clever man, a very clever man."

Lester Leith glanced at the door through which the irate officer had vanished, sipped his coffee, and smiled. "Not so hot, Scuttle. Not so hot."

The Girl With The Diamond Legs

CHAPTER I

Beauty and the Mouse

During the course of his entire career, Stacy Middleton did but three things which met with the unqualified approval of his wife. The first was to acquire some two million dollars, profiteering on war contracts. The second was to take out a million dollars in life insurance. The third was to die.

Mrs. Middleton was too fat to look well in black. Her period of mourning was, therefore, quite brief. Within two weeks following the death of her husband, which was as soon as she could arrange for the collection and investment of the insurance money, she left for Europe. Upon her return, two years later, she had developed into a full-fledged follower of cults, a seeker of publicity, and a simpering, fleshy, foolish widow who religiously believed all the flattery which was poured into her ears by fawning fortune seekers.

Even the most imaginative person on earth could hardly see how such a woman would enter into the life of Lester Leith, that debonair connoisseur of crime whose activities caused the police such exasperating unrest.

But Mrs. Stacy Middleton purchased a diamond necklace in Berlin, and the fabulous value of that diamond necklace was commented upon from time to time in the newspapers. And Mrs. Middleton took up parlor magic and entertained her select friends.

Those two facts, standing alone, would never have caused Lester Leith to take an interest in her case. But it happened that on one stormy March night, Mrs. Middleton arranged an entertainment for a select group of friends, and part of the program included a spring dance by Dorothy Delano, a beautiful chorus girl, and an exhibition of parlor magic by Mrs. Stacy Middleton.

Those facts, welded by fate into a composite whole, attracted the attention of Lester Leith in due course and gave rise to the adventure of the vanishing diamonds.

As has been mentioned, the night was stormy. Dorothy Delano had not, as yet, done her spring dance. She had not even dressed for it. Her simple costume, consisting principally of flowing veils, reposed in a very small hand bag.

A buffet supper was being served. Mrs. Stacy Middleton, standing upon a little platform at one end of the room, simpered in the rays of a well diffused spotlight.

"I will now give you a little demonstration of spiritism," she said. "Of course it's not genuine. It's just magic. I'll be tied and placed inside a little cabinet on a chair. And yet you will see spirit hands, hear bells ring, hear a drum beat, hear a revolver shot. Then the cabinet will be opened and I will appear still bound tightly to the chair.

"Will a committee from the audience come forward and see that I am bound securely to the chair?"

Dorothy Delano fought back a desire to yawn, and toyed with a salad. She wished heartily that the old fool would get it over with. Dorothy had a heavy date at midnight.

Several men, decorously garbed in conventional evening dress, moved listlessly but politely to the stage to see that Mrs. Stacy Middleton sat down on the chair which a liveried servant placed in the center of the platform.

It was noticed that the lights glittered and gleamed from the double string of diamonds which circled the fat neck.

The tying was completed. The liveried servant slipped the folding cabinet around her. The volunteer committee left the stage, one at a time. The last to go paused for a final look at the bound figure.

The servant snapped the fastenings of the cabinet in place, and signaled with his hand for the lights to dim to that weird blue glow which Mrs. Middleton always used as a background for her spiritualistic tricks.

The lights dimmed. The place was flooded with a ghastly blue light which robbed beautiful ladies of the bloom of youth, and made them fidget uneasily and avoid the eyes of their escorts.

All eyes were on the cabinet.

Nothing happened. There was no ringing of bells, no beating of drums, no firing of shots.

Then the silence was broken by the piercing scream of a woman. Dorothy Delano, the actress, jumped to her chair. "A mouse!" she screamed, and elevated her silken skirt. The display of hosiery attracted the attention of every masculine eye in the room. The eyes of the women followed those of the men. The men looked in ill-concealed admiration.

At that moment the lights went on.

A mouse scuttled for shelter, a dark streak of scampering fear. Other women contented themselves with screaming and wrapping their skirts tightly around their knees. Only one or two went as far as Dorothy Delano.

Some of the women laughed, some craned necks curiously. Some lifted their noses in scorn. One rather slender and nervous woman screamed in actual fear.

Then the mouse vanished, and the room echoed to masculine laughter and the shrill comments of the women. Several minutes passed before anyone thought to inquire about Mrs. Stacy Middleton.

Then the liveried servant ran to the cabinet.

Mrs. Middleton sat as she had promised she would, still tied to the chair. But now she was also gagged. The glitter of diamonds was gone from her bare neck. Only her eyes caught the reflections of the lights and scintillated indignant lightnings.

The cowbell, the drum, the revolver with its blank cartridge were all untouched, lying upon a shelf of the cabinet which had dropped down when the cabinet was latched into place.

They untied the bonds, took off the gag.

"My diamonds!" screamed Mrs. Stacy Middleton, and her voice rasped with harsh indignation.

A man arose from the center of the room.

"Ladies and gentlemen," he said, in a rich, throaty voice, "it is obvious that something has happened. I was one of those who went on the stage to inspect the bonds which tied Mrs. Middleton to the chair.

"I realize that if anything has happened to those diamonds, we are all under suspicion. In justice to ourselves, I propose that all doors be locked, and that everyone in this room submit to an immediate and thorough search!"

Mrs. Middleton nodded her head emphatically. Here and there a mutter of protest was swallowed in a chorus of affirmation.

The search was made, first by the guests themselves, later by the police. The diamonds were not found.

All of which was why Lester Leith, super-crook deluxe, became interested in the affair of Mrs. Stacy Middleton.

CHAPTER II

The Scavenger Business

Lester Leith, sprawled at silken ease in his bachelor apartment, blew a smoke ring and watched it float upward toward the ceiling of the room.

His six-foot valet, ponderous as a steam shovel, surreptitious as a prowling weasel, in reality no valet at all, but a police spy, set to watch over the suspected criminal, thumbed the newspaper clippings in his fingers.

Those clippings gave all the facts of the Middleton robbery as the newspaper reporters and the police had been able to gather them.

"Who suggested the search, Scuttle?" Lester Leith asked. Edward H. Beaver, undercover agent of the department, writhed under the nickname of Scuttle, bestowed upon him by Lester Leith through some fancied resemblance to a reincarnated pirate.

But when the spy spoke, his voice and manner were letter-perfect imitations of the well-trained valet.

"That was Steven Slone, sir, press agent for Dorothy Delano, the actress, who was to give a spring dance later on in the evening."

"Ah, yes," commented Lester Leith, his voice drawling in lazy good nature. "Doubtless knew he would be considered an outsider, and, therefore, the first to lie suspected. Tell me, Scuttle, why didn't the spiritualistic cabinet do its stuff?"

"The way she was tied, sir. It was a trick chair. One of the rungs in the back was made to come out of its socket and let Mrs. Middleton get her hands loose. It just happened that someone had bungled the tying and got the rope around two of the rungs, holding them firmly together. Then a gag was slipped around her mouth and the gems lifted.

"She thinks it was the servant when he adjusted the cabinet, but she can't be certain. She was held in such a position that she couldn't even turn her head. It must have been either the servant or some member of the committee."

Lester Leith nodded.

"Suspicion, of course, attaches to the press agent?"

"So I gather from the newspaper clippings, sir. Either him or the servant. Yet the diamonds were not actually taken until about the time the actress screamed at the mouse, sir."

"I see. That would implicate the actress, eh, Scuttle?"

"The police have grilled her, sir. She's always been deathly afraid of a mouse. They've established that much, sir. And there doubtless was a mouse."

Lester Leith nodded. His eyes were lazy-lidded and laughing. "By the way, Scuttle, save me those newspaper clippings, will you?"

"Yes, sir."

Lester Leith blew a smoke ring and traced its perimeter with a well-manicured forefinger. He seemed to be chuckling inwardly, as though at some joke which was plain enough to him, yet obscure to others.

"If the gems weren't taken until the woman screamed at the mouse, there's no real reason to suspect any member of the committee, Scuttle."

"Why, sir?"

"Because the committee was off the stage by that time. The guests were being served a buffet supper, I understand, Scuttle?"

"Yes, sir."

"And I presume the food was left untouched in the excitement which followed, Scuttle."

"Yes, sir. One of the papers even comments upon that fact, sir. There were great bowls of punch, of salad, plates of rich food, all untouched save for such food as the police consumed."

Lester Leith's eyes slitted in thought. "I wonder who collects the garbage out there, Scuttle? It's rather an exclusive residential district, eh?"

"Yes, sir. I believe someone has the concession. The food goes to hogs, sir. The garbage is collected at night, sir, so the residents won't be annoyed by the sight of the ugly wagons, sir."

Lester Leith nodded dreamily.

The police spy was watching him like a hawk. It was during such moments that the master mind of Lester Leith conceived the ingenious schemes which had hitherto baffled the police. But the police were learning much of his method of working out these mysteries. Daily the invisible net was growing tighter. Daily the police were becoming more efficient in their surveillance.

"Scuttle," said Lester Leith, at length.

"Yes, sir?"

"I think I shall go into the show business. I am going to back a show—preferably a musical comedy."

The valet's eyes widened. "Become an angel, sir!"

"Tut, tut, Scuttle. I haven't been any angel in the past, and I don't know what there would be about backing a musical comedy which would make me grow wings. If there's anything in environment, Scuttle, one might expect quite the opposite."

"Pardon me, sir. I didn't mean it that way, sir. An 'angel' is what the theatrical profession refers to when it means a rich man who backs shows. Usually—er—ahem—the angel backs a show in order to star a certain young lady in whom he has taken an interest."

Lester Leith let his eyes beam in ingenuous enthusiasm. "That's just it, Scuttle! You've hit it exactly. This Miss Delano, Scuttle, is going to have some trouble, being mixed up in this Middleton mess. It will undoubtedly affect her career, Scuttle; and it seems a shame that the career of an innocent woman should be affected by so trivial a thing as a mouse."

The valet was decorously deferential, but doubtful. "Yes, sir," he said.

"Yes, indeed, Scuttle. And there's one other thing I propose to do. I want to go into the scavenger business."

"Into the scavenger business, sir!"

"Yes, Scuttle. Not that I shall make it a permanent profession, Scuttle. But I shall dabble around in it a bit. I think I shall start in on the route which comprises the best houses, such as the Middleton house, for instance."

"But, good heaven, sir, you can't just go into the business that way, sir. Those garbage routes are highly profitable. They are all contracted for. The Middleton garbage is collected around midnight, sir—twice or three times a week, sir. You couldn't simply start hauling it away."

But the valet's eyes were narrowed with a shrewd suspicion, and he was watching Lester Leith as a cat watches a mouse hole.

"But," drawled Lester Leith, "suppose one should simply take over the garbage route? Suppose one should hijack the garbage? They couldn't stop one from doing that, could they?"

"No, sir. I guess not, sir. That is, sir, I suppose it could be arranged, sir. But what you'd want of the garbage is more than I know, sir."

Lester Leith stretched and smiled. "Certainly, Scuttle."

"Certainly what, sir?"

"What I want with the garbage is more than you know. But, Scuttle, would you mind arranging for a garbage truck? And you'd better have it lined with galvanized iron, Scuttle, so that nothing can leak out. Once the garbage is placed in the truck, Scuttle, I should dislike very much to have any of it, no matter how small, leak out. Do you understand, Scuttle?"

The valet leaned forward, lowered his voice.

"Yes, sir. I think I do, sir. It will be a pleasure to help you, sir. I've often mentioned that I could do a great deal more for you, sir, if you'd just take me into your confidence, sir."

Leith nodded, casually, carelessly.

"That's fine, Scuttle. And now, if you'll lay out my afternoon clothes, I think I shall take a stroll. By the way, Scuttle, better ring up Dorothy Delano, tell her who you are, and tell her that your master has become interested in backing a musical comedy. Ask her if she would care for the leading part. She would pick her own players from first to last, have charge of the rehearsals; in short, be the one to handle all details."

Edward H. Beaver, police spy, smiled, a suggestive smile. "Oh, yes," he said. "Yes, indeed, sir. I shall fix everything up in the approved manner."

Lester Leith stared at him gravely. "The approved manner, Scuttle?"

The valet-spy coughed. "Well, sir, at least in the usual manner, sir."

Lester Leith's eyes remained cold.

"You will confine yourself, Scuttle, to transmitting the message I gave you to transmit. That will be all, Scuttle."

CHAPTER III

A Break

Sergeant Arthur Ackley mouthed a cigar between his thick lips, and scraped a spade like thumbnail along the angle of his jaw, a mechanical gesture of meditation. The thumbnail scraped the bristles of a grizzled beard, and gave off little rasping noises, particularly irritating to the ears of Beaver, the undercover man.

"So you think he's got a line on those Middleton diamonds, eh, Beaver?"

"I'm sure of it," said the ponderous spy.

"But how could he? He hasn't been to the place, doesn't know the facts!"

Beaver grunted. "You know the way he plays the game. He figures the newspapers give all the facts that are necessary to solve a crime in a lot of the cases. He never starts on a case unless the newspaper clippings give him some lead.

"Well, now, I think I know his lead in this case. He figures the actress, Dorothy Delano, engineered the whole thing. When the stage had been set just right, she yelled at a mouse, probably one she'd turned loose herself, and climbed on a chair.

"The girl made a good job of it. Most of the people in the room were looking at her silk stockings. The rest were all excited.

"An accomplice pulls the robbery and drops the gems into a bowl of punch, or into a salad or some such place, or, perhaps, sticks them into a roll.

"Now the man who pulled that robbery will try to get back to the house to pick up the stones. Leith intends to prevent him some way or another, and then he figures the stones will find their way into the garbage. He's going to hi-jack the garbage route, and go over all the stuff with a fine-toothed comb. He expects to get the diamonds."

Sergeant Ackley grunted. He rolled the cigar from the left side of his thick-lips to the right side, grunted again, and then fell to drumming on his desk with heavy fingers.

"Humph," he said. Beaver waited.

"Humph," grunted the sergeant.

"The idea has possibilities. And the girl's accomplice?"

"Her press agent, of course. Who else would it be? He was one of the men to go on the platform to tie up Mrs. Middleton. He was in a position to work hand-in-glove with the girl, and was about the only one in the place the girl knew at all well."

Sergeant Ackley took a card from his desk, studied it. "Name's Steven Slone. He's married. His wife is jealous. Used to be on the stage himself, doing ventriloquism. Has no criminal record. Been publicity agent for several minor actors and actresses, been with Dorothy Delano for six months. Looks like the wife is jealous of Dorothy, too."

Beaver nodded.

"I think he'll let me go with him this time," he said, lowering his voice. "Handling garbage requires an assistant. I think he's getting ready to take me into his confidence."

Sergeant Ackley grinned.

"Yeah. Looks like we're getting a break after all. Tell you what you do. You go on the garbage wagon with him. When he acts as though he's got the stuff, you work a flashlight. I'll have the shadows ready to throw a raid. We'll tackle the garbage and beat him to the rocks. Then we'll slip him the works!"

The two men shook hands.

"I've got to get back to my job. Looks like we've got him, sergeant!"

Sergeant Ackley beamed. "There's a promotion in it for you, Beaver!"

CHAPTER IV

The Proposition

Lester Leith regarded the beautiful Dorothy Delano, and Dorothy Delano studied the debonair visitor over the tip of a smoldering cigarette.

"It'd take a lot of money," she said.

Lester Leith nodded, casually waved his right hand. "That," he said, "I had expected."

The golden eyes of the girl regarded him in a tawny appraisal. "What made you come to me?"

"I think you've got everything that's necessary to success on the stage."

They were seated in a little restaurant where a curtained booth gave them privacy. It was a restaurant noted for the tact of its waiters as well as for the quality of its food.

The girl crossed her legs casually. "You mean — figure?" she asked, her tawny eyes glowing.

He shook his head.

"Not entirely. You have a beautiful figure, and you have a beautiful face. Those things, of course, are necessary to success on the stage. But you have more. You have a charm of personality."

She straightened. "Let's be frank," she said. "Let's get things settled definitely."

He nodded. "That's fair. I want to be convinced that you can act."

"Can I act?"

"In the love scenes."

"You'd want a demonstration?"

"Yes. I'd want to see that you could act the part of a woman in love—act it convincingly."

"Get ready, big boy, here I come!"

Lester Leith held up a hand. "No, no. Not with me!"

The tawny eyes widened in surprise. "Say," she demanded, "what's your game, anyway?"

"Your photograph," said Lester Leith, "was in the papers in connection with that Middleton affair. In fact, one of the tabloids had you posed in the same position you took when you first saw the mousie. It was rather a compelling pose.

"I saw at once from those photographs, that you had charm, appeal, personality. I suspected that you had talent. My idea in backing a musical comedy of which you are to be the head, is to make money. Simply, solely, entirely, to make money.

"Now you naturally are grateful to me for the opportunity of giving you a chance to star in a play. Therefore, it would not be too hard for you to make love to me. But that would not be acting. What I want to see is a demonstration of your ability as an actress where I know that you are acting."

The girl sighed. She studied him intently through her golden eyes, and then shook her head.

Lester Leith smiled.

The girl drained her glass, lit a fresh cigarette from the stub of the old one. Lester Leith consulted his wrist watch. His smile became a grin.

"Well?" said the girl.

"I have arranged with Steven Slone to join us here in ten minutes. I shall want him to help us dope out the publicity stunts for our new venture. He is, I believe, your press agent?"

The girl sighed.

"That bozo!" she said. After a few moments she elaborated. "He ain't so hot as a press agent. And he can't give good service because he's got a jealous wife. She's got a triple chin and an eye like a rattlesnake. Every time we'd be in the middle of a conference over something new the telephone would start ringing, and Steve would have to go bye-bye to his fat mamma. If we're going to invest a bunch of your dough in something that is supposed to go across, let's get the best talent we can afford."

Lester Leith blew a smoke ring. "You're not so hot for Steven Slone?"

"Baby, I'm not even lukewarm—"

"Is he personally attractive?"

"What, that guy? You ain't seen him, I guess. He's lived a hard life and he shows it. He's got footballs under his eyes, and his cheeks sag down into his collar. He's fat, and tries to pretend he ain't. He wears all sorts of rubber contraptions to keep his stomach from flapping around and hitting him in the back when he turns quick, and he insists on wearing collegiate clothes.

"He's a typical bozo who's all done and don't know it. I could like the bird if he'd be himself, but he's always trying to play the part of the twenty-year-old rah-rah just out of the sheepskin factory. He gives me a pain!"

Lester Leith nodded.

"In the neck," supplemented the girl, and smiled at him with her tawny eyes.

"That," said Lester Leith, "makes it very nice. He is the one on whom you can demonstrate."

The girl set down her glass. "Huh?" she asked.

"You can act as though you love him. If you can act convincingly, then I am sold on going ahead with the show. If you can't convince me that you are acting so convincingly that you have convinced him you are not acting at all, then I'm finished."

The girl took a deep breath. "Me, make love to Steve Slone?"

"Yes. And convince him you mean it."

"Why he and I have just had a business relationship for six months. He tried to get fresh the first week, and I slapped his face.

"He let it go at that until he had me a little jingled on a sizz party one night, and then he tried to strong-arm me. I had to leave my finger-nail marks down each side of his fat face. He went to a drug store and got the clerk to bandage up his whole head, and told his wife he'd been in an automobile accident.

"After that we got along fine. It's been strictly business. If I should start in falling for him now he'd sure think I'd gone batty."

Lester Leith rubbed his hands together.

"That's fine. It couldn't be better. It will require consummate acting upon your part. He will arrive in a few minutes. It will be your job to start in by degrees, warm up to him so gradually you carry conviction all the way, yet wind up in exactly one hour having him so infatuated he agrees to run away with you and leave his wife."

The tawny eyes were wide now. "How about the new play? He wouldn't run away if he knew I was starring in a new play and he was to do the publicity."

Lester Leith nodded gravely.

"At the proper moment, when you kick my leg under the table, I shall announce that I have changed my mind, that I am not going ahead with the play until next year. Then you can strut your stuff. If you dare him to meet you in front of the Palace Theater at precisely ten-eleven to-night, all packed and ready to run away with you, then I shall consider you have demonstrated your ability as an actress, and I will finance the show. Otherwise, the proposition is off. I shall then have to look around for some other promising actress who has talent and beauty."

The girl sighed. "You'll find plenty of 'em who are strong on the promising part," she said.

"Doubtless," he commented. "You're in this to make money?"

"Yes."

"Only that?"

"Yes."

"Then I can tell you about the B. F.," she said.

"The B. F.?"

"Yeah. You know, the boyfriend."

"Oh," said Lester Leith.

The girl sidled over closer to him, placed an intimate hand on his arm, looked up into his face with her tawny eyes softened with emotion.

"He's got the most wonderful hair, and his mouth is so adorable.

His eyes just do things to my heart, and he's so tender, and so intelligent. He's the most wonderful boy in the world."

Lester Leith regarded her in stern disapproval.

"Don't forget you've got to make Steven Slone fall for you—and fall hard. Thinking of your boyfriend isn't going to be the best preparation for your act."

She snuggled up to him with a kittenish intimacy.

"Oh, don't worry about me. What I wanted to do was to tell you about the B. F. and the script."

"The script?"

"Yes. He's a playwright. He's written a musical comedy that's a scream. 'Three Strikes and Out' is the name of it. I want you to use it."

Lester Leith smiled gravely.

"Don't you think it would be better to get one of the better-known playwrights to turn out a script that would be designed to star you, than to purchase the play of an unknown? I take it this play has been offered and turned down."

She nodded.

"Turned down by every damned producer in the world, and it's a knockout. I swear it is! A real knockout! The B. F.'s a genius!"

Lester Leith patted her shoulder.

"Very well," he said, "we will use 'Three Strikes and Out.' If you're for it, I'm for it."

The curtains parted, and a man stood in the entrance. "Hope I'm not intruding, folks."

CHAPTER V

Just a Meal Ticket

"And this is Leith, the new backer, eh?" asked Steven Slone. "Mighty glad to know you, Mr. Leith."

Dorothy Delano turned up yellow eyes brimful with grateful moisture.

"Mr. Leith," she said, "this is Steve Slone, a great little press agent."

Gravely, the two men shook hands.

Steven Slone was one of those men who go through life making others feel at home. He had a booming voice, a perpetual smile, a ready hand. His figure was contained within a worsted suit of youthful cut. He gave the impression of a sausage that had been stuffed too tightly and was ready to burst. Yet there were no bulges of fat upon him. His stomach was compressed into the vest until it seemed the surplus fat must be squeezed out at his neck and ankles.

And that was exactly the impression both neck and ankles gave. The neck wash-boarded above a tight collar. It did not seem that the fat of that neck had slipped down from the pink jowls, but rather that it had drifted up from under the collar. The ankles were thick and flabby. The feet were rather small.

"Mighty glad to know you, Leith. Looks like you're a genius when it comes to picking 'em. I've seen 'em come and I've seen 'em go, but Dorothy here has got more on the ball than any of 'em I've seen in a decade, and I've seen some pretty big ones.

"That's the reason I coppered to her. I could have got jobs by the hundred managing some of the beauties that have already arrived. But they're on the wane. What I wanted to do was to pick a comer, and skyrocket to the top with her. She'll be packing 'em in like sardines in another year. You'll see her name all over Broadway in electric lights. She'll be endorsing cigarettes, toilet soaps, and hair tonics at so much per endorse. She'll be eating health foods at so much per eat. I can look ahead right now and see it just as plain as plain can be!"

And Steven Slone drew up a chair and sat down. Lester Leith let his mouth sag open just a bit. "You certainly carry conviction," he remarked.

Steve Slone reached forth a pudgy hand, grasped the sleeve of Lester Leith's coat. "Lis'n," he begged in a booming voice that fairly quivered with sincerity. "Lis'n, I know what I'm talkin' about. I'd bet all the money I ever saw that this little kid is going to knock 'em dead. You back her and you'll be the king of the white lights in six months, a multi-millionaire in a year!"

Dorothy Delano glanced once at Lester Leith, glanced swiftly, surreptitiously, then her hand stole out to rest on Steve Slone's hand.

"Steve," she said, "I been kinda mean to you."

The press agent turned his cautious eyes down upon the girl, and he half turned so that he could see her more plainly.

"That's all right, girlie. I'm just an old friend, married happily, taking a platonic interest, an' a business interest. Don't forget that business interest. I want to cop big when the time comes. But nobody don't need to think I'm foolish enough not to know which side of the bread's got the butter. Nobody'd ever need to get jealous of me. I'm strong for you, kiddo, but it's just business. Nothin' but!"

The tawny eyes swept reproachfully over his face.

"Mr. Leith says he don't care nothing about me either. He wants to make money. He don't want me to even smile at him."

The breath whooshed from Steven Slone's taut waistcoat. His startled eyes surveyed Lester Leith in a stare of utter incredulity.

Lester Leith nodded.

Steven Slone blinked his eyes a few times. "I," he said, "will be damned!"

The girl glanced up into his face.

"And then you come along and tell me I'm just the same as a meal ticket to you, that you don't enthuse over me any more than so much pasteboard. I must be getting old or something. You used to get a thrill out of me."

Steven Slone was cautious, but responsive.

"Say," he said, "you're the one that turned me out in the cold world. Remember that 'automobile accident' you got me into?"

She moved a trifle closer to him.

"Aw, Steve," she crooned. "Don't you remember? You said that when a woman struggled with you it brought out all the primitive in you? And I wanted to be cave-manned, and so—so—so I struggled. And you got mad and went home."

Steven Slone glanced once more at Lester Leith. There was a certain apprehension in his gaze.

Lester Leith was busily engaged in lighting a cigarette. Apparently the conversation was of no interest to him.

Steve Slone's arm went around the girl's shoulders, drew her to him with a pressure which seemed to stretch the vest buttons to the point of bursting.

"Say, listen, baby. From the first time I ever looked into those gold eyes of yours, I felt my heart go for a loop. So don't string me along unless you mean it, because I'd fall hard. I don't know what you may be to other people, but to me you're the cream on the top of the milk pitcher, the cat's whiskers, the snake's hips. You're the last word!"

She pouted, and the pout made of her mouth a kissable temptation which could have been ignored by no man under ninety-two.

Steve Slone bent down. The narrow cut of his coat stretched under the strain of the shoulders until it seemed the cloth would burst. Dorothy's tawny eyes looked up into the gleaming ones of the press agent, the lips half parted, as though to make some comment, and remained half parted as Steve Slone's mouth met them. There was a moment of silence. Then Steve looked apprehensively at Lester Leith.

That individual was consulting a notebook.

"The name of the play we have decided upon is 'Three Strikes and Out,'" said Leith.

CHAPTER VI

"Baby, I'll Be There!"

Slone straightened his figure, pushed the girl to one side. "That rotten thing!" he yelled.

The girl clutched at his shoulder. "Please, Stevie, dear!"

He looked down at her. "Say, you know it's rotten as well as I do. You're just falling for it because of the guy that wrote it! Why don't you get a play we can do something with, instead of petting some long-haired down-and-outer who has a flop that's been turned down..."

The girl's bare arm crept up and around his neck.

"I promised him. Stevie—before—before I knew you cared. Now he's going to lose me, and you wouldn't want to see him lose out on the production as well, would you? It's a good play. I could go over big in it. He wrote it for me. And it would break his heart to lose out on the play and to have you—to have you—" She didn't finish the sentence, but pouted again, her lips upturned.

Steven Slone bent down.

There was a discreet knock. An apologetic waiter stood in the doorway, holding a desk telephone in his hands.

"I'm very, very sorry," he said, "but there is a call for Mr. Slone. She says it's important, imperative. She knew you were here, sir, gave the number of the booth, even, told who you'd be with. So I thought it best, sir. You can plug the telephone in on that plug there."

Steven Slone sighed, straightened, reached for the telephone. The waiter snapped the plug into the hollow receptacle in the wall.

"Hello," said Slone.

There was the sound of a feminine voice rasping questions.

Steve Slone talked with the soothing insincerity some adults use with young children. His voice fairly dripped.

"Yes, dearest...Just a few minutes ago...Yes, he's here ...Of course, she's here...No, no, she's talking with him ...Not very late, dearest...Just as soon as I can get away...Business...Of course... Naturally. Ain't he the angel?...Just as soon as I possibly can...Yes, sweetheart...Good-bye!"

He hung up the telephone, turned back to his companion at the table, scooped her to him.

Dorothy Delano started to cry. "I hate that woman!" she exclaimed.

Steve Slone looked at her with widened eyes. "Why, honey?"

"I can't help it. Maybe she is your wife, and I should respect her rights, but she's always interfering. You love her. You know you do. You love her more than you do me!"

And she pillowed her head on his shoulder, and burst into an ecstasy of weeping.

After the manner of a man who has learned his technique from many similar experiences, Steven Slone pushed aside his water glass, plate and napkin, cleared elbow room on the table and gave himself over to the situation with serious attention.

"Why, honey, how can you think that? I married her before I ever saw you. Why, she isn't in your class at all. She's been a thorn in my side for the last two years. I can't stand her. She doesn't understand me. She's cruel. She stifles my ambitions. If I could get the grounds, I'd have divorced her long ago. I'd run away if it wasn't for this new job."

Lester Leith winced as the toe of a pointed shoe made a direct connection with his left shin bone.

"We've decided not to actually open the show until next season," Lester Leith said. "Dorothy Delano's salary will start from the signing of the contract. But there won't be much actual work for the first few months."

Dorothy Delano raised a tear-stained countenance.

There could be no doubt of the moist nature of those tears. They had ruined the make-up on her eyelashes, had streaked down her cheeks, leaving glistening trails of ruin behind them.

"Then we…can…run…away," she sobbed.

Steven Slone hesitated for perhaps two long breaths, then reached his decision.

"Okay by me, baby. We'll start tonight. We can divorce the wife in Reno or Mexico, and come back here for the rehearsals. Unless that's going to make Mr. Leith change his mind."

Lester Leith beamed a blessing.

"Not at all, not at all. It'll be great publicity. Of course, I shall want to keep in touch with you, and I'd want to have Dorothy pick the supporting cast for the show. Reno would do very nicely."

Dorothy Delano grasped her publicity agent by the sides of his fat cheeks. "Will you meet me at ten-eleven in front of the Palace Theater to-night, all packed and ready to go?"

Steven Slone nodded emphatically. "Baby, I'll be there!"

Lester Leith arose and extended his two hands in a gesture of benediction.

An apologetic waiter again knocked, bowed deferentially. "She's on the line again, Mr. Slone. I'm very sorry, sir, but she insisted—"

Steven Slone pulled the receiver from its hook with a savage gesture of impatience. But his tone contained that same drooling insincerity.

"Hello, smile-eyes…Yes, dearest…No, sweetheart, of course not…Yes, precious, right home…As soon as this conference is over…It's quite important…Yes….Yes…Yes…Of course. Bye, bye, honey."

He hung up.

"You didn't tell her," wailed the girl.

"Huh," grunted the publicity man, "she'll find it out fast enough. With that baby you don't need to tell her anything. Just try to keep it to yourself and see what happens. I'm going to toddle along and get some things together, precious. I'll see my baby at ten-ten."

She shook her head. "Ten-eleven."

He smiled. She pulled his head down to hers savagely. "Try cheating on me, and I'll carve your heart out!"

He held her in a long, clinging embrace, straightened, sighed, felt with a questing forefinger around the line of his collar, straightened his tie, grinned.

"Baby," he said, "have you got half a century to cover the tickets and stuff?"

She looked at Lester Leith. "How about an advance?"

Lester Leith took out a well-filled wallet, handed each of them a hundred-dollar bank note.

"There'll be more as soon as I can get a look at the script of the play and have my lawyer make out a contract," he said.

Steve Slone pocketed the bill, shook hands with Lester Leith.

"On my way," he said, and vanished from the booth. The girl eyed Lester Leith in teary triumph.

"Well?" she said.

Lester Leith studied the tawny eyes. "You've convinced me you can act," he admitted, "but I'm afraid I'll never trust a woman as long as I live."

The girl indicated the telephone.

"That's the way with you men. You're always yelling that women are deceivers and two-faced. But how about the lies that man told over the telephone? How about his wife waiting for him to finish a business conference?"

Lester Leith grinned. "It's a great life," he admitted. "When do I see 'Three Strikes and Out'?"

"Tomorrow. Do you want me to meet Steve at ten-eleven to-night?"

"No. I'll see him and leave a message from you."

She got to her feet, gave him her hand. Her tawny eyes were puzzled.

"You're a queer one," she said, and melted from the booth into the corridor with its row on row of green curtains masking similar booths where couples dined and discussed matters not quite so complicated as those Lester Leith had discussed with the tawny-eyed actress.

CHAPTER VII

The Signal

Edward H. Beaver fastened his obsidian eyes upon the man he had grown to hate.

"You mean we'll start gathering garbage to-night, sir?"

Lester Leith nodded. "Promptly at nine-three we leave here. We'll take in several blocks on both sides of the Middleton mansion, then there won't be any particular suspicions raised."

The spy shifted uneasily on his huge feet.

"You mean that you're going to take me with you, sir?"

Leith nodded, adjusted the tie about the collar of his evening shirt, donned coat and vest.

"Certainly, Scuttle. You will gather in the garbage. I'm not particularly versed in the etiquette of garbage-collecting, but I presume it is not done in evening clothes. I presume one should wear overalls and gloves. You have overalls and gloves, Scuttle?"

The valet nodded. His eyes were glowing with the fire of enthusiasm which comes to the hunter when the quarry is almost within range.

"You're going to take me into your confidence, sir?"

Lester Leith nodded.

The spy sighed. "I've always been willing to do anything to help you, sir—anything. I only asked that you give me a chance to cooperate."

Lester Leith surveyed the man gravely.

"Scuttle, give me your word of honor that you'll never repeat that which I am about to tell you."

The valet raised his right hand. "I swear it, sir. On my word of honor. I cross my heart and hope to die, sir."

Lester Leith nodded, consulted his strap watch, which was set right to the second.

"Scuttle, did it ever occur to you that the binding of Mrs. Middleton was not accidental? That is, Scuttle, the roping of that rung in the chair so it couldn't come loose wasn't merely a coincidence. It was done deliberately.

"Therefore, Scuttle, we are dealing with someone who has a knowledge of stage magic. We are also dealing with someone who has ability to use his hands, as well as his head."

The valet-spy nodded eagerly.

"You mean Steven Slone, the publicity manager!" he blurted.

"Precisely, Scuttle."

"And the girl was an accomplice!"

"I am inclined to think not, Scuttle. It seems she is genuinely afraid of mice. This, of course, is another link in our chain of clews. Only Slone was likely to have been aware of that fact, as far as the occupants of that room were concerned. It was exceedingly simple for him to smuggle in the mouse, turn it loose at the proper time, sneak back on the stage, grab the diamonds, and then hide them."

"Hide them, sir?"

"Yes, Scuttle. Obviously he would not keep them on his person. He knew there would be a search, at least of the committee who went on the stage. So he beats them all to it by suggesting such a search himself; and he suggests that everyone in the room be searched.

"Now, Scuttle, obviously, a man with stage experience, one who has mastered at least the rudiments of legerdemain, would naturally slip those diamonds in some place where he could count on finding them at a later date, but where they would remain undisturbed until he wanted them.

"Now it's readily apparent that any other guest could have counted upon returning to the house, upon some pretext or other. Perhaps, just to pay a social call. But Slone was there, not as a guest, but in an official capacity. His chances of again entering that house were almost nil.

"Therefore, Scuttle, it's almost certain that he would place the necklace where he could trust it would be brought to him. In other words he would place it in some article of food that was partially consumed; say a baked potato, or a half-eaten roll.

"In the excitement of the robbery there would be no thought of food as far as the guests were concerned, once the alarm had been raised."

The valet-spy was nodding his head. "No wonder they call you a mastermind!" he exclaimed. "That's bound to be what happened! It's the only logical thing, When you see it, it all fits in together perfectly. It's so simple I wonder the police haven't tumbled to it."

Lester Leith listened to the spy with a cordial smile, lit a cigarette, blew a smoke ring at the ceiling.

"You'll get the garbage, find the necklace, and hijack it, sir?" asked the valet eagerly.

Lester Leith shook his head, regarded the last smoke ring with a frown. "Not at all, Scuttle. I shall, of course, turn it over to the police."

"Huh!" said the spy.

"Certainly," commented Leith, trying another smoke ring.

"That ain't the way you built up that big trust fund for widows and orphans. And, what's more, the stones were insured. Mrs. Middleton has hid her head in shame. She didn't mind the loss of the diamonds nearly as much as she did the publicity about her spiritualistic trick. She won't be able to stage any more amateur magic again. She's collected from the insurance company, or will, and won't bother about the stones. She won't want to see them any more."

Lester Leith tossed the cigarette impatiently to one side. "Scuttle, there's something wrong about the blend of this tobacco. The smoke rings don't hold together as they should. However, that's neither here nor there. Let's start hijacking the garbage, Scuttle."

The valet was on his feet. "Yes, sir. Let me get some coveralls and gloves, sir. I have them in the garage. I won't be but a minute, sir."

Leith nodded.

"You've attended to the garbage truck, of course, Scuttle?"

"Oh, yes, sir. Yes, indeed, sir. I have it all ready."

"And you can drive it, Scuttle?"

"Of course, sir."

"Very well. Suppose you meet me on the corner, three blocks south of the Middleton residence. I'll do some scouting and make certain the coast is clear. This is the night the garbage is collected, around midnight. We'll get there at nine-twenty. By that time the garbage will be out. but we'll beat the regular truck by three hours."

The valet nodded. A cunning look crept into his eyes.

"Yes, sir. But you might attract attention if you rode on the truck in your evening clothes, sir. Suppose you go in the roadster and meet me as I drive up. It'll take me a little longer, going on the truck, sir."

Lester Leith nodded, carelessly, casually. "Okay, Scuttle. You're willing to help me?"

"Indeed I am, sir!"

"And you won't tell a soul?"

The valet looked hurt. "Didn't I promise, sir? On my word of honor, didn't I promise?" Lester Leith looked gravely apologetic.

"Pardon me, Scuttle," he said and donned his silk hat and top coat, took his stick and gloves, consulted his wrist watch.

"You must leave here in precisely two and one-half minutes, Scuttle," he said.

The spy nodded.

"I'll get the coveralls and gloves. I'll meet you there, right on the minute!"

Lester Leith slammed the door.

The valet made a dive for the closet where the telephone was housed. He moved with the frantic fixity of purpose with which a football player hurtles himself toward the goal line.

Sergeant Ackley's voice answered his frantic call.

"It's all fixed, sergeant. This is Beaver. It came out just the way I doped it, only Leith has reasoned it out so fine there ain't a chance for a slip-up.

"And he's taken me into his confidence, all except that he won't admit he's going to keep the necklace. He claims he's going to turn it over to the police when he gets it. Of course that's hooey!

"But I'm starting right now on the garbage truck. You have your men out there. When we get the garbage from the Middleton house, you can trail along. He'll stop right along in there somewhere to go over that garbage. I'll have a flashlight. When he gets the sparklers, I'll flash the light. As soon as your men see that, make the pinch!"

Sergeant Ackley grunted.

"He might have a flashlight, too. Better make it a signal. You put the flashlight on your face, hold it there for a minute. That'll be the signal."

"Okay, sergeant."

"Okay, Beaver. There'll be a promotion in this."

"Thank you, sir," said the undercover man, and grinned into the telephone.

CHAPTER VIII

"I Arrest You"

The wide street, given over to pretentious houses, showed vast and majestic in the half-light which came from the street lamps.

Here and there lighted windows, a scattering of parked cars, attested the progress of some party. The garbage truck seemed a sacrilege as it rumbled its odoriferous and unclean way to the corner and stopped.

Lester Leith, his silk hat gleaming in the street lights, strolled from the shadows, climbed to the side of the driver. "Take the alley on the left, Scuttle."

"Very good, sir."

They turned in at the alley, rumbled to the back entrance of one of the mansions. There was an assortment of cans collected near an alley gate.

The valet jumped from the seat, picked up the cans. One by one, their contents tumbled into the galvanized iron interior of the truck's bin.

The valet-spy worked for some five minutes with the cans, then clambered aboard the seat. "Phew," he said.

The truck jerked into motion and rumbled forward. Another assortment of cans greeted them, and Beaver brought the truck to a stop, repeated the process of emptying them. When he returned to the driver's seat he was breathing heavily, and his forehead was beaded with perspiration.

"One more block and then we come to the Middleton mansion," said Lester Leith, lighting a cigarette.

The police spy glanced back over his shoulder. He fancied he saw vague shadows moving furtively forward, the police, following the truck, closing in the net which was to finally terminate the activities of this master criminal; and the pseudo-valet smiled, a smile of smug satisfaction.

The truck crossed an intersection, wended its way to another assortment of cans.

"I'd hate to do this sort of thing regularly," said the spy.

Lester Leith laughed. "Think of the reward."

The valet clenched his fist, picked out the exact place on Lester Leith's jaw where he intended to swing that fist when the time came.

"I am thinking of it," he said, grimly.

He hoisted in the contents of the cans. The truck moved on. The next house was the Middleton residence. The police were closing in now.

"Careful with this garbage," said Lester Leith.

"You bet I'll be careful," agreed the spy.

"Maybe I'd better give you a hand," said Leith.

The valet grunted. "I've done it all so far. You just sit still." And he climbed stiffly to the ground.

He grasped the sides of the pails with his wet gloves, elevated them one at a time to the truck. Perspiration rolled from the face of the valet as he finished dumping the last of them.

Under cover of the truck's body, he flashed the beam of his spotlight in the agreed-upon signal. Almost instantly silent shadows glided forward with purposeful menace. The truck was surrounded.

Sergeant Arthur Ackley, himself, boomed forth the fateful words. "Lester Leith, I arrest you in the name of the law, for the possession of stolen property, for conspiring with Beaver, your valet, for the commission of a felony. Anything you say will be used against you."

There was no reply.

"Go get him, boys, and don't be too gentle." rasped Ackley, and he himself swung up on the side of the truck, his big hand clenched into a swinging fist.

The truck seat was empty.

From the other side came the perspiring face of the spy.

"Where is he?" asked Ackley.

The valet looked surprise. "He was here when I got down."

Ackley grunted.

"He could have slipped off one side of the seat when you got down the other."

Edward H. Beaver began to curse, a monotone of heartfelt profanity.

Sergeant Ackley laughed.

"What do we care? We've got him dead to rights. You can testify he got you to get the truck, that you delivered it to him, that you went out and gathered in the garbage at his direction and under his supervision. We only have to find the diamonds and then make the pinch."

Edward H. Beaver rubbed the sleeve of his coveralls across his moist forehead, looked meditatively into the back of the truck.

"I'd rather he'd stayed to sort over the stuff," he said.

CHAPTER IX

The Search Narrows

Steven Slone, an overcoat setting nattily on his shoulders, a stick swinging idly at his side, a suitcase and bag on the pavement beside him, surveyed the crowds that milled up and down the well-lit thoroughfare.

He glanced at his watch. It was precisely eleven minutes past ten.

A car purred in to the curb. A well-tailored man, garbed in faultless evening clothes, opened the door of the car.

"She asked me to pick you up," said Lester Leith.

Steven Slone extended a cordial hand, after the best showman manner. "Leith, by George! It's a pleasure. And you're right on the dot. She's waiting?"

Leith nodded.

"You're all ready for the train?"

"Yes."

"Climb in."

Stephen Slone flung the suitcase and bag into the car. "Mighty good of you," he mumbled.

"Not at all," said Leith. "She had a hard time getting packed. She's to pick up the train at Two Hundred and Seventy-Sixth Street. You folks have a drawing-room. I have the tickets here." He patted his pocket.

"Fine," said Slone.

The man was perfumed, shaved, massaged, manicured. His glossy hair emanated the odor of a particularly fragrant hair tonic. His eyes glowed with the light of one who has come to believe in the irresistible power of his own attractions.

The car slid smoothly away from the curb, out into the stream of traffic. Steven Slone lit a dark perfecto and sat back, prepared to enjoy life to the limit.

The street intersections whizzed by.

"Heard anything more about the Middleton diamonds?" asked Lester Leith.

"No, I haven't. Most unfortunate. Mighty glad I suggested that a search be made, right at the time."

"Yes," said Leith, "that was fortunate. Let's see. You used to do a little stage magic yourself, didn't you?"

"Oh, just a bit."

"Enough to know about those trick chairs?" The perfecto tilted just a trifle upward.

"Say," said Steven Slone, "what are you driving at?"

"Oh, nothing in particular. The technique of the crime interested me, that's all. You see, it had to be someone who knew Dorothy Delano was afraid of mice, someone who knew about the chair, someone who could get on the stage, fix Mrs. Middleton's trick so it wouldn't work, and then liberate a mouse at the crucial instant.

"More than that, it had to be someone who knew enough about sleight of hand to palm off the diamonds where they wouldn't be found while he was being searched so he could pick those diamonds up afterward, and walk out of the house."

Steven Slone reached up and took the perfecto from his lips. His whole frame seemed to have stiffened.

"Yes?" he asked softly.

"Yes," said Lester Leith. "There seemed to be only one person present who possessed those qualifications. So I thought it would be well to ask him about the diamonds. Now, of course, a man who was clever enough to engineer such a crime would have the necklace hidden where the police would never find it.

"It would be worse than useless to try and make a search for it as long as that man had it in its hiding place. But it occurred to me that if I could get that man to plan on running away on such short notice that he could lake only a very few of his most valuable possessions with him, I might narrow down the scope of the search."

Steven Slone took a deep breath. His right hand moved casually toward the lapel of his coat, then stopped as he felt a pressure against his side.

He looked down to see that Lester Leith was driving with one hand, that the right hand was pressing a barrel of blued steel against his side.

"We have narrowed down the search quite a bit," suavely supplemented Lester Leith. "Just your person, the suitcase and the bag."

Steven Slone thought for a while.

"Dorothy Delano?" he asked.

"Was merely giving me a demonstration of her ability as an actress. She wasn't in on it at all. I used her as an unconscious accomplice, just as you did when you freed the mouse."

Steven Slone kept both hands well in the air. "You're not nervous?" he asked.

"Not in the least, as long as you don't resist," said Leith.

"After you get the diamonds, then what?" asked Slone.

Lester Leith's smile was cheerfully urbane.

"Then we go right ahead producing the show. You draw a salary as a press agent. I have an idea you'd make a good one. It has occurred to me that you dabbled in crime only as a side line because you saw such excellent opportunity. I have a hunch you were more puzzled what to do with the diamonds after you got them than you were over any other phase of the matter."

Steven Slone heaved a great sigh.

"Damn it, you're right. They're in that grip. I figured out what a cinch it would be to cop those sparklers, and then, after it came off just the way I figured, I didn't know what to do with them.

"I turned the mouse loose, slipped up on the platform during the excitement, grabbed the diamonds, slipped them in a bowl of fruit punch. Then I suggested the search.

"After I'd been searched, I walked right over to the punch bowl in front of every one, stirred the ladle around on the bottom, managed to scoop up the necklace, and dumped it into my cup.

"I drank it, got the necklace up my sleeve, and walked out. It was just that simple. The police were all goggle-eyed. Nobody had any idea of what was going on."

Lester Leith laughed.

"Dorothy Delano?"

"You described her—an unconscious accomplice of mine, just as she was of yours."

Leith slowed the car to a stop. "The police will probably question you later on to-night. Do you suppose you can hand them a good song and dance?"

"Can I? They've nothing on me."

Lester Leith nodded. "That's true. But, perhaps, if you were to take the train for Reno, just as you planned, it might make things a little better. That would enable Dorothy Delano to give you an alibi if she were questioned."

Steven Slone sighed.

"I should have known I was getting out of my line, anyway. But, having been a stage magician, I thought I could pull the stuff ..."

Lester Leith parked the car.

"You'd better let me have that gun. You're not used to carrying it. It's going to spoil the shape of that tight coat."

Steven Slone held his hands high above his head. "Take it," he said.

Lester Leith took it, took also the diamond necklace from the bag.

"Your train," he said, "leaves in exactly ten minutes. I will drive you there. If you should be questioned you will remember that the police have nothing on you except suspicions. If you should mention that I had taken the necklace from you, you would be making yourself liable for about a twenty-year jolt."

Steven Slone struck a match, re-lit the perfecto. "I'm not a damned fool," he said.

CHAPTER X

Very Simple

Sergeant Arthur Ackley, his uniform soiled, his eyes smoldering with rage, burst into the apartment of Lester Leith.

"What the heck made you slip off that truck?" he demanded.

Lester Leith was sprawled at silken ease on the cushions of the reclining chair, blowing smoke rings. He got to his feet, the silk lounging robe billowing about him as he moved forward.

"My dear sergeant! Phew! So you've been in the scavenger business, too, eh? Well, well, well! Just fancy that! Now you had a question. What was it, sergeant? Oh, yes, why did I slip off the truck?

"Dear me, so the police know that, do they? Do you know, sergeant, the police seem terribly efficient? They know so many things. But you want an answer, sergeant. Why did I slip off the truck? The answer, my dear sergeant, is 'Three Strikes and Out.'"

The sergeant glowered at Lester Leith.

"Three strikes and out? What the heck are you talking about?"

"The name of a play I'm putting on. Dorothy Delano is going to star in it. And, during the course of the performance, a mouse is going to run across the stage. You can imagine what a kick the audience will get out of that.

"And I wanted to get some unusual publicity for it. I didn't know how to do it at first, and then I remembered about the Middleton robbery. So I decided to get Scuttle, my valet, to act as an amateur detective. I gave him a perfectly impossible solution of the Middleton affair, and had him start out to run it down.

"Then I telephoned the newspaper reporters and told them to be on hand with cameras, and they'd see Scuttle making a recovery of the Middleton diamonds.

"I hope they fell for it. Because, you see, the more publicity I can give to that story, and the episode of the mouse, the more free advertisement I can get. Then, tomorrow, when I announce the starring of Miss Dorothy Delano in the new play 'Three Strikes and Out,' all of the public who read the papers will remember the episode of the mouse.

"You see, Miss Delano was an unconscious accomplice in that affair. But the fact remains that her legs were so shapely they enabled the thief to get away with the diamonds, undetected.

"One couldn't ask for a more splendid endorsement of the young lady's figure. By the way, sergeant, I'm presenting you with a pass to the show. Drop in whenever you like. Perhaps we might even allow you to appear at dress rehearsal…Dorothy Delano, the girl with the diamond legs! Pretty nifty, what?"

Sergeant Ackley clenched and unclenched his odoriferous hands.

"Well," he said, "the damned reporters were there on the job all right. They'll be wild when they find out it's just a press stunt. How the hell did you get Beaver to fall for it?"

Lester Leith lit a cigarette.

"Oh, it sounded reasonable to him. He has a mind of child-like simplicity. Any sane person would have realized that, even if the thief had secreted the diamonds in some article of food that would go into the garbage, he'd have removed those diamonds after he had been searched and before he left the house.

"But Beaver's simple. He doesn't think of those things. So I made Beaver an unconscious accomplice to get me some free publicity ... By the way, sergeant, you certainly didn't get fooled? You weren't an unconscious accomplice?"

Sergeant Ackley clenched his hands. "Oh, no. Certainly not," he said.

Lester Leith laughed.

"Poor Scuttle! It must have been a show to see him searching for that necklace."

Sergeant Ackley forced a grin. "It was," he said.

"Ha ha!" said Lester Leith.

Sergeant Ackley took a deep breath, towered over Lester Leith for a moment, then turned and strode toward the door.

"Ha, ha!" he echoed, and banged the door with a force which threatened to tear it loose from the plastering.

Behind him, Lester Leith smiled and blew a smoke ring at the ceiling.

'The sergeant," he muttered, "seems discomfited."

Nor did it add to the peace of mind of Sergeant Ackley when it subsequently turned out that "Three Strikes and Out" was the comedy hit of the season, nor when the public fell for Steven Slone's clever press-agenting and referred to Dorothy Delano as "the girl with the diamond legs."

All of which brought additional dollars into the well-tailored pockets of Lester Leith.

Lester Takes the Cake

CHAPTER I

Lemon Pie and Layer Cake

Lester Leith stretched forth a graceful arm and jabbed an impatient finger upon the electric bell button.

The bedroom door opened and disclosed a surprised valet. "What is it, sir?"

Lester Leith motioned toward the window. "Machine guns, Scuttle. I dreamt I was in a battle."

The valet grinned. "Oh, that, sir, that's just an automatic riveter working on some steel framework next door."

"Scuttle, don't ever refer to anything that makes such an infernal racket as 'just an automatic riveter.' And another thing. Don't look so damned cheerful. What time is it?"

"Nine o'clock, sir."

Lester Leith sat up in bed, reached languidly for a cigarette. "Scuttle! Do you mean to tell me any one gets up at such an ungodly hour?"

"Yes, sir."

"Yes, indeed. So it seems. And not only do they get up, but they insist upon raising the devil with my sleep. What can we do about it, Scuttle?"

The valet leaned forward. His beady black eyes glistened like twin chunks of obsidian. His lips twisted eagerly.

"The crime news, sir. There's been a most wonderful crime, sir."

Lester Leith yawned. "Tut, tut, Scuttle. I like to read of crime during the evening for intellectual enjoyment. But now's no time for thought. It's the middle of the night. Nine o'clock in the morning! How horrible! How atrocious!"

The valet lowered his voice, made the tones seductive. "A ten-thousand-dollar diamond necklace, sir."

"Indeed, Scuttle. Now you begin to interest me. Am I to infer that this diamond necklace disappeared and has not been recovered?"

The valet nodded, rubbed his hands, twisted his great sweep of black mustache in an oily smirk.

"Yes, sir. And the police can't find it. It vanished right under their noses."

Lester Leith straightened, threw back the covers. "Indeed, Scuttle, I am interested. Give me the details."

But the valet was suddenly wary.

"Your bath first, sir. Then some coffee, sir, and a little crisp toast and bacon, with just a bit of that tart marmalade, sir, and then you'll sit in your chair by the fireplace and I'll give you all the clippings, sir."

Leith yawned, stretched, nodded, grinned.

The valet watched him narrowly through hostile, squinted eyes. Did Lester Leith realize that the supposed valet was, in reality, a police spy? Did he know that the reason for switching the conversation to the living room was because there was a cunningly hidden dictograph concealed there? That every word spoken within that room was relayed two floors down where Sergeant Ackley sat with two police stenographers, waiting, tense, expectant, drawing the net ever closer?

But if Lester Leith knew he gave no sign. He tubbed, rubbed down, shaved, dressed, ate and sprawled in the big easy chair, directly under the eager disk of the concealed dictograph.

"You were mentioning a crime, Scuttle?"

The valet pussyfooted his huge form to a place where his voice would register clearly over the hidden wires and purred an eager acquiescence.

"Yes, sir. At Goldman's, sir."

"Tut, tut, not Goldman, the jeweler?"

"Yes, sir. Goldman, the jeweler."

"And what happened? Ah. I see you have the clippings in your hand!"

"Yes, sir. Just a moment, sir. Shall I read them or shall I give you a summary of the facts?"

"Give me a running summary of the facts, Scuttle, and then I'll glance over the clippings if the crime seems to have its points of interest."

"It all started over George Cripely, sir. He was employed at Goldman's, and he was discharged. They rather fancied he'd been getting some of the smaller stones at rather less than cost. At any rate, sir, he was discharged."

Lester reached for a cigarette.

"At rather less than cost, eh, Scuttle? Come, come, you're developing tact, diplomacy. Too bad our dear friend, Sergeant Ackley, couldn't have heard that!"

And the valet, pausing only long enough to flick his boiled-lobster eyes toward the spot where the dictograph was concealed, nodded, wet his lips with the tip of a nervous tongue, and went on:

"Yes, sir. Cripely was discharged, sir. Then he returned to the store yesterday, sir. He had with him a companion, sir, a Miss Nell Spratt. He walked up to the counter, bold as brass, sir, and said he wanted to purchase a diamond necklace. The girl was rather striking, sir. Very striking, in fact, sir. From the newspaper account, one gathers that the employees all watched her. She had a beautiful figure, and the newspaper states that—let's see just how it was the newspaper did state it, sir—ah, yes, here it is: 'The suspect was accompanied by a companion whose well molded figure had taken full advantage of latest styles to proclaim itself to the masculine world.'"

Lester Leith chuckled.

"Rather neatly turned, eh, Scuttle?"

"The expression, sir?"

"No, the figure."

The valet glanced up sharply, but Lester Leith's lazy-lidded eyes seemed devoid of guile. "Yes, sir, so I gathered, sir."

"And then what happened?"

"The clerk brought out the diamond necklaces, sir. He had, of course, no means of knowing who Cripely's companion was. And she carried a package, sir, a package that she sat down on the counter. From subsequent events, sir, it seemed that the package contained an alarm clock.

"Well, sir, as I said, sir, Cripely looked at the necklaces. The companion glanced at them, over his shoulder, picked out several for comparison.

"And the store policeman came on the job, sir."

CHAPTER II

An Alarm Sounds

Lester Leith, who had been listening to the account, blowing smoke, the while, straightened in his chair. "What's that, Scuttle? The store policeman?"

"Yes, sir. You see, sir, on account of Cripely having been discharged, and on account of the suspicions that the management held, sir, the clerk pressed the button which summoned the special officer on duty at the store, sir.

"That officer wasn't intrusive. There was a chance Cripely held no hard feelings and had brought a very valuable customer to the store, sir. Such things have happened, sir. So the officer merely watched the couple.

"Well, sir, Cripely became more and more attentive to the necklaces. The woman seemed to lose interest and wandered about the store. And then the package, which had been left on the counter, sir, let out the very devil of a noise, sir. It was the alarm clock, sir. It had been wound and set, sir.

"Cripely grabbed the package, sir, ripped off the wrappings and silenced the alarm clock. Naturally, when he did that, he tossed the necklaces down to the counter, sir.

"And that was where the clerk was wise, sir, or else stupid, sir. They can't tell. For he immediately inspected the necklaces. And one of them was an imitation, sir.

"He made a sign to the officer, and the special officer placed Cripely and his companion under arrest. Cripely was searched, but they couldn't find any trace of the necklace.

"And they detained the woman, of course. Finally they were all sent to headquarters, and there the woman was searched by a matron. The search was most complete. Yet they failed to find the necklace."

The valet finished his recital, gazed with fixed intensity at Lester Leith.

"Ah, yes, Scuttle. Yes indeed, rather strange. You made a remark I didn't quite gather. You said that the clerk was either quite clever or quite stupid when he called the officer and when he inspected the necklaces. Just what did you mean, Scuttle?"

"I meant this, sir. The clerk might have been the one to make the substitution. No one thought of searching the clerk, sir. You see, because Cripely had been discharged, he was somewhat under suspicion, sir. And the clerk was considered absolutely honest.

"But Cripely claims he had telephoned the store that he was coming in with a customer, asked for a commission. He claims he talked with this clerk who waited on him. And he claims that the clerk, seeking to capitalize on the circumstances, had switched necklaces as soon as the attention of every one was distracted by the alarm clock, and that the clerk had pocketed the original.

"Of course, the clerk was running around in the excitement that followed the arrest. And, of course, he had ample opportunity to have ditched the necklace. Cripely didn't, and yet they couldn't find any trace of the necklace on Cripely or on his companion."

Lester Leith blew a smoke ring. Then he blew a smaller smoke ring through the first. Once more his chuckle rattled through the tense silence of the room.

"I see, Scuttle. And if the clerk had waited until after Cripely had left the place before making his discovery, the police would never have suspected him. It was only when they failed to find the gems on Cripely and knew that he had had no chance to dispose of them that they began to heed Cripely's story and suspect the clerk? Is that it?"

"Yes, sir."

"Yes indeed, Scuttle. And the further fact that the other suspect was a woman. That complicated matters. The store hardly cared to assume the responsibility of having its special officer search the woman. They were almost forced to wait until they got to a matron."

"Yes, sir. And now the police feel that there may be something in Cripely's story. They say it was a physical impossibility for him to have ditched the necklace anywhere."

"I see, Scuttle. They searched the package that the alarm clock was in, of course?"

"Yes indeed, sir. They even took the alarm clock to pieces and searched it."

Silence fell on the room. Lester Leith continued to blow smoke rings. "I have heard," he said, after awhile, "of crooks pulling a swindle something like that. One of them chews gum and sticks the gum to the underside of the counter. The other pushes a gem up into the gum. Then, later on, he comes back to the store and pulls the gum from the counter."

The valet snorted.

"Old stuff, sir! The police have gone over the under sides of the counters. And you've got to remember, sir, that this was no mere isolated stone. This was a necklace of diamonds. Not very large stones, to be sure, yet fairly large and well matched."

Lester Leith nodded, yawned. "Well, what other crimes have we?"

The valet's face darkened. "Nothing, sir. I thought you'd be interested in that crime, sir."

"Why, Scuttle?"

"Because you always are, sir, in crimes where the loot isn't recovered, and—er—"

Lester Leith finished for him.

"And Sergeant Ackley thinks I solve such crimes, go out and locate the missing loot, hi-jack the criminal out of it and return to my life of lazy indolence, eh, Scuttle?"

The valet squirmed, gulped.

"Yes, sir. That's about the size of it, sir."

He waited for further comment, but a series of twisting smoke rings that drifted toward the ceiling was his only response.

"Do you think the clerk was guilty?" asked the valet, after a bit.

Lester Leith yawned.

"It's hard to say, Scuttle. This is once where the newspaper hasn't given sufficient details to interest me. And there are so many ways in which Cripely could have committed the crime that it's hard to tell just what did happen."

"So many ways in which Cripely could have committed the crime!" echoed the astonished valet. "Why, sir, the police simply can't figure out a single way in which he could have possibly committed the crime. That's what makes them suspect the clerk."

"Yes?" drawled Lester Leith. "How about the woman? She was wandering all around the store. She wasn't searched until sometime later. Cripely might have slipped the stones to her."

"But the clerk swears he is certain the stones were all genuine up until the moment the alarm clock went off. And, while they didn't search the woman at once, sir, they did keep her under such close watch that it was impossible for her to have slipped anything from her person, or to have planted anything."

Lester Leith stretched, yawned, threw the cigarette into the fireplace.

"It is really too early to take any great interest in anything. And I don't like the sound of that damned riveter. I'm afraid I shall have to go out—and I don't know where to go.

"By the way, Scuttle, one point. Was that imitation necklace rather cleverly made, or was it very crude?"

The valet jumped, snapped to rigid attention. "Why do you ask that question, sir?"

"Because I want to know, Scuttle."

The valet flushed.

"That's one of the peculiar features of the case, sir. The imitation was so crude that it's hardly conceivable any one could have been imposed on by it even for a minute. It was nothing but glass, sir, strung on a thread, and the particles of glass weren't even cut to make them glisten. It was a frightfully crude piece of work."

Lester Leith reached for another cigarette, lit it, inhaled a great drag and sent twin streams of blue smoke pouring from his nostrils.

"Ah, yes," he drawled, and there was something in his tone that was like the purr of a stalking cat approaching its prey. "Do you know, I rather fancied as much."

"But," protested the valet, "that's the point that baffles the police."

"It would," smokily agreed Leith.

"But," continued the valet, conscious of that spying contrivance which reported the conversation to the listening police, "If they were going to use an imitation at all, why not use a good one? Whoever used that imitation must have used it to cover up the theft. Why not put in an imitation that would not have been discovered for an hour or two, perhaps a day or two?"

CHAPTER III

Lester Makes a Wager

Lester Leith blew a smoke ring, traced its perimeter with the tip of a well-manicured forefinger.

"You haven't answered my question, sir," muttered the valet, reproachfully.

Lester Leith grinned. "I haven't, have I, Scuttle?"

The face of the spurious valet purpled with rage. "Probably because you don't know," he gritted. "It's damned easy to sit there and blow smoke rings. You can sit in an easy chair and patronize the police, but if you were put in their place you couldn't do any better!"

Lester Leith half turned to one side to survey his enraged servant.

"Tut, tut, Scuttle. There seems to be a certain feeling in your remarks. One would gather that you had a certain sympathy with the police."

The valet, conscious of his slip, reminded also that the critical ears of his superior had been listening in on the conversation, became suddenly humble, cringing:

"I'm sorry, sir. I didn't mean it that way, sir, but I have a beastly headache, sir, and I'm a little nervous. I couldn't help but think that you hadn't made a single constructive suggestion. In fact, sir, you never do. You read the newspaper accounts of crime, sir, but, if you find any solution, you don't communicate it, sir. You use it yourself—er—that is, sir, you keep it to yourself."

Leith smiled.

"Therefore, you think that I haven't found anything out? H'mmm!

Well, now, Scuttle, I'll just make a bit of a wager with you."

"Yes, sir?"

"Yes, I'll just wager I could go into that same jewelry store, with a female companion, and work exactly the same crime on the same clerk, in the same manner. And I'll bet the police couldn't find a single clew, couldn't find the necklace I stole."

The valet gasped, that raised his voice so that no word of the incriminating conversation would be lost upon the ears of the stenographers in the police room below.

"Do—you—mean—that—you—would—steal—a—necklace?" he asked, pausing carefully between each word so there could be no possibility of talking too fast for the stenographers.

Lester Leith walked blithely into the trap he had avoided for so many weeks.

"I mean that exactly, Scuttle. I could go down to Goldman's, have a female companion, look at necklaces, steal one of the necklaces, and the police, summoned instantly, of course, would be unable to find a trace of the gems. Of course, Scuttle, I would have to introduce a little variation, just a little. I wouldn't have my companion carry an alarm clock into the store. I would have her carry something else."

The coarse lips of the police spy quivered in their slavering anxiety.

"You mean to actually steal? Not to take as a joke, not to subsequently return, but to actually steal?"

Lester Leith sighed. "Tut, tut, Scuttle, you're painfully obtuse this morning. Perhaps it's the early hours. Perhaps it's that automatic riveter. Yes, I said steal, and I meant steal. Of course, Scuttle, I'd want your word of honor that you wouldn't betray me."

The eager valet nodded. "Oh, yes, sir, of course. That would go without saying."

Lester Leith smiled. "Quite right. That would go without saying."

"You—er—you'd keep the diamond necklace, sir?"

"Of course I would. Come, come, there's no need for all this beating around the bush. For a long time you've really suspected I was the mysterious phantom hi-jacker that's been flitting around here in criminal circles, robbing crooks of their loot.

"You might as well admit it, Scuttle. Deep down in your heart you've felt that I had you read these crime clippings for a purpose. Come now, haven't you?"

The valet nodded. "Yes, sir, I have. If you'll just confide in me, sir, I promise you that I'll assist you to the limit, sir. To hell with laws.

They're made for the rich to usurp the poor. I wouldn't hesitate a minute to help you break the laws!"

Lester Leith sat bolt upright in his chair. He himself began to talk with slow, distinct articulation.

"Tut, tut, Scuttle. Let's not misunderstand one another. I am telling you nothing. I admit nothing. I only offer to wager you that I could, now mind you, I don't say that I will, I only say that I could, go to the same store and commit the same sort of a robbery."

The valet sneered. "I thought so! Always leaving a loophole, always hedging. I offered you loyal support, and what do you give me? Nothing except a lot of cheap talk. Talk's cheap. All right, if you're so confident you could go down there and rob a diamond necklace, let's see you do it!"

Lester Leith hesitated.

"Go on," taunted the valet, his purple face thrust close, the lips twitching, the eyes glittering, the veins on the forehead corded into ridges. "Go on! You made your play. I'm calling you. I'll bet you couldn't do it. All you could do is talk about how it could be done. Let's see you actually do it! I'll accept your wager. Put up or shut up."

Lester Leith regarded his valet gravely.

"Scuttle, you forget yourself! I might offer to wager with you, but you are still my valet, and you must keep your place. I'm sorry now I mentioned the matter. But, since you seem so doubtful of my sincerity in the matter. I'll just wager you an even hundred dollars that I can and will go down there, take a diamond necklace, and the police will never be able to convict me."

"Done!" yelled the valet.

"Very well, Scuttle, it's done. But there's no need for so much noise, no occasion for such an unseemly racket. And, of course, your attitude in this matter has become such that you'll understand a continuation of our relations is practically impossible.

"Your taunts, your insolence is hardly that which one expects from a servant in the way of respectful attention. This a servant must have to be valuable. Having lost that attitude, Scuttle, you have lost your value."

The valet blinked.

"Excuse me, please, sir. I assure you, if you overlook it this time I won't offend again. It was a mere slip, because I differed with you so strongly, sir. It's a physical impossibility to commit the crime, the way you outline it, sir. Why it couldn't be done on another jewelry store, to say nothing of being handled in the same way with the same clerk in Goldman's store, sir.

"And I felt so positive, sir, that I was perhaps a little out of place, sir. But I beg your pardon, sir."

Lester Leith sighed. "For the present, Scuttle, your apology will be accepted. But we'll discuss the matter later. I'm afraid you're losing some of your respect for me. Perhaps it's those constant accusations of Sergeant Ackley's.

"However, let it pass for the moment. We have other things to do. If I'm going to win that wager I'd better be getting about it. I shall need certain things. Of course there'll be the female companion—and then there'll be certain packages she will have to carry, and then there'll be the crude necklace to be used as a substitute.

"Do you know, Scuttle, I think I should have two paper bags. In one of them I want a lemon pie and in the other a layer cake. And I shall want bits of glass strung together."

"A lemon pie, sir!"

"Yes, a lemon pie. And in a paper bag, Scuttle."

"And a layer cake?"

"Yes. A layer cake. That, also, should be in a paper bag."

"But what, in heaven's name, sir, do you want with a lemon pie and a layer cake in a paper bag?"

"Not in *a* paper bag, Scuttle. That denotes a singular. I want them in paper bag*s*, Sound the *s*, meaning plural, two or more bags. I want a layer cake in one paper bag, and I want a lemon pie in the other paper bag. And don't forget about the glass necklace.

"I shall leave these matters up to you, Scuttle. As my valet you must assist me, whether your interests as an adverse party to the wager suffer or not."

The valet gulped. "Yes, sir. And the female companion? How about her, sir? I can get you a very attractive girl, sir?"

CHAPTER IV

Fine Work, Beaver

Lester Leith shook his head in stern negation.

"No, no, indeed, Scuttle. A gentleman must always insist upon consulting his personal tastes in the matter of his neckties and his women.

"No, indeed, Scuttle, I shall get my own accomplice, and I rather fancy I shall get a brunette this time. I shall want a woman with fire, a woman with glossy black hair, a woman with full lips, a woman with an undulating walk. Her every motion must be an invitation, her glance a caress.

"No, Scuttle, I should hardly trust you to find such a woman. It will, in fact, keep me pleasantly occupied during the rest of the morning. And the difficulty is enhanced by the further fact that such women as I have described are rarely abroad in the morning—unless their sleep is disturbed by a riveter, Scuttle, and that's hardly likely."

The valet watched him with puzzled eyes.

"A layer cake, a lemon pie, paper bags, glass necklace," he muttered.

"That's right. You attend to those details, and I will see about the young lady. If I should send one up here to wait, please see that she's made comfortable. I shall probably canvass the employment agencies. Good morning, Scuttle!" And Lester Leith, clamping a soft hat upon his head, grasping his stick firmly in his right hand, twisted the knob of the door and shot into the hall after the manner of a man who has urgent business awaiting him.

Behind him, the spurious valet knitted his brows in puzzled thought, waited a few minutes, then opened the door and oozed into the hall.

Tiptoeing his ponderous way down the carpeted treads of the stairs, the police spy descended two flights, paused before a door and gave a certain scratching signal upon the panels.

The door flung open.

Sergeant Ackley's beaming features smiled upon his spy. "Fine work, Beaver! Fine work! You've got him nailed to the cross. But get a bigger bet. Put me down for a couple of hundred, hell, yes, five hundred, a thousand!"

The grinning sergeant drew the spy into the room, kicked the door shut.

At a long table two stenographers were waiting, notebooks covered with pothooks and angles before them. A plain-clothes man tilted a chair against the wall and surveyed the newcomer with languid interest. Sergeant Ackley sank back in his swivel chair, still beaming.

"Aw, the bet don't cut no ice," rumbled Beaver, the man whom Lester Leith had nicknamed Scuttle.

"The hell it don't. Look here, the bet is that the police can't convict him of a crime after he lifts the necklace. Why, it's a cinch! Even suppose he was so damned slick he could lift the necklace and we couldn't find it on him. We've still got him. This talk you've had amounts to criminal conspiracy. When he steals the necklace that's an overt act. We can use his own statements and get a conviction, even if he could work out some scheme by which he could make the blamed necklace vanish into thin air.

"Look alive, Beaver. Look alive! I don't believe you know how good a break you've got. You just stumbled into it by accident."

The spy grunted.

"Yes, I did! Fat chance! I've been worming my way into his confidence for six months. I've been drawing his bath water and pressing his clothes, cooking his breakfasts, cleaning up his cigarette stubs, and putting up with his infernal air of patronizing ridicule. He Scuttles me this, and he Scuttles me that, and he Scuttles me the other, and I'm supposed to keep my temper no matter what happens."

Sergeant Ackley nodded grimly as he twisted the end from a black cigar and scraped a match across the bottom of the table.

"A good man. Beaver, never lets his personal feelings interfere with what he's doing in the line of duty. A good man never loses his temper. Remember that. Beaver. Write it down if you have to. It's your one vice.

"Lord, how I wish the bird had fallen for your suggestion to furnish the broad. We've got a couple of police lures that work the streets for mashers that'd do the job to the queen's taste. But we've got him anyway. I'll be down at Goldman's myself, and I'll have a couple of picked men—no—I guess I hadn't better attract too much attention. I'd better handle it alone."

The spy scowled. "Aw, sergeant, don't hog it all. I've worked hard on this thing, and I'd ought to be in on the killing. It won't hurt you none."

The plain-clothes man tilted his chair forward, opened his eyes, started to say something, waited. "No. You don't understand. It's not because I wish to hog the credit. It's simply because too many men will excite suspicion. You forget there's already a special on duty at the store. No. I shall handle it alone."

The plain-clothes man sighed, tilted his chair back against the wall and resumed his gum chewing.

One of the stenographers flashed the other a broad wink. Beaver, the spy, bowed his head. "Very well."

"And you'd better get busy getting those things, Beaver. A layer cake and a lemon pie! Bah! He's gone nutty."

Beaver straightened, his hard, round, boiled-lobster eyes glittered meaningly into Sergeant Ackley's face.

"You'd better get busy and figure out what he wants that stuff for. He's never made a slip yet. He always asks for some fool thing that sounds plumb crazy on the face of it. But, before he gets done, it comes in handy. You'd better watch out or he'll slip it over on you again."

Sergeant Ackley jerked the soggy cigar from his mouth, spat out a mouthful of smoke and jerked his thumb toward the door.

"That'll do, Beaver. I know how to handle this case. Don't spoil a good record by impertinence, and remember what I told you about losing your temper. That's going to make a bad blot on your record someday.

"You can get them to fix you up a glass necklace at the department, or there'll be some glass stuff at the five and ten. Get him something awfully crude. That's what he said he wanted, and that's what we'll get.

"In the meantime I'm going to drift down to Goldman's and explain the case to the manager. I'll be back here though. I want to get a line on the broad he picks.

"On your way."

And the spy, wordless in chagrin, half opened the door, oozed his bulk into the corridor and flat-footed toward the elevator.

Sergeant Ackley followed after an interval of a few moments.

CHAPTER V

A Sweet Little Girl

It was two o'clock when Lester Leith opened the door of his apartment, bowed, ushered in a striking brunette.

"Right in this way, Miss Rayon. Scuttle, the valet, will make you comfortable."

The girl turned snapping, black eyes to Lester Leith. There was a subtle invitation in the very manner in which she turned her head, in the angle of the chin as it topped the rounded point of a perfect shoulder.

"Scuttle! What a funny name!"

Lester Leith nodded. "It's a nickname. I never did learn his real name. But he looked so much like a reincarnated pirate that I christened him Scuttle—ah, here he is now.

"Scuttle, this is Miss Jean Rayon, an actress, temporarily out of employment. You'll observe that she fits into the description I had worked out for my accomplice.

"And I want her to understand the terms of our bet, Scuttle. I am to go to Goldman's Jewelry Store, stand at exactly the same counter, and in exactly the same place that George Cripely stood. I am to lift a diamond necklace, leave a glass necklace in place of it, and I am to conceal the genuine necklace so the police can't find it. We have a wager of one hundred dollars on the outcome. Is that right?"

The valet could hardly take his eyes from the seductive figure, but he glanced at Lester Leith, shook his head. "No, sir, the bet was that the police wouldn't be able to pin a case on you." And his eyes went back to the brunette.

Lester Leith laughed.

"Right you are, Scuttle. Miss Rayon will hold the stakes. And don't stare so. I can assure you that Miss Rayon, in private life, is a very estimable young woman. But she's playing a part now. She's assuming the part of a vamp for the afternoon, and I warn you, Scuttle, not to succumb to her wiles, or you'll have a broken heart.

"But to get back to the stakes, Scuttle. Get your hundred dollars. And I'll put up a hundred."

The valet reached in his pocket, pulled out some bills. "There's sixty dollars here, sir. If you'd advance me forty— there'll be a two weeks' salary payment due on Saturday, sir."

Lester Leith's hand flashed to his pocket. "Not at all, Scuttle, not at all. It's a pleasure. I'm glad to see you betting. It's a sign of an adventurous disposition, isn't it, Miss Rayon?"

The girl flashed her dark eyes to Scuttle's face.

There was, in the glance, a tangible something, almost as perceptible as in the caress of a dog's tongue. She deliberately swept her eyes from chin to forehead, forehead to chin. Her half parted, red lips disclosed a fleeting glimpse of pearly teeth, a red tongue.

"I simply adore adventurous dispositions," she said and gently elevated the tip of her shoulder.

The valet gasped.

"Come, come, Scuttle. Look alive. You have the layer cake, and you have the lemon pie?"

"Yes, sir."

"And the glass necklace?"

"Yes, sir."

"Very well, you may get them for us. We'll be leaving. And, by the way, Scuttle, what do you think of Miss Rayon's wearing apparel? That is, do you think it matches the newspaper description of the wearing apparel of George Cripely's female accomplice?"

"My God, yes!" exclaimed the valet.

"We have had the best shops in town working frenziedly," beamed Lester Leith. "There are trivial imperfections which could not be remedied in the short time allotted, but, on the whole it's rather striking.

"Well, we'll be off. And please, Scuttle, don't make the mistake of confusing Miss Rayon's stage personality with her real self. As I told you, she's acting a part."

Lester Leith gathered up the paper bags, peered at their contents, inspected the glass necklace, then held the door open for his accomplice. "All set, Miss Rayon."

At the door, she turned, swung her very short skirt in a half circle as her tilted head regarded the valet over shoulders that slanted seductively. "I just *adore* tall men with mustaches!" she breathed, and the very whisper was a caress upon the ears.

"Wait a minute!" yelled Scuttle. "Let me warn you, Miss Rayon—"

But Lester Leith had the girl by the arm. The door slammed. The police spy sat down in a chair. "Oh my God!" he exclaimed to himself.

Then he arose, walked to a mirror and preened his sweeping mustache with thumb and forefinger.

The door banged open.

"Scuttle, we've overlooked something."

"Yes, sir. What is it, sir? Do come in, Miss Rayon."

Lester Leith jabbed the tip of his cane toward a pile of newspapers.

"We were to stand at exactly the same place George Cripely stood, have exactly the same clerk wait on us. And I haven't the name of the clerk, and I don't know just where it was that Cripely stood. Do the newspapers give any photos, and diagrams of the store, the name of the clerk?"

Scuttle nodded.

"Yes, sir. I have them here. The clerk was Robert Farley, sir, and the parties stood at the extreme southerly end of the second counter on the west of the store, sir. That's where the diamonds are kept, it seems, and Mr. Cripely remained right at the corner of the counter. The woman wandered around some, looking at various things.

"Might I have a word with Miss Rayon, sir? Just a suggestion I might make to her, sir, so that, if you—er—if you lost the bet, sir, she wouldn't be involved, sir?"

Lester Leith shook his head, firmly, emphatically. "No, Scuttle, it wouldn't be fair. Come, Miss Rayon." And he drew the protesting girl into the corridor.

"But I'd simply adore talking with him. He's such a splendid specimen—"

The banging of the hall door clipped off the sentence, Scuttle cursed, went to the telephone, called Goldman's Jewelry Store and asked to speak with Sergeant Ackley. "They're on their way, sergeant, and go easy with the young lady. She's just an innocent little kid that he's roped in to do his crooked work—Yes, they're coming—No, no, she's not a common type—Rather striking and her skirts are very—er—stylish: but she's as sweet and refined as any girl you ever saw—No, no. How in hell would I know how he made her fall for him! It's just his way, damn him!"

And the spy slammed the receiver viciously into place.

CHAPTER VI

A Few Swift Gestures

The arrival of Lester Leith made quite an impression at Goldman's. The clerks had been repeatedly warned to act natural, comport themselves as though nothing out of the ordinary was happening. They overdid their parts. There was in evidence too much elaborate carelessness.

But Lester Leith seemed not to notice. He turned, held the door for his companion.

Masculine eyes swept over Jean Rayon in swift appraisal, and continued to appraise.

The girl's walk was slightly exaggerated. Her close-fitting skirt, revealing a perfect figure of rounded curves and supple motion, was daringly short. The limbs that were disclosed were graceful, well formed.

"I am looking for Mr. Robert Farley, and we wish to purchase a diamond necklace," announced Lester Leith casually to the elderly gentleman who bowed him a welcome to the store.

"This way, sir," said the gentleman.

And his were the only masculine eyes in the place that did not dwell upon Jean Rayon as she walked down the aisle.

At the second counter from the end on the west side of the store, Lester Leith leaned against the counter, hooked his cane over the edge of the showcase, and gripped the corner of the molding with well-manicured hands.

"You are Mr. Farley?"

"At your service, sir."

"And the diamond necklaces?"

"Are here, sir."

The tray of necklaces was placed upon the counter, each nestling in a special case, each case fitted into a tray, all sparkling, glittering, scintillating.

And then instructions were forgotten. The entire store crouched tense, expectant.

In the inner room, his eyes glued to a special peep hole in the polished walnut paneling. Sergeant Arthur Ackley held his breath. His face twisted and writhed, unconscious evidence of the inner suspense, the nervous strain under which he labored.

The girl stood slightly to one side. Her languid form draped against the showcase would have ordinarily arrested attention. But now all eyes were fastened upon Lester Leith.

Slowly, deliberately, with a tantalizing disregard of time, Lester Leith inspected the necklaces.

"This is a beautiful one." he said, at length. "What is the price?"

The clerk lowered his voice.

"Ten thousand dollars."

"Ah, yes, yes indeed. And this other one?"

"That, also, is ten thousand dollars The tray contains ten-thousand-dollar necklaces. Now we have another tray of necklaces at fifteen thousand dollars, if you should be interested."

Lester Leith shook his head. "No. I think these are as high as I should care to go. Let me see now if I understand you. This tray contains necklaces each of which is priced at ten thousand dollars."

"Yes, sir."

"Yes, indeed. Therefore, if I should pay you twenty thousand dollars in cash—cash, mind you, I would have the privilege of picking out and purchasing any two necklaces now on the counter?"

The clerk's eyes widened. "It's rather unusual, sir."

"Yes, yes, my dear man. I am an unusual character. But my understanding is correct, is it not? Twenty thousand dollars in cash and I can pick out any two of the necklaces now on the counter?"

"Yes, sir."

"Ah," muttered Lester Leith, and his tone was as the purring of a cat approaching a dish of cream. "Here, then, is your twenty thousand dollars."

He flipped a slender, well-manicured hand into an inner pocket, brought out a billfold. From that bursting bill fold he took crisp one-thousand-dollar currency.

"One thousand—two thousand—three thousand—four thousand—ten thousand—fifteen thousand—eighteen— nineteen— twenty thousand dollars. Would you mind verifying the amount, my good man?"

The clerk counted the money. "Yes, sir. The amount is correct, sir."

"Yes, indeed, and I now have the privilege, or perhaps I should say, the duty, of selecting two of the necklaces now on the counter?"

"Yes, sir. It's rather unusual, sir, but—"

There was the piercing shrill of a woman's scream as it knifed the air. The clerk looked up.

Jean Rayon, lounging against the counter, her arm stretched along the wooden molding of polished mahogany which rimmed the heavy plate glass, had upset one of the paper bags.

The lemon pie tilted out, hung poised on the edge of the counter.

As she screamed, the pie toppled over, hit her dress, slid down her stockings; plumped to the floor, a shapeless mass of soggy, sticky sweetness.

The girl gave another scream, darted back from the counter. Too late. The falling pie had smeared her clothes.

She raised the skirt, held it before her for inspection. And then her laugh rang out, a rippling cadence of genuine amusement. And the laugh was like the woman. In its throaty abandon there was a certain voluptuous note that arrested attention. Men ran to her, everybody shouted at once. Only the clerk at the diamond counter held his place.

Lester Leith reached her side, not as promptly as the others, however; he had hesitated for a moment while his hands had made certain swift gestures. A glittering necklace skidded upon the glass counter as he flung the bauble from him to go to the girl's assistance.

"My dear Miss Rayon! This is indeed a shame! I shall telephone a modiste immediately. Perhaps Mr. Goldman can give us a dressing room where you can wait—"

A masculine voice raised in a hoarse shout. "We've been robbed. Grab that man!"

Lester Leith turned, his face showing an expression of courteous inquiry.

"Robbed?" he asked.

"Robbed!" yelled the clerk. "Grab him! Hold them both!" There was a patter of running feet. The special duty policeman hurtled forward, grabbed the unresisting Lester Leith by an arm. The clerk rounded the counter, his finger pointing. "He switched necklaces. Left a glass necklace. Search him!"

A glass necklace dangled from the finger of the pop-eyed clerk.

"It happened during the excitement! Just the same as Cripely did yesterday!"

"I say, my man," drawled Leith. "aren't you getting a bit impertinent?"

CHAPTER VII

Not Robbed, But—

Abe Goldman, veteran of many a confidence racket, waddled out from an inner office. His shrewd face was stamped by years of business successes and reverses. His deep eyes carried great pouches beneath them. Those eyes flitted from Leith to the girl, from both to the special duty officer.

"Bring them into the office," he said.

And Lester Leith was swept into that inner office as a ship is swept on the crest of an incoming tide.

"Search him!" yelled the clerk. And Abe Goldman nodded.

Eager hands explored Leith's pockets, brought out a various assortment of objects. There were money, keys, cigarette lighter and case, fountain pen, pencil, handkerchief, knife—no trace of a necklace.

Abe Goldman twisted the cigar in his paunchy lips, twitched the puffs under his eyes, a bit as his cheek muscles tightened.

"Where's that other guy?" he asked.

Lester Leith smiled. "Rather laid yourself open for a damage suit, haven't you, Goldman?" he drawled.

Goldman never flickered so much as a flash of expression. His eyes were as steady as ever.

"We were warned about you," he said. "Where's the other guy?"

And Sergeant Arthur Ackley, striding into the room with his chest expanded, a satisfied smile on his face, answered the question. "Here I am, sir, Sergeant Arthur Ackley, ready to expose one of the slickest thieves in the country."

"You!" exclaimed Lester Leith.

"None other—in person!" gloated the sergeant.

"The man has no necklace on him," said Goldman in steady tones. "On the strength of your warning I ordered a search. I hope you haven't laid us liable to a damage suit, sir."

Sergeant Ackley laughed. He pulled the moist cigar from his lips, tried to blow a smoke ring, failed, sneered at the man before him.

"Well, I'm Sergeant Arthur Ackley, and I don't make mistakes. I told you this man was going to pull a fast one. Every one of your clerks was on the job. Your special duty officer was on the job, and still he pulls the wool over their eyes."

"There's no necklace on him," said Goldman. "I ordered him searched. How about the woman? Did he slip it to her? Shall we have a matron come? There is a great responsibility in this searching business, you know."

Sergeant Ackley laughed, then he thrust that laughing, gloating face close to the expressionless mask of Lester Leith's features.

"Ha, ha, ha! Another triumph! But it was nipped in the bud. You didn't know that I was ready for you, did you? Just shrewd detective work, that's all. I figured you'd read about Cripely's arrest. It was a toss-up whether Cripely or the clerk was guilty. If you could stage the same game with the same clerk and make it stick they'd come to the conclusion the clerk was the guilty party.

"And you sure were slick about it. But I was on the job, watching with my face against a little window. Didn't know that, did you? Well, you've come to the end of your rope."

Abe Goldman interrupted. "You can keep the praise for the papers, sergeant. Tell it to the reporters. I want to get my store cleared. This business isn't helping trade. Where is the necklace? It's missing. There's a glass substitute. The man hasn't got it on him. How about the woman?"

Sergeant Ackley shook his head. "You could search her until the cows came home!" he gloated. "There isn't a thing on her."

Then he laughed at the look of mystification which came upon their features. Sergeant Arthur Ackley was living one of the supreme moments of his life and he sought to prolong it.

But Goldman was impatient, and Sergeant Ackley hungered for their praise, their eager adulation. So he sprung his little surprise.

"The bag with the layer cake," he said. "When the woman screamed and held out her skirts all of you men looked. I didn't look. I was on the job. I did my duty. I kept my eyes on Lester Leith.

"What happened? Ha! I'll tell you what happened. Lester Leith made a swift pass with his hand toward the layer cake. There was something in his hand that glittered. After an instant he took his hand out of the bag. Nothing glittered. Clerk, get that bag!"

They regarded him in awestruck silence.

The bag was produced. Sergeant Ackley ripped open the paper. Ostensibly the cake was as before, save for a certain dent in the frosted surface, a little ridge on either side.

"He stuck his forefinger into that cake. From the palm of his hand the necklace dropped into the hole. Then his thumb smoothed back the frosting!"

"Incredible," said little Abe Goldman, short, paunchy, unemotional.

"Be careful with that cake, sergeant," warned Lester Leith in a drawling tone of calm superiority. "It's a birthday gift."

"Yeah! You would want me to be careful! Well, look at this!"

And he took a knife from his pocket, opened the small blade, probed into the cake as a physician might probe a wound.

The knife blade grated. Sergeant Ackley's wrist twisted, and a glittering string of scintillating gems came into the light, a trifle smeared with moist cake, but sending their sparkling coruscations glittering through the somber room. "Identify them!" yelled Sergeant Ackley in triumph.

The clerk leaned forward. "Those are the ones. The price-tag's still on them."

Sergeant Ackley set down the knife with its pendant string of glittering gems. Slowly, deliberately, conscious that the eyes of every person in the room were upon him, he pulled handcuffs from his hip pocket.

"A long, long time I've waited for this moment," he said. "I pray that you resist me, you damn, drawling, sneering, dirty double-crossing crook!"

"Tut, tut, sergeant. There are ladies present, and aren't you getting just a bit premature?"

Sergeant Ackley shifted the handcuffs to his left hand. His right hand bunched into a fist. His gloating eyes fastened in malevolent hatred upon Lester Leith's finely chiseled features. Abe Goldman took the cigar from his mouth. "None of that. Not in here. Farley, are you absolutely sure of that necklace?"

The clerk nodded. "It's the one."

"What one?"

"The one he stole."

Goldman sighed. His shrewd mind grasped that here was something that was not what it seemed on the surface.

Lester Leith turned toward the clerk.

"The one I *what*?"

"Stole!" snapped the clerk.

"Tut, tut," cautioned Lester Leith, "you've got your verbs mixed, my man. That necklace was the one I *bought*."

And the clerk, suddenly reminded, jumped a foot, let his jaw sag while his eyes widened until they were about to drop from their sockets.

Sergeant Ackley's right fist slowly opened. The left hand with its glittering handcuffs dropped to his side.

"*Bought!*" said Abe Goldman. "How's that, Farley?"

The clerk nodded, tried to speak, failed, gulped again.

"My God, he's right! It *is* the one he bought!" Goldman's eyes suddenly became hard as agates. "Then why did you accuse him of theft?"

The clerk leveled a trembling forefinger at Sergeant Arthur Ackley.

"The cop. He came in here and described this chap, said he'd come in and lift a necklace from me. He came in and bought two necklaces. Then there was excitement, and he dropped a glass necklace on the counter, mixed it in with the others. I had my attention on the girl. I looked back at the counter, saw the glass, remembered what the officer had told me. and—and—well—"

Abe Goldman shifted his glance toward Sergeant Ackley. "There may be a damage suit in this," he said dryly.

Sergeant Ackley's face suffused with color. He twisted the moist cigar in nerveless lips, lips that trembled. Abe Goldman was in right with the city administration.

"But why," demanded Sergeant Ackley, in a voice that was but a feeble echo of his usual booming tones of rasping authority, "did this guy stick that necklace in the cake and drop another fake necklace on the counter?"

Goldman's eyes shifted to Lester Leith's, stared hard at him for a full minute. "That's what a judge would want to know, if you started a damage suit against us for false accusation," he said.

Lester Leith's face was a mask of pained surprise. "Dear, dear," he said. "I never thought of that. But it's the most simple explanation in the world, gentlemen. You see, this is Miss Jean Rayon's birthday. I wanted to surprise her with the gift of a diamond necklace, and I wanted the surprise to be genuine.

"So I pretended I was going to come here and try to steal a necklace. I even made her think so. And I made my butler and valet, a chap I call Scuttle, think so. I even made a trifling wager with Scuttle.

"I intended to buy the necklace, stick it in the cake when nobody was looking and then have the clerk wrap up the glass necklace for me. Of course, Miss Rayon would know that the necklace I was having wrapped up was glass, and she'd be completely mystified. Then when I parted company with her, I was going to say: 'Jean, you take the cake,' and I was going to give her the cake. Then she'd find the diamond necklace in it when she came to eat it. I even thought we'd have a little party in my apartment and I would serve her the piece that had the diamond necklace in it.

"It was a most tasty little surprise, and now you sleuths have ruined it!"

Abe Goldman sighed.

"That," he remarked judicially, "is a damned lie. But you look just goofy enough so some fool jury might believe it!"

Lester Leith became haughty. "I am afraid I care to have no business dealings with your house, sir. Will you please instruct your man to return my twenty thousand dollars? My attorney will continue this discussion."

Abe Goldman chewed the cigar. "There's more to this than appears on the surface," he muttered.

"There will be," promised Lester Leith.

Jean Rayon held out her sticky, soiled dress. "And how about poor little me?" she shrilled.

Abe Goldman looked, sighed, looked again. Lester Leith extended a protecting arm.

"Not here," he said. "We will go directly to my apartment to change. Mr. Goldman, will you please compensate in some measure for the damage done us by calling a cab?"

Goldman sighed, jerked a thumb toward the special duty officer.

"Get'm a cab, Bob. Just the same, mister, I'll fight any suit for damage you bring. The whole thing smacks too much of a frame-up. I won't pay a plugged nickel for compromise!"

Lester Leith shrugged.

"I had hardly intended to commercialize the incident, but I did intend to exact an apology to the young lady, and, perhaps, a new costume for her."

Abe Goldman's eye lit. "That all you want?"

"That's all I want."

Goldman's hand shot out.

"Damned if I don't believe you. Leith. I apologize, Miss Rayon, you'll find a credit slip mailed you, care of Mr. Leith, at the best shop in town for the most expensive outfit in the place."

And he broke off as twin arms snapped around his neck, drew the paunchy face toward half parted red lips.

"You *dear*!" she exclaimed.

Five seconds later Leith coughed apologetically. "Air?" he asked.

Goldman jerked his red countenance away, suddenly embarrassed. "Bob, where the hell's that cab?"

"In front, sir."

Sergeant Ackley. moving on rubber heels had sneaked toward the door.

"No, you don't!" yelled Abe Goldman. "I've got something to

take up with you! Farley, give this man back his money, see him into his cab. Sergeant, you sit down. I'm going to talk to you."

Lester Leith bowed suavely. "Ah, good day, gentlemen, and—Jean, you take the cake!"

They entered the cab, Lester Leith carefully counting the twenty thousand dollars. Just before the special duty officer slammed the door, Lester Leith thrust out a detaining hand.

"My glass necklace," he said. "They've forgotten that."

And the officer trotted into the store, returned with the crude glass gewgaw. Lester Leith took it, smiled his thanks. The cab door slammed, the vehicle lurched forward and moved away. Within a few blocks he ordered the driver to halt, and, excusing himself to the girl, sauntered around a corner into a bank, where he obtained access to a safe deposit box listed under a name that neither Scuttle nor Sergeant Ackley would have recognized.

CHAPTER VIII

Ackley Has an Inning

The valet stared at the bedraggled form of the girl, her dress and stockings smeared with the remnants of a lemon pie.

Lester Leith, in the doorway, snapped the man's attention back to earth.

"Scuttle, Miss Rayon has met with an accident. It's impossible to get her accurately fitted, but we have here a ready-made dress we've picked up, also some stockings and shoes. Will you kindly draw a bath and lay these things out for Miss Rayon?"

The police spy glanced his dumb amazement, then nodded.

"And may I caution you," remarked Lester Leith in his dry voice, "that Miss Rayon has been acting a part. In reality, Scuttle, when she's not in character, she's a very modest and very estimable young lady of unimpeachable character."

The valet gulped, nodded. "This way, ma'am."

The girl followed him. Her soiled skirt was lifted in her hand. Her red lips parted in a smile of good-natured recognition of the spectacle she made.

There was the sound of running water, the murmur of voices, and the valet oozed his bulk back into the room. "I wonder—" he began.

The words clipped off as the door banged open. Without the formality of knocking, Sergeant Ackley slammed his way into the room. His face was livid, his lips writhing in an ecstasy of rage.

"Tut, tut, my dear sergeant," remonstrated Lester Leith. "You grow more and more intolerant of my rights. You usually go through the formality of knocking. Scuttle, the night latch please. Let's have no more heavy-fisted policemen walking in upon us."

Sergeant Ackley stopped the pseudo-valet with a gesture. "Cripely's confessed!" he snapped.

"Indeed?" Lester Leith's tone was a combination of superior condescension and mild exasperation.

"Yes, damn you, indeed! He confessed while I was at Goldman's and they telephoned the confession to me there!"

Lester Leith reached for a cigarette, lit it, flung himself into a chair.

"Indeed?" he asked again, his voice masked in utter unconcern.

The police spy, masquerading as a valet, caught the significant look in Sergeant Ackley's eye, and moved closer.

"Yes," rasped Sergeant Ackley, "and he told the whole scheme. He went to the store with his woman companion. The episode of the alarm clock served to distract attention for a second. That was all the time he needed."

Sergeant Ackley paused.

Lester Leith blew a smoke ring.

"George Cripely had been a wood joiner at one time. When he knew he was to be discharged he became bitter in his resentment and resolved to get even. So he put in his spare moments when no one else was about in working over the wood molding on the corner of the diamond showcase. He hinged a section some five inches long, hollowed it out, fixed it so it would flip back and forth by a gentle pressure, and he joined the wood so cleverly it was almost impossible to detect the flaw."

Lester Leith blew another smoke ring, traced the whirling perimeter with the tip of a well-manicured forefinger.

"Really, sergeant," he drawled, "if you came here in such excited haste just to tell me this, your efforts have been in vain. I deduced as much as soon as I read the newspaper account of the crime. It was obvious—particularly when I knew the man had two weeks' notice of his discharge.

"If he hadn't arranged some clever hiding place he'd have had the imitation necklace—one that would have fooled the clerk until after he and his companion had left the store. As it was, he wanted the theft to be discovered in time to be thoroughly searched before he had left the place. Under the circumstances, there was only one deduction."

Sergeant Ackley rasped an oath.

"Of course, you knew it, and you went to the store with this elaborate stage setting of yours. And while you were buying the necklace, you fooled around until you found the section of the counter that had been tampered with."

CHAPTER IX

Scuttle Gets Slapped

Lester Leith stifled a yawn with a courteous palm. "Indeed?"

"You're damn right, indeed. They telephoned me from headquarters when Cripely confessed, and I went to the counter myself. I found the place, but the necklace was gone!"

Lester Leith tried sending a small smoke ring through a large smoke ring. Sergeant Ackley's face was a purple mask of wrath.

"And so you played it damned slick. You were careful to ask if you could buy any two necklaces on the counter for twenty thousand dollars. Then you put up the twenty thousand.

"Where you fooled us was when you stuck your hand into the cake. You put in two necklaces. One of the ones the clerk had been showing you, and the other the one Cripely had hidden, and you were damned careful to have the Cripely necklace down underneath the one you'd been looking at.

"If nobody had tumbled to the hiding place you'd have walked out with both necklaces and later demanded your twenty thousand dollars back.

"If anyone had tumbled to the place where the missing necklace was as I did—you had a perfect defense—you'd bought it. And if I'd had sense enough to probe down and find the second necklace, you even had a defense for that. It was on the counter, and you'd purchased it.

"It was one of those damned crimes where you had a perfect defense all the way through—"

Sergeant Ackley broke off, leveled an accusing forefinger. "Lester Leith, where's that cake?"

Lester Leith shrugged his shoulders. "Miss Rayon took it."

Sergeant Ackley glanced at Scuttle. "It's in the paper bag," he prompted.

Scuttle nodded. He oozed his bulk through the bedroom door. From the bathroom beyond could be heard the splashing of water.

Lester Leith smoked in contemplative silence. The pseudo-valet returned with the paper bag. "She carried it in," he muttered.

Sergeant Ackley pulled out the cake, thrust a forefinger into the hole which remained plainly visible in the frosting. For a second a look of startled, fierce incredulity suffused his features, then he gave an exclamation of joy.

"Trapped, by God! I thought, of course, they'd ditched it!"

And his grimy forefinger pulled to light a cake-covered bit of glittering jewelry.

"Trapped!" he yelled. "Run to earth!"

Lester Leith moved no muscle. He remained in his chair, calm, relaxed, the smoke eddying up from the end of his cigarette.

"By God, this is the time I've outsmarted him!" yelled Sergeant Ackley. "Get the handcuffs. Get the girl. Get the wagon. Get the plain-clothes men up from below. Get Goldman on the phone. By God, I'll show—"

His voice trailed off into silence. The wind whooshed from his lungs as though someone had smashed him in the stomach.

Lester Leith sighed, moved the end of the cigarette to lips that were parted in a half smile.

"The damn thing's glass!" exclaimed Sergeant Ackley.

"Quite so. sergeant." soothed Lester Leith. "You'll remember I sent back for my glass necklace. I really couldn't think of a better place to put it than to drop it into the hole in the cake. Sorry you were fooled, sergeant. Better luck next time, eh?"

Sergeant Ackley muttered an oath.

"You put it there just to tantalize me some more, you damn, drawling, sneering, smoke-ring-blowing crook!"

He drew back his arm, held the cake poised for a moment, then dashed it into the fireplace. The cake shattered against the sooty wall, dropped to the hearth. Lester Leith never moved.

"Scuttle," he said, "you'll have another mess to clean up. The sergeant's lost his temper again."

There was no answer.

Lester Leith half turned in his chair. "Scuttle, where's Scuttle?"

There showed only the half open door into the bedroom. There was now no sound of splashing water. "What the devil?" drawled Lester.

There was the sound of bare feet, the smack of a blow that sounded explosively loud. Scuttle oozed from the half-opened door with sudden speed. Upon his left cheek were stamped the livid marks of four fingers, the unmistakable imprint of a woman's hand, swung in a terrific slap.

Lester Leith laughed. "I told you, Scuttle, that Miss Rayon, when out of character, was a very estimable young lady of unimpeachable morals."

And then Lester Leith turned lazy-lidded eyes to the glowering sergeant.

"You know, sergeant. Jean is a very remarkable girl. You have to hand it to her, sergeant, she takes the cake!"

There was an oath, the banging of a door.

Lester Leith was alone. Sergeant Ackley had stormed through the front door in a rage. The humiliated, crestfallen police spy who posed as valet, had oozed through the door into the kitchenette.

"Under the circumstances," mused Lester Leith. "I think Scuttle will concede the bet."

And he blew a smoke ring, traced the whirling edge of the curling smoke with the tip of a delicate forefinger.

His chuckle was plainly audible to the mystified police stenographers who waited, two floors below, taking down the sounds that came to them over the telltale wires of the dictograph.

The police might suspect what they pleased, but there could be no conviction unless they actually found the stolen necklace in Leith's possession. Without corroborating circumstances they dared not even make a formal accusation. They had only the word of a self-confessed crook that the necklace had ever been placed in that counter with its concealed hiding place in the molding. And any one of half a hundred men might have removed that necklace, the janitor, the clerk, even Sergeant Ackley himself.

Thieves' Kitchen

CHAPTER I

Fifty Thousand in Diamonds

Lester Leith, his well-knit form arrayed in faultless evening garb, drew on his gloves, and surveyed the police spy who masqueraded as his valet, with eyes that were clouded in thoughtful speculation.

"Not more than ten minutes, Scuttle?" asked Lester Leith.

"No, sir. Ten minutes will suffice, sir, and I can assure you that it's most unusual."

Lester Leith glanced at his wrist watch. "But, Scuttle, I've repeatedly told you that I'm no longer interested in crimes. I collected crime clippings on unusual cases for a while, it's true; but I did it merely to satisfy a private curiosity. It afforded me a certain intellectual stimulus, Scuttle.

"I have always contended that a man should have some mental exercise to develop his brain, just as he uses a physical exercise to develop his muscles."

The spy nodded eagerly.

It was apparent that he was trying with all of the wiles at his command to interest Lester Leith in the matter he was about to present.

"Yes, sir, quite so, sir. And you're right, sir. And this matter I have to discuss, sir, is one of the most unique of all crimes. It's going to be a most celebrated case. There are more than fifty thousand dollars in diamonds missing, sir.

"And the murder of the woman was so cowardly, so utterly brutal..."

Lester Leith yawned, patted his mouth with four polite fingers to conceal the yawn, reached for a cigarette.

"But, Scuttle, you overlook the main fact," he remonstrated. "This over-zealous, bungling, heavy-handed Sergeant Ackley got wind, somehow, of the fact that I was interested in crime news; and he immediately jumped at the conclusion that I was solving crimes in advance of the police, ferreting out the criminal, stripping him of his ill-gotten gains, and using the proceeds to swell the funds I gave to charity, despite the fact that a large portion of those gifts are to the Police Protective Association. Those last funds, Scuttle, are for the exclusive benefit of the widows and orphans of officers killed in the line of duty.

"Now I like to turn my mind on crime problems, Scuttle, but Sergeant Ackley is a boor, a bore and a boob, I don't like him, and I don't like the type of officer he stands for. There are lots of good men in the department, Scuttle, but this Ackley person has declared a private feud with me. They say he neglects everything else to harass me, hoping to get..."

The valet who was not a valet; but an undercover man, acting under the direct orders of this same Sergeant Ackley, broke in on the conversation.

"Yes, sir, I know, sir, and I know you'll pardon me, sir. But if I'm to give you the details of this crime in ten minutes, sir, I'll have to begin immediately, sir!"

"Well put, Scuttle, well put, indeed! I grudgingly give you ten minutes to impart information, and then start railing against the police force. Go ahead, Scuttle. I'll wait. What is it?"

And Lester Leith flung himself down in a reclining chair, crossed his ankles, tilted his head back and regarded the curling smoke from his cigarette with meditative eyes.

The spy, big, broad-shouldered, bull-necked, with little gleaming black eyes which peered suspiciously at the world from under bushy black brows, bowed deferentially.

"Yes, sir, thank you, sir. The crime is the robbery and murder of Mrs. Conrad Steele."

Lester Leith flicked a quickly questioning glance to the spy's face.

"I read something about it, Scuttle. The woman went to her home, I believe. Robbers had entered the house searched for the stones, found that the woman was wearing them, and deliberately awaited her return. When she entered the little reception hall they struck her down from behind, stripped the gems from her, and then made their escape. Is that the case?"

The spy twisted his thick lips in a smile. "Well, now," he said "that's part of it."

"Indeed?" he commented.

The spy nodded, an emphatic nod of oily affirmation, of ponderous emphasis.

"Yes, sir. There have been more recent discoveries. For instance, sir, the chauffeur, Bert Meggs, sir."

"What about him, Scuttle?"

"You remember that the back window had been forced with a bar, sir? Well the edge of that bar had a peculiar dent in it, and that dent impressed itself upon the soft wood so that the police were able to know exactly what bar it was that was used to force the window

"They found the bar in the garage. It had the fingerprints of the chauffeur on it.

"You'll remember, sir, that the police were tipped off to the crime. That is, there was a telephone call. If you read the newspaper accounts of the crime, you'll remember that the police received their first intimation of the murder by this mysterious call.

"The man on the other end of the line seemed all excited. He said he had gone with two other men to steal some diamonds from a house, that the diamonds weren't there, that while they were waiting in the house for some coffee to get hot there was a sound at the door and the woman came in, wearing the diamonds.

"He said that the other two men struck her down and ripped off the jewels. That made it first degree murder for all three, but this man wouldn't have anything to do with it. He ran out, refused to share in the loot, telephoned the police.

"Well, sir, the police have about concluded that this call came from the chauffeur. Their theory is that the chauffeur trapped Mrs. Steele, took two professional crooks into his confidence and was to split the spoils with them.

"Then, when they murdered the woman, instead of just robbing her, the chauffeur got frightened and ran away. Anyhow, the bar that opened the window had been used by the chauffeur. The chauffeur was missing. They finally located him. He refused to talk about the case.

"But, sir, when the body of Mrs. Steele was being examined at the inquest, the coroner found a note tucked in her stocking, down at the sole of her foot. That note was from the chauffeur, Bert Meggs, and shows that he and the woman had an appointment at the house. She was to go to the reception at Mrs. Stanwood's, pretend to be taken ill, go home early.

"Mrs. Steele's husband, Conrad Steele, the lawyer, was working at his office, dictating an important brief that had to be in the hands of the printer in the morning. He had arranged with his secretary to be there and work all night.

"So the chauffeur and the wife were to meet in the man's own house. Those were the plans. The note's in the chauffeur's handwriting. There's no question of that. It was addressed to the wife under an assumed name and sent through the mail. That is, the envelope had the false address, but the note started out 'Dear Vivian,' and it was to the woman all right, was in the chauffeur's handwriting, and mentioned that he knew Conrad Steele was going to be working until well after midnight.

"That's enough to hang the crime right on the neck of this Bert Meggs. He knew it and skipped out, but the police caught him and took him to jail."

The spy paused, watching Lester Leith's face. That face contained no faintest flicker of interest, so the spy thrust forward the bait once more.

"The diamonds, sir! They're worth fifty thousand dollars, sir. They're even insured for forty thousand."

CHAPTER II

A Love Pirate

Lester Leith blew a smoke ring, watched the twisting smoke spiraling upon itself, nodded, and finally spoke. His tone was cold and distant.

"Tut, tut, Scuttle. You're getting a tabloid mind. I've warned you against it before, Scuttle. You become interested in problems of the eternal triangle, of love nests and beauty. You gloat over the discovery of women in compromising situations. You want to pry into things which are none of your dammed business.

"So far as I am concerned, I regret very much that Mrs. Steele is dead, I regret ten times more the fact that the circumstances of her death were such that her name can be bandied about by a morbid population which gloats upon scandal."

The valet wet his lips.

"You forget the diamonds, sir," he reminded, reproachfully.

Lester Leith shook his head. "I forget nothing, Scuttle. I am not interested."

He got to his feet, straightened out his coat, glanced at his wrist watch.

"But the crime, sir. The newspapers are simply crammed with it. There are photographs, diagrams, interviews."

Lester Leith yawned, and this time made no attempt to disguise that he was yawning. He started for the door of his sumptuously furnished bachelor apartment.

The spy followed him.

"But there's still another angle, sir. A beautiful woman was the accomplice of the chauffeur. And it may be the real motive of the crime wasn't robbery at all. The pilfering of the diamonds was merely an incident, sir."

Lester Leith paused, hand on the knob of the door. "Let's hear it, Scuttle."

"The secretary of Mr. Conrad Steele, the lawyer, was in on it too, sir. She had said that she didn't know the chauffeur, had never met any of the members of the attorney's family, sir. That was when the police first interrogated her, just as a matter of routine, sir.

"Then, when the chauffeur was arrested, a woman called up and wanted to get in touch with the chauffeur. She seemed very much disturbed. She didn't want to give her name.

"In a case of that sort, it's customary for the police to run down every clew, particularly every woman element, so the police held the woman on the line and trace the call. It was coming from a pay station in a drug store.

"The police asked the woman if she had any particular interest in the man, and she said she was his wife. So they told her they would let her speak with the chauffeur if she would hold the line until they got him from his cell. They left her holding the line and rushed a patrol to the drug store.

"They found the woman still waiting at the telephone. And when they arrested her, sir, and took her to headquarters, they found that she was really the woman who worked in the attorney's office, the one who had sworn she had never even met Bert Meggs."

The spy paused, waiting to see if this last bit of information had proven of interest.

Lester Leith remained, hand on the knob of the door. "When they arrested her, did you say, Scuttle?"

"Yes, sir."

"The police arrested her, Scuttle?"

"Yes, sir. Of course, sir."

"Why, of course, Scuttle?"

"Because they have an entirely new theory now, sir. They feel that the chauffeur might have had a rendezvous with the lawyer's wife, that the girl who worked as secretary for the husband might have been wise, might have caught the pair together and struck down Mrs. Steel. The rage and hatred of a woman under such circumstances, sir, knows no bounds. There are many cases on the police records to prove that.

"Then the police feel that Meggs might have made up with the girl, that they might have stripped the corpse of the jewels, and tried to make it appear that the crime was the work of burglars, instead of being a crime of vengeance.

"They did that be ransacking the place, jimmying a window.

Then the girl rushed back lawyer's office. The chauffeur telephoned the police with the story about the three men who had broken into the house, and then tried to run away.

"It's the old story, sir. The man had a charm fatal to women. He preyed upon them. But when he was caught by the secretary, when the lawyer's wife had been murdered, then the chauffeur decided to play the hare that would draw the hounds off the real criminal—the woman who worked in the lawyer's officer."

Lester Leith's hand dropped from the doorknob. "Scuttle," he said, "you are beginning to interest me."

Relief flooded the concerned face of the spy. "Yes, sir," he said, and sighed.

Lester Leith frowned thoughtfully. "So the police are going to make the lawyer's secretary the goat, eh, Scuttle?"

"Not the goat, sir. If she's guilty, then the police will ferret it out, and she'll have to pay the penalty."

Lester Leith made a wry face.

"And in the meantime she'll be the goat of the press. Her good name is all gone right now. The public will lick its chops over the girl's predicament...What's her name, Scuttle?"

The valet spy smirked. "The name that she goes by, sir, is Jean Joy."

"Why say it in that way, Scuttle, the name she goes by?"

"Because, sir, it's undoubtedly an assumed name. It's the sort of the name a motion picture actress would assume."

Lester Leith sighed. "And what are the police doing, Scuttle?"

"They are giving the chauffeur the works, hoping that he'll crack."

"And has he cracked, Scuttle?"

"Not entirely. Not on the major points. But the police raided his apartment over the garage on the Steele property, and found a trunkful of love notes. There were notes in the hand-writing of Mrs. Steele, and notes in the handwriting of this Jean Joy, as well as notes from forty or fifty other women. He was regular love pirate. That's what he was, sir!"

Lester Leith nodded.

"Doubtless, Scuttle. I'm not particularly interested in him. But I *am* interested in this Jean Joy. Mark you, Scuttle, she does nothing save allow her emotions to be ensnared by this love pirate, and calls up to find out about him at the jail—and that's only natural, Scuttle—and the police swoop down upon her.

"It gives the police a lot of free publicity. It solves the mystery and saves the police the embarrassment of locating the two robbers who were in the house, awaiting the return of the attorney's wife.

"That's typical police reasoning, Scuttle. If their first theory is correct, and the chauffeur was the one who telephoned in the tip about the murder, then the chauffeur was the innocent one. Not in the eyes of the law, perhaps, since he'd entered the house feloniously, along with the other two, And, as I understand the law, Scuttle, when a man does that, and one of his associates commits murder in furtherance of the joint felony, then it becomes first degree murder for all of them.

"But mind you this, Scuttle. If that same police theory is correct, then the two who actually struck the fatal blow, the two who actually stole the diamonds, are the ones that are missing.

"Then this girl shows up. She has been unfortunate in an affair of the heart. And what happens? She is immediately thrust forward as the one who did the murder. The police act on the theory that the other two bandits weren't there at all. They were, claim the police, just a stall on the apart of the chauffeur to protect the secretary! Bah!

"The real truth of the matter, Scuttle, is that the police know there's no romance and no advertising in having a pair of thugs kill a woman and strip off her jewels. But there's opportunity for any amount of sob sister stuff in the business of a secret wife killing another woman over her husband's affection."

And Lester Leith made snorting noises of disgust.

CHAPTER III

Hungry Crooks

The spy fidgeted during the arraignment of the police, muttered under his breath, but preserved the outward semblance of servility. "Yes, sir," he said.

"And, of course," added Lester Leith, "the police have the added advantage with this new theory of having the culprit they want to convict behind the bars. It might prove embarrassing for the police if they threw out a dragnet for the other two robbers, and then couldn't find them."

"Yes, sir," said the spy.

"Tell me," said Lester Leith, "was this secretary really his wife?"

"Probably not, sir. There was a sort of common law marriage, but it's not legal. The police want to be certain that it wasn't really legal, sir."

"Why, Scuttle?"

"So they can force the chauffeur to confess and testify against his wife. Under the law, a husband can't testify against his wife."

Lester Leith smiled without amusement.

"So the police will show the marriage is illegal, eh, Scuttle?"

"Yes, sir."

"But what time was the murder committed, Scuttle?"

"About ten o'clock, sir."

"But, Scuttle, this girl, Jean Joy was in the attorney's office. Wasn't she writing on this brief? Can't Steele himself give her an alibi?"

The valet shook his head. "He claims he can, sir. The police claim he can't."

"Why, Scuttle?"

"Because Steele was in his private office with the door closed and locked, dictating to a dictating machine. The girl was in the outer office transcribing the records that Steele brought her from time to time.

"That's the way Steele dictated his briefs. He would shut himself in, get a whole bunch of wax cylinders, and work on his brief. When he had a bunch of cylinders dictated, he would take them to the outer office, give them to the girl. Then he'd go back and dictate some more.

"Now he claims that the girl was working steadily. He says he could hear her typewriter going all the time. He was in his own room, dictating, but the sound of the typewriter could be heard through the closed door.

"The police claim that the girl could have had a confederate who slipped in, put the tubes of the transcribing machine to her ears and went right on with brief.

"Steele admits that he started on a fresh batch of records around nine thirty, and that he didn't emerge from the office with them until the police had called him on the telephone to notify him of the death of his wife. And the police can prove that, because the dictated cylinders are still there.

"So that's the way it stands, sir. The lawyer feels that his secretary is innocent, and is going to try and swear to an alibi for her. The police feel she is guilty. The chauffeur holds the key to the situation."

"I take it," said Lester Leith, his eyes shifted in thought, "that they will be sweating this chauffeur, Scuttle."

The laugh of the spy was harsh and vindictive.

"Sweating him is right, sir. That man's going to get a third degree that'll make him think he's been some place. You can't hold out on the police. A crook has to cave, sooner or later. There never was a crook who didn't crack some time or other, or would have, if the police could have had him long enough without some lawyer butting in."

Lester Leith paced to the window, stared out at the street lights, glanced down at the passing automobiles, pursed his lips and nodded.

"Yes, Scuttle," he said, "I am interested in that case. Do you know, Scuttle, in many ways it's a curious case. It offers an opportunity for speculative mental exercise."

The valet spy was never more at sea than when Lester Leith drawled at him in this patronizing tone. But it was apparent that he had achieved the result he had started for. Lester Leith was going to turn his mind on the problem of this case. So the police spy bowed deferentially, as became a well trained servant, and said tonelessly:

"Yes, sir."

Lester Leith walked to the reclining chair, dropped into it again, lit another cigarette.

"Do you know, Scuttle, the thing that started my interest in this case was what I read in the newspaper account about the woman's purse."

The spy raised his eyebrows. "You mean the large sum of money it contained, sir?"

"Partially, Scuttle. The report said that the purse had over five thousand dollars in bills, a compact, a bottle opener, a latchkey to the front door, a lead pencil, a fountain pen, some visiting cards and a check book."

The spy nodded.

"Yes, sir. I believe so, sir. The purse was untouched, sir. Robbery was the motive of the crime right enough, sir; but it was robbery of the diamonds, sir."

Lester Leith regarded twisting smoke spirals.

"The murderer must have known her habits intimately, Scuttle."

"Yes, sir. So it would seem."

"Funny that he'd not think to look in the purse."

"You say 'he,' sir."

Leith nodded. "I can't bring myself to that hypothesis that the woman did it."

"You mean then that the chauffeur must have done it?"

"No, Scuttle. I am inclined to take things at their face value. That is where I differ from the police. The police never take things at their face value. The police always believe everyone is lying. Now why not believe, Scuttle, that the persons who have been so unfortunate as to become involved in this affair are telling the truth. In other words, Scuttle, why not look for the two robbers who are missing, the two men who broke into the house?"

The police undercover man was dubious. "That's all very well, sir," he said; "if you want to fall for that line of hooey. The police have about abandoned that theory of the case."

Lester Leith said nothing for several minutes, but below small smoke rings which went hurtling through larger smoke rings.

"What clews are there, Scuttle, to the missing men? It seems to me that I read in the paper something about these men having cooked themselves a lunch, or robbed the ice box or something."

"Yes, sir," said the spy. "That is correct. The three men broke into the house, searched for the jewels, and could not find them. Then they sat down, apparently to await the return of the woman. They cooked coffee. There were three cups with dregs in them, which gave the police the theory that there had been three men. There was an apple pie in the ice box, and the men ate it all up. They also drank a bottle of milk, and ate half a chocolate layer cake."

"These men, then," said Lester Leith, "must have been hardened criminals."

"Yes, sir," said the mystified undercover man.

Leith frowned into his cigarette smoke, pursed his lips, stroked his chin, Then his eyes twinkled into a smile. He slowly nodded his head, after the manner of a man who gradually sees the light of reason and logic, breaking through a cloud bank of mystery.

"Yes, Scuttle, I think I have it," he said.

"Have what, sir?" asked the spy eagerly.

"Have the correct method of procedure. You see, Scuttle, there were three crooks. Let us act upon the assumption that one of these crooks has eliminated himself. He was either the chauffeur, in which event the police have eliminated him from our search; or else he was not the chauffeur, in which event he has fled in a panic.

"What's more, Scuttle, that third man, regardless of what the law may have to say on the subject, isn't really a murderer. He telephoned the police, and he refused to share in the spoils. Therefore, Scuttle, we should eliminate *him* from our search.

"What we should search for, Scuttle, is a pair of seasoned crooks who have a fondness for apple pie and chocolate layer cake."

CHAPTER IV

The Garbage Can Business

"Now it's almost a certainty that men who could do a murder with such casual disregard of human suffering are men who are old hands at the game. They've probably served terms before.

"Now we know that this pair didn't get any money from their loot. They couldn't sell those diamonds right now. The stones are hot. They dare not move them. And they overlooked the money that was in the purse.

"Therefore, Scuttle, these men are broke. They are looking for an opportunity to lay low for a while, until they dare to dispose of their hot diamonds.

"So I think we'll start a new philanthropy, Scuttle. We'll open an employment bureau for ex-crooks. We'll cater only to tough guys, Scuttle. We'll try and get men who have served at least one term in some penitentiary.

"And we'll have a free lunch, Scuttle, just like in the days of the old saloon. And that lunch will have, among other things, chocolate layer cake and apple pie and milk. Also, Scuttle, we'll have coffee.

"Now we'll have an intelligent girl, one who's beautiful enough to attract attention anywhere, to serve the pies and cakes. And she'll keep a little record, Scuttle, under the counter where it won't show. It'll mark the amount of pie and cake each man eats. In that way we'll find out the crooks who are particularly fond of pie!"

And Lester Leith regarded the spy who posed as his valet, with that expectant look which a child gives to its mother when it has just done something for which it anticipates praise.

The spy gulped a couple of time. "I was not joking, sir," he said with dignity. "This is a murder case, and most unfortunate."

Lester Leith let his eyes widen with synthetic astonishment. "But, Scuttle," he said in a tone that held every whit as much of wounded dignity as had that of the spy, "*I* was not joking."

The spy wet his lips, spoke with a voice that quivered slightly. "Of course, sir, you have the right to make sport of me if you wish, sir. I am in your employ, and you can do as you damned please. But if you think all of this apple pie stuff—"

"Scuttle, please listen to reason. Remember, in the first place, I don't want actually to solve any crime problem, not practically. That is the purpose of the police. And also remember, Scuttle, that I have no authority such as the police have. I have no organization. The police would round up every man with a criminal record, put them through a third degree, to make them account for the way they spent their time on the night of the murder. Then they'd weed out their suspects by getting the ones who couldn't tell where they were, and sweating them. That procedure would sound entirely logical to you, Scuttle. Am I right?"

The man blinked. "Yes, sir," he said.

Lester Leith smiled affably.

"Quite so, Scuttle. That is because that particular method has been used so often that you have become accustomed to it. Now my methods have to be makeshifts, Scuttle, because I haven't any organization to back me In fact, Sergeant Ackley has the entire force at his disposal hampering and harassing me in everything I do. Therefore, Scuttle, I have to employ other methods, and, bearing in mind all the time that I do not want to catch any criminal but merely work out a possible, theoretical solution for a crime problem. Do I make myself plain, Scuttle?"

"Er...yes, sir. I guess so, sir."

Lester Leith beamed.

"That's fine, Scuttle. Then you'll understand. Now I'll want to talk with this husband, the lawyer. But I wouldn't want to intrude upon his grief. It would be indelicate to walk in upon him in his private office, and say; 'You'll pardon me, I'm not a real detective, nor am I a reporter. I'm just a man who wants to intrude upon your private affairs through a sense of curiosity.' That sort of an approach wouldn't do, Scuttle. But I could approach him as a salesman, perhaps, and solicit his business.

"Ah, Scuttle, I have it. I noticed in a mechanical magazine, devoted to inventions, that a man had invented a new form of garbage pail. Instead of the ugly, galvanized iron receptacle, which gets all smeared up and smelly after use, this man has invented a very fine, white enameled garbage can which enameled garbage can which contains some mixture which keeps the flies and ants away. Then the garbage isn't put in this pail at all, but in a paper filler which hangs in the pail from specially designed clamps.

"The garbage man merely lifts this paper receptacle from the pail and slips in a fresh one when he comes by to collect the garbage. There are no smells, no soiled hands, no spilling of some food. The paper is treated in some way to make it a deodorant.

"Do you know, Scuttle, that sounds so neat and gentlemanly and I think I should like to have an interest in that business. I clipped out the article at the time. Here it is. You might go to this man, tell him he can keep the patent, but I want the sales agency for this city, and I'll pay enough for it to give him some working capital.

"He lives right here in the city. You see his name is listed here. And you could arrange with him that I'd pay him one thousand dollars for the sales rights for ten days, another thousand dollars at the end of that time, and then a thousand dollars a month for each month I keep the sales rights.

"But have it understood I can quit at any time, Scuttle. And arrange for a dozen cans and paper containers to be sent to my order right away. And you'd better speak to Sergeant Ackley, Scuttle, and tell him I'm interested in those two robbers who escaped from the house. I've had so many misunderstandings with the Sergeant, let's let him in on the ground floor this time.

"And about the pies, Scuttle. Were they home-cooked? You know the ones I mean, the ones that were in the Steele residence."

The spy nodded.

"Mrs. Beechwood cooked the pies, sir. She's the housekeeper, and then there's Shinshara Kosimosto, the Japanese houseboy. They were out the night of the murder. It was their night off, you know."

Lester Leith nodded.

"Yes, Scuttle, and, as I remember the account of the crime which I read in the newspapers, Mrs. Steele was attending the reception when the telephone rang. Someone asked for her. She went to the telephone, and returned, white to the lips, said she was ill and asked to be excused. Isn't that right?"

"Yes, sir."

"Did anyone trace that call? Or did it sound as though it came from a Japanese?"

The valet shook his head, his eyes wide.

Lester Leith yawned, as though bored by the whole affair. "No matter, Scuttle. Just a fancy I had, a sort of a hunch. Forget it. You go ahead and make the preliminary arrangements. You needn't wait up for me. I'm going to that confounded dinner dance. I promised them I'd be there personally, and I hate to back down on a promise. But this crime interests me so much. It gives me something to think about. Ask Sergeant Ackley what he thinks about mental exercise for strengthening the brain. After all, he's on the job every day, wrestling with these crime problems. Ask him, Scuttle, if he thinks it's developed *his* brain. And now, Scuttle, good night!"

And Lester Leith adjusted his tie, took his gloves, cane, hat, coat, smiled at the spy and banged the door behind him.

CHAPTER V

The Bird Dog

Sergeant Ackley and the spy sat in a room that was blue with smoke. The Sergeant, a massive figure of a men with suspicious eyes and a spade like thumbnail that scratched the bristles along the angles of his bony jaw when he was thinking, spoke positively.

"That's the play, Beaver. I've got it doped out."

The spy made a grunting noise.

"You just think you've got it doped out. Nobody ever dopes out anything on that bozo. He acts sensible for a while, and then he seems to go plumb crazy. He acts like a guy that was about half shot trying to burlesque a detective. But, so help me, it's when you think he's crazy that he's using sense. This thing sounded so crazy to me that I thought he was kidding me. But he ain't. He'll slip the thing around somehow so that it'll all click into place, and, presto, he'll have pulled another fast one, right under our noses!"

Sergeant Ackley smiled, a paternal, patronizing smile.

"I can see just how you feel about it, Beaver. When he baffles a man with that chain lightning mind of his, it's mighty confusing. But when you get to see through his little schemes, they aren't complicated at all."

The spy made a single withering comment. "Oh, yeah?" he drawled.

Sergeant Ackley nodded. The smile was leaving his features now. "Yeah," he grunted, "and you don't need to be so damned skeptical about it, Beaver. The trouble with you is that this man gets on your nerves and makes you so mad you can't think. He never calls you by your right name, you tell me, but by that nickname he wished off on you because he says you look like a reincarnated pirate. That's part of his game. A man who's mad can't think. He keeps you mad all the time. And when he's slipping over a fast one. He tries to make us all madder than ever.

"He used to fool me, and I used to get mad. But no more. He can't make me mad now, not at all.

"I see through his little schemes.

"He plays them funny, yet with a certain system. He slips over a fast one, but he wraps it up in so much honey that we don't pay attention to it.

"Now take this little scheme of his right now, all about the crooks and the apple pie. It's all just a big lot of hooey. What he really wants is a chance to interview the servants. He doesn't give a damn for anything else.

"And he's probably right. There's something in the business that's fishy. And the servants may be in on it. It was their sight out, but we've never checked into things very strongly to prove their alibis "

"Now he senses that that's where we've slipped up. He'll talk pies to the housekeeper, and get her to make him a bunch of apple pies, but, back of it all will be some scheme to shake her down.

"She might have been pretty close to the mistress, you know. Servants take sides in every household. And servants ain't so dumb as husbands when it come to certain things.

"I bet you anything you want to bet that this housekeeper, Mrs. Beechwood, knows the whole thing about the affair between the lawyer's wife and the chauffeur, and even knows about the affair with the secretary."

"And I've got some more news for you, another funny development. The chauffeur has caved."

The spy sat up very straight, rigid at attention. "Yeah? What'd he say?"

"Well, he said that had a date with Mrs. Steele all right, and then the note she had in her stocking was in his handwriting, all right. He admitted that they'd been making dates through the maid. She was getting her mail under an assumed name, the name that was on the note.

"And he says he came there to meet her, that he was on time to the minute. That everything was all fixed up, she'd let the servants go for the night, and she'd pretended to be sick so she would slip back from the reception. The chauffeur came up to the house, just the way he'd intended to.

"He said the front door was locked with the night latch, which was the way they always kept it. That he gave the low whistle that would let Mrs. Steel know that he was there. And there wasn't any answer. He kept whistling, and then the very silence of the place surprised him, and make him feel that everything wasn't right.

"So he sneaked around the house, and saw a window open. He crawled through the window, and found the remains of the evening meal on the table. He was just about to heat it, when he glimpsed the woman's foot through an open door.

"He ran to her, and found she was dead. She'd been batted on the head right after she'd entered the room. The body was lying just the way we found it, just inside the little reception hallway. Well, he beat it. He knew he'd be dragged into it somehow, and he just made tracks. That's his story."

"Did he telephone the police?" asked the spy.

"Nope. Claims he didn't."

The spy yawned.

"Hell!" he said. "If he's cracked that much, he'll crack the rest of the way. He'll be confessing the whole business before noon tomorrow."

Sergeant Ackley frowned.

"That's the funny thing," he said. "He caved all the way before he made this admission. You know how he was sweating and pacing the floor. And the boys were shooting questions at him, and he'd hesitate before he answered, and all of that business.

"Well now he acts just like a man who had got it all off his chest. He snaps answers out to questions, and he seems like a big load was off his mind. You can't trip him up anywhere along the line, and he rings true all the way along."

Beaver shook his head skeptically. "Well, that ain't the story. He may claim it is right now, but you keep sweating him, and he'll be singing a different tune."

Ackley scratched his chin.

"Well, Captain Walker's in charge of that end of the case. And you know how Walker is. He's one of those two-fisted guys that jump all over a guy when he's lying, but when he starts telling the truth, Walker'll stick up for him. And Walker claims this chauffeur is telling the truth now, and says he is going to stick up for him."

Beaver made a single exclamation.

"Hell!" he said, scornfully. "How about the broad?"

"The broad's sitting tight. Can't shake her story a damned bit. She says she was working in the office. That when she heard the chauffeur had been arrested she wanted to talk with him just to tell him she loved him. That's her story, and damned if she ain't got old E. R. Walker sold on that."

Beaver frowned.

"What's gettin' into Walker? He usually knows when they're tellin' the truth."

Sergeant Ackley shook his head. "Hard to tell," he grunted.

Beaver leaned forward. "We can get farther by pinnin' the crime on the broad. The newspapers'll eat it up. The secretary in the office, in love with the chauffeur, trying to get him a make their marriage legal. The chauffeur, trifling with the love of the wife of his employer, stalling off the honest working girl!

"Gee, it'll be a wow. Every office girl in the city will be grabbing for the papers. And all the society dames will be digging for new dirt. It'll be smeared all over the papers and we'll get a lot of publicity for the efficient police work."

Sergeant Ackley grunted. "Hell, Beaver, you ain't tellin' me nothin'. But how about the diamonds? We gotta have the diamonds. And then look at old Walker. That bozo has got the idea we ain't got the real facts yet, and he's riding the whole damned department to uncover more evidence. He's going to fall for that idea of the three crooks before he gets done, and let the advertising value of this case slip right through his fingers. That's why I telephoned you to get Leith interested on this case. He's been a pretty good bird dog before, pointing out the real crook to us, and usually getting the swag all copped for himself.

"This time we'll use him to uncover the diamonds. Those are the key to the whole business. Whoever has got those diamonds is going to get the hot squat. The possession of those stones will fry the guy that's got 'em."

The spy got to his feet. "Well, all I gotta say is watch him. He'll slip over another fast one. And you'd better frame up something on the broad. She's the one that's the logical defendant in the case. It'll make a swell case if we try her, and not so hot if we try someone else. Hell, I'd plant some of the diamonds on her!"

Sergeant Ackley's suspicious eyes glittered. He lowered his voice. "You get Leith working on that case, let him find the diamonds. Then we cinch Leith for having the stolen property. And we get the diamonds. When we've gone that far, you can trust me to see that the diamonds are planted where they'll do the most good, some of them, anyway.

"The men have wanted to bust into the jane's trunks and all that stuff. I've held 'em off. I figure that if we can get the stones, and it looks like a good case otherwise, we might help the D. A. a little with the evidence. Get me?"

Beaver leaned forward. "Hell!" he said, "maybe the stones are in her trunks!"

Sergeant Ackley grinned. "Nope. I wouldn't let the boys make a search, but I got some pass keys and snooped around.

"We can't help the D. A. with the evidence, until we can get some evidence to sprinkle around for him. So you get Leith working on this case, then when we get the stones, we'll know what to do with 'em. Get me?"

The spy nodded. "Yeah, I get you, okay. I got your instructions. But I had a hell of a time getting this bozo to work on the case. He just wouldn't get interested in it. You've been too rough with him. You scared him off. Every time I have more trouble getting in trap baited."

Ackley nodded casually. "Well, this'll be the last time. We'll cinch him on this job."

"You've said that before," reminded the spy.

"This time it's a cinch. He ain't never seen the guy that invented this garbage pail, has he? Well, it's dead easy. We'll get the real inventor out of the way, and we'll run in one of our boys as the inventor. That'll give us a man that'll be right with him in the deal without his smelling a rat.

"And then we'll have another guy in the house as a servant. Tell him that you forgot to list the butler when you mentioned the servants because the butler had been away on a vacation.

"And we'll get hold of Steele and tell him we've got to plant a dick in his house. We'll run in a guy as a butler. See how soft it'll be?

"Now you beat it and get things lined up, and keep me posted on what's doing. Remember to keep Leith all hopped up over those sparklers. We need 'em in our business."

Beaver, the police spy, grunted affirmation, banged the door.

CHAPTER VI

Dead Game

Lester Leith, dressed faultlessly, as was his custom, strolled down the aisle which led to the employment desk of the big typewriter company.

On either side of that aisle, girls sat. As Lester Leith progressed toward the desk, eyes followed him in silent appraisal. Here and there a face with hope. Here and there listless eyes brightened perceptibly.

The woman who sat behind the desk was one of those women who are crisply efficient, yet never seem to do anything with their efficiency besides making a nuisance of themselves.

She smiled at Lester Leith, a mechanical smile of welcome which would have been cordial had not it conveyed the impression that it had been perfected by five minutes a day before a mirror.

"Good morning, sir, and what can I do for you, if you please?"

"I wanted to ask about a girl," said Lester Leith.

The hard, metallic eyes behind the spectacles snapped with anticipation.

"Ah, yes. In times such as these we're only too glad to get a chance to place one of our young women. And what was your name, please, and the address?"

And she slid a pad of paper, printed into various paragraphs of questions with blanks for answers, across the top of the counter, held a pencil poised.

Lester Leith shook his head. "I wanted to get information about a *certain* young lady," he said.

The woman's pencil dropped. Her eyes lost their expression of metallic eagerness, and became, instead, dulled with disinterest and caution.

"What was her name?" she asked. Lester Leith leaned forward.

"That's what I want to know. I have only the description. She was employed for a while during the rush of the business boom, but she hasn't been able to hold her job since. She's rather an attractive girl, very friendly and good-natured, knows her way about, but just can't get along with the typewriting and shorthand. She's got some dependents she's been supporting the best she could, and she's pretty hard up, pretty shabby, but she comes in every day to see if there's anything for her, and she always manages to keep cheerful.

"The way times are right now, you're almost afraid to recommend her, even if there was an opening for just her type. She's a good scout, loyal, friendly, but a rotten stenographer. She can smile, but she can't spell…"

The woman interrupted.

"The only one I know is Lois Webber. She doesn't fit all the description, but she fits most of it. I hope she hasn't been getting into any trouble. You aren't an officer, are you?"

Lester Leith shook his head. "Where can I find Miss Webber?"

The woman consulted a card-index.

"She was in here in hour ago, but she went out. She keeps plugging right along, looking for work, but she's not getting anywhere. We all like her, only she's hopeless as a stenographer.

"Let's see. Here's her address. I'll write it down and slip it across to you. I wouldn't want the other girls who are waiting, to think I was letting a prospective employer take some girl who wasn't waiting here."

Lester Leith took the slip of paper.

"She hasn't been doing anything wrong, has she?" asked the woman.

Lester Leith shook his head, turned, and walked down the long aisle. Feminine pulchritude, arrayed in postures which showed that pulchritude to advantage, stared at him with scornful eyes, their facial expressions showing lofty disdain.

Leith found the elevator, got his roadster, drove to the address he had been given. It was in a district where a dollar could be counted upon to bring a full one hundred cents worth of the necessities of life. The district was cheap but efficient.

Leith climbed a rickety flight of stairs, came at length to a little room which was sandwiched in under the stairs, opening on a court. He knocked on the door.

There was the sound of someone moving, the springs of a bed creaked, and the door opened a crack.

The girl was young and blond, wrapped in a kimono. She held a needle and thread in her hand, and a torn dress was lying on the bed, evidently in process of mending.

The room was so small that the bed filled its center, leaving barely room for a cane-bottomed, straight-backed chair in one corner, a little bureau with a mirror that gave a sickly, wavy reflection in another corner. There had been a pathetic attempt at decoration, a cheap pennant hung at an angle on the wall, flanked by two colored prints.

The girl was shaking her head. "Not today. I can't make any payment today. You'll just have to put me out if you can't wait."

Her eyes were friendly, frank, but her mouth was grave, unsmiling.

Lester Leith smiled affably. "I came," he said, "to offer you employment."

The girl swayed slightly, as though something had pushed her back into the room. Sheer surprise flooded her features. Her eyes widened with incredulity.

"The hell you did!" she exclaimed.

For a moment the significance of her own words did not seem to strike her, and then she gasped.

"Oh, I didn't mean that! That is, I didn't mean it that way. What I meant was that I'd come to the conclusion there wasn't any work to be had in the whole city…Come in. Pardon the negligee. I've got one dress, and I snagged it getting off a high curb. I was going to mend it and then start out again. I've been looking for work."

Lester Leith bowed, entered the tiny room. The girl left the door open, perched on the bed, indicated the chair.

Lester Leith sat down.

"What sort of work?" asked the girl.

"Rather a responsible position," said Lester Leith.

The girl nodded. "I can fill it."

Leith studied her face. "Can I count on your loyalty, on your unfailing good nature, on your keeping a closed mouth?"

She nodded. "When does the work start?"

"This afternoon."

"How…how much salary?"

"We'll discuss that a little later," said Lester Leith, "after I've had an opportunity to see how you fit in."

She stared at him.

"Aw, gee," she said, "let's not beat around the bush. I'd do almost anything to get a job, but—well—well, I'm no good as a stenographer. I held a job when business was good, but I can't spell for sour apples, and I can't read shorthand notes after they get cold. You're a good scout. I can tell by looking at you. You hunted me up to offer me a job, and that's something nobody ever did before…"

Lester Leith got to his feet. "There's no need of discussing things further," he said.

She blinked her eyes, twice, rapidly as though fighting back moisture, then smiled, a wistful smile, gave him her hand.

"Thanks for coming," she said "Get some girl that can fill the bill .You're too good a scout to hand a lot o' taffy to…"

Lester Leith shook his head, smiling.

"No. I didn't mean that you wouldn't do. I meant you would. There's no use wasting time on that. I want character more than ability. I want a girl who is a dead game little trouper, who can stand on her own two feet and be frank and honest. You've shown that you're just what I'm looking for."

She stared at him. "It's on the level?"

"It's on the level," said Lester Leith.

He took out a wallet, counted out two tens and a five, handed them to the girl, together with a card, bearing his address.

"Here's an advance on salary. Here's my card. Come to that address within a hour if you can, and I'll explain your duties. You start at five hundred a month."

CHAPTER VII

Jobs for Ex-Cons

She was staring at the card and the money as Lester Leith gently closed the door and sought the stairs.

He waited, inconspicuously lounging against a cigar stand entrance at the corner. He waited for less than five minutes. The girl emerged from the rooming house, walked with quick steps and clicking heels, looking neither to the right nor to the left.

Lester Leith followed her.

She went directly to a telegraph office, filled out a money transfer blank, and sent twenty dollars by telegraph. Then she came out, walked to a restaurant, sat at a counter and ate a double order of ham and eggs, had three cups of coffee, and ate ravenously a double order of toast.

Lester Leith smiled, sought his roadster and returned to his apartment. He had found the girl he wanted.

Beaver, the spy, held forth a newspaper. "Yours, sir?"

His big, bony forefinger indicated an ad in the classified department. It was boxed in, printed in heavy type commanded attention of the casual eye:

EX-CONVICTS WHO WANT WORK ARE GOING TO BE GIVEN A CHANCE TO REHABILITATE THEMSELVES. FREE BOARD AND ROOM WHILE WAITING FOR EMPLOYMENT, OFFICERS WILL NOT MOLEST. A LEGITIMATE OPPORTUNITY FOR THE MAN WHO HAS SERVED A TERM IN THE BIG HOUSE AND WHO WANTS TO GO STRAIGHT, DO NOT APPLY UNLESS YOU HAVE A CRIMINAL RECORD. ADDRESS SOCIETY FOR REHABILTATION. BOX 534. GIVING DETAILS.

Lester Leith nodded his head.

"Yes, Scuttle, that's mine. I put it in late last night. It made the first editions this morning. I left word with the paper to bring over the replies in bunches, three times a day. The messenger should be showing up with the first batch."

"He has, sir, just a few minutes ago, sir," said the valet, and pointed to an assortment of folded papers, ragged envelopes of various sorts and description, lying on the writing desk.

Lester Leith chuckled.

"Ah," he said. "I didn't know but what the gentry would be suspicious and smell a trap. But, evidently, the signature of the ad did the trick. The Society for Rehabilitation, and the offer of free board and room without police molestation sounds good. Let's see what we've got."

There followed a ten-minute period of silence, broken occasionally by the rustle of paper as Leith unfolded another message, classified it, placed it in a pile, either at his right or left hand.

Leith finished the last answer, chuckled. "Would you believe it, Scuttle?"

"Believe what, sir?"

"That these men are all innocent?"

"Are they, sir?"

"Yes, Scuttle, all of them innocent. They all served terms in various penitentiaries, but they are all utterly innocent of any crime."

The police spy snorted.

"You get to fooling around with a bunch of crooks, sir, begging your pardon, sir; and you'll find yourself with trouble on your hands. Once a crook, always a crook!"

Lester Leith smiled, a patronizing smile. "Tut, tut, Scuttle, you overlook the main factor in the situation."

"And what is that, sir?"

"These men aren't crooks, Scuttle. They just served terms in the penitentiaries of the country. That's all. They weren't guilty of any crime. They say so themselves. I've got their written statement, over their signatures, Scuttle."

The valet snorted, his face turning a dark red with anger. "I wasn't joking," he said, and glared angrily.

There came a knock on the door. Lester Leith raised his eyebrows.

Then the electric doorbell whirred its alarm. The sound of beating knuckles on the panels became annoyingly audible. Lester Leith motioned toward the door.

"Seems to be devilishly impatient, Scuttle. Let's see who it is."

The valet went to the door, flung it open.

A broad-shouldered man with a big jaw, heavy shoes, fists that were as hams, and a slouching attitude of sneering self-assurance, stood on the threshold.

"Where's Leith?" he said, and walked into the room. The spy bowed.

"Well, well, it's Mr. Lamont, inventor of the Lamont Patent Garbage Container. Do come in, Mr. Lamont. This is Mr. Leith."

The broad-shouldered man moved over toward Lester Leith.

"So you're Leith, eh? And you want to handle my garbage containers, and are putting up a thousand bucks as a first payment, eh?

"Okay. I've talked with your man here and reached an agreement. I just wanted to drop in and look your joint over, and see the sort of a man I was working with."

Lester Leith indicated a chair. "Do sit down, Mr. Lamont."

The broad-shouldered man sank into a chair, fished a cigar from his waistcoat pocket, put the tip in his teeth, gave a wrenching motion with his right hand, spat out the tip of tobacco, scraped a match across the sole of his shoe, and scowled at Lester Leith.

"Only I got one condition about the deal," he said.

"What is that?" asked Lester Leith.

"I want to be with you at the start and watch the way you work. I want to see how you go at selling these garbage containers, and I want to make certain that you savvy how they work.

"A lot depends on the way a guy puts the stuff on the market, an' I ain't going to have my invention ruined by being put on the market the wrong way."

And he glowered at Lester Leith. Leith was urbanely smiling.

"Quite all right, Mr. Lamont. But your attitude is rather unusual for an inventor. Inventors are usually dreamy, unpractical sort of chaps. You seem to be most practical, aggressively so." And Lester Leith beamed at the man.

Beaver, the spy, seeing the danger, made frantic and surreptitious signals to the police detective who was masquerading as Lamont.

That individual changed his tactics a little.

"I ain't aggressive," he said. "I'm just prudent. That Lamont garbage container is destined to revolutionize the garbage industry, and I ain't going to see it flop because it ain't put across right.

"I ain't sore or nothin'. I just dropped in to shake hands, and tell you that when the first garbage containers are delivered I'm going to come right along with 'em, and stick around until I see how they've put across."

Lester Leith bowed appreciatively.

"Your assistance in the matter will be appreciated," he remarked.

Silence fell upon the room. There seemed nothing left for anyone to say. Lamont lurched to his feet.

"When do you want the first shipment of cans?" he asked.

"This afternoon, at four o'clock."

"Okay, brother, only I come with 'em."

Leith nodded. "Do," he invited.

The broad-shouldered man paused in the doorway, as though conscious of the fact that his impersonation of the investor had left something to be desired. He shifted uneasily on his feet, trying to think of something to say that would be in keeping with the character of the inventor, opposed to the character of an officer.

Suddenly his face lit with inspiration. "Thanks," he said, and closed the door.

CHAPTER VIII

Desperate Men

The knock at the door was timid.

"No one seems to be finding the bell button today, Scuttle," said Lester Leith.

"The light in the hallway is a little confusing at first, sir, to one who leaves the brilliant light of day and ..."

Lester Leith waved his hand. "Open it," he said.

The spy opened the door.

Lois Webber smiled affably at him. "I was to report," she began.

Lester Leith was on his feet, pushing the spy aside. "Quite all right, Miss Webber, quite all right. Do come in and sit down. This is my valet. I believe his real name is Beaver, but I call him Scuttle because he looks so much like a reincarnated pirate.

"And this, Scuttle, is Miss Lois Webber, the young lady who is going to have charge of our thieves' kitchen."

The spy bowed. The girl stared directly at Lester Leith.

"Thieves' kitchen?" she asked.

Leith nodded.

"Yes, you see I have come to a conclusion in regard to crooks. I believe that ex-convicts want to go straight. But they never have the chance. Society turns thumbs down on them, kicks them around. That either breaks their spirit or else makes them fight.

"Now what I propose to do is to fix up a regular kitchen for the thieves. I want a home for crooks that'll be sort of a club. You can understand, Miss Webber. A crook goes to the penitentiary. While he is there he is cut off from all of his outside friends, has to form friendships within the walls. He comes to regard the place as his club. It's a sort of lodge. All of his friends are there.

"That's what brings him back. He may hate the restraint of the place, but his friends are all there, and friendships are the most binding things in the world, Miss Webber. Do you understand?"

The girl regarded him with frank eyes, then grinned. "Am I supposed to understand?" she asked.

Leith indicated a chair. "Not unless you want to."

"I don't want to, then. I got enough on my mind. Go ahead and tell me what I do, and don't worry about the explanations. I'm going through with this job. So shoot the works."

Leith nodded. He picked up the pile of correspondence that had arrived in response to the rather peculiar ad he had inserted in the paper.

"Now here are the addresses and letters of a lot of innocent men who were unjustly imprisoned. Here is some expense money. You'll hire what help you need, go to this house, open it up as a boarding house and sort of club room. You'll write to these crooks, or call them on the telephone where they've left a number at which they can be reached and you'll invite them to come and join the club.

"You'll impress upon them that the club is founded by a philanthropist who wants to keep his name out of the papers, that the club is secret and confidential. And you'll see that there is a big free lunch counter with roasts and sandwiches, and salami…and lots of chocolate layer cake and apple pie.

"Now those crooks will start hanging around that lunch counter. You'll be there to serve them and assist them. Down underneath the counter you'll keep a notebook, and in that book you'll mark down the names of the men, and opposite each name you'll write just what that man takes from the counter.

"I want to know exactly what diet these men prefer. I want to know every sandwich they take, every piece of pie, every slab of cake. Now can you do that, Miss Webber?"

The girl nodded.

"Sure I can. Gosh, this is a cinch. I was afraid it was going to be another one of those jobs where a guy spouted out a lot of words I'd never heard before and I was supposed to write 'em down in shorthand, and tell what they were afterwards.

"I never had any education to speak of, except what I picked up, and I faked most of my shorthand. And the typewriter always did seem to have a jinx as far as I was concerned." And she grinned at Lester Leith.

"Some of those men may be desperate," warned Leith. "You can hire what assistance you need. I would suggest you get a couple of men to act as general help and as bodyguards. You'll get a caterer to furnish the food."

The girl laughed.

"Shucks," she said, "all men are desperate. I was in a road show for three years. I oughta know. I can handle 'em. As a matter of fact, a guy that's been down on his luck himself will come nearer giving a girl a break than a bird that's rolling in the lap o' luxury."

Lester Leith nodded.

"I see that you are a philosopher and an observer of life," he said.

She smiled, shook her head.

"Not me. I just been around a bit, an' heard most of the lines that get slung at a girl's ears. When do I start?"

"Right now," said Lester Leith.

She got to her feet, started to count the bills which Lester Leith handed her for expense money. Her eyes widenedin surprise. "This can't be right!"

"It is right. I want those men to be well treated. I want the food to be the best money can buy. I want them to have lots of it. I want you to make them feel right at home, break through their reserve. And then I want you to telephone me every day the results of the experiment, what the men are eating. I am particularly interested in the men who eat the most pie and the most chocolate layer cake. Get the four high men on pie and cake.

"There'll be some more replies to my ad a little later. I want you to send some of the men out to round up the others who reply. Get them all down there. The doors are open to everyone. If you need anything, buy it."

The girl stared silently at Lester Leith.

For some ten seconds the appraisal continued, a searching stare from steady eyes.

"Guy," she said softly, "my ears warn me that you ain't on the level, but everything else I got tells me that you stack up a hundred percent, an' my eyes don't lie to me. I'm with you. So long."

"Any questions?" asked Lester Leith. "Have I made myself clear?"

"It all sounds goofy to me, but I'm the baby that rushes in where the angels fear to tread. I'm away to a flying start. G'bye."

But she, too, paused in the doorway, as the detective had done. She stared at Lester Leith, and there was something wistful about the stare, a suggestion of moisture in the corners of the eyes.

And she said exactly the same word which the detective had said, as he had paused in the doorway, trying to think of something which would convince Leith that he was the man he pretended to be, Lamont, the inventor.

"Thanks," she said.

Then the door closed, gently. The latch clicked. The spy started to say something to Lester Leith, but the ringing of the telephone interrupted him.

He strode to the instrument.

As he took down the receiver and said, "Hello," the voice of Sergeant Ackley came to his ears.

"Steady, Beaver, don't tip this off, but we're on something hot. We've been checking up on the servants, and the moves of Shinahara Kosimosto, the house boy, don't check out at all. He looks fishy.

"Maybe that's where Leith is going to shift his guns. We ain't doing anything except putting the houseboy under surveillance. But I think maybe that's where Leith is figuring on pulling his fast one. G'bye."

And the line went dead.

The spy turned to Lester Leith, placed the receiver back on the hook. "A wrong number, sir."

CHAPTER IX

Fingerprints on a Pie Plate

Lester Leith held the shiny surface of a new tin pie plate to his face, studied the reflection.

"Almost as good as a mirror, Scuttle."

The valet was noncommittal. "Yes, sir."

"Yes, indeed," said Lester Leith, and picked up a plate, not so new. He regarded the bottom of that pie plate with scowling features.

The spy watched him as a hawk might watch a rabbit. "Scuttle."

"Yes, sir."

"From time to time you've mentioned certain things the police were doing. In fact, Scuttle, you seem to have a certain familiarity with police methods…"

The valet interrupted in nervous haste. "Only because I happen to be friendly with a certain young lady who is also friendly with a member of the force, sir. I pick up a lot of things from her. You'd really be surprised, sir."

Lester Leith's tone contained no hint of sarcasm. "Doubtless I would, Scuttle," he agreed.

"Yes, sir," said the spy. "I've come to know quite a bit about the police and the crime situation, just from what she tells me."

Leith nodded again.

"Then, Scuttle, perhaps you can tell me something about fingerprints. Now take these two pie plates for instance. One of them is old and the other new. Now I can readily understand how a finger pressed upon the shiny surface of this new pie plate would leave certain lines of moisture which would remain for some time. But I don't see how in the world the police could ever find a fingerprint on this old pie plate. I press my finger against it, and it leaves no mark whatever."

The spy smiled, a wise smile. "You just think it doesn't. It really does."

"No, Scuttle. It does not. I've tried."

The spy radiated an amused air of superiority. "You'll pardon me, sir. I think I can show you that it does. Now see here. I press my finger against this new pie plate. You can see the imprint, sir?"

"Certainly, Scuttle."

"Very well. Now I press my finger against this older pie plate. Do you see the impression?"

"No, Scuttle, there isn't a line."

"If you wouldn't mind marking the place, sir," suggested the valet, "I think I can show you something. It happens, sir, that I once took a correspondence course as a detective, and I believe I still have, among my things, the fingerprint outfit they sent me. If you'll pardon me for a moment, sir."

And the police spy walked heavily to his room, returned in a very few moments with two bottles.

"Now, sir," he said. "If you'll be so good as to watch what I do, I think I can show you how the police work."

And the valet proceeded to develop the latent print until, dusted with aluminum powder, it showed up startlingly plain, every ridge and whorl.

Lester Leith stared in silent wonder.

"Scuttle," he said, at length, "you surprise me. You're really clever. I knew that some of the fingerprint experts became very capable in such matters, but I didn't know that you possessed such a complete education."

The valet endeavored to look modest. "Oh, sir, it's nothing, mere routine, that's all—er—may I ask how the thieves' kitchen is coming along, sir?"

Lester Leith set down the pie plates, bottoms up. He talked rapidly, as one talks when he is riding a new hobby.

"Scuttle, it's wonderful. Those men are making a regular club out of it. It's been going for two days now, and that Lois Webber girl is a wonder. She's calling all the men by their first names, and she's got every piece of pie and cake tabulated. She knows exactly how many pieces of pie and cake each man has taken, and she knows the exact size of each piece.

"These crooks aren't a bad sort at all, Scuttle. I went down there, and they gave me a big hand. The girl acted as hostess and introduced me, and the men cheered, Scuttle! Think of it! They cheered!

"These down-and-out crooks, many of them starving because they couldn't get work, aren't a bad sort at all. You'd be surprised, Scuttle, to find how friendly they are."

The valet nodded impatiently. "Yes, sir, doubtless you're right, sir. But you'll remember that the object of the thieves' kitchen was to pick out the pair that ate the most pie and cake, sir."

Lester Leith let the smile fade from his face.

"By George, Scuttle, you're right, and I've got the figures right with me. Two of those men are veritable fiends for pie and cake, Scuttle. They all eat a lot, but there are two ... great Heavens, Scuttle, I'm glad you reminded me! I have work to do!"

And Lester Leith, scooping the pie plates to him, wrapped them very carefully in a piece of paper, grabbed his hat, catapulted from the room.

The slam of the door gave the spy his cue. He made a bee line for the telephone, to acquaint Sergeant Ackley with the fact that the watched pot was continuing to simmer, would soon, doubtless, come to a boil.

But Sergeant Ackley was prepared.

Outside of the apartment two police cars were ready to shadow Lester Leith to whatever destination he might choose. The man had slipped through the fingers of the police often enough before so that the sergeant was taking no chances.

But Lester Leith was quite open and above-board in his moves. He made no attempt to shake off the police shadows, but went at once to the store room where the police detective who posed as Lamont, the inventor of the patented garbage container, was guarding the first two dozen garbage cans which had been delivered as sales samples.

"I've got a swell idea," said Lester Leith.

The man who posed as Lamont was lacking in enthusiasm. "Yeah?" he said.

"Yes," said Lester Leith. "I'm going to start a sales campaign on these cans, and each salesman is going to be an ex-convict."

The police detective frowned.

"Say," he snarled, "what's the idea?"

"Publicity," said Lester Leith. "Come on. Let's load these cans on a light truck and get them delivered. I'll telephone the transfer company. We're going right now to put on a sales talk. You're going to explain the fine points. Then we'll advertise.

"Get the idea? We'll ask the public to give the crooks a chance to be honest. We'll explain that every salesman is a former convict. It'll attract a lot of attention. Old Man 'Pro-Bono-Publico' will write in the People's Forum in the newspaper and give us hell for finding work for crooks when honest men are out of employment. And then Miss 'A-Constant-Subscriber' will write in and answer him and say she thinks it's a lovely idea.

"And all the time it'll be netting publicity for us. We'll be selling these garbage cans as fast as you can make them. People will talk, and talk means interest, and interest means sales.

"Come on. Get your hat. We'll go see the salesmen. They're a fine bunch of boys. You'll like them. I've been feeding them apple pies, and they're bearcats when it comes to eating them."

The broad-shouldered man regarded Lester Leith with a sneer. "Say," he snarled, "are you cuckoo?"

Lester Leith became frigidly dignified.

"Of course," he said, "I merely proposed that you come because you said you wanted to come. After all, Mr. Lamont, under our agreement you are to manufacture the cans. I am to sell them through any channel or through any organization I see fit. If you don't feel enthusiastic, don't come."

Lamont gripped a cigar in his teeth.

"I'm enthusiastic," he said grimly. "Hurrah, hurrah, *hurray*! Try and *keep* me from coming."

And he jammed a businesslike derby down low on his forehead, glowered at Lester Leith.

Lester Leith became very dignified and businesslike.

"I will telephone the transfer company," he said and put through the telephone call, left explicit directions as to the manner in which the cans should be delivered, and then turned to the man who was masquerading as Lamont.

"Very well," he said, "we will go in my roadster."

And he drove the detective in the place which he had branded as his "thieves' kitchen," climbed the stairs to the clubroom.

CHAPTER X

"You Show Up!"

There were some eighteen men lounging around. They smiled at Lester Leith, came crowding forward to shake hands. They stared at the man who posed as Lamont, and had no difficulty whatever in piercing his disguise. A sudden cold restraint fell over the men.

Lois Webber had been playing poker with a group of five of the convicts. She frowned slightly as Lester Leith introduced her to the man who gave his name as Lamont.

Lester Leith walked to the free lunch counter, helped himself to a piece of apple pie, ate it, rapped sharply for order.

"Men," he said. "I've gone into business. I'm going to sell a new form of garbage container. Any of you men who want to work with the company can do so, and can have a territory assigned to him. That holds good for every man of you. There's only one thing that you've got to remember. That is that any man who handles this garbage pail is going to be branded an ex-convict. I'm going to put it across as an advertising stunt.

"This man, Lamont here, is the inventor of the can. There'll be a dozen or so of the sample cans come in within the next few minutes. Lamont will explain the features of the can to you."

There was a moment of silence as Lester Leith quit talking. Two or three lowering glances appraised the broad-shouldered man who claimed to be the inventor. Those glances were decidedly hostile.

There was a commotion at the door. A man called a message through the corridor. That message was relayed to Lester Leith.

"The garbage cans are here."

"Send them up," directed Lester Leith. "Suppose some of you boys give the men a hand."

There followed a brief period of bustle and confusion. Under cover of that confusion, Lois Webber approached Lester Leith.

"The boys like you fine, but they don't fall for your little playmate."

Lester Leith raised his eyebrows. "Indeed," he said, "the man's a perfect gentleman, save for a few minor points."

The girl snorted.

"He looks like a dick to the boys."

Lester Leith shook his head. "He's an inventor…Tell me, have you got plenty of apple pies and chocolate cakes?"

"Of course. There's enough on the counter to last for quite a while, and a dozen of each in the shelves underneath."

Leith nodded.

"I'm going to keep out of the picture," he said. "I want Lamont to have a chance at the boys when I'm not around." And Lester Leith slipped unobtrusively into a little private lounging room the door of which was equipped with a spring lock, the only key to which dangled on Leith's key-ring.

There was a telephone in that room, and he used it, when he had seen that the door was locked and fastened, to call Conrad Steele, the lawyer, husband of the murdered woman.

"I think," said Lester Leith over the in low tones, "that I can show you evidence that'll demonstrate the guilt of your chauffeur, and free your secretary."

Steele's voice was harsh, rasping, stern. "Who is this talking?"

"A private investigator who's uncovered something worthwhile."

"Well," rasped the voice, "come on over."

"No," said Lester Leith, "you've got to look over two men without letting them know that you're looking at them. If I get your cooperation in this thing, I can show you some results. You'd better plan on being absent from your office for three or four hours."

"I can't," rasped Steele. "I'm busy."

"Say-y-y-y," snarled Lester Leith, "what's eating you? Why are you so anxious to pin this crime on your secretary?"

"I'm not."

"Well, you're acting funny. This business is the most important piece of business you've got, right now."

"What's the address?" asked the attorney, using a milder tone of voice.

Lester Leith gave him the address.

"Ask for Mr. Leith," he said, "and don't tell anyone who you are or what you want to see me about. And make it snappy. I think we can have your secretary out in a couple of hours if you play cards right."

"I'll be over," promised the attorney.

"Okay," said Lester Leith. "See that you show up, or the cops'll use it against you."

The attorney flared into rage.

"What are you talking about?" he bellowed.

"You," said Lester Leith, and hung up the receiver.

He opened the drawer in the little desk in the room and took out a pile of imitation diamonds. They were excellent imitations. Purchased wholesale, they amounted to a neat sum, but they would have deceived any save a careful eye. Lester Leith placed these diamond imitations on the table, covered them over with a handkerchief. Then he opened another drawer which contained a gun, and put a glove on his right hand. He selected a cigarette with his left, leaned back in the chair, smoked, and waited.

It was precisely eleven minutes and forty-three seconds after he had hung up the telephone receiver that a timid knock came on the door of the little office like room. Lester Leith slipped the bolt, opened the door a few inches.

Lois Webber slid through the opening in the door, into the room.

"There's a man outside who won't give his name, and he's mad as a hornet," she whispered. "I'm afraid he may do something to you. He's sputtering and popping like a bunch of firecrackers."

Lester Leith smiled.

"Show the gentleman in," he said.

"But he might hurt you!"

"I think not. Show him in."

The girl held the door open. "This way, please," she said.

A small man, vigorously aggressive, his black eyes snapping beneath heavy black brows, barged into the room, his shoulders swinging, his lips clamped in a straight line, his black hair ruffled.

"What the devil did you mean by that last crack of yours?" he stormed.

Lester Leith waved a conciliatory hand.

"I wanted to make certain you came. That's all."

The man glared at him.

"Well, that's a hell of a way to get a man to come. I'm fed up on the whole batch of you detectives. The detectives, the reporters, and the police, all make me sick ..."

Lester Leith motioned to Lois Webber. "Get out," he said.

The girl closed the door behind her, slowly and reluctantly. The spring lock clicked into place.

Lester Leith reached out toward the handkerchief which covered the pile of imitation stones.

"I think," he said, "that I have recovered your wife's diamonds. That's why I was so insistent upon your dropping your business affairs and coming over."

The man's black eyes widened a bit. "Recovered the diamonds!" he said.

"Exactly," said Lester Leith, and snatched the handkerchief from the glittering pile of imitation diamonds.

The man checked a startled exclamation, clapped his right hand to his side, near the bottom of his vest, leaned forward, pushed the imitation stones about with the forefinger of his left hand.

"No," he said, "those aren't the stones."

Lester Leith's face showed disappointment. "Are you certain, Mr. Steele?"

"Certain."

Lester Leith frowned, after the manner of one who is checking and rechecking certain conclusions.

"The chauffeur didn't have a latchkey to the front door," he said, almost dreamily; "that's why he had to jimmy the windows."

"Naturally," said the attorney. "I don't trust my hired help with keys to the front door. The only latchkeys were those which my wife and I had."

Lester Leith pursed his lips.

"Now don't mistake me on this thing," rasped the lawyer in a harsh voice. "I know that convention requires that a man be all broken up over the murder of his wife. I want to see justice done. I want to see her death avenged. But I am not going to be a damned hypocrite. The woman was double-crossing me, and she met her death because of that fact.

"I'm sorry she's dead. I want to see her murderers brought to justice. I don't want to see an innocent person convicted. But I'm not prostrated with grief.

"Her life was insured in my favor. I shall not touch one penny of that insurance money. The diamonds were insured. I shall insist upon the payment of that insurance money, unless the stones are recovered. I paid for those diamonds, and it's only fair that I should be reimbursed for them. I suffered a loss on them.

"The insurance on the life of my wife was to compensate me in a measure for the loss of her society and affection in the event she should die. I now find that the value I placed upon that society and affection were vastly overrated. I shall, therefore, request the insurance company to refund the premium paid. That's all."

He got to his feet.

"Just a minute," said Lester Leith. "I have here a diagram showing the various carat sizes of stones. Will you indicate the approximate size of the diamonds your wife wore?"

And Lester Leith slid a diagram across the table. That diagram was in glass covered frame, similar to the printing frames used by photographers.

"This size," said Steele.

"Which size?" asked Leith.

"This one."

"Which one?"

"This one right here," said the lawyer, and pressed an emphatic and impatient forefinger upon the glass.

"Ah," said Lester Leith, and there was something sinister about the tone of his voice. It was a purring indication of something ominous to come.

The lawyer stared at him.

Lester Leith unfastened spring clips in the back of the frame, removed the glass, taking great care to use his right hand, which was gloved, whenever he touched the glass. He took a small bottle of aluminum powder from a drawer, dusted it over the place where the lawyer's finger had pressed. Then he placed the glass against a black background in the shape of a piece of velvet cloth.

The marks of the fingerprint stood out startlingly distinct.

CHAPTER XI

No Proof

Lester Leith took out the package of pie plates which he had taken from his apartment. He placed the pie plate that had the developed latent of Beaver's fingerprint upon it, immediately next to the piece of glass. He adjusted a magnifying glass, started checking the two latents.

The attorney paused, took a hesitant step, sat down in a chair. His piercing, black eyes were narrow now, and the color of the face was a shade whiter than it had been.

Lester Leith nodded from time to time.

"Well?" asked the lawyer, "what are you doing?"

Lester Leith glanced up, surveyed the attorney. "If," he said, "there were only two latchkeys to the front door of your house, and your wife's latchkey was found in her purse when she had just stepped inside of the reception hall, the answer is obvious."

The lawyer swallowed with difficulty. "Precisely what," he asked, "do you mean?"

"I mean," said Lester Leith, "that when a woman carries her latchkey in her purse, and opens a door with that key, she naturally has to take the key out of her purse. And she wouldn't be able to replace it in the purse and close the purse after opening the door until a second or two had elapsed.

"If, therefore, that woman were found, just inside of the locked door, murdered, with the key in her purse, and it was apparent from the position of the body and the fact that there had been no struggle that she had been murdered just as soon as she opened the door, I would deduce that someone had been with her. I would further deduce that someone had a key, and that the door had been opened with that key."

The lawyer stared at Lester Leith, his face set, defiant. "Are you trying to accuse me?" he asked.

"And," went on Lester Leith, "it would be natural to suppose that if robbery had been the motive, the five thousand dollars in the purse would have been taken. *But* if jealous rage were the real motive of the crime, and the diamonds had been taken merely in order to strengthen the hypothesis of a hold-up, it would be only natural for the murderer to overlook the purse—particularly if he expected to inherit its contents in any event.

"But let us suppose for the sake of the argument that such a person had struck the woman down, and he wanted to make it appear that the crime had been done by someone else he only had to go to the garage, get a bar that had been used as a jack handle, and was, therefore well covered with the fingerprints of the chauffeur, jimmy a window, and then ransack the interior of the house.

"Then, deciding that he'd gild the lily a bit and paint the rose, he went ahead and made it appear three persons were concerned in the stick-up. That was easy. He had only to set three places at the table in what appeared to have been a hasty lunch.

"Then this person slipped out, went to a public telephone, called the police, told them that he had been one of a group of three who had conspired to rob the woman, that the others had resorted to murder, and that this person disclaimed any responsibility.

"Now such a telephone call is mysterious, and puzzling. If it had been placed by the person who claimed he had been one of three, and had been a genuine confession, the person could have gained nothing. On the other hand, it undoubtedly *did* give the police a chance to discover the crime several hours sooner than would otherwise have been the case.

"Now why should the criminal be concerned as to the time the crime was discovered? One would naturally conclude that it was because the murderer had a good alibi he could use in the event of the police suspecting him.

"Now, as a matter of fact, Mr. Steele, your wife didn't go home to meet the chauffeur. She went home because someone telephoned her. As soon as she received that telephone message she pretended she wasn't feeling well, excused herself from the reception and went home.

"Those facts are uncontradicted. Now let's analyze them a bit.

"Let's suppose, first, that your wife had received the letter from Bert Meggs, your chauffer, making a rendezvous at the house. Then let us suppose some other person had telephoned her, telling her he had to see her at once. She would never have taken such a person to the house, because she knew the chauffeur was to be there.

"On the other hand, there was no occasion for the chauffeur to telephone, because he thought she already had his note. The explanation, therefore, would be that your wife did not receive the note which the chauffeur sent her, but that some other person told her something over the telephone, sufficiently important, to make her plead illness and return to her home at once.

"And it's reasonable to suppose, at least as a working hypothesis, that such a person met her somewhere between the reception and her home and that this person had a latchkey to the front door."

Lester Leith smiled urbanely.

Steele sneered, but there was just the faintest suggestion of pallor about his face.

"When you consider that the note Meggs sent was actually found in the wife's possession, and that I have a complete alibi," he said, "this theory of yours wouldn't seem to hold much water."

Lester Leith's smile became a grin.

"Ah, yes," he said, almost soothingly, "your wife did have the note in the sole of her stocking, didn't she? And that's pretty conclusive evidence that you were the murderer. You intercepted the note, baited your own trap, then pressed the note down into the stocking where it would be found by the coroner.

"The evidence shows she didn't know Meggs expected her there. Yet she would have known Meggs was to be there had she received the note. Yet the note was found on her body. That would indicate the note had been intercepted, delivered after her death.

"And as for your alibi, it works both ways. If you couldn't give an alibi for your secretary, she couldn't give one for you."

"But," said Steele, speaking rapidly, "I was dictating steadily. The number of records I sent out on the brief would show that."

Lester Leith smilingly shook his head.

"Cylinders on a dictating machine can be made at any time. You could have dictated that brief in the afternoon, simply sent out the cylinders during the evening."

The lawyer took a deep breath.

"You can't *prove* a thing! You can only pull some fancy conversation. That's all!"

Lester Leith shrugged his shoulders, returned his attention to the fingerprints. In utter silence he checked various points of real or pretended similarity in the two prints, exclaiming under his breath, little whispered comments of satisfaction.

"You overlooked a bet here," he said, "and this is *proof!*"

The lawyer stretched back his arms, yawned.

"Yeah?" he said, as though the thing interested him not at all. "Is that so? And can't I leave a fingerprint on a pie plate in my own home if I want to?"

Lester Leith shrugged his shoulders without looking up. "That's for you to tell the jury… And there's another thing."

Lester Leith whirled about, faced the lawyer as he snapped out the last of his accusation. "I have an idea you're a gambler, one of the whole-hog-or-nothing guys. You knew the officers would be searching every place they thought the diamonds might have been hidden. With supposed thieves in your house, that meant your house would be searched. With a chauffeur suspected of murder, that meant the garage would be searched. With a secretary also accused of murder, that meant your office would be searched. So I have a hunch you carried those diamonds where they'd be safe from discovery unless the police should suspect you! And your relied on your ingenuity to keep them from suspecting you."

And Lester Leith swung back for a final inspection of the fingerprints.

CHAPTER XII

Red-Handed

There was a sudden rustle of swift motion.

Steele made a lunge. His hand darted out to the drawer. The clutching fingers grasped the butt of the gun, slipped, fumbled, grasped again. He leaped backwards, fangs showing, black eyes glittering, mouth twitching. The gun was in his hand, pointed at Lester Leith.

"All right, damn you. I won't be taken alive. They can only burn a man once. I may as well eliminate you and your damned fingerprints. That'll destroy the evidence of Vivian's murder. Then I'll take a chance on yours, damn you!"

Lester Leith faced him, hands up.

"Don't do that, Steele," he pleaded. "I'll listen to reason. I'll make you a proposition..."

"Baloney!" snapped the lawyer, squinted deliberately down the sights, and pulled the trigger.

The hammer clicked.

The lawyer pulled the trigger again. There sounded another click.

"Empty," said Lester Leith with a smile. "I left that empty gun in the drawer. Thought you might betray yourself with it. The shells for it are in the pasteboard box. Now *this* gun is loaded." And Lester Leith's gloved hand darted beneath his armpit, brought to light a wicked looking automatic.

The lawyer caved into a sitting position. The whites of his eyes were showing now, around the black irises, as the whites show in the eyes of a fighting horse. He was breathing hard as thought he had been running.

Lester Leith pushed across a typewritten sheet of paper. "A confession for you to sign," he said. "It covers all the major points."

The lawyer stared. Beads of sweat were on his forehead. "You," he snarled, "can go to hell!"

Lester Leith shrugged his shoulders. "Very well," he said. "I'll call the police."

He got from his chair, started toward the door. The attorney, vicious as a cornered rat, lunged.

Lester Leith stepped back. His motion was as well-timed as the footwork of a professional boxer. The lawyer smashed down with the gun, using it as a metal club. The blow whizzed past. Lester Leith's right travelled a matter of eight inches. The slender form of the attorney stiffened as the blow contacted with his jaw.

Lester Leith eased the man back into the chair, opened his vest and shirt, pulled open the pockets of the money belt which was next to the skin.

From those chamois pockets he extracted diamonds, dumped them into the pockets of his own coat. Then he fastened the shirt and vest, sat down to wait.

He smoked two cigarettes before the attorney's eyes flickered open. There was a moment or two during which Steele stared with punch groggy eyes that refused to focus. Then realization and expression flooded his eyes.

Lester Leith made sure the man was in full possession of his faculties.

He got to his feet.

"I'm going to lock you in and summon the police," he said.

He opened the door, slammed it shut behind him, leaving the attorney in the office.

That office was locked from the outside, but the spring lock could readily be opened from the inside.

Leith walked to the counter where the pies were placed, back of the counter, paused, chatted a few moment with Lois Webber.

The ex-convicts were standing in little knots, talking in low tones. Half a dozen garbage containers were in the center of the floor. There were more along the sides. Here and there some of the men were toying with them. The man who had posed as Lamont was standing out near the center of the floor. His attitude was charged with suspicion. His hand was near the hip pocket of his trousers.

He glowered at Lester Leith, walked purposefully toward him. There was no further pretense of being merely an inventor. The man snarled his question.

"What were you saying to Steele in there?"

Lester Leith became confidential. "Do you know, Lamont, I

have an idea Steele murdered his wife. I have accused him of it. I have left him in there with a typewritten confession. I felt that if he was alone with his conscience it would be a good thing for him. You know, a little of the subtle third-degree stuff."

Lamont gasped. His eyes grew wide, and the pink interior of his mouth showed as the sagging jaw dropped.

"What?" he yelled.

"A fact," said Lester Leith. "If was apparent, right from the start, that the woman hadn't used her latchkey to get into the house with. Now if the chauffeur was to meet the woman there, and wanted to rob her, why break in the window? She was going to let him in. And why have accomplices? He didn't need them. If, on the other hand, he had robbed her, why overlook the coin in the purse?

"Then there were other discrepancies. I've pushed them home to Steele. I firmly believe he's going to weaken."

Lamont managed to get his jaw back into position, his eyes narrowed down.

"The diamonds?" he asked.

Lester Leith nodded.

"I believe," he said, "the man has the diamonds with him."

Lamont took a deep breath. "I'm going in there," he said.

Lester Leith shook his head, emphatically.

"Don't do it. The man's a crook. You start crowding him, and—"

"You go to hell," said Lamont, and strode toward the door of the inner office. He wrenched the knob, flung his weight against the door.

"Hand me the key," he called back to Lester Leith.

"Nothing doing," snapped Lester Leith. "That man's a murderer. He might kill you."

Lamont banged on the door. "Open up! This is the law!"

His answer was the roar of a gun, a tearing slug that crashed through the panels of the door.

"Don't let a man leave this room," called Lamont, brandishing his gun, covering the men who paused, uncertain of what course to take, ex-convicts who were hardened to conflict, trained to think quickly with cunning minds.

Lamont shot the lock of the door off, reached out with his foot, kicked the door. A slender shape came rushing from the room, shooting as it came. Lamont ducked behind a garbage can, fired. The running figure staggered, whirled, shot at Lamont, dove through the door.

"Stop him!" yelled Lamont, and ran in pursuit.

He paused at the doorway, raised his arm, fired twice.

Lester Leith turned to Lois Webber. "Run into the office and hide," he said. She stared at him.

"But—"

"Please," said Lester Leith, "do as I say, and take the boys in there with you."

He raised his voice.

"Into the office, everybody. Clear this room. The police will be coming…"

They scattered at his words. Some of them made for the door. There came the sound of police whistles. The men turned back. Lois Webber ran into the office.

"Follow me," she cried.

Lester Leith ran toward the door.

Shots sounded from the foot of the stairs. Then a shot from the stair head. There was the thud of a falling body. Lamont jumped up from behind a packing case.

"I got him," he said.

There were cries from below. Feet sounded on the lower floor. A man shouted. A police whistle blew. Lamont took the stairs two at a time. Lester Leith was on his heels.

Steele lay in a crumpled, inert heap at the bottom of the stairs. Lester Leith was at the side of the detective who had posed as the inventor of the garbage can when that individual knelt by the side of the corpse.

"Dead," said Lamont.

"Through the back of the head," said Lester Leith.

A door banged open. Sergeant Ackley with a plainclothes officer at his side came thundering up on a flat-footed gallop.

"What the hell?" asked Sergeant Ackley.

Lamont looked up. "This man murdered his wife, Vivian Steele. He stole the diamonds."

Ackley pointed his finger at Lester Leith. "What are *you* doing here?"

Lester Leith got to his feet.

"Just a theory of mine, Sergeant, that seemed to work out. You know most of my theories are just academic solutions. They're possible, but I've never had a chance to follow them up. On this case I managed to stay with it—all the way."

Lamont looked at Sergeant Ackley, nodded. "He called the turn, Sergeant."

Lester Leith glanced down at the body.

"He framed his wife, cracked her skull as she entered the house. Then he arranged plates of grub so it looked, as though the house had been entered. He stole the diamonds."

Sergeant Ackley sneered. "Where are the diamonds?"

Lester Leith shrugged his shoulders.

The man who had posed as the inventor made a swift search of the corpse. Sergeant Ackley kept his eyes on Lester Leith. A door opened and three more men came in, joined the group.

They regarded the dead man on the floor with casual interest. Sergeant Ackley indicated Lester Leith. "Watch him," he said.

The men moved forward, silently, efficiently, purposefully. Lamont straightened.

"A money belt," he said, "empty."

"Maybe," suggested Lester Leith, "he left the diamonds in the room upstairs. I left him in there with a confession. Lamont busted in the door and started the party. If Lamont hadn't been so impetuous we might have had a signed confession."

Lamont stared at Lester Leith.

"You left him in there with a gun," he said accusingly.

Lester Leith shook his head. "The gun," he said, "wasn't loaded."

Lamont spat an expletive.

Leith added: "But there were some shells in another drawer in the table. He must have gone through the drawers, found the shells, loaded the gun and started to shoot."

Sergeant Ackley pointed to Lester Leith.

"Frisk him," he said.

Two of the men made swift motions. Lester Leith put his hands up.

"This is an outrage," he said. "You haven't a warrant."

Sergeant Ackley laughed, and the laugh was without mirth.

"Damn you! I'll find those diamonds if it takes a year. This time I've caught you red-handed. You've mixed yourself up in a pretty mess, and…"

He stopped abruptly as a woman screamed.

CHAPTER XIII

Evidence to Convict

"Who's up there?" asked Ackley, pointing a finger toward the upper floor from which the scream had sounded.

"A frail and a bunch of hard-boiled eggs," said Lamont.

Sergeant Ackley hesitated. "Go on up, Bill," he said to one of the men. He turned back to the two who were searching Lester Leith.

"Go on with this baby. He's the one I want. He's got fifty thousand dollars' worth of sparklers on him somewhere."

Lester Leith's tone was low, earnest.

"Sergeant, you're making a big mistake. All this is costing you…"

"Shut up," said Sergeant Ackley. "Pop him on the buzzer if he yips again, boys."

The woman screamed again.

There were running steps. Then a man's voice bellowed excitedly: "Sergeant! This way. Bring the men!"

Sergeant Ackley cursed.

The two who had been searching Lester Leith turned and reported to Ackley. "He's clean," they said.

Ackley cursed again. "How the hell *can* he be clean? He's got those sparklers. He …"

Lester Leith interrupted. "I might have had them, Sergeant, if Lamont hadn't been so impulsive. Then I could have turned them over to the authorities and the case would have been closed—"

"Sergeant—quick!" yelled the voice of the detective who had gone upstairs. There was the sound of a shot, of blows, of the tramp of feet that surged forward in a concerted mêlée of motion.

Then the feet avalanched across the room, broke into running steps. The woman screamed again, then again.

Lamont straightened, stared at Sergeant Ackley with unfriendly eyes.

"To hell with you," he said. "I'm going up!"

He ran for the stairs. One of the men who had searched Lester Leith followed.

Sergeant Ackley tugged handcuffs from his pocket, eyed Lester Leith.

"Put 'em out," he said.

Lester Leith's lips clamped.

The detective who remained with Lester Leith and Sergeant Ackley pulled a blackjack from his hip, swung it suggestively. Lester Leith put out his wrists. The handcuffs clicked.

"Okay," said Sergeant Ackley. "I'll hold him. You go up, Fred."

The man thundered up the stairs.

Sergeant Ackley hesitated, stared at the dead man on the floor, then at Lester Leith. There were running steps coming down the stairs. The second detective who gone up came down, holding Lois Webber by the wrist. Her face was white, her lips bloodless. She stared at the man on the floor, at Lester Leith.

"This baby," said the detective, "saw the whole thing. She was the first into the room after Steele ran out. The diamonds were in a pile in the center of a table. She kept yelling for us to come. There were eighteen hard-boiled ex-cons up there. They copped the ice. The girl tried to stop 'em. They flung her into a closet.

"She got out and screamed. The cons were dividing the loot. Bill came up. He was in on the tail end of it. He yelled for help and drew his rod. The cons rushed him, smashed him down and beat it out the back."

"They won't get far," said Sergeant Ackley. "I've got men scattered all around the block."

"The hell they won't," said the detective. "These boys weren't amateurs. They all had records."

"How did that happen?" asked Sergeant Ackley.

Lester Leith answered the question.

"My fault," he said. "I hand-picked them. I was running a thieves' kitchen."

Lamont came down the stairs. The detective who had first gone up was battered and bloody. He glowered at Sergeant Ackley.

"If you'd sent the boys up when I yelled, we might have stopped 'em!" he said, bitterly.

Sergeant Ackley thought for a moment. "Did you *see* the diamonds?" he asked.

"They were splitting them when I came in," said the detective. "I tried to hold 'em. They rushed me. I had time for one shot."

Sergeant Ackley sighed

"Anyhow," he said, slowly, "I've solved the Steele murder mystery."

Lamont stared at him with wide eyes. "*You* have!" he exclaimed.

Sergeant Ackley gritted his answer. "I have," he said, staring straight at Lamont, "and jobs are damned hard to get right now."

There was a silence.

Sergeant Ackley stared at the others. "And that goes for you, too—all of you."

He took a key from his pocket, unfastened the handcuffs around Lester Leith's wrists.

"And a damned lucky break you got, too. If this guy hadn't disregarded order and bungled the case, you'd have been caught with the goods on by this time."

Lester Leith arched his eyebrows. "Was Lamont a detective?"

Sergeant Ackley sneered.

"He was. Maybe he'll keep on being one. Maybe not. I didn't give a damn about the rest of it. I wanted *you*. I told this McNutt to play it that way. He lost his head."

Lester Leith sighed.

"I didn't *think* he was an inventor," he said.

Captain E. R. Walker stared at Sergeant Ackley through level-lidded eyes. The stare was unfriendly.

"Grand jury, hell!" he said. "You'd be the laughing stock of the city."

Sergeant Ackley slammed a glittering bit of hard stone on the battered desk. The stone bounced, rolled, fetched up against an inkwell, came to rest. The rays of the morning sun glinted from it. "See what it is? It's imitation. I rounded up three of those ex-cons who were in that thieves' kitchen. I made 'em cough up. The stones they had were imitations. Now Steele took those stones in that building. They weren't on him when he was croaked. Lester Leith was in that building. I want an indictment."

Captain Walker's eyes took on little crows' feet as his lips twisted in a smile. "But you searched Leith right away, even before the stones were stolen," he said.

Ackley snorted. "Know what he could have done? I reasoned it all out. He ducked down behind the pie counter when the shooting started. He could have shoved all those stones into the apple pies. Afterwards, they dumped all that stuff in the garbage and took it away. Leith showed up and said he owned the garbage containers. Lamont was with him. They took them all away. He *could* have done it. He was there, and he had the opportunity."

Captain Walker's smile was dry.

"Sergeant," he said. "I've reminded you several times that it takes evidence to convict. If you hadn't bungled that whole case, you could have gone on up in time to cop those imitations. Then you could have searched the pies. But your damned personal grudge against Leith stood in your way. You bungled the whole case."

Sergeant Ackley pressed the point. "Yes," he said, "and there were exactly eighteen two- and three-time losers in the room who could have done it."

"This is once he outguessed you, Sergeant. I won't let the force be made the laughing stock of the newspapers. Not one suspect, but eighteen, and all of them trying to be guilty of stealing the diamonds, and you standing at the foot of the stairs, searching the one man in the house who didn't have a criminal record.

"No, Sergeant. It takes evidence to convict."

Captain Walker picked up an envelope, toyed with it, pulled

out a tinted oblong of paper. "That is particularly true." He said softly, "of a man who has just made a fifty-thousand-dollar donation to the Police Protective Association. The net result, Sergeant, is one murderer brought to justice without the expense of a trial for the state to pay; one innocent woman removed from suspicion; one innocentchauffeur, ditto; credit to the police department for having solved a baffling case in record time—and fifty thousand dollars for the wives and orphaned kiddies of brave men who gave their services to the state.

"This Leith fellow may be a crook as you say. But, Sergeant, if we had about fifty more crooks like him we'd have a city that was free of crime, and a fund for orphaned kiddies and hungry widows that would make me sleep a lot better of nights.

"And that, Sergeant Ackley, closes the subject!"

There was a glitter in the eye of Captain Walker which was very significant to those who knew him. Sergeant Ackley knew that glitter. He straightened, bowed.

"Yes, Captain," he said, and closed the door very softly behind him as he went out.

Captain Walker, treasurer of the Police Protective Association was endorsing the check, and he disliked the sound of slamming doors when he was writing.

Put It in Writing!

CHAPTER I

"What About the Dog?"

Lester Leith, attired in silk pyjamas of violent hue, toyed with a cigarette case and beamed at his valet.

"Scuttle, I should like something novel in the way of a crime."

"Yes, sir?"

"Yes, Scuttle. Crime is getting monotonous. Really all crimes are mere repetitions. The only thing that is different is the victim and the criminal. Greed or revenge is the motive. There are crimes of violence and crimes of cunning. But nearly all the crimes are bungling affairs. I wonder if we couldn't find some really artistic crime, something new in the way of a crooked scheme, something where the motive was so obscure as to be baffling."

The valet straightened to his full six feet plus of beef and regarded the sprawled figure with glittering eyes. "You know, sir, if you don't mind my saying so, sir, this mania of yours for criminal news is going to get you in jail, sir."

Lester Leith flung back his head and laughed.

"My *dear* Scuttle! You are so delightedly ponderous! You amuse me! Tut, tut, Scuttle, here we have been suspected by the police for over a year. Why, we even found, only last month, that Sergeant Ackley had gone so far as to install a dictograph in my rooms. Lord knows how long it had been there. Think of it, Scuttle, all of our private conversations were recorded by the police. One might say that my innermost thoughts were open to police inspection.

"And why did they do all this? Merely because they knew I was interested in the newspaper accounts of crime, that I liked to work out theoretical solutions, based purely upon newspaper reports. Can you imagine anything as puerile as the police, Scuttle?"

And the valet, because he was in reality a police spy, working "under cover" as Lester Leith's valet, squirmed uncomfortably.

"*Somebody,*" he said in a tone which was accusing in its lugubrious doggedness, "is able to work out actual solutions from the printed reports of crime. And that somebody, sir, beats the police to a solution, hijacks the swag from the crook and makes a perfect get-away every time."

Lester Leith chuckled.

"Yes, Scuttle, I'm beginning to think you're right. At first I thought this nebulous hijacker was a figment of Sergeant Ackley's imagination. But now I'm beginning to believe he's an actual person. But, of course, Scuttle, the fact that the police have concealed a dictograph on *us*, have made repeated searches of our persons—those things, Scuttle, should demonstrate our innocence, even to the police mind."

Lester Leith took out a cigarette, tapped it on his thumb nail, and regarded the valet through lazy-lidded eyes that twinkled.

"Think so, Scuttle?"

The valet gulped, nodded. "Yes, sir," he said, and a deep-seated hostility glittered from his ebony black eyes.

"Yes, indeed," purred Leith, "and, now that my innocence is established. I can fling myself into my hobby, the *theoretical* solutions of crime from newspaper accounts.

"What have you clipped from the papers lately, Scuttle?"

The police spy, posing as a well-trained servant, moved his great bulk with catlike tread, opened a drawer and returned with sheaf of clipping.

"A daylight robbery, sir. The Fifth Avenue branch of the—"

Lester Leith patted his parted lips to stifle a yawn. "Come, come, that's getting positively monotonous. Pass it. Get something else, something with a dash of mystery in it, something that has romance."

"The murder of Stella Rutland, sir."

"What about that?"

"She was killed by one of two men, but the police can't tell which. She went riding and never returned. Her body was found, frightfully mutilated, seated in an automobile. The automobile had been stolen. Evidently it was a romantic affair. She had gone into the night with some—"

Lester Leith straightened in his chair, fixed his servant with an accusing glare.

"Scuttle, I'm sure of it—positively certain!"

"Sure of what, sir?"

"That you've been devouring the tabloids again, Scuttle. How many times have I told you to save me only the reports that come from the most conservative newspapers? I must have accuracy. I can supply my own sob sister stuff when it's necessary."

The servant turned a brick red.

"Well, damn it, I guess I can—"

He remembered himself, choked off the words of red rage.

"Tut, tut, Scuttle. You must be more careful; apoplexy, Scuttle.

And there's no need for any resentment. I spoke to you as a friend who is interested in your mental development. Come, come, we're digressing, and that's the sign of failing concentration. Let's return to the crime news. What else?"

"A wife poisoning, sir."

"Pass it."

"A husband shooting, sir."

"Let it go. There's always one of them."

"A mysterious murder in an apartment. The woman—"

"Young or old, Scuttle?"

"Rather elderly, sir."

"Was the motive clear?"

"Yes, sir. There was a necklace, sir—"

"Pass it. I've worked on so many necklace cases I'm getting tired of the damn things. Come, come, Scuttle, there must be some crime that's intriguing. I want something with a dash of mystery. I want something with a hidden motive. In short, I want something complicated, and with a little romantic interest attached to it."

The valet shook his ponderous head. "I'm sorry sir. There's nothing, sir."

Lester Leith took a deep drag at the cigarette, held the smoke for a while, looked at the ceiling, frowned, then exhaled as he spoke, clothing the words in a smoky aura.

"Can you fancy that! And the police complain about the increase of crime. Ever since I can remember, Scuttle, the police have been 'coping' with a 'crime wave,' and the newspapers have been talking about the annual increase in crime. And here we can't pick the crime we want. It's like going to a restaurant and not finding a thing on the menu that fits the appetite."

The valet said nothing.

Of a sudden Lester Leith sat erect, as one does when one has an inspiration. "Scuttle!"

"Yes, sir?"

"I have it!"

"Yes, sir?"

"Yes, Scuttle. We'll dig back into the old, unsolved murders. Surely we can pick the sort of a case we want out of the past ten years' record!"

"Perhaps, sir, but, I fail to see how you can solve a crime where the clews have been covered by time, where—"

"Tut, tut, Scuttle. I am only after a *theoretical* solution."

"Yes, sir."

"Yes, indeed. By the way, how about the Marigold murder? Was it ever solved?"

"No, sir. It never will be now. The jury acquitted Bradbury in that case and the police have marked it as a closed file. Bradbury was guilty, of course, but the police couldn't convince the jury."

"There was a romance in that case, wasn't there?"

"There most certainly was, sir. Little Margy Marigold, the most romantic figure that ever came into crime circles, sir."

"In what way, Scuttle?"

"She was married to Bradbury, in California, sir. They lived near Los Angeles for three years, then she got a divorce. It was pretty well established that there was another man, the man she subsequently married, Harley Marigold, sir.

"But she couldn't cheat, sir. While she was married to Bradbury she remained absolutely above reproach. The divorce case was bitterly contested, yet that fact established beyond any doubt."

Lester Leith had dropped back to the cushions of the reclining chair. He sent a thin streamer of blue smoke drifting upward. His eyes were half closed, lazy with attentive listening.

"Go on, Scuttle."

"In California, sir, they give an interlocutory decree of divorce. A year later they grant a final decree. The parties can't remarry until after the final decree.

"And little Mrs. Bradbury disappeared right after the interlocutory decree. Both men were frantic. Bradbury wanted to effect a reconciliation, Marigold wanted her to go to Mexico and be married. Bradbury threatened prosecution for bigamy.

"Both men employed rival detective agencies to find her. Both men threatened each other. There was a suit pending for alienation of affections, another for defamation of character.

"All in all, it was a frightful mix up. Both men disappeared from time to time, running down clews that their detectives had unearthed. But neither man ever found anything of value. The detective agencies were forced to bring their reports into court at the murder trial, sir."

"Yes, yes, Scuttle, go on!"

"Well, sir, exactly one year to the day after the interlocutory decree, little Margy Bradbury showed up in this State. She wired her attorney in California to get the final decree. She wired Marigold to come on for the wedding.

"And she granted interviews to the newspapers. She said a woman could never hold the love of any man unless she made that man respect her. She said that she knew she loved Marigold far too much to resist his entreaties to go to Mexico and be married, yet she knew the marriage would be nothing except a legal mockery.

"So she concealed herself until the year was up and then made that dramatic appearance right here in town with a little house all furnished, ready for the new romance.

"She secured the house through an agent, and she picked out the furniture in a single afternoon. Then she got the license and wired Marigold.

"Of course he was wild with joy. He came on by fastest train. And Bradbury also came on. He took an assumed name, ditched the reporters as well as the detectives Marigold had shadowing him, and took the train following the one Marigold was on."

Lester Leith sighed, flipped the cigarette end into the fireplace.

"Scuttle, this is *it*! This is *the* crime! Go on!"

"But there's no mystery, sir. The police couldn't have solved the crime. Anything that has all these subtle motives of characterization couldn't have been solved in a routine way."

"Pray proceed."

"Yes, sir. I happen to remember the case very well, sir. It's been four years ago, sir, but I know all the details. It was striking, dramatic.

"Marigold reached town first. They were married. They went to the little cottage she had picked out. Newspaper reporters refused to give them any honeymoon. They swarmed all over the place, but the bride and groom were most gracious about it.

"They posed for pictures, sir, they gave interviews, and Mr. Marigold asked the reporters to be sports. He had given them all the story he could, and he asked them to leave him alone. And the reporters promised a twenty-four-hour recess. They had their stories. They had their pictures. They had their interviews. They knew everything, except just one thing."

"What was that, Scuttle?"

"Where she had been during the year. The newspaper reporters were never able to find that out. During the trial of the case the police moved heaven and earth. They were never able to find it out. She had simply disappeared and she remained disappeared. The detective agencies Marigold and Bradbury were tracking down vague rumors. Neither one had the slightest success."

Lester Leith lit another cigarette. His eyes were soft now.

"This woman, Scuttle, must have been a rather remarkable woman. She had strength of character, and she was able to keep her mouth shut. She never told, never gave a clew?"

"Not a word, sir."

"I see. Then what happened?"

"The newspaper reporters came to the house the next morning. They were ready for another story of the honeymooners. They got a story—ugh!"

"Yes, yes, Scuttle, go on. What was it they got?"

"The house was closed tightly, sir. They knocked and they hammered and they go no answer. Finally they arrived at the conclusion the newlyweds had given them the slip and gone away.

"Naturally, sir, they were peeved, since they'd have watched the place all night if Marigold hadn't been so decent about it all. They'd sort of put him on his honor. And the city editors wouldn't understand the situation.

"So they decided to get in the house, sir, and see if there wasn't some little clew that would tell them where the pair had gone."

"Yes, yes, Scuttle. Go on."

"Well, sir, you'll remember what they found. Marigold was unconscious, tied to a chair. The woman was in bed. She had been strangled. Evidently the tragedy had occurred sometime before midnight. Margy Marigold had just retired for the night. Harley Marigold had his coat and shirt off, was in his stocking feet.

"Of course they made a great uproar over it. It was such a horrible finish for a romance. And poor Marigold was almost prostrated when he regained consciousness. And the police surgeons rather fancied there had been some drug administered to him as well as the blow on the head.

"He could tell almost nothing of what had happened. He had approached a closet in the bedroom to hang up his coat. There had been the rustle of motion. A dark figure had leaped out, and that was the last Harley Marigold remembered until he regained consciousness some twenty-four hours later.

"He was knotted in a most clever manner. It must have been a sailor who tied those knots. And Bradbury had been a yachtsman. The police caught Bradbury. He had been out all night. He claimed he had tried to see the dead woman, that Marigold had ordered him from the premises, threatened to call the police, and that he had walked the streets all night.

"Marigold branded that as a lie."

The police spy, who posed as a servant, came to a conclusion of his recital, stared at the man he was trailing with glittering eyes.

"*That's* a crime for you, sir."

Lester Leith nodded.

"Solve that crime, sir, and you'll be solving something."

"Yes, yes, Scuttle. There were other facts, though. There was something—let me see, there was some touch of pathos other than the tragedy itself. What was it?"

"No, sir, I've told you the entire facts, sir. But they discovered other facts afterward, sir. There was the man who saw Bradbury sneaking away from the house shortly before midnight. He identified him positively."

"Yes, yes!" exclaimed Lester Leith impatiently. "I remember all those, but there was—ah, I have it! The dog!"

"The dog, sir?" Scuttle's brows were puckered.

"Yes, Scuttle, the dog. It was featured in one of the newspaper articles."

The valet shook his head.

"I'm afraid you're mistaken, sir."

"No, I'm not, Scuttle. You go out and dig me up a file of papers showing the reports of the crime, and I'll try and check through them. That's the worst of the police, Scuttle, they get a theory of the case and they cram the facts into a mold to fit that theory. The newspaper reporter is more discerning. He sees facts and reports them. He gives all the facts and reports them. He gives all the facts as he sees them. The police only see the facts that tend to support their theories."

"But, good heavens, sir! You don't contend that Bradbury wasn't the murderer?"

"The jurors didn't think so, Scuttle."

"Shucks, sir, the jury! Why, the jurors fell for his play acting."

"Possibly, Scuttle. It has been known to happen. Tell me, what was done with the body?"

"Taken to Indianapolis for burial, sir. Her folks lived there. The husband took the body back for burial in the cemetery where her father was buried."

"Very touching, Scuttle, very touching. It does the husband credit. But all this isn't solving the crime. You go get me the newspaper files that covered the crime. Get me the photographs. I particularly want clear photographs."

"Yes, sir."

And the big valet, his face wearing a look of puzzled bewilderment, opened the door and oozed into the corridor. But he did not immediately go on his various errands. Instead he made a telephone report of the situation to Sergeant Ackley, received implicit instruction.

Only after that did he put in an afternoon gathering the data Lester Leith had suggested.

CHAPTER II

Scuttle Goes Traveling

It was evening. The fire crackled in the open grate. Lester Leith, attired in faultless evening raiment, sat with his feet stretched toward the fire, a cigarette in his lips.

The valet shifted uncomfortably from one foot to the other.

"So you see, Scuttle, I was right. There was a dog, and its presence was important."

The heavy forehead of the valet wash-boarded. "But I don't see, sir—"

"Tut, tut, Scuttle. You wouldn't."

Lester Leith picked up a glossy surfaced print of a newspaper photograph.

"You see I was right about the dog, Scuttle, and about the dog's importance."

"But what's important about the dog, sir? It was just a stray, sir, bearing a license from a town in Indiana. Mrs. Marigold took it in and fed it. There's nothing unusual in that, sir."

"No, Scuttle, but the dog was sick with grief after the tragedy. Now this photograph shows the bride with the stray dog in her arms. It's a clear picture. The dog is a Boston bull and the photograph shows the dog license, Pickets, Indiana, Scuttle."

"Doubtless some country town, sir."

"Doubtless, Scuttle."

The valet squirmed again.

"Are you making fun of me, sir?"

"Indeed, no, Scuttle. I am merely suggesting that you go to Pickets, Indiana, and buy a dog. I should like a rather large fox terrier, Scuttle. And I wish you would call him 'Bobo,' and get a collar suitably engraved. Just the name, 'Bobo.' No address. And be sure you purchase a license.

"And then I wish you would get me a furnished apartment, and then go to one of the best beauty shops, if the town has a beauty shop, and get me a jar of cold cream, a curling iron, and an electric blowing machine, such as is used for drying hair.

"And I'd like you to get me a hammer and a cold chisel, and a little anvil. You know what I mean, Scuttle, one of those little affairs such as jewelers have.

"And I guess that's all for the present, Scuttle."

The man stared at him with sagging jaw. "Good God, sir, are you crazy?"

"That is hardly a fair question, Scuttle. All medical authorities agree that persons afflicted with insanity think they are sane. Therefore, if I should tell you I was sane, it would not prove anything. In fact it would merely give an impartial observer some grounds for thinking I might not, in fact, be sane."

"But—but—why should I go to Pickets, Indiana, and get a dog, an apartment, and all the rest of that junk?"

"Simply for the change, Scuttle, and, because I have requested you to do so. The fact may have altogether escaped your mind, Scuttle, but it happens that I'm paying you your salary—ah, yes, you *had* forgotten that, hadn't you Scuttle?"

And Lester Leith beamed upon the spy with an expression so smilingly urbane that the man whirled on his heel, walked abruptly toward the bedroom.

"Shall I start at once, sir?"

"At once, Scuttle."

And, for once, the valet went through a door without his customary oozing of stealthy caution. He jerked open the door, strode into the bedroom, slammed it with a jar that made the plastering quiver.

But Lester Leith took no notice.

His face had suddenly become as hard and as keen as a razor blade. His eyes narrowed to mere slits. The cigarette burned in his hand unnoticed, the smoke spiralling towards the darkened ceiling.

Those who knew only Lester Leith the polished, urbane mocker, would have been dumbfounded at the glittering eyes, the quivering nostrils, the thin lips, the concentration of the features.

From time to time he nodded his head after the manner of one who is blocking out a strategic campaign in which every single move must dovetail with existing facts.

Finally he relaxed and smiled.

And, at that moment, there was a rattle of knob and the valet stood in the doorway, a valise in his hand.

"You're in earnest, sir?"

"Certainly, Scuttle."

"But, sir, there isn't a thing in the newspapers, sir."

Lester Leith whirled.

"Scuttle, you will do as I say. I have one more request. You will go to the head of the police force at Pickets and ask him if there has been a murder committed within the past four or five years that has been entirely unexplained, one in which there was no apparent motive. If there has been, you will wire me at once, and begin to carry out my instructions; if there has not been you will wire me and await my telegraphic orders."

"Murder ... four years ... surely, sir, you don't think. "

Lester Leith made a little jabbing motion with the cigarette in his fingers.

"Listen, Scuttle, the police theory of the Marigold murder was not the correct theory. The dog is important. Stray dogs do not pine for persons who have adopted them within a few days of their deaths."

"And, if you will notice the sob sister article in the *Bugle*, Scuttle, you will note this paragraph:

"The little dog, Bobo, whines piteously for the mistress whose kind hand took him in from the homeless highways. Only one person can comfort him, and that is the heartbroken husband. Animal psychologists say it is a case of the animal recognizing the grief of the husband and being united to him through the bond of joint suffering."

The valet nodded. "Yes, sir. I remember that paragraph."

"Very well, Scuttle. Perhaps you'd better clip it and take it with you. You might find time to study it on the train. Also ponder the expensive collar with the engraved name."

The valet grunted.

"But, if you think this Bobo dog came from Pickets, and you want to work a dummy, why in hell don't you get the same sort of a dog? Why not let me get you a Boston bull? I could get one just like the picture."

And Lester Leith, suddenly letting his face slip into that patronizing smile which the valet found so irritating blew a smoke ring at the ceiling, then answered almost musingly. "Ah, yes, Scuttle, why in hell don't I? That, Scuttle, is my little secret. Be sure that he is a fox terrier. Under no circumstances get a dog that is anything like the pictured Bobo."

The valet turned and swung toward the door.

"I'll wire you," he said, and, for the second time that day, found occasion to slam the door after him.

CHAPTER III

A Little Game of Cards

It was three days before Lester Leith received a wire from his valet. At that time the valet sent two wires. The one to Lester Leith was rather complete:

Arrived Reported chief police and find woman named Martha Striker was murdered sometime in June of 1926. Her body was not found until several months later, but identity established by dental work and broken bones in one leg. Husband offered reward of ten thousand dollars for murderer, but no clew to date. Rented apartment, secured fox terrier named Bobo, got collar and dog license, curling iron, cold cream, hair dryer, cold chisel, hammer and anvil.

(Signed)   Beaver.

The second telegram was sent to Sergeant Arthur Ackley at police headquarters:

Interest in Marigold murder was only a blind to get opportunity to investigate murder of a Martha Striker here in June of 1926. There is chance Leith was the one who guilty of this murder. Have secured apartment and wired him, and he will probably take next train out. Have him shadowed all the way, as he is planning to slip over a fast one.
(Signed)   Beaver.

The two telegrams were duly delivered. The next limited train saw Lester Leith comfortably ensconced in a compartment.

Police officers had shadowed him to the station, had secured his reservation numbers as soon as the compartment had been engaged. Police pull had secured the adjoining compartment for Sergeant Ackley and a plain-clothes detective. By the time the train had been made up the officers had not only settled themselves in their quarters, but had bored two tiny holes through the steel partition. These holes were hardly the diameter of a needle, but they enabled the officers to secure a very fair view of the interior of the adjoining compartment.

They had been careful to board the train while the car was still in the yards, far in advance of the time when ordinary passengers were allowed through the gates. But they might well have spared themselves the trouble, for Lester Leith did not enter the car until precisely two minutes before the train pulled out.

Sergeant Ackley heaved a sigh of relief.

Lester Leith stretched himself comfortably in his compartment, took out one of his monogrammed cigarettes, lit it and sent little spirals of smoke trailing upward.

His eyes were, for the most part, amused, lazy-lidded. But occasionally, as some thought flitted across the matchless mind, those eyes went through a subtle change of color. At times they were a warm gray. At times they were a deep hazel, and, at times, they glittered with that indescribable color which cold sunlight brings forth from a floating iceberg.

The train rumbled out of the yards, gathered speed as it hit the open country, roared along the banks of a river, snorted up long grades.

Lester Leith propped the door of his compartment open. Passengers who strolled past always gave a second look at the well-knit figure that sprawled in such easy indolence. There was something feline in the luxurious relaxation of the body.

But Lester Leith paid no attention to them.

Not until a waiter was summoned to the adjoining compartment, did he take any notice of what was going on about him. Then, when the waiter returned with a tray, loaded with viands, bordered with two silver foiled cigars, Lester Leith got up from his seat, adjusted his tie before the mirror, brushed his hair, straightened his coat, and knocked upon the door of the adjoining compartment.

The door flung open.

"I told you we didn't want to be distur— " That was as far as Sergeant Ackley got before the words stopped coming. His crestfallen eyes took in the smiling debonair countenance of the man he was trailing.

"Well, well, sergeant, this is indeed a pleasure. I had looked forward to a rather lonesome trip. Fancy meeting you here! And you have a friend with you. Doubtless er ... a business associate, a co-worker, eh?

"And do you play poker, sergeant?"

The red-faced officer glanced back of him at the table, the sumptuous repast, the gaping face of his subordinate. "How in hell did you know we were here?"

Lester Leith laughed, and there was a cooing note of patronizing assurance in that laugh which caused the flush to deepen upon the sergeant's cheeks.

"Tut, tut, sergeant, you give me credit for absolutely no brains. I surmised you might try to follow me. I even surmised you might use your influence to get a compartment close to me. But it was an absolute certainty that you would wait to order your meal until you were on the train.

"A police officer is a highly trained opportunist, my dear sergeant, and when he travels he puts his meals on the expense account. When he eats within the limits of the city where he is employed he pays for his own meals.

"Therefore, sergeant, when I saw a loaded tray, a grinning waiter, two foiled cigars ... well, my dear sergeant, here I am. Go ahead and finish your meal, then do, by all means, drop into my compartment and we'll while the time away with a little poker."

And Lester Leith bowed and withdrew.

Thereafter he derived much enjoyment from applying his eye to one of the secret peepholes Sergeant Ackley had bored in the steel partition, and watching the expressions upon the faces of the men who were shadowing him.

It's a poor peephole that won't work both ways. A fact which Sergeant Ackley had overlooked in his confusion, for the little metal covers which had been arranged to slip over the holes remained unadjusted, and Lester Leith was able to secure a very good view of a worried officer who lost his appetite for the very good meal, which was being paid for by a municipality not ordinarily liberal with its employees. After the waiter had removed the tray, Sergeant Ackley tilted the half-consumed cigar at an aggressive angle and knocked upon the door. Lester Leith opened it with a bow.

The officers found a table, a deck of cards, poker chips.

Lester Leith shook hands, inquired the name of the subordinate.

"Fawkes, eh?" he remarked when Sergeant Ackley had mumbled an introduction. "Well, well, I always had something of a warm spot in my heart for that name. Guy Fawkes, you know, of historical importance. Tortured and hanged, he was, for conspiracy, and what a conspiracy it was! I don't know your first name, Fawkes, but, out of deference to your ancestral line, I shall call you Guy. You won't mind if I do call you Guy, will you, Guy?

"Do come in and be comfortable."

Sergeant Ackley grumbled a growling comment. "That's a hell of habit you've got of calling people names that happen to strike you. You call your valet, Beaver, by the name of Scuttle because you think he looks like a reincarnated pirate. He don't like the name. "

Lester Leith paused in the act of shuffling the cards and stared with polite interest at the speaker.

"Indeed, sergeant, I wasn't aware that you were so intimate with the likes and the dislikes of my servant."

The sergeant gulped, swallowed some of the smoke from his cigar, coughed, leaned over, spat, wiped his face with the back of his hand.

"Yeah, oh, yeah. That's all right. Just happened a friend of his happened to mention it to somebody or other in my hearing. Go ahead and deal, Leith. I'm going to open the first pot. I feel lucky."

Leith sent his trained fingers racing over the edges of the cards.

"You should feel lucky after a meal like that!"

"Aw, don't rub it in. It was my birthday. I was celebrating."

The sergeant words were blurted out, failed to ring true, but Lester Leith extended a well-manicured hand in congratulations.

"Sergeant," he said, gravely, "I shall promise you a fine birthday present."

"Yeah?" asked the sergeant, suspiciously.

"Yes. I shall make you a feature of the national news within a fortnight. More, my dear sergeant, I shall give you a chance to capture the murderer of a woman, a very baffling crime. Here has been a reward offered of ten thousand dollars for the arrest of the murderer, sergeant. I shall place evidence in your hands which will lead to a conviction if the man is placed on trial before a jury."

Sergeant Ackley glanced at Fawkes.

"That's a damned good birthday present," he said significantly. "I'll try to cooperate with you and see that I *get the dirty skunk!*"

Lester Leith smiled urbanely.

"And now, my dear sergeant, permit me to remind you that you promised to open the first pot."

And Lester Leith picked up the five cards which he had dealt himself.

CHAPTER IV

"Smuggle Him In"

Some twenty-four hours later the local train, completing a two-hour journey of rattling annoyance from the main line, deposited the three men on the station platform of a wooden structure which bore a big sign, on which was painted Pickets.

Beaver, called "Scuttle" by his urbane employer, gazed wide-eyed.

"Tut, tut, Scuttle," remarked Lester Leith, "don't tell me that you're surprised to see our good friend, Sergeant Ackley. Use your head a little, Scuttle, and you'll realize that the real ground for surprise would have been in the event he had *not* come.

"I trust, Scuttle, that our apartment is big enough to accommodate Sergeant Ackley and his companion as our guests? It is? Very well. The hotel accommodation will probably be quite poor here.

"Scuttle, shake hands with Guy Fawkes. Be careful not to refer to him as 'this guy, Fawkes,' for he wouldn't like that. Just call him Guy. He's an associate of Sergeant Ackley. As far as I know he has only one vice in the world, the habit, Scuttle, of raising on two pair when there's a stripped deck in play. Aside from that he's an admirable man."

The three men exchanged glances.

In the eyes of each of those three was an inarticulate, burning rage. These men had long been goaded by the tongue of Lester Leith. Fawkes, a comparative newcomer, had, in addition, lost his next month's salary. Not that he ever intended to redeem the I.O.U.s which Lester Leith held in his pocket; but it would have been so much nicer had the winnings been the other way.

But each of the three appreciated the advantage of maintaining an outward semblance of friendship. It would make it so much easier to shadow the man they wanted.

And so the three grinned cheerfully, concealed their real feelings as best they might, and went to the apartment which Lester Leith had rented through his pseudo-valet.

"And now, Scuttle," remarked Lester Leith, when they were seated in the cheaply furnished living room, "we'll hear about the murder of Martha Striker."

The valet grunted.

"Nothing much to it. Striker and his wife lived here in town for quite a while. Everybody liked 'em. Striker was in the insurance business. His wife was devoted to him. She disappeared. She left a note saying she was running away with another man, a chap named Colby who had an apartment in the same building.

"Striker was wild. He engaged detectives, made an awful stink when the police wouldn't interest themselves. He offered rewards, personally ran down clews and did everything. He vowed to shoot Colby on sight. But he never got the chance. He never saw Colby.

"Two or three months after the disappearance, some boys were prowling around a lot of pasture land and they came on something suspicious. They dug and found a human leg, a woman's leg.

"They called the police. The police dug. The whole body was found in various places in that pasture, buried in rather shallow soil. When they found the head they identified the corpse.

"It was Martha Striker. She had been cut up into pieces. Nobody knows why. The body was in awful state, but the teeth furnished a good identification. A local dentist had just finished a lot of work on her teeth. And there was an old fracture in the right leg that checked out.

"Then the cops got busy. They never got any place. Colby skipped out. They ain't ever seen him again, not since the day he left with the jane."

Lester Leith nodded slowly. "Striker was rather wealthy?"

"Seemed to be, although nobody knows much about his business affairs. He always talked about his big holdings. Never kept much in the bank here, though. Said his property interests were scattered around. Told several friends he was worth around half a million. He offered a ten-thousand-dollar reward for the arrest of the murderer."

Leith stroked his chin.

Sergeant Ackley and Fawkes watched him with eager eyes.

"Tell you what, Scuttle, you'd better get out the curling iron, the hair drying blower, and the cold cream. And the dog, Scuttle—how about the dog?"

"He's in the yard, sir. The landlady positively refused to allow him to enter the apartment."

"Tut, tut, Scuttle, that only goes to show how extremely narrow-minded landladies can become. A good dog, Scuttle, is much better than a poor man. Let's have him in. You can smuggle him in under your coat. Surely with these gentlemen of the police here there can't be anything wrong with having a dog in the apartment."

Sergeant Ackley scraped back his chair.

"Do you mean—" he bellowed, then stopped at the look of surprised innocence upon Lester Leith's face.

"Merely that you'd use your influence with the landlady, my dear sergeant," said Lester Leith, smiling. "No offense, sergeant. No offense."

The valet left the apartment. Soon he could be heard, laboriously ascending the wooden stairs. He entered, a suspicious bulge over his chest. The coat opened and the bulge became a chain-lightning streak of white puppy that scampered over the floor in an ecstasy.

"Ha, little fellow," said Lester Leith, and the dog, recognizing a subtle something in the voice, came bounding to his lap.

Lester Leith quieted him with tender fingers which scratched back of the cars, and stroked the neck. "A very nice dog, gentlemen. What I wished to call to your attention in particular, is the collar and license."

And Lester Leith slipped off the collar from which dangled

a dog's license, granted by the municipality of Pickets, bearing a number, and the name of the city. There was no date.

"Rather a habit with smaller cities," remarked Lester Leith. "They don't stamp any dates on the licenses. They get them all made up at one time. They use different numbers for different dates. For instance, let us say, to take an arbitrary figure, that numbers one to fifty represent licenses issued in nineteen twenty-five; numbers fifty to a hundred those issued in nineteen twenty-six."

"What," growled Sergeant Ackley, his heavy forehead puckered into a scowl, "has that got to do with?"

Lester Leith regarded the man for several seconds. His keen eyes flickered over the somewhat heavy features of his guest, the high cheek bones, the bushy brows, the small eyes, the oily skin, the thick lips, the impression of unwashed grime which the oily skin always gave.

"Sergeant," he said, "you surprise me. It has everything to do with it."

"With what?"

"Ah, now, sergeant, you're getting nearer to the point. With what, indeed? I wish I was certain, sergeant."

The officer's face flushed.

Fawkes hatched forward to the edge of his chair. "It's a long lane that ain't got a turn in it," he said. Lester Leith smiled at him pleasantly.

"It is, isn't it? And, do you know, Guy, Sergeant Ackley has been having rather hard luck of late. I fancy this is going to be turning point. I think the dear sergeant is going to cover himself with glory.

"By the way, Scuttle, where is this man, Striker?"

"I have his address, sir. He's in Valparaiso, Indiana. That's a place about fifty miles from here, sir."

"Has an office there, Scuttle?"

"Yes, sir. He seems to have concentrated his holdings, sir, and he's quite well fixed. He owns quite a bit of real estate in the town, business property, income-producing and what not."

Lester Leith nodded gravely. "Scuttle, go in the kitchen and see if you can find me a bit of mineral wool, and a cruet of vinegar."

The valet flashed one swift glance at Sergeant Ackley, then vanished. In a few moments he was back with the articles mentioned.

Lester Leith took them, slipped the collar from the dog's neck. "You got the name Bobo engraved on the collar very nicely, Scuttle," he said. "I wonder what's under the nickel name plate."

"Brass," growled Ackley. "Brass takes a plate well."

"Let's see," remarked Lester Leith, and began to rub the plate with the mineral wool. Within a short time there was the gleam of yellow, and then a strip of brass was exposed. "Quite right, sergeant, quite right. You nearly always *are* right. Mind you, though, sergeant, I said *nearly*. By that I mean that I know of no man who is better able to pass upon brass than you are. But when it comes to the questions of guilt or innocence—but then, again, why bring that up?

"Scuttle, has the local chief of police a good description of this man, Colby, with whom Martha Striker ran away?"

"Yes, sir, of course, sir. The police are not as dumb as some people think, sir. This chief of police, C. A. Lambertson, is a very intelligent man—for a country officer.

"He realizes, of course, that Colby is the probable murderer of the woman. In fact, it almost goes without saying that Colby is the murderer. And Chief Lambertson has secured a very fair snapshot of Colby, together with an excellent description."

Lester Leith glanced up from the dog collar to study his valet with quizzical eyes.

"Ring him up, Scuttle. Tell him to wire the description to the warden of San Quentin prison in California, and see if the description doesn't tally with that of a confidence man who was discharged sometime in the last part of twenty-five or first part of twenty-six."

The valet gulped, swallowed, cleared his throat, glanced at Sergeant Ackley.

"Are you serious, sir?"

"Certainly, Scuttle, why not?"

"But how could you possibly know that Colby was an ex-convict, and that he was confined in San Quentin penitentiary?"

"Tut, tut, Scuttle. I don't know it. Otherwise I wouldn't have Chief Lambertson waste the expense of a telegram. And would you mind doing as I say without asking questions, Scuttle? Of course, I realize it may be quite a request to make, but you must remember that I am paying you your salary, Scuttle. Not much of a salary, perhaps, but enough, nevertheless, to entitle me to your cooperation upon such minor matters."

And Sergeant Ackley echoed Lester Leith's disapproval with a deep scowl. Since it was vital to the police to have Lester Leith shadowed at all times, it became imperative that the undercover agent must restrain his feelings in order to keep the job. If he should be dismissed, the police would have great difficulty in seeing that the man's successor was also a police spy.

Beaver oozed through the door to the telephone.

Lester Leith turned to the dog collar again. "Now a drop or two of vinegar, my dear sergeant."

"What's that for?" growled Ackley.

"To furnish an impression of age, of course. You know vinegar and salt will polish brass. But a little vinegar left on brass will turn it green after a bit."

Sergeant Ackley leaned forward.

"Look here, Leith, there was a murder of a Margy Marigold that has never been cleared up. She had a dog she'd adopted a day or two before the murder. That dog was named Bobo, the same as this dog. And it seems to me he came from out here some way. Seems like it was some little town in Indiana."

Lester Leith's smile was oily in its suave benignity. "Yes, yes, sergeant. What a wonderful memory you have. You interest me strangely. Or, perhaps I should say, strangely, you interest me. Because there's so much of the time when I'm not interested in your conclusions. Pray, go on."

"Well, that dog was a Boston bull," blurted the officer.

"What of it?" asked Leith.

"Simply this. If you want to plant a dummy dog some place so it will look like that dog, why in hell don't you get the same kind of a dog?"

Lester Leith nodded smiling acquiescence. "Yes, indeed, sergeant. Do you know, my valet, Scuttle, or Beaver, as you call him asked me the same question in precisely the same words? It's rather a unique instance of similar minds running in the same channel."

Fawkes glanced at his superior, gathered his feet in under him, ready to spring for Leith's throat at a word of command.

"But," muttered Sergeant Ackley, restraining his temper in part, "that's not answering the question."

"Quite right, my dear sergeant, quite right. It's *not* answering the question. And the answer, sergeant, is, of course, that I'm not trying to make a dog take the place of the Bobo that figured in the Margy Marigold murder. That's why I was so particular in selecting a fox terrier. Even a police mind couldn't possibly figure that I was trying to make a fox terrier substitute for a Boston bull—no personal reflections, of course, sergeant. I merely had reference to the vast organization of which you happen to be a sergeant. But tell me, am I right in thinking that even the police would hardly suspect me of such an attempt?"

"What attempt?"

"That which I just mentioned, of trying to substitute a fox terrier for a Boston bull."

"No. Nobody's going to think that."

"Well, sergeant, since you're here, and since I'm here, would you mind giving me that in writing."

"Giving you *what!*"

"A statement that even the police wouldn't think I was trying to make my Bobo take the place of the Boston bull Bobo that figured in the Marigold murder case?"

"I'll give you nothing in writing," growled the irate officer.

"Tut, tut, sergeant. A man should never make a positive statement unless he is willing to put his name to it. However, we'll let the matter pass for the present.

"Now this license. You'll notice it carefully, sergeant, because I intend to do things to it."

And Lester Leith detached the license from the collar, placed it upon the little anvil, took a cold chisel and began to tap little crisscross marks upon the soft brass, marks which almost completely obliterated the number of the license.

"What in hell you're doing that for is more than I know," said Fawkes, booming into the conversation with a voice of deep-throated hostility.

"I surmised as much, Guy," said Lester Leith, without bothering to raise his eyes from the anvil.

Sergeant Ackley placed a surreptitious, but, nevertheless, firmly restraining hand upon the tense arm of his subordinate. Catching the blazing eyes, he shook his head, intimated by pantomime that the conversation was to be left entirely in his hands.

CHAPTER V

"Sure I'll Sign It"

"Seems like you're going to a lot of trouble with that job," said Ackley, in his most ingratiating manner, "You're not helping the looks of the dog license any."

"It's my dog license, isn't it?"

"Oh, yes, of course. No call to get sore about it."

"I'm not, not in the least, sergeant, I merely wanted to know if it was not my dog license, my property, mine to do with as I liked."

"Sure it is."

"You're an officer. You'd ought to know."

"I *do* know."

"And it's mine?"

"Naturally. You paid for it."

"And I can do what I want to with it? I can mutilate it. I can throw it away. I can give it away, or can sell it."

"Sure."

"Ah yes, my dear sergeant, and would you mind putting that in writing?"

"Putting what in writing?"

"That it's my dog license."

A look of cunning came over the features of the officer. "Sure I'll put it in writing, provided you'll sign the writing along with me."

Lester Leith nodded. "I'm always willing to sign any statement I may make."

Whereupon Sergeant Ackley beckoned toward the valet. "Get me paper and pen, Beaver."

"Ah yes, and a carbon paper, Scuttle," added Lester Leith. "It might be well to have carbon copy, you know."

The man brought the things with suspicious alacrity.

With the pen pausing over the paper, Sergeant Ackley glanced at his assistants purposefully and intoned the legal formula which would make the document admissible in evidence against Lester Leith.

"You are making his statement of your own free will and voluntarily, and with the understanding that it may be used against you?"

"Why, sergeant, I fancied you were the one who was making the statement?" inquired Lester.

"But you're joining in it!"

"Oh, certainly, my dear sergeant. But it should be capable of being used against either or both of us if it's a joint statement. I'll tell you what, let me dictate what I want and then, if it's my own dictation there can be no question but what it's free and voluntary."

"And can be used against you?" persisted Sergeant Ackley.

"Oh, by all means," murmured Lester Leith.

"Very well," said the officer, with a triumphant glance at the other two men, "You remember that, Beaver. You remember it, Fawkes."

"Yes, sir," said the valet, leaning forward, his glittering eyes fastened upon the paper.

"You're damn tootin'," grumbled Fawkes, his eyes flitting to the waistcoat pocket over Lester Leith's well molded torso, and in which pocket there reposed certain I.O.U.s signed by Fawkes, and amounting to precisely one month's salary.

"Very well," agreed Lester Leith, "We are ready. Here is the statement:

"It is agreed that the undersigned Lester Leith is the owner of the dog collar upon which appears the word 'Bobo.' It is further distinctly understood that he is the owner of a license issued by the City of Pickets, Indiana. The undersigned Lester Leith admits that he is the owner of these articles, that they were procured for him at his special instance and request. The undersigned Sergeant Ackley bearing in mind the Marigold murder case, admits that the undersigned Lester Leith, being the sole owner of these articles, may sell or otherwise dispose of them as he sees fit, and that he has the police consent to do so."

Lester Leith paused, glanced about him. "That covers the situation, sergeant?"

"Yes," breathed Sergeant Ackley.

"Very well. I'll sign, and you can sign, and we'll have witnesses. You should sign in your official capacity, naming your station and rank, sergeant and the municipality of which you are an officer."

Sergeant Ackley signed as he was directed, passed the paper over to Lester Leith.

That individual signed his name with a flourish.

Sergeant Ackley carefully passed the paper over to Fawkes. "Sign," he commanded.

"With your official office and title," prompted Lester Leith.

Fawkes signed.

Sergeant Ackley blotted the signature, folded the original, put it in his pocket, passed the copy over to Lester Leith.

"No, sergeant, I must have the original. You see my word might not go very far, and a carbon copy can be erased much easier than a pen and ink writing. Your official station would preclude any one from raising a question that you had tampered with the document."

Sergeant Ackley hesitated.

"Otherwise I would retract my signature," suggested Lester Leith.

The officer promptly exchanged copies.

With that written admission that the collar and license had been procured at the "special instance and request" of Lester Leith, he felt certain of his case. Once before he had felt that Lester Leith was trapped, but that individual had slipped from the trap by calling attention to the fact that the mysterious articles, which had finally figured so dramatically in the shaking down of a firebug, had been procured by his valet without any suggestion on the part of Lester Leith.

In the present case the articles had also been procured by the valet. Now Sergeant Ackley had a written statement which admitted Scuttle had been acting under the orders of Lester Leith.

It would be wonderful advertisement to release that statement to the press when the time came, showing how the clever sergeant had matched wits with the suspect,had managed to get a statement which incriminated the defendant without said defendant having any idea of the noose into which the clever officer had managed to get him to put his head.

"And now," Lester Leith, "for the jar of cold cream and the hair dryer."

He took the jar of cold cream while Ackley watched him with eyes which were mere pin points of glittering suspicion.

"Ah, yes, the jar bears the name of the town's leading department store. Very nice. Very nice indeed."

He removed the cover, scooped out a part of the contents with his fingers, flipped the mass into a wastebasket, regarded the contents critically.

"No, Scuttle. This is too oily. It won't serve. What I need is more of a massaging cream."

The valet nodded his head after the manner of one who thoroughly appreciates his own importance.

"Yes, sir. I got several different kinds so you could have the exact kind you wanted sir. Here's a jar of massage cream."

Lester Leith took the new jar.

"I know very little about such matters, Scuttle, but this is the sort, I believe, that dries upon the face and is rubbed out of the pores of the skin."

"Yes, sir."

"Very good, Scuttle. We'll try it."

And Lester Leith unscrewed the top of the jar, scooped out some of the contents, regarded the balance with a critical eye, smelled the jar, extended it to Sergeant Ackley.

"Rather a gooey mess, sergeant. Just dip your finger in it. No, no, take the little finger, press it right down into the jar."

The sergeant pressed his finger into the jar. "Feels just like any other cream to me," he said.

Lester Leith regarded the depression where the finger had rested.

"Seems to be awfully thick to me," he growled. "See the way your finger left a deep print. You can trace every ridge, every whorl of the fingertip. Might be a good thinking to keep fingerprints in, sergeant."

"No better than an inked impression," snapped the officer, nettled that he was unable to figure out what Lester Leith could possibly want of the jar of cream, or, for that matter, with any of the other things he had been so anxious to obtain.

Lester Leith connected up the blower, adjusted it so it was sending out a current of warm, dry air, directed that current upon the top of the jar.

"Notice how rapidly it dries," he said.

The surface of the mass assumed a slightly different color, drew away from the sides of the jar. The depressions made by reaching fingers shrunk in size, but remained perfect as to detail.

"Humph!" said Lester Leith, after a few moments, and screwed the top back on the jar. "You brought me a curling iron, Scuttle."

"Yes, sir."

"Let me see it."

Lester Leith took the curling iron. From his pocket he took a flask, a little glass phial of colorless liquid that looked like water.

Very carefully he touched the cork, moistened with this liquid to the prongs of the curling iron. Almost instantly there was a peculiar, acrid odor, the trace of little smoke curls, winding up from the steel.

"What's that?" asked Sergeant Ackley.

"A very powerful and very poisonous acid," remarked Lester Leith. "It has the effect of oxidizing steel or other metal. In a few minutes there will be particles of rust form all over the curling iron. But if that were to be taken internally, sergeant—"

He spread out his hands, palm upward, in a gesture of the utmost finality.

"How did you—"

Sergeant Ackley did not finish the sentence. There was an imperative pounding on the door. Before the valet could open it, the knob turned and a figure stood on the threshold.

CHAPTER VI

Affixing the Seal

He was a great hulk of a man, pot-bellied, bull-necked. His thick lips were quivering beneath a stubby mustache of untrained bristles which sprouted from underneath wide nostrils. A big hat surmounted the head. Gray eyes bored into the faces of the occupants of the apartment.

Sergeant Ackley jumped to his feet.

"What in hell do you mean by busting in on—"

The valet coughed.

"This, gentlemen," he said deprecatingly, "is C. A. Lambertson, the chief of police of Pickets."

"And," murmured Lester Leith, with more than a faint trace of glee in his tone, "he is following a custom possessed by all police officers, of busting in wherever they damn please, whenever it suits their purposes."

For an instant Sergeant Ackley seemed about to eject the newcomer. Right when he was trapping Lester Leith into admissions which would put him in the power of the police. And this hick officer had to butt in!

"Say, you birds," bellowed the bull-necked one, "who in hell do you think you are? And what's the big idea? You guys are mixed up in that Striker murder too thick to suit me. You're going to come over to the station house, and—"

"Steady," cautioned Sergeant Ackley, and swept back his coat, showing the gold star which gleamed from his vest. "I'm the sergeant of a police force which numbers more men than your whole town can scrape up in the way of citizens. And Mr. Fawkes here is a plain-clothes detective assigned to me for work on a most important case."

The chief gulped his surprise. The belligerency melted away from him, leaving him rather awed.

He advanced, read the lettering on the sergeant's badge. "Any credentials?" he asked, suspiciously.

Sergeant Ackley took a billfold from his pocket, showed him commissions, photographs, signatures, letters.

"Sorry, sergeant," said the chief, "but you sure got a hell of a way of working on a case with me. You come to town and don't tell me anything about it, and then one of your men gives me a ring and tips me off Colby was discharged from San Quentin, and—"

"Mr. Beaver," said Sergeant Ackley, speaking hurriedly, "has no connection with the police department. He is the valet of Mr. Lester Leith, the gentleman who is fingering the dog collar."

And Sergeant Ackley closed one eye in a portentous wink, jerked his hand in a gesture, shrugged his shoulders, pursed his lips, and gave other evidences of stealth, caution, secrecy and warning.

All of which various gestures, being perfectly visible to Lester Leith in a wall mirror, caused that individual to become seized with a fit of coughing.

"Well, what I want to know," continued the chief, "is how in heck you fellows got all that information about Colby."

His voice was cautious now, too cautious to fail to alarm a wary quarry, and Sergeant Ackley made haste to inject himself into the conversation.

"That tip came from Mr. Lester Leith without my knowledge. Leith takes a great interest in crime news. He's always working on some crime or other."

(Here Sergeant Ackley took advantage of Leith's modestly lowered eyes to inject some more pantomime.)

"And he took an interest in the Striker murder, apparently. He sent his valet on ahead to get certain information. And then Leith came on. It happened that I was *accidentally* on the same train, and Leith has kindly invited us to be his guests for a few days."

"Oh," remarked Lambertson, "I see."

And his lips pressed together so tightly that the mustache bristles scraped against his nostrils. The big hand swept to the broad-brimmed hat and jerked it off. "I see," he said again, and dropped into a chair.

"Was there—er—anything to the tip—about Colby?" asked Sergeant Ackley, anxiously.

"Was there! Say, d'yuh want to hear?"

"Yes, but—er—well, tell me the main facts. You can let the details wait."

"This Colby was convicted from Los Angeles under the name of Tillotson. He's one of the slickest confidence men that ever got into jail, and he swindled his way out. He got some of the witnesses against him to withdraw their statements and got the parole board to let him out. It turned out later on that the witnesses had been bribed to make those retractions with some mining stock that they thought was worth a million, and then the stock deal turned out to be a bigger swindle than any of 'em.

"They're indicting the witnesses for perjury, but they didn't dare prosecute 'em without Tillotson because it looked like the poor victims were being sent to jail while the crook was at liberty.

"It's a hell of a mess, and California would give a good deal to get this same Tillotson, alias Colby, back where they wanted him. And now I've got a good murder rap on him. And to think I let the damned crook slip through my fingers!"

Sergeant Ackley's eyes glittered.

"Of course," he said, "while Leith had the tip telephoned to you. I—well, er—that is, I had a pretty good idea about this chap, Colby. Apparently Leith got the same idea very shortly after I did."

"But how did you know?" asked the perplexed chief.

Ackley waved a hand toward Leith. "Tell him, Leith. I dare say your reasoning processes followed the same general lines mine did."

Leith bowed.

"Tut, tut, my dear sergeant. I really didn't have any reasons. I simply wanted to keep Scuttle out of mischief. The devil finds mischief for idle hands, and this apartment doesn't give Scuttle very much work to do. It was just a coincidence as far as I was concerned.

"But apparently *you* reasoned it out. It was a devilishly clever thing to do, if you just reasoned it out. Do tell the chief how you reasoned. I'm most interested."

And Beaver, he who had worked with Sergeant Ackley for years, and knew only too well how that individual was always a hog for grabbing any credit that he thought he could get, how he always appropriated the ideas of others as his own, became suddenly seized with a spasm which necessitated his abrupt departure from the room.

Sergeant Ackley's face turned a brick red.

"I'll talk with you later about that, chief. The important point is that we know. I don't want to divulge too many details, as yet."

And Sergeant Ackley jerked his head significantly toward Lester Leith.

"Oh, by the way chief," said Lester Leith, apparently failing to appreciate the significance of that jerk of the head, "we were signing a document before you came in, and I'd like to have have your signature on it as well."

And Lester Leith pulled the folded paper from his pocket. Chief Lambertson glanced at Sergeant Ackley.

Sergeant Ackley nodded.

Chief Lambertson grasped the proffered fountain pen in his thick fingers. He read the document, his thick lips forming the words as his eyes slowly went from line to line.

"Well, of all the damn foolish—"

But Sergeant Ackley's fist prodded him in the fat back with an insistence that was not to be denied.

Slowly, laboriously, he drew the letters that formed his name.

"And now," said Lester Leith, "I wonder if we can't call in a notary public to have these various signatures acknowledged."

"Why, hell, everybody knows—"

But Sergeant Ackley interrupted Chief Lambertson's remarks.

"Certainly, surely. We can acknowledge that's it's our free and voluntary statement," he said, and winked once more at the country officer.

A notary public was summoned, a rather hatchet-faced girl with nose glasses, a hopeless droop to the mouth, pop eyes which were filmed with perpetual moisture, and hands which were long and tapering, terminating in slim, sentient fingers which seemed independent entities, each capable of individual motion. They were hands which were unique, utterly fascinating.

Lester Leith watched them with skilled appraisal as she affixed a notarial acknowledgment, signature and seal.

"You play the piano, don't you, Miss Garver?"

The girl's face lit up with an expression of enthusiasm. "Oh, I love it. I've always wanted to study in the city, but I've never been able. I've only had the advantage of country music teachers. You see mother's crippled with rheumatism."

Lester Leith nodded gravely.

Sergeant Ackley cleared his throat after the manner of one who embarks upon a carefully rehearsed speech. "If you folks are going to talk music," he said, "I'll take Chief Lambertson and Fawkes into the other room for a minute. I want to talk over some stuff with 'em, about catching a N'Yawk crook. It ain't anything that you're interested in, Leith; just a matter of police routine, an' I won't bore you."

"Certainly," said Lester Leith. "Walk right into the bedroom and make yourself at home. I'll have Scuttle wait on you with tea, Scuttle, make the gentlemen some tea.

"And I'm going to play for Miss Garver. Probably this piano, which is furnished with the apartment, may be a bit out of tune, but it'll serve the purpose."

And Lester Leith approached the instrument, swung a piano stool into proper adjustment.

"As a matter of fact," said Miss Garver, "it's in perfect tune. I know the folks who had the apartment before. They just lived for music—"

CHAPTER VII

The Music Lesson

Lester Leith's trained fingers crashed down upon the keys, and a volume of harmony emerged from the instrument which would have been ample had Leith been giving a concert performance. His foot jammed down the loud pedal. His hands went up in the air once more, crashed down.

Ackley led the way into bedroom, leaving the door slightly ajar so that he could peer into the sitting room. The valet, under guise of getting an order for tea and cakes, finding out who liked tea, who coffee, who toast, who cake, managed to hover over the group, finding occasion to put in a word here and there.

And Lester Leith, seated at the piano stool, paid them absolutely no attention, but sent his fingers flying over the board while Miss Garver's moist eyes became more misty than ever. Her mouth sagged and an expression of rapture was on her features.

"Get this," hissed Sergeant Ackley. "That guy's the slickest crook the country ever turned out. He can pull jobs right under the noses of the police, and they can't get him."

Chief Lambertson indicated the valet. "Better get rid of this guy—"

"He's all right, chief. He's one of our men. That's why I tell you how dangerous this fellow is. Why Beaver's been undercover as his valet for a year. We've had him shadowed day and night, and we've had a dictograph in his apartment and taken down every word he's said, and he still manages to pull his crimes. He can slip shadows as easy as a duck slips water, he—"

Chief Lambertson lurched to his feet, felt the holstered weapon at his waist.

"Well, he can't slip me, and he can't pull stuff here. I sometimes have trouble finding a crook, but when I get him tagged, it's curtains, that's all."

Sergeant Ackley did not trouble to suppress the smile which wreathed his features.

"Well, this one's rather different. He even uses the police to help him pull his stunts."

"Say," demanded the country chief, "are you guys crazy?"

In the silence which ensued there came to their ears the music of the piano, a tinkling, roguish tune of soul-stirring propensities.

"Listen to him," said Ackley. "He plays like a fiend."

They listened for several minutes, so fascinating was the music. Then they fell into a whispered discussion of plans. After some ten minutes the pseudo-valet backed from the room.

"Very well, gentlemen," he said. "Two coffees and one tea, with lemon. Cream with the coffee. Two toasts, one tea wafers. Yes, sirs."

He turned, and then fell back in sheer amazement.

Miss Garver sat at the piano, playing as though her very soul's salvation depended upon the correct rendition of the music. She was alone in the room.

The valet gained the bedroom with a single stride.

"Gone!" he said.

"He's playing the piano, you sap," said Sergeant Ackley.

The undercover man snorted.

"Look."

They looked, Sergeant Ackley, his mind suddenly grasping the situation, rushing for the player. Fawkes standing open-mouthed in the doorway, Chief Lambertson laboriously and slowly tugged the weapon away from its hip holster, his face very red as he strained to get his hand back to the hip, the gun from its holster.

Miss Garver screamed as Sergeant Ackley's rough hands grasped her shoulders. Then she turned and the color drained from her face.

"Why! Where...what?"

Her amazement was so utterly genuine that it immediately exonerated her, even in the eyes of Sergeant Ackley.

"What happened?" he asked.

"Why!" exclaimed the girl. "Why, I never in my life! Why!"

"Quick!" rasped Ackley.

"Why, he played for me a bit and then asked me to finish the piece. He bet me that I couldn't sit on the stool beside him and take up the playing where he left off without interruption and without missing a note."

And then the pop eyes swam in tears.

"And he told me that if my technique seemed good enough, he'd send me to New York to study, and, later on, to Paris!"

But no one was paying any attention to the girl.

The open door to the kitchenette, the open back door, the streaming sunlight from the back yard told their own story. Sergeant Ackley found time to grin at Chief Lambertson. "So they don't ever get away from *you*?" he asked, and the sarcasm of his tone was far greater than the situation called for, acute as it was.

"Well, by cripes, he can't make it stick," bellowed Chief Lambertson. "Gimme the telephone, and I'll close up this town on him like a clamshell in ice water!"

And he proceeded to telephone various and sundry people, using much force and profanity. Bit by bit, after the single-handed fashion of a limited police force, he closed various avenues of escape.

He telephoned railroad men, inter-urban ticket offices, bus stations, cab drivers, drive-yourself stations.

"Now, gents," he announced ponderously, "this town's sealed up as far as that crook's getting out. This ain't like a city the size of N'York. We got him so he can't get out, an' now all we gotta do is stroll down on the street. If he's on the streets we can find him inside of ten minutes."

Which last statement was readily apparent.

His broad-brimmed hat tilted back at an angle, the stubby mustache bristling over one of Sergeant Ackley's cigars, the pompous official waddled with belligerent assurance to the street, and began a search which lasted not ten minutes, but half an hour.

At the end of which time sheer accident aided them in picking up the trail of Lester Leith.

Casual conversation with an automobile dealer developed the fact that a well-dressed stranger had called at the display room, purchased the demonstrator, paid for it with cash, waived all formalities of transferring title, and had driven out of town at a rate that indicated the foot throttle was pressed well against the floor boards.

"Where could he be going?" demanded Ackley.

"He got a road map to Valparaiso," said the dealer.

"Come with me. I got a car with a siren an' a red light," said Chief Lambertson, and ran with the waddling pace of the very fat whose joints are also very unlimber.

The party hurried out, attracting attention as their feet pounded the cement sidewalks.

Lambertson slowed to a puffing walk, placed a hand over his heart, gasped for breath, pointed melodramatically at the opposite curb.

Sergeant Ackley followed his glance, and then exploded into a single epithet.

The red car which was parked at the opposite side of the street, equipped with red spotlight and siren, the car which the municipality of Pickets placed at the official disposal of its corpulent chief of police for the running down of criminals, was a model "T" of the vintage of around 1925.

CHAPTER VIII

Lester Works Fast

Lester Leith confronted the lean man with the catfish mouth. "You're Sidney Striker?"

"Yes, yes, you're Leith then. Your wire was rather peculiar, asking me to remain in my office all the afternoon of this day."

"Couldn't help it," said Lester Leith. "Couldn't tell just what time I could get away. Where can we talk?"

"In here, Mr. Leith. You wanted to see me about purchasing the Wiker block, your telegram said?"

"That's what my telegram said."

The lean man whirled, gave a suspicious glance at his visitor, then led the way into a private office.

"And what the telegram said was correct, I hope." Lester Leith shrugged his shoulders, settled in a chair, took a cigarette from its case, tapped it on his thumb nail and reached for a lighter.

"I wished to discuss the matter of a ten-thousand-dollar reward I understood had been offered for the arrest of your wife's murderer."

The man started as though an electric current had contacted him.

"That's been four years ago. I fancy the reward has outlawed."

"Possibly," agreed Leith, blowing a smoke cloud toward the ceiling, "but the murder has not outlawed. Murder never outlaws."

Sidney Striker clamped his catfish mouth into a thin line of alarm.

"Exactly what do you mean?" he asked.

"When you murdered Margy Marigold there was no apparent motive. That's why the police missed the significant clew."

Sidney Striker gave a gasp, a hissing expellation of breath. His thin lips blued. The eyes blinked. He gasped, choked, inhaled, and then regained some semblance of composure.

"That's slander. I'll make you prove that statement."

"With pleasure. In the course of a criminal career covering many years, I've encountered lots of skunks, Striker, but you're the worst. You lived under the name of Marigold and won the love of Bradbury's wife. She divorced Bradbury to marry you, and even then you were tired of her. You slipped away, both of you, came to Pickets and took the names of Mr. and Mrs. Striker. You lived happily, outwardly. But, all the time, you were planning black murder.

"You mentioned your great property interests, and you secured a joint insurance policy of fifty thousand dollars on your life and that of your wife. Then you persuaded her it would be fitting to have it appear she had vanished. So you made frequent trips to California to engage detectives to hunt for the woman whom you had concealed in Pickets. And all this was part of a most diabolical scheme of murder. You wanted to collect that insurance policy in such a manner there could never be any comeback on you.

"When the year was up and Margy Bradbury was entitled to her final decree in California, you were careful to be there on the job. In accordance with your prearranged plan, the woman who had been Margy Bradbury, who had masqueraded with you as Martha Striker, met you in the east and became Margy Marigold.

"Then you secured the services of a swindler, an ex-convict whom you helped swindle out of jail. You had him in your power. You persuaded him to live in an adjoining apartment in Pickets under the name of Colby. Then he was to disappear and take your 'wife' with him. That would account for the disappearance of Martha Striker, and pave the way for a reappearance of Margy Bradbury.

"That's what you told Colby. And you told him, also, to follow you east, to come to your little bungalow and rob you, tie you up, and leave you. You planned on luring Bradbury to the vicinity of that cottage. And you told Colby you would identify Bradbury as the assailant. You told him that would put Bradbury in enough hot water to keep him out of mischief.

"What you didn't tell Colby was that when he was tying you, your wife was dead in the adjoining room, strangled by your own hands. The drug that was to have been administered to Margy Marigold, to keep her asleep, wasn't necessary. You took it to make your unconsciousness the more pronounced.

"When Colby read what had happened, he knew you had tricked him. But he had to flee. If he had been caught then he'd have been accused of the woman's murder. Even he didn't know what your motive was.

"You took the body of Margy Marigold to Indiana and butchered it, hid the pieces where they would be discovered sooner or later. Then you went about your business as Sidney Striker, the bereaved husband whose wife had eloped with another man. And you knew that, if the worst ever came to the worst and you were suspected, you had only to dig up the criminal record of the absent Colby, and that would again turn suspicion to him. But you didn't intend to do that except as a last resort, because with his fingerprints and photos, they might capture him."

Sidney Striker watched the mouth of Lester Leith with fascinated eyes, as though he must not only hear the words, but see them spoken.

"But I never accused Colby," he said.

"Because it wasn't necessary. The fact that your wife had eloped, plus the positive identification of the remains, was all the insurance company needed.

"They thought you had acted in good faith with that insurance policy. They paid the money. You invested and reinvested. Today you are a fairly wealthy man."

The catfish mouth parted to give vent to a rasping laugh. "Rather a wild story. How about proof?"

Lester Leith opened a black hand bag he carried.

"Curling iron, left in Pickets, identified as that of your wife, rusted, fingerprints. Jar of stale massage cream. Also left in Pickets apartment. Note fingerprint. That fingerprint tallies with fingerprint of Margy Marigold. Note dog collar.

"Ah, that *does* give you a start. You'd almost forgotten the dog, eh? Yes, the woman nearly upset all your carefully laid plans by having a dog. She wouldn't leave it behind. You couldn't insist without arousing the suspicion of everyone. So you had her take the dog, pretend to find it as a stray. After you removed the body to Indiana you 'disposed' of the dog. That collar and the license tag gives you something of a start, doesn't it?"

There was no need of the question. The sallow face was twitching spasmodically.

Suddenly the lean hand flashed into an arc of motion.

Up from under the desk came a blue steel automatic. "Damn you, yes! You know enough to—die!"

Lester Leith spoke rapidly, his eyes on those of the other. "Don't be a fool. I'm not going to betray you."

Beads of unclean perspiration welled out of the taut skin across the man's forehead.

"What—"

"Certainly not. I'm going to sell you this evidence."

"Humph, then start the police on the trail. There are too many angles by which they could check up. You're right about my needing a convict as an accomplice. I needed a man with a criminal record. That was so I could turn around and accuse him if anything went wrong. But that's the point of danger. I went bond for Tillotson, alias Colby. That's a matter of record. They can uncover this from the California end."

Lester Leith flipped over the document which was signed by himself, by Sergeant Ackley, by Fawkes, and by Chief Lambertson.

"Read that. The police are in on this shake-down. They're selling you immunity."

A look of dazed relief crossed the thin features.

"Honest?"

"Look at that, read it. See, it's acknowledged. They wouldn't let you have anything like that, would they— not unless they were prepared to talk business. I'm their emissary."

Striker gulped.

"How much?"

"How much quick cash you got in the bank? Don't lie. We can check it up if you do."

"Thirty-odd thousand dollars."

"I'll take thirty even."

"Good God, man, that won't leave me with enough to pay my monthly expenditures!"

"You *might* prefer to check it to a lawyer to defend you on a murder charge that can't be beaten," suggested Lester Leith, softly.

"It's a holdup!"

"Certainly. But it's less than you got from the insurance. One word of this and the insurance company comes down on you for fraud and collects not only the money, but all of the profits you've made with that money. The police throw you in jail and prove a murder charge. You sizzle in an electric chair like a sausage in a frying pan."

"I'll never be taken alive."

"No? Well, frankly, Striker, or Marigold, or whatever name you want to be called, I don't give a damn for you. You make me sick. If you want to be a damned fool go ahead."

"I could kill you and take that paper from you."

"Ha, ha, the police knowing, unofficially of course, that I was here? Bah. I either give them their split of thirty thousand or they close in on you. They're posted at all the street corners now, waiting."

"But—the police are crooks!"

"*You* should call the kettle black! They have to live. If they'd tumbled to the facts three years ago they'd never have made you this proposition. But now the public has forgotten about the case, and there's a chance for the case, and there's a chance for the ones on the inside to made a little money."

Striker considered the situation. Slowly, he pocketed the gun.

"That's sensible," said Lester Leith. "We go to the bank. You draw out the money. We come back here, make a bill of sale for the articles of evidence, and I deliver the document signed by the police to you. Then I wait for the police to have a divvy. After that you keep that document in a safe deposit vault. The police dare not double cross you while you have that. That's your assurance that everyone is playing fair."

Sidney Striker had experienced a whirl of emotions in the last fifteen minutes that had drained his every ounce of strength. He could hardly walk, much less think straight. He had seen the spectre of a dead past beckon him to the grave. He had heard himself sizzling in an electric chair like a sausage on a hot stove. He had a hope, a chance of salvation. Thirty thousand dollars was but a fraction of his wealth.

He grasped the arm of Lester Leith for support. Together they went to the bank.

CHAPTER IX

The Police Arrive

"Important business deal," muttered Striker as he handed in his check over the counter. "Large bills."

The teller showed evident surprise, but he cashed the check. The two men repaired once more to the private office. Here Lester Leith made out a bill of sale, delivered the articles of "evidence," also endorsed over the document signed by the police officers.

"So you'd never be taken alive?" he asked.

Striker shook his head.

"Don't blame you, but, perhaps you might not get a chance to shoot."

Striker shrugged his shoulders.

"I always carry a phial of poison," said Lester Leith, taking the phial from his pocket. "I have enemies who might want to take me for a ride. I always resolved I'd take that poison if I ever got in their power."

Striker snorted.

"Don't think you're the only smart one. I always carry tablets. They'd never electrocute me while I got these." He took out of his pocket a small glass bottle.

Leith nodded.

"I was hoping you carried something like that," he said cryptically. "Now I'm going to wait in your outer office. If you hear voices, simply listen at the keyhole. That will show you how I fix things with the police."

And, with no other word of farewell, he went to the door, slammed it, took a seat in the outer office.

Ten minutes passed. The inner door opened. "I don't understand—" began Striker.

Lester Leith waved him back.

"Naturally you wouldn't. But the police have to make sure of a fair split. That's why I can't leave this office until they come for their cash. Otherwise I might ditch some of it. They'll be here in a moment. Get back."

Striker withdrew.

Within less than sixty seconds there was the pound of feet on the stairs. The door burst open. Sergeant Ackley's florid face thrust into the room. The eyes lit on Lester Leith, sprawled contentedly in a chair.

"Ah, sergeant, beat me to it, eh? I'd hoped to leave a nice little chat with Striker before you arrived. He isn't in at present."

Sergeant Ackley leaped into the room. Behind him came Fawkes. Chief Lambertson could be heard, patiently toiling up the stairs. Soon he, too, puffed his way into the room.

"So Striker was the murderer of his wife, and you wanted to shake him down?" accused Ackley.

"Tut, tut, sergeant. Who said anything about wanting to shake him down? I wanted to find out certain details. But my interest in crime solutions is purely academical, as I've told you many times.

"Now Striker not only murdered his wife, but his wife and Margy Marigold were one and the same."

"What!" yelled Ackley.

Behind him there was the faintest sound of rustling motion at the keyhole of the inner door. But Ackley was too excited to hear it, and Lester Leith began to talk rapidly, trying to cover up that noise.

"Certainly. There was no motive for the murder of Margy Marigold save jealousy. But there was a motive for the murder of Martha Striker. That was why Striker arranged things as he did. He really is the same person as Harley Marigold.

"It was the dog that was the clew, Boston Bulls do not stray all the way from Indiana to make up with a chance mistress who takes them in, and then become inconsolable over the death of that mistress. Nor, under those circumstances, is it a strange man who can give such animals their sole consolation?

"No, my dear sergeant, the clew of the dog should have given you all you needed. It did not. As a result, Sidney Striker was able to collect fifty thousand dollars on the death of Martha Striker, whose body was so readily identified by the recent dental work she had so opportunely had done—at his suggestion. A moment's thought would have given you the lead. It only needed to secure a picture of the supposed Martha Striker to make the chain complete.

"And, aside from the dog, there was the matter of the woman. A woman who loves as this woman loved, does not banish herself from the man she loves when a divorce is granted, call it interlocutory or any other name."

Sergeant Ackley's jaw sagged. "Good God!"

Lester Leith lit a cigarette, calmly blew a smoke ring. "There are a few details I haven't cleared up, as yet," he said, "but for the most part I've reached a theoretical solution—and, by the way, sergeant, I've sold that dog collar and license."

"Sold it!"

"Yes, indeed."

"Who'd you sell it to?"

"Striker. Can you imagine? I asked him thirty thousand dollars for it, and the damned fool paid, largely, I think, on the strength of the fact that you had given me written authority to dispose of them."

"You—you—you've seen him then."

"Oh, yes."

"Does he know your suspicions?"

"Oh, yes, he admitted his guilt."

"Where is he?"

"I don't know. I *left* him in that office."

In a single bound Sergeant Ackley was at the door. He flung it open. The door thudded against something soft and inert. "Dead!" exclaimed Ackley.

Lester Leith nodded. "He always carried poison. He said he'd never be taken alive."

Sergeant Ackley snatched the bit of paper from the dead hand. "By God, Leith, I can send you up for life on this evidence. That's blackmail. You didn't inform the law, that's compounding a murder."

Lester Leith shook his head.

"Quite the contrary, my dear sergeant. That's why I was so anxious to see that it was *not* evidence that I sold. That's why I insisted that my dog couldn't even be of the same breed as the dog, Bobo, who figured in the Marigold case. That's why I got your written permission to sell my property."

Sergeant Ackley gasped.

"But the fox terrier was of the same *size!*"

"Doubtless the collars *looked* somewhat alike. You should have thought of that before you gave me permission to sell them."

CHAPTER X

Dead Lips

Chief Lambertson had been puffing from his exertions. Twice he had tried to speak. Each time the labouring lungs refused to supply sufficient air to give the words sound. Now he managed to get enough breath to fill his lungs, open his mouth, and then a sardonic laugh rasped from his heaving diaphragm.

"The city police!" he chortled.

"By Gad!" Sergeant Ackley glared.

"Shut up! Your signature's on that paper, too!"

Lester Leith shrugged.

"As for the other angle, that of withholding the information from the police, sergeant, I waited in the outer office for you. You must admit I told you as soon as I saw you."

Sergeant Ackley looked at the lifeless form. "And knew this chap was listening. You knew he'd kill himself."

Lester Leith made a deprecatory gesture with his hands. "Of course, one doesn't always follow the best course. There are no books of etiquette giving guidance in such cases. I rather thought it would be better to tell you, rather than to have you burst into that room without knowing.

"You see, the man had a weapon, and he threatened me with it. Under the circumstances I felt it would be decidedly better to let you know the man was a murderer before you jumped into the room."

Sergeant Ackley sneered. "All very pretty. Yet you knew this man would kill himself!"

"How very much better to have him kill himself, sergeant, than to have him kill *you*. I'd almost lose my interest in the theoretical solutions of crime problems if I didn't have you to make it so very interesting for me. No, sergeant, I couldn't spare you.

"And as far as this man is concerned—well, sergeant, the law would have killed him, very bitterly, very painfully, very deliberately. And, do you know, sergeant, I've never met a criminal for whom I felt less sympathy. He had the love of a good woman, a regular little pal, and he killed her for a lousy bit of money! Bah! I can't even sympathize with him in anything he did, not even fooling the police."

Sergeant Ackley scratched his head. "But you must have had some clew beside the dog!"

Lester Leith smiled. "That, and that the police had already run down every possible clew based on any disclosed motive. I told Scuttle not to bother unless the records of Pickets disclosed a murder within a certain definite time period. When he told me that, I knew I was sure of my ground. And, of course, I made it a point to get pictures of the various parties concerned by dropping in to a friendly police station as an interested citizen and going over their files."

"Humph," grunted Ackley. "You're talking pretty freely for you. You're under arrest. I'll make a case out of this somewhere."

Lester Leith's eyes suddenly narrowed to cold slits. "On the contrary, sergeant, you'll do nothing of the sort. You won't even arrest me!"

Sergeant Ackley's jaw sagged. "Won't what?"

"Won't arrest me, won't try to make out a case. You see, my dear sergeant, I asked the newspaper reporters to drop up here for a story at precisely four o'clock. They'll be here soon.

"If you try to press a case against me you'll establish these things: first, that you gave me this fool paper saying I could sell the things you now try to make appear as a criminal sale; second, that *I* solved the Marigold-Striker murders, and that you were just suckers who followed along.

"On the contrary, if you tear up this acknowledged paper, you can claim the credit of the solution. You'll be nationally known. You'll get a promotion. You'll get more pay. You'll be written up in newspapers and magazines as the greatest sleuth of the department. And, lastly, it won't appear that the fingerprint in the dried massage cream is of *your* little finger."

Ackley turned a startled face to confront the questioning eyes of his companions.

"The notary?" he asked.

"Is going to Europe to study music," assured Lester Leith. "She leaves on the train with me tonight. She has rare talent."

There was the sound of hurried steps on the stairs outside of the office.

"Quick, the reporters," said Lester Leith.

Sergeant Ackley swooped. With a swift motion he grabbed the dead man, felt through his pockets. When he straightened he had the dog collar, the massage cream, the curling iron, the signed, acknowledged document, and he thrust them all in his pockets.

A man stepped into the outer office. "You said you had a story? A telephone, I believe?"

"Yes," snapped Sergeant Ackley. "I'm Sergeant Arthur Ackley. This is my assistant, Mr. Fawkes. The other gentleman is Chief

Lambertson, of Pickets. The other chap doesn't matter."

"Good Lord!" yelled the reporter, catching sight of the body. "It's Striker!"

"On the contrary," said Sergeant Ackley, with drawling insolence, mimicking Lester Leith's tone as nearly as he could, "it's not Striker. It's Marigold. That man is the murderer of Margy Marigold, and he's the murderer of Martha Striker. *I* have solved the case, with the aid of a dog's photograph."

"And *my* assistance," reminded Fawkes.

"And your able assistance," conceded Sergeant Ackley.

"And you couldn't have done it without *me!*" proclaimed the pompous chief of police of Pickets.

"You, too, are entitled to credit," agreed Ackley.

The reporter gazed with goggled eyes, then made a dash for the telephone.

"Oh, my God, what luck! It's broken for me. I'll sell this yarn to every newspaper in the country. Gentlemen, stay right where you are until I can get a photographer and a line to the papers."

Grabbing the telephone receiver, he jiggled the hook in an ecstasy of haste.

Sergeant Ackley, his forehead wash-boarded, turned to Lester Leith.

"Leith, did you tell Striker of your suspicions before or after you got the money?"

It was a seemingly innocent question, but Lester Leith smiled. "After, of course, my dear sergeant."

Ackley cursed inaudibly under his breath.

"And the only lips that can contradict that ..." he began, then glanced at the corpse.

"Are dead," supplemented Lester Leith, as smilingly debonair as ever.

Cold Clews

CHAPTER I

Sergeant Ackley Sends a Visitor

Lester Leith, stretched at indolent ease upon the reclining chair in his bachelor apartment, regarded his valet, who besides being a valet was a police undercover man spying upon him, and smiled.

"Scuttle, there is altogether too much emphasis placed upon the detection of crime. In reality it's a simple matter."

The "valet" straightened to attention. Six foot two of him, there was, with a heavy face flanked on either side by the sweep of black mustaches. His black eyes were round and bulging, like the eyes of a boiled lobster. "I've heard you say so before, sir."

Lester Leith reached for a cigarette with a lazy gesture of utter disinterest with life.

"Yes, indeed, Scuttle," he remarked, and tapped the cigarette upon the arm of his chair.

The valet cleared his throat. "What made you say so at this particular time? If I may ask, sir."

"Because I just happened to think of it, Scuttle. I was thinking of the general inefficiency of the police department."

The big man flushed beneath the sallow skin of his bulging cheeks. His lips opened as though to emit some blasting bellow of rage, but he took a deep breath and controlled himself.

"Perhaps the police are more efficient than you think, sir."

Lester Leith lit the cigarette, extinguished the match with a single smoky exhalation; took another deep drag and exhaled the smoke in twin streams through appreciative nostrils. "Perhaps," he agreed lazily.

But the valet did not let it drop at that. He was bristling, like a huge dog looking for trouble.

"You don't know what the police are up against, sir; if you don't mind my saying so, sir. You have me save the crime clippings from the newspaper. Every so often I read them to you. You pick out some particular crime which interests you. It's your theory that many times the newspaper accounts contain enough facts to enable the crime to be solved."

Lester Leith stretched his well-knit arms high above his shoulders and yawned prodigiously. "Well, Scuttle, what's all that got to do with it?"

"Just this, sir. You hand-pick a particular crime and go out and solve it from the data given in the newspaper clippings. The police can't do that. They have to take every crime that comes along. You pick one out of a hundred or more!"

Lester Leith half turned in the chair and surveyed the police spy with lazy-lidded eyes in which there was a glint of inscrutable humor.

"Tut, tut, Scuttle. Don't say 'go out and solve' the crimes. What you mean is that I study out an academic solution from the newspaper accounts."

The valet, still bristling, stuck doggedly to his guns. "You always go out, sir."

Lester Leith took another drag at the cigarette, sent a twisting spiral of smoke toward the raftered ceiling. "Before, or after the solution of the crime has been worked out, Scuttle?"

The valet blurted his reply in unthinking haste. "I wish to God I knew!"

Lester Leith took the cigarette from his month and surveyed his valet with eyes that glittered frostily. "What was that, Scuttle?"

The valet squirmed. "What I meant to say, sir, was that Sergeant Ackley believes you solve the crimes, and then go out and hi-jack the criminal of his spoils. Therefore, he thinks you solve the crime first, and then go out."

Lester Leith laughed outright. "The dear sergeant! How simple he is! And how utterly asinine. Why, Scuttle, the very idea is preposterous. For more than a year now he's had shadows tailing me, following me every place I went. He's hounded me to death. Surely, if his suspicions were justified he'd have proved his case before now."

The valet was not so certain, but he concealed his feelings under a mask of awkward diplomacy.

"Yes, sir. Of course, sir. I wasn't insinuating there was any ground for his suspicions. I merely mentioned that he had them. Of course, sir, you must admit there is some mysterious hi-jacker who is, beating the police to the solution of important crimes and robbing criminals of their plunder."

Lester Leith blew a smoke ring, watched it twisting and turning upon its writhing course upward toward the dark shadows of the ceiling.

"Possibly, Scuttle. Sergeant Ackley claims to have proof of it. But I'm not concerned. In fact my sympathies are with this hi-jacker. After all he's only punishing criminals as they deserve. But we digress, Scuttle, and digression is a dangerous habit since it indicates lack of concentration.

"You were speaking. I believe, about how the police had to consider every crime that was committed, while I only picked out particular crimes for consideration."

The valet nodded, his eyes glittering with hatred. "Yes, sir."

Lester Leith blew another smoke ring, traced its perimeter with an idle forefinger. "Perhaps you're right, Scuttle," he said with that patronizing air which was so irritating to the police spy. And then, after a long moment, he added, almost dreamily, "But I don't think so." And he resumed his smoking.

The valet's face purpled. He started to say something, choked back the comment, and was seized with a fit of coughing.

"Really, Scuttle," drawled Lester Leith without looking around, "you must do something for that cough. Cough drops, perhaps. I've never tried them, but there's a certain charm about the rugged faces of the bearded brothers as they appear on the box that seems to be an assurance of remedial efficiency."

The valet took a deep breath. His great hands clenched into twin fists. The taut skin over his knuckles showed drawn and white.

And, at that precise moment, as though the interruption had been timed, there sounded a buzzing noise from the reception hallway.

"Someone at the door, Scuttle." drawled Lester Leith.

The valet seemed to welcome the interruption. He strode toward the door with swift haste. Lester Leith continued smoking, not bothering to give the valet so much as a glance. There was the sound of the outer door opening and closing. The valet's heavy voice rumbled some comment, and was answered by a soft feminine voice.

The valet thrust his head into the door of the living room. "Miss Rhoda Bromley to see you, sir."

"Have her come in, Scuttle, have her come in!" said Lester Leith, and got to his feet with that rippling motion of easy grace which bespeaks a strength and muscular coordination far above the average. As the young woman entered the door, Lester Leith bowed formally, from the hips.

"This is Mr. Leith, Miss Bromley."

"Will you have a chair and explain to me if there is of some way in which I can be of service to you?"

She walked directly to him and regarded his face with anxious eyes. Then she put out her hand.

Lester Leith took the hand with a gesture of courtly deference.

"It is indeed a pleasure," he murmured, and escorted the young woman to a chair.

From the chair she continued to study him with clear gray eyes that were entirely frank in their appraisal. Then she settled back, crossed silken knees and smiled. "Sergeant Ackley said you would help me."

"Sergeant Ackley!"

And something in Lester Leith's tone caused the smile to fade from her face.

"Why, yes. I—er—I gathered you were great friends. He said you were the only man in the city who had sufficient ability to help me, and that you were one student of crime who thought the police were wrong about nine-tenths of the time!"

And swift tears moistened the gray eyes. Suddenly she shook her head and smiled again.

"I mustn't bawl about it. Gimme a cigarette and I'll quit the baby act. After all, if there's been a mistake made, it's my fault. I thought you were a detective."

CHAPTER II

Leith Takes a Case

The valet moved forward with the box of cigarettes, but Lester Leith was at her side in a single stride, extending his jeweled cigarette case.

"My dear Miss Bromley, pardon me if I seemed rude. It happens that the dear sergeant was indulging in a little sarcasm, and you doubtless took his comments at their face value. But that's neither here nor there. If there is some way in which I can help you, you have only to suggest it."

She took a cigarette, lit it and inhaled with the satisfaction which comes only to women who smoke because they like it rather than because they have cultivated the habit as an intriguing gesture to the opposite sex. "He's arrested my brother," she said.

Lester Leith bowed. "He would," he remarked, and his tone contained a contempt which indicated that Miss Bromley's brother must be—like the wife of Cæsar—above reproach.

She smiled her thanks.

"Evidently your opinion of Sergeant Ackley's intelligence is about the same as mine."

Lester Leith returned to his chair, shrugged his shoulders.

"Sergeant Ackley's intelligence is like that of so many of the policemen who have been selected for brawn rather than brains—virtually nil."

And the valet, standing in the background, bat ears strained to catch every word of the conversation, was seized with another fit of coughing.

"Precisely what," asked Lester Leith, "did Sergeant Ackley arrest your brother for?"

Her eyes blazed with indignation. "For nothing but walking down the street! That's the honest truth. Carl was walking along the sidewalk, maybe he was running a little bit. He had a date, and he wanted to get the street car at the corner.

"A police machine came skidding around the turn, slammed on the brakes and two officers jumped out, grabbed Carl and started to curse him. They accused him of having held up Mr. Riggers, the jeweler, and taken a rare necklace. They flung him into the police car, took him to jail and had Mr. Riggers come down to see him.

"They put him on a platform and turned bright lights on him, and asked Mr. Riggers if that was the man. And Mr. Riggers made what they call a 'partial identification.' He said the man who had robbed him wore a suit of almost that color, and that his shoes were the same type, and that he was about the same build and general appearance as Carl. And they locked Carl up on suspicion."

Lester Leith looked at her with eyes that were closed to mere slits. "You're not telling me all," he said.

"Well," she admitted, "Carl was in trouble once before, a matter of a check that wasn't good, and the police were very hard-boiled about it. I made up the check out of my account, but they insisted upon going ahead with the case and putting Carl on probation."

Lester Leith nodded.

"Yes," he said, "that's typical police reasoning. If a man ever gets in trouble and happens to be found near the scene of a crime, no matter if it's years afterward, then he must be the criminal. I take it that Riggers was robbed near the place your brother was picked up?"

She shook her head in a gesture of swift negation. "Not even that. But I guess the real robber was near there all right. You see he escaped in a stolen car, and the car didn't have much gasoline in it. He ran out of gas and coasted into a service station and asked for some gasoline in a hurry.

"The police had lost his trail, but were cruising around, looking for a car of that description. The robber was standing at the gasoline tank, holding the hose. The service station man was turning the pump, when, all of a sudden, the police drove on the scene.

"Even then they might not have noticed the parked car in the gasoline station. But the boy had a guilty conscience, and he started to run. It looked as though the police were going to catch him easily. But it happened there was a motor cycle rider who came up to the service station at just that moment and got off his motor cycle. The robber hopped on and started away. That time he ditched the police for good."

Lester Leith's eyes clouded in thought. "The man at the service station," he asked, almost dreamily, "does he identify your brother as the man who got the gasoline?"

"Yes!" she blazed, "and he's a dirty, pimple-faced liar! The police have coached him. I know they have. You can tell it from the shifty-eyed way he looks at you when you talk with him! He says he thinks it was Carl all right, and then he shifts his eyes all around the room. He just won't look you square in the face and say it was Carl."

Lester Leith nodded slowly.

"The police have been known to do things like that. You understand that identification is a very difficult matter. Many times a man is in doubt about identifications. But by the time the police get a witness in court he's positive, invariably positive…Carl, of course, says he knows nothing about it?"

She nodded.

"And," continued Lester Leith, "Sergeant Ackley sent you to me?"

"Yes. I can see now it was just his idea of a joke. I told him that I thought the police were a bunch of boobs, and he said that you were another one who had the same idea, that you would undoubtedly be glad to cooperate with me in proving they were mistaken about Carl.

"I asked him about your fees, if they were high, and he laughed in that coarse way he has, and said I wouldn't have any trouble with you over that, none whatever. I didn't get his meaning at the time. Now…"

She broke off and a flush suffused her cheeks. "Oh, well," she said, and sighed, "it's all in the day's work. Guess I'll ankle along and try another lead."

Lester Leith raised his hand in a gesture of restraint. "You're working?" he asked.

The gray eyes regarded him steadily. "Yes. I'm a dancer, a stage dancer."

"Playing here in town?"

"I have the lead in a burlesque show at the Baltimore Theater." And the gray eyes seemed to be waiting for something. Lester Leith bowed his head. "You have talent and intelligence," he said, "you'll succeed in the dramatic profession."

She sighed. "Well, you're about the first man that ever gave me a break. Usually when I tell 'em I'm in burlesque they start wise-cracking right away. 'I'll have to get a ticket. I'd like to see more of you'—that's one of their favorite lines. As a matter of fact, I studied dramatic art and studied it hard. When I tried to crash in, all I could land was a job in the burlesque. I've worked up, though, out of the chorus, into one of the leads.

"It's not what I care for, but I started out to be an actress, and, by God, I'll be an actress if I have to crawl on my hands and knees through every dance hall in the city!"

Lester Leith nodded his approval. "Oh, Scuttle," he drawled.

The eager valet leaned forward. "Sir?"

"You've been saving the crime clippings, Scuttle?"

"Yes, sir, of course, sir."

"And you're familiar with the facts of this Riggers robbery, Scuttle?"

"Yes, sir, as the newspaper gives them, sir."

"Yes, Scuttle. You were commenting, I believe, that it was rather easy to hand-pick a crime and work out a solution. Let's see what we can do by taking them as they come, the way you said the police had to."

The valet wriggled his head and neck in a gesture of assent, eager assent that caused his eyes to sparkle. "Yes, sir."

"When did the crime take place, Scuttle?"

"Yesterday afternoon, sir."

"Get me the newspaper clippings."

The big valet nodded and oozed from the room.

The gray eyes of the actress regarded Lester Leith frankly.

"Listen, I came to you because Sergeant Ackley got smart. I can see you're wealthy." She broke off to wave her hand in an inclusive gesture at the rich furniture of the sumptuous apartment. "So let's not have any misunderstandings about … about compensation."

And the eyes regarded him with unfaltering frankness.

Lester Leith smiled.

"We won't have any misunderstandings, Miss Bromley, not about anything. I like to study crime and look for a possible solution just as some people like to solve chess problems, others to play cards. It's my hobby."

She took a deep breath. "If you help me you'll be paid for it—understand?"

He bowed. "To help you would be ample compensation—and, then again, think how gratified the dear sergeant would be if we were able to demonstrate that he was wrong again. He would be so pleased to think he had sent you to me!"

She laughed at that, and settled herself in her chair, seemed to relax. It was as though she was commencing to feel very much at home with Lester Leith.

CHAPTER III

Stolen Diamonds

Scuttle pussyfooted his huge bulk into the room with half a dozen newspaper clippings. "Shall I give you a summary, sir?"

"Yes, Scuttle. Get Miss Bromley a glass of that prescription port, and put some cigarettes at her elbow. Then tell us the gist of the newspaper reports."

The valet moved swiftly, brought out the bottle, the glasses, placed the cigarettes, laid the clippings in order on the table.

"Mr. Samuel Riggers, sir, is a well-known jeweler." Lester Leith nodded, dreamily, sipped his wine.

"He deals very largely in large transactions, sir. He purchases collections of stones, and pays for them at good prices. His establishment has been in operation for years and he is known throughout the world.

"That is why Señor Jose Camulos, coming from South America with a very fine string of diamonds, arranged in advance for an appointment with Mr. Riggers, sir. It seems the necklace was very valuable, and Señor Camulos had used every precaution to conceal the fact that he had it with him.

"He went at once to the office of Mr. Riggers, and there exhibited the necklace. Mr. Riggers was examining it to ascertain what sort of an offer he could make on it, when the door of his private office was thrown open and a masked man entered the room. He had an automatic and he demanded that both men raise their hands.

"He looked desperate and they surrendered the diamonds to him. He turned and ran from the office. Mr. Riggers shouted an alarm, but the man made good his escape."

Scuttle pawed the newspaper clippings. "Here's a sketch plan of the store and a dotted line showing the course taken by the man as he ran from the store, sir."

Lester Leith took the newspaper clipping, but did not look at it immediately. "How about the clerks in the store, Scuttle? Did they see the man who committed the crime?"

"They saw him when he went in, but no one seems to have noticed him particularly. When he went out he ran down some back stairs, through a work room and out into an alley. No one seems to have seen his features clearly."

"But surely, Scuttle, a masked man would have attracted attention, entering the store!"

"Yes, sir. That's where he was clever, sir. He didn't put on the mask until he had entered the office where the two men were examining the diamond necklace."

Lester Leith nodded musingly. "And he didn't take anything other than that necklace, Scuttle?"

"That's all, sir."

"And he escaped in a stolen car?"

"Yes, sir. He had stolen an expensive car belonging to Mr. Charles Petterman, the lawyer, sir. Mr. Petterman is one of the most successful of the corporation and probate lawyers in the city. The thief had stolen his automobile earlier in the day. It was a stock model, two years old. It had a distinctive red band around the upper part of the body, and the people who ran into the alley after the holdup saw that car quite plainly.

"They tried to follow, but were unable to keep the car in sight. The police were notified and they started cruising around the district. It was then, and quite by chance, that they discovered the car some two miles from the scene of the crime, filling up in a gasoline station."

Lester Leith nodded.

He looked at the newspaper sketch diagram, selected another cigarette, lit it, and sent spirals of smoke drifting upward. Finally he chuckled.

"Scuttle," he said, "telephone Mr. Charles Petterman, and get the exact details surrounding the theft of his car, where it was taken from, how long it was stolen before the crime was committed, and ask him if he has any theories as to why a thief should take a distinctive car of that type with the red stripe running around the body."

"But what has that to do with this crime, sir?" the valet inquired.

Lester Leith regarded him with a candid smile. "Really, Scuttle," he said softly. "I haven't the faintest idea. Have you?"

"No, sir."

"Ah, yes, that simplifies matters and enables you to carry out my request without further delay."

The valet's face was brick red.

"Yes, sir," he gritted, turned on his heel and strode into the closet where Lester Leith had recently housed the telephone.

The girl regarded Lester Leith over the smoldering tip of her cigarette. "You're a funny man," she remarked, after a few seconds.

Lester Leith shook his head. "On the contrary, it is other people who are funny. When you get to know me better, you'll realize that I go directly after what I want, where other people waste time in milling about on detours."

The girl raised her glass. The gray eyes regarded him speculatively over the rim.

"Here's to knowing you better, then," she said, and smiled.

Lester bowed an acknowledgment.

There followed an interval of silence. The actress clasped her silken knees and pulled her feet to the edge of the chair, studying Lester Leith. Lester Leith sent little smoke rings through big ones, and regarded them with thought-slitted eyes. From time to time, he nodded his head; little brief nods as though he were checking off a complicated campaign in his mind, checking each point as he came to it.

The door of the closet opened and the valet stood staring at Lester Leith.

"There's something uncanny about you, sir!" he exploded.

Lester Leith opened his narrowed eyes. "Indeed?" he asked.

"How did you know that the car had something to do with the mystery?"

"How do you mean?" asked Lester Leith.

CHAPTER IV

The Hoodooed Car

"Mr. Petterman, sir. He says his car has been stolen three times within the last month. That it's been used for joy rides, and recovered each time. He not only locks the transmission and ignition, but he locks the doors, and each time someone borrows the car without any more bother than if it had been unlocked.

"He says it was taken yesterday from in front of his office where it was parked against the curb, with the doors, ignition and transmission locked. He says, further, that even last night someone was prowling around his garage where he has the car stored, and that he had to notify the police."

Lester Leith lit a fresh cigarette from the tip of the old one.

"Indeed, Scuttle. That's interesting, isn't it?"

The valet's eyes were still big with wonder. "But how did you know that the car figured so much in the case, sir?"

"I didn't," said Lester Leith with a smile. "That's why I had you telephone to Mr. Petterman."

The valet shook his head as one shakes his head when some phenomenon of the physical universe challenges his credulity.

"Well, it's got me stopped, sir. Mr. Petterman is all worked up about it, sir. He says he's going to sell his car and buy another. He thinks his car is hoodooed."

Lester Leith blew a smoke ring. "Hoodooed, eh? Tell you what, Scuttle, call up Mr. Petterman again, and tell him Mr. Leith is going to call on him with reference to the purchase of a new car."

The valet regarded Lester Leith with sagging jaw. "You, sir?"

"Certainly, Scuttle. I am going to become an automobile salesman for one of the new car agencies. After all, we have a hot tip here. Mr. Petterman wants a new car. Business is quiet. The automobile agencies are finding things very slow indeed. If I show up and offer to work as a car salesman and guarantee the immediate sale of a new car, they'll probably give me a nice commission."

The valet rubbed his ears. "*You*, sir! Work as a salesman, sir!"

Lester Leith nodded casually. "Yes, Scuttle. You heard me perfectly. And if you'll hurry up with that call you'll catch Mr. Petterman before he goes out. Tell him I'd like an appointment with him for…let's see. It's now two o'clock. Tell him I'd like an appointment with him for four o'clock."

The valet sighed, turned back to the booth.

"Tell him," called Lester Leith, "that I will give him an allowance on his old car that's within one hundred and fifty dollars of the price that he paid for it,"

The valet halted mid-stride. "It's two years old, sir!"

Lester Leith smiled his thanks. "Under those circumstances, Scuttle, since you doubtless know more than I do about the matter, you'd better make it two hundred dollars less than the purchase price."

"A thousand would be more like it!" blurted the valet.

"Two hundred, and that's final," said Lester Leith, and waved his hand toward the closet where the telephone was located.

The girl continued to hug her silken knees up under her chin. "You," she said, "are either the craziest or the brainiest man I know!"

"Thank you," remarked Lester Leith. "One always likes to excel."

And he again returned to a brown study, nodding his head from time to time. The valet found him so when he emerged from the closet.

"At four, sir." he said, stiffly. "Mr. Petterman was only too pleased, only too much pleased."

Lester Leith's nod was dreamy. "Very well, Scuttle. I think we will start work on the case."

The valet cleared his throat. "Such clews as there are, sir, and there aren't many, are rather cold by this time. Particularly since the police have already jailed the culprit."

Rhoda Bromley's knees snapped downward. She was on her feet, gray eyes blazing.

"What's that! You mean to insinuate Carl is guilty?" The valet flushed, squirmed, cleared his throat.

"Sergeant Ackley is very efficient," he said lamely. "I was merely explaining to Mr. Leith that this case was hardly a fair test of the demonstration he was to make."

Lester Leith, also, got to his feet. "Scuttle, you forget yourself. I did not ask you for any opinion as to whether the case was difficult or whether the clews were cold or hot.

"However, Scuttle, since you think the clews are cold, we'll get a stove and warm them up."

The valet blinked. "Do what?"

"Get a stove and warm them up. I want an iron stove, Scuttle, a coal stove that weighs about three hundred pounds. I want a big stove, a heavy stove, a strong stove. And I want a watch dog, twenty-eight dice, a yard of silk cord, a small vise, a portable drill, and a small emery wheel.

"But first I want the watch dog. He should be a bulldog, quite savage looking. And I shall want my walking stick, my hat and my gloves, Scuttle. You can get the dog at the kennels half a dozen blocks down the boulevard. I noticed their ad in the paper. Better get them on the telephone, Scuttle, and tell them to deliver the largest and fiercest bulldog they have. Price, of course, Scuttle, is no object.

"Then, when the bulldog comes, you can start out after the stove and the dice and the drill, the vise and the emery wheel."

The valet's feelings mastered him. "One of us." he blurted, "is stark, staring crazy."

Lester Leith nodded approvingly. "I've thought so at times, too, Scuttle. I'm glad you agree with me."

He turned to the actress. "Within the next twenty-four hours. I shall have news for you. I believe, Scuttle, that is the police formula. I notice that the newspapers always quote some police official as predicting 'an arrest' within the next twenty-four hours. They never say one day, or to-morrow, but it's always within another twenty-four hours. And where can I reach you when I have news, Miss Bromley?"

She handed him a card upon which had been scribbled a telephone number. "That's my apartment. The number's on the card."

Lester Leith took her hand, bowed low over it. "So nice of Sergeant Ackley to send you here," he remarked, and personally escorted her to the door.

CHAPTER V

Bobo

The bulldog arrived, escorted by a puzzled trainer from the kennels, within the next twenty minutes. The dog looked fully capable. He was a huge animal, squat, powerful, bowlegged, and his jaw was thrust out at such a sharply aggressive angle that the upturned nose seemed almost incapable of feeding enough air into the animal's lungs. Great fangs protruded from either side of the upper lip, like the tusks of a walrus.

"This here dog," proclaimed the trainer, "is valued at two hundred and fifty dollars. You said as how—"

And he broke off, for Lester Leith had taken a roll of currency from his pocket, and was counting off bills of large denomination.

"You'll have to take it easy with him," said the trainer, as he pocketed the bills. "He's been trained to bite."

Lester Leith nodded easily. "Just walk past me, and hand me the end of the leash," he said, "and I'll show you a trick I learned from Larry Trimble, the trainer of Strongheart."

The man walked toward him. The bulldog growled throatily. Leith extended his hand and took the end of the leash. The dog crouched.

"Now walk away," said Leith, his eyes fastened upon those of the growling dog.

The trainer walked away doubtfully. "For God's sake, sir, don't do that!" he warned, but Lester Leith, speaking reassuringly to the dog, was pulling him toward him, hand over hand.

The dog pulled back, braced his feet.

Leith turned to Scuttle and commented quite casually. "Be sure and get a heavy stove, Scuttle, and get it right away. I'll telephone your instructions about delivery later. And don't forget the other things."

The valet nodded, his eyes on the dog.

"My hat and gloves, Scuttle."

The valet brought them. The growling of the dog subsided.

"I'll be hanged!" muttered the trainer.

Lester Leith waved him toward the door. "If you'll get started now, it will simplify matters."

The trainer left the room. Scuttle cleared his throat. "That dog, sir, is dangerous."

"I don't think so—not to me," said Leith.

"His name is Bobo," said the trainer as he slammed the door.

Leith nodded, took a handkerchief from his pocket, tossed it in front of the dog's nose. "Guard!" he said.

The dog stiffened.

"Now, Scuttle, would you mind picking up that handkerchief?"

The valet stepped backward. "Sir?"

"Yes, Scuttle, come forward and pick up that handkerchief."

"But, sir!"

"You heard me, Scuttle."

The valet advanced timidly. The bulldog growled.

"Come on, Scuttle."

The valet took another step and the dog rushed.

Lester Leith, on the end of the leash, dragged him back. "That's all right, Bobo. That's all right." And he reached forward and patted the head of the dog. Then he picked up the handkerchief.

"You see, Scuttle, he knew it was mine. And he knew the leash had been surrendered to me. It only needed that little touch to make him accustomed to guarding my things...Come, Bobo."

And Lester Leith led the dog to the door, paused. "Don't forget the stove, Scuttle," he said, and walked out, the dog trotting at his side.

CHAPTER VI

Lester Becomes a Salesman

Booth Garner, manager of the automobile agency, regarded Lester Leith with puzzled eyes. "Of course, Mr. Leith, you could undoubtedly sell cars to your friends in club circles. But selling cars is a specialized branch of sales effort.. We require our salesmen..."

Lester Leith interrupted. "You want business, don't you?"

"Yes, of course, but..."

"Very well. Here's five hundred dollars in currency. Keep it as an evidence of good faith. I will start work at once. On any day I fail to sell one new car you are at liberty to terminate the employment and keep the money. I will work on commission alone."

The automobile dealer's eyes bulged. "Why, you couldn't do that..."

"Do you wish to accept the offer, or shall I make it to some other dealer?" And Lester Leith got to his feet.

"I'll accept it," snapped Garner. "Don't say I didn't warn you."

Lester Leith bowed gravely, snapped his fingers at the dog. "Come, Bobo. We've got to get to work."

The dealer regarded Leith speculatively. "I wish I knew just what you have in mind," he said, and he tightened his grip upon the five one-hundred-dollar bills which Lester Leith had left by way of deposit.

Leith smiled frankly. "Just the sale of new cars. One hears so much about business being quiet, you know. I wanted to see if it were at all true.

"It's a little after three o'clock now. If you'll give me a new car ready for delivery, I'll take it out and try to make a sale by quitting time."

The manager scowled at the dog. "You'll have to tie your dog up and leave him here."

Lester Leith smiled his acquiescence. "Oh, yes, indeed. One wouldn't put a dog in a new car, would one?"

And something in his tone brought the trace of a frown to the forehead of the automobile dealer, but he led the way to the show room and pointed out the models on hand.

Ten minutes later Lester Leith was at the wheel of a new, shiny creation, driving it slowly out of the garage. Behind him a puzzled dealer regarded five hundred dollars in currency and a surly bull-dog, tied to a bench in the workshop.

"Crazy as a March hare!" he said.

But Lester Leith, tailored to the minute, sure of himself as only those are who have social position and wealth, drove the new car to the curb opposite the office building where Charles Petterman had his office.

He noticed a car with a red stripe running around the upper part of the body, and parked the new car directly behind it.

A doorman stepped forward.

"Parking reserved for tenants of the building, sir," he said.

Leith motioned toward the other car.

"Quite all right. I'm delivering this new car to Mr. Petterman and taking the old one in exchange."

The doorman bowed. "Very well. Whatever Mr. Petterman says. I'm particularly charged with watching this automobile. Mr. Petterman thinks it's a hoodooed car. He said something about selling it this afternoon, and cautioned me to keep my eye on it every minute. He doesn't want anything to happen to it until it gets safely sold."

Lester Leith smiled, and looked up and down the street. Charles Petterman had his office in one of the newer buildings which are springing up on the wide arteries of commerce within the cities where automobile traffic is at once a problem and an asset. The boulevard was wide. There was ample parking space, and the stores seemed to have that comfortable appearance of having plenty of elbow room with which to display their merchandise in commodious show windows.

Still smiling, Lester Leith made his way into Petterman's office.

Petterman was of the cautious, conservative type that is frequently selected to pilot the legal affairs of large corporations.

He rubbed a fat hand over a very bald head, and fastened gimlet eyes upon Lester Leith. Those eyes were the eyes of one who takes nothing for granted.

"Over the telephone," he said, "you offered me within two hundred dollars of what I paid for the old car."

Lester Leith nodded.

"Isn't that rather a high allowance?" ventured Mr. Petterman.

"We can lower it if you feel it is unfair," remarked Lester Leith.

Petterman's lips damped into a thin line.

"You're the one that's making the figure," he snapped.

"Precisely," said Lester Leith. "We are making the figure rather high because it is to our advantage to be able to point to customers who buy our cars year after year. You can step to the window and see the new car. It's in front."

Mr. Petterman heaved himself from the chair. After the manner of corporation lawyers who have spent their profitable lives at desks and in directors' rooms, he waddled to the window, looked down at the street.

Lester Leith joined him.

He could see the old car with the doorman guarding it, could see the new car behind it, and, across the street, he saw two cars parked, cars which contained drivers who were staring across at the office building.

Lester Leith regarded these men with a smile. They were police shadows, delegated by Sergeant Ackley to tail Lester Leith and report on his every move. Many times before, Lester Leith had managed to give the police shadows the slip, and this time Sergeant Ackley had arranged an elaborate plan to have Leith under espionage virtually every minute of the time.

"That's a new car?" asked Petterman, suspiciously. "It isn't a demonstrator, or a car that was sold once and came back?"

"Absolutely not. You can pick out any other car on our floor if you don't like this one."

"I think," remarked Petterman, "I'll just drive down to the agency and look the other cars over. I want to talk with Mr. Garner about this deal, anyway."

Lester Leith was cheerfully acquiescent, as became an automobile salesman dealing with an important customer. "Certainly. There's one little matter that I've got to check up on, though. Mr. Petterman. I've got to make a complete examination of your old car before I confirm that offer."

"But you already made the offer."

"Subject to the car's being in ordinary condition."

"Well, it's A-1 !"

"Very well, but I have to look it over to make a report. I wonder if you'd mind coming downstairs with me while I check it over. It won't take over a few minutes."

Petterman reached for his hat. "Won't be back any more this evening," he called to his secretary. "I'm buying a new car. If Blanchard calls up about his minute book, tell him it'll be ready tomorrow. Good night." And he waddled his portly way in portentous dignity to the elevator.

The elevator operator spoke to him obsequiously. The starter wished him a good night as he left the building. The doorman raised his hat.

Charles Petterman crawled behind the steering wheel of the new car. "Seems all right," he said.

Lester Leith nodded and started about the examination of the old car. Across the street, the two police shadows made notes of everything Leith did.

And his examination was, to say the least, peculiar.

He took a pressure gauge from his pocket and tested the pressure in the two front tires. He took a hydrometer from another pocket and sampled the specific gravity of the water from the radiator. Then he took a bit of stiff wire, went to the gasoline tank, and seemed to measure the gasoline in the tank. Next he lifted the hood and pulled one of the wires from the spark-plug, stared owlishly at the contact point, muttered something, replaced the wire and lowered the hood.

"Yes," he said to Mr. Petterman, "I shall be pleased to confirm the offer on the car."

"Okay," said the lawyer. "I'll drive this new car to Garner's. You drive the old car. I won't touch the damned thing again. It's hoodooed."

Leith nodded, climbed into the car with the red stripe around the upper part of the body, and stepped on the starter.

CHAPTER VII

A New Car—Second-Hand

As he purred away from the curb, the cars of the police shadows fell in behind him. Nor did they make any attempt to conceal the fact that they were shadowing him.

In the past Lester Leith might have slipped through their lingers, but this time they were going to see that nothing of the sort happened.

Lester Leith took them for a nice little ride. He didn't go directly to the automobile agency of Mr. Booth Garner. Instead, he swung out into the boulevard, put the car through its paces, and tried the brakes as well as the acceleration.

Hence it was that he arrived at the automobile agency fully ten minutes after the corporation lawyer had arrived. And there was an irate reception committee to greet him.

The portly lawyer with florid features was wiping the perspiration from his indignant forehead. The manager of the business was fairly dancing in his rage.

"What sort of a sap are you!" yelled Garner. "You can't make that sort of a thing stick. Mr. Petterman is a lawyer, and he says you can't."

"What sort of thing?" asked Leith innocently.

"Guaranteeing to sell a car a day and then going out and making damn-fool trade offers. Any fool could sell a car every five minutes if he offered to take in a two-year-old car at two hundred dollars off its list.

"I'll have you understand, Mr. Society Smartaleck, the salesmen don't have a damned thing to say about the trade-in price of the old cars. I have an appraiser who makes that price, and that price will be exactly what Mr. Petterman receives for his old car.

"But, since you've nearly ruined a good customer's business for me, and since I happen to have five hundred dollars of your money on deposit here. I'll just make up the difference between the appraised value of this car and the price you quoted Mr. Petterman out of that five hundred dollars, and take the balance from your commission!"

And the voice of the automobile manager rose to a roar. "That," said Lester Leith with a smile, "impresses me as being entirely fair. How does it impress you, Mr. Petterman?"

The lawyer's jaw sagged.

Booth Garner acted as though he could not believe his ears.

"And," said Lester Leith, "if the margin is still inadequate, I will make it up in cash. Has Mr. Petterman selected his car yet?"

Booth Garner looked about him sheepishly.

"I," said Mr. Charles Petterman, "will be damned!"

Lester Leith got from the old car. "Will you kindly send out the appraiser, Mr. Garner?" he asked.

And because Booth Garner was primarily an automobile merchant who knew his profession well and thoroughly, the sale from that point proceeded with neatness and dispatch. A puzzled, but satisfied corporation lawyer drove a brand-new automobile from the show room. An appraiser tied a pink slip of pasteboard to the steering wheel of the second-hand car and Lester Leith took it into the garage where second-hand cars were stored, walked to his dog, untied the leash, and ensconced the bulldog into the rear seat of the car with the red body stripe.

Then he went into the office of Booth Garner.

The automobile manager regarded his new salesman with a dour look.

"Now." he said, "what's the idea?"

Lester Leith was mild but firm.

"In the future," he said, "let's not stage our quarrels in front of our customers. It isn't good business."

Mr. Garner flushed. He didn't need to be reminded of that.

"I fixed what I thought was a fair price on the car," said Lester Leith. "Your appraiser was hundreds of dollars too low."

Garner was on familiar ground now. He sneered.

"That's what the salesmen always say. Perhaps you've forgotten that I'm the one that's running this business."

"Not at all," said Lester Leith. "As you mention, you're the one that's running it." And he smiled, then added, "You didn't say in what direction."

Garner's face purpled with rage. "Of all the damned crazy, exasperating—"

Lester Leith held up his hand.

"To show my good faith in the matter. I am willing to buy the old Petterman car. I will buy it at the price I quoted Petterman. I had that in mind all along, if your appraiser was too low."

And Lester Leith took a well-filled billfold from his breast pocket and started counting out money.

"But," he added, raising his eyes to Mr. Garner's startled countenance, "you must remember that the car is mine, and that if there's any profit on it, I make it, subject, of course, to a deduction of the usual sales commission if any other salesman closes the deal."

Garner sighed. "Look here, Leith," he said, not unkindly, "you may mean all right but you don't know a damned thing about business, and you're simply crazy on this deal. You'll lose more money than you'll make in two months of hard work."

Leith nodded absently, passed over the money.

"With my five hundred dollars, and the sales commission on the new car, this makes the balance of the purchase price. Will you kindly execute the necessary documents to pass title to me?"

Booth Garner sighed. "You'll never learn any younger," he said, and reached for his pen.

Lester Leith smoked while the automobile manager made out the necessary transfer, passed it across.

"It is now past five o'clock. I don't think I can sell any more cars tonight," said Lester Leith. "I'll leave my car here, and I'll leave my dog in the car. I don't think they'd care to have me keep him in my apartment until after I'd made arrangements with the janitor. I'll be back to feed him. There's a night man on duty?"

Gamer nodded.

"Kindly give me a note to the night man, telling him I'm a new salesman, and that I own the car with the red stripe."

Once more Garner scribbled a note. "Don't think I'm taking advantage of you on that deal, Leith," he said, not unkindly. "It was your own proposition."

Leith nodded. "And when I sell it at a profit don't think I'm taking advantage of your low appraisal," he said. "By the way, I guess I'd better put the new resale price on that car."

And he walked back into the shop, took out his pencil and crossed out the figure which the appraiser had placed on the red ticket, and put in its place another figure.

Garner leaned forward to read that figure and then gasped. It was seven hundred and fifty dollars more than the car had cost when it was new.

"You," he said with the certainty of absolute and final conviction, "are crazy!"

Lester Leith smiled at him. "That," he said, "is precisely what my valet thinks. And good night, Mr. Garner."

He spoke to the dog, strolled to the street, and caught a passing taxicab.

Garner, almost willing to believe his eyes had deceived him, reached for the price ticket once more. There was a growl and a flash of motion. He jerked his hand back just in time to avoid the clashing jaws of the ferocious watch dog. "Damn!" said the profane and utterly exasperated Mr. Garner.

CHAPTER VIII

An Early Customer

Lester Leith smiled at his valet as he adjusted the tie on his evening clothes.

"Do you know, Scuttle, I enjoy working for a living very, very much."

The valet was bursting with curiosity, but he managed to control himself. "Yes, sir."

"Yes, indeed, Scuttle. And I made the sale to Petterman this afternoon. Now I've got to look around for a prospect for tomorrow. I wonder if Sergeant Ackley would be interested in a new car."

The valet coughed. "I hardly think so, sir."

"Well, Scuttle, can't you think up some prospect for me?"

"I'm afraid not, sir."

"Tut, tut, Scuttle. You should be of more assistance. You got me the stove?"

"Yes, sir."

"The dice?"

"Yes, sir."

"The drill?"

"Yes, sir. There's no need to go over it item by item, sir. I got everything you asked for. The vise, the silk-cord, the drill, the dice, the stove, everything."

"Very good, Scuttle. Where are they?"

"The stove is at the hardware company, awaiting instructions for deliverers. The rest of the things are here."

Lester Leith nodded, gave his reflection a last survey in the mirror.

"But you were telling me about your experiences selling automobiles," reminded the valet, eagerly.

Lester Leith smiled benignly at him. "Yes, Scuttle, I was, wasn't I?"

And with nothing more than that to encourage the eager ears of the spy, he put on his hat and coat and went out into the night. Behind him, the valet shook a ham-like fist at the door and cursed bitterly.

On the lower floor two police shadows picked him up, followed him to a restaurant where he ordered a large portion of choice steak and some bones wrapped up in paper, paid for the same, and took a taxicab to Booth Garner's automobile agency.

The card which Garner had given him, a cigar and a good-natured greeting, contrived to make a friend out of the night man in charge.

Lester Leith walked back to his red striped car and was gratified to notice that Bobo, the savage watchdog, wagged his stump of a tail at the approach of his new master.

Lester Leith took him from the car, let him run for a few minutes, saw that the dog was well fed from the rich meat he had secured at the restaurant, placed a pan of water in the car, and bedded the dog down for the night.

Then, while the attention of the night man was taken from his duties, while the two police shadows watched the exit of the garage, waiting for their man to come out, Lester Leith walked about the automobile with a polishing cloth, rubbing it tenderly and without regard for the fact that his spotless evening clothes were hardly the proper garb for a man polishing an automobile.

The light was poor in the garage, and Lester Leith was as a flitting shadow. If he did anything to the car beside polishing it, it was impossible for the night man to notice it—as the night man afterward very truthfully confessed to Sergeant Ackley.

After Lester Leith had puttered around his new car for some thirty minutes, he went out, consulted a uniformed officer as to the location of the nearest telephone, called Miss Rhoda Bromley on the phone, found that which he might have known, that she was at the theater, and called a taxicab to take him to the Baltimore Theater. There was in everything he did a wide-eyed candor which made things exceptionally easy for the men who trailed him. He saw the performance, applauded vigorously at intervals, and waited at the stage door for Miss Bromley.

She met him with a smile, and a wise crack that was duly noted by the shadowing officers. "Well, you had to see more of me, I observe."

Lester Leith's bow was a model of courtliness.

"Your talents will not long be wasted here," he said. "You have rare dramatic talent."

She sighed. "Thank God for someone who can look higher than my legs! Are we eating?"

"We," Lester Leith assured her, "are eating."

Thereafter the reports of the two operatives, duly filed in headquarters, snowed that Lester Leith and his lady friend passed a very enjoyable evening with much laughter and dancing. He returned her to her apartment at two o'clock in the morning, refused her invitation to run up for a moment, and engaged a taxicab which took him directly to his bachelor apartment.

The shadows took up a lonely vigil over that apartment house until they were relieved at six o'clock in the morning. Lester Leith had not left the place.

In fact, Lester Leith did not even arise until after nine o'clock. At that hour a frantic ringing of the telephone brought Scuttle to the instrument. He listened in puzzled perplexity, and then tiptoed to the bedroom where Lester Leith was deep in serene slumber.

"I'm sorry to disturb you, sir, but it seems quite important." And he took Lester Leith by the shoulder, and shook him none too gently.

Lester Leith snapped his eyes open, and, for the moment, there was a frosty look of cold hostility in those eyes which sent the police spy back a step, as surely as though he had been struck with a club.

"I take it, Scuttle," said Lester Leith, speaking in close clipped accents, "that there is a fire in the apartment house."

"No, sir," said the abashed valet, "it's your job, sir. You were supposed to be on duty at eight o'clock, sir."

Lester Leith reached for a cigarette lit it. "And the time now, Scuttle?"

"Nine-fifteen, sir."

Lester Leith groaned. "The middle of the night, Scuttle, the middle of the night!"

The valet nodded.

"But there's a customer for your car, sir, and the bulldog won't let anyone come near it. They can't demonstrate it, they can't even move it."

Lester Leith nodded casually. "Ah, yes, the dog. I must get up to give the doggie a walk, Scuttle."

"Yes, sir. Mr. Booth Garner is on the phone, sir. He seems very much annoyed, sir. He says there is a young lady who actually desires to pay the price you have marked on the tag. He didn't mention the amount, sir, but I gathered from his tone that it was very much more than the car was worth. He seems eager to make the deal."

Lester Leith yawned prodigiously. "Scuttle?"

"Yes, sir."

"Present my compliments to Mr. Booth Garner, and tell him to have the young lady return at two fifteen, at which time I will demonstrate the car. In the meantime no one is to be allowed to touch it.

"And tell Mr. Garner that I am ill; that I won't be able to work until this afternoon."

"Yes, sir. If Mr. Garner asks what is the matter with you, what shall I tell him?"

"Tell him that an unexpected and unwelcome interruption has interfered with my sleeping; that I passed virtually a sleepless night. Tell him that the interruption was in the nature of an unwelcome telephone call at nine fourteen this morning, and that I'm afraid I'm not going to be able to go back to sleep. Tell him, also, Scuttle, that I requested him to go jump in the lake until two fifteen."

The valet nodded, walked from the room on tiptoes.

Lester Leith sighed, slipped from the covers, flipped the end of his cigarette into a fireplace, and engaged in setting-up exercises. Then he filled his own bath and was whistling merrily by the time the valet returned.

"He seemed most angry, sir."

"He would, Scuttle, he would. I've started the bath water, Scuttle. You may ring up Miss Rhoda Bromley, and ask her if she cares to have breakfast with me. Tell her I think we are about due to get some definite results in our case. She can come over here, if she doesn't mind, Scuttle. Tell her we'll eat in about forty-five minutes, and that I have some work upon which I would like to have her assistance.

"And telephone the hardware store and ask them to deliver the stove to the Cadillac Branch operated by Mr. Booth Garner. They'll find a car belonging to me there. They can put the stove right back of this car."

The valet nodded doubtfully.

"Yes, sir. Mr. Garner didn't sound overly cordial, sir."

"Quite right. My shaving things are ready? Very well, Scuttle, you may place the calls."

CHAPTER IX

The Stove Gets Damaged

Lester Leith worked with swift efficiency that morning, shaving himself after a cold tub in record time. He was dressed, ready for the street within less than twenty minutes.

"I am taking a run down to the garage to give my doggie a little exercise, Scuttle. I'll be back almost as soon as Miss Bromley gets here. Ask her to wait."

And Lester Leith opened the door into the outer corridor and pushed the elevator button.

In the apartment, the police spy raised the curtain and lowered it several times, signal to the waiting shadows that their quarry was about to emerge.

By the time Lester Leith gained the sidewalk, the two shadows were ready for action. Leith looked about him for a taxicab, saw none, and walked to the garage where he took out his high-powered red roadster, and gave the detectives something of a chase.

But he went exactly where he had said he was going, to the branch agency operated by Booth Garner, parked his car, and was confronted by that irate gentleman. "Well, what did you show up for? Your party's gone!"

Lester Leith nodded. "I just dropped in to exercise the dog. Being cooped up in a car all night must cramp his legs."

"Well," retorted the red-faced Mr. Garner, "nothing seems to cramp your style any!"

"No," smiled Lester Leith. "It doesn't. By the way, there's a stove to be delivered here for me. Will you see that it's put back of my automobile when it comes in?"

Garner's voice fairly dripped sarcasm.

"Yes, my lord. The stove has already arrived, and has been parked as your lordship directed. Were there any other orders you have? A stove! Perhaps you'd like to park an elephant in the garage. It's a privilege that's usually extended to salesmen."

Lester Leith yawned, shook his head. "No. No elephant, just stoves. And, by the way, Garner, do you want my services or don't you? You made a nice little profit on a deal I closed yesterday afternoon."

Garner fidgeted.

"Oh, go to it. You've got to sell a car to-day or you're out, under your own proposition."

Lester Leith nodded casually, strolled toward his car.

The bulldog wriggled his hindquarters in enthusiastic greeting. Lester Leith spoke soothingly to the dog, rubbed his hand over the back of the dog's ears, got in the car and drove from the garage.

Booth Garner watched him go with mixed emotions depicted upon his countenance.

Leith did not drive far. There were some vacant lots within a mile, and he went to them, produced a rubber ball, and for ten minutes threw the ball for the dog to retrieve. Then he returned the dog to the car and drove back to the garage and new car agency.

He had been followed every inch of the way by the detectives. His every move had been noted and written down. Later those reports would come into the desk of the puzzled Sergeant Ackley.

It was when Lester Leith was backing the car into its stall that the vehicle seemed to live up to its reputation as a hoodooed car. The car was in reverse, Leith was looking behind, slipping the clutch, when something happened.

His foot slipped off the clutch pedal. The gasoline lever caught on his coat sleeve. The car leaped backward in reverse, propelled by the powerful motor racing at top speed.

There was a crash which echoed through the garage, and then the car came to a sudden stop.

Lester Leith jumped from it. Employees of the garage ran forward. An irate manager rushed to the spot. "I'm afraid," said Lester Leith, "that I've broken my stove."

"Stove, hell!" roared Garner. "Look at that gasoline spurting out from the tank. Shut off the motor! Shut off the motor! *Shut off the motor!*"

Someone ran to the motor and shut it off. White with rage, Garner faced Lester Leith.

"You're finished. Get out and stay out. Don't ever come in this place again. Of all the supercilious, doubly damned dude fools, you take the cake!"

Lester Leith regarded the stove, broken into half a dozen pieces, the fragments squirted with gasoline. He looked at the circle of curious faces who surveyed the scene, noticed the watchful eyes of the two detectives.

"Very well," he said, meekly. "But this is my car, you know.

Can I get it repaired here? There doesn't seem to be much wrong with it except the broken gasoline tank. That tank can be soldered, can't it?"

Booth Garner laughed. "Solder that tank! You're good! Yes, my dear Mr. Leith, you are a customer here. You can get service, provided you pay for it. I will put you on a new gasoline tank for exactly fifty dollars, cash."

Lester Leith opened his wallet. "Very reasonable," he said, and handed Garner a fifty-dollar bill.

"Oh, Lord!" groaned the suffering manager, and turned to one of his shop foremen.

"Bill, get a new gasoline tank on this bus and get it out of here. Put all the men on it you need to, but get it out. Don't ever let it come back. The car's a hoodoo and the man's a hoodoo and I'm going crazy if I ain't careful!"

The foreman immediately motioned two of the men. "Get your wrenches, boys," he said.

Lester Leith took the dog, tied him to the steering wheel, and supervised the operation of changing gasoline tanks. When the new tank had been fitted into place Lester Leith picked up the old tank.

"I get credit for this?" he asked.

Booth Garner was properly sarcastic. "Oh, yes," he said, "twenty-one cents."

Lester Leith shook his head. "It's worth more than that, some junk company would give me three or four dollars for it."

"Take it then!" stormed Garner. "Take it! Put it in the back of your damned hoodooed car and get the hell out of here!"

And Lester Leith did just that, while the plain-clothes men shadowed him.

But Leith did not go directly to the junk men. Instead he drove to his apartment, leaving his red roadster parked in front of the agency. He put the car in his garage, and he left the dog in the car. Then he closed the garage doors and went to join Miss Bromley in his apartment.

"Well," she greeted him, "you're a nice one. Had an appointment with me for breakfast almost an hour ago! Got me out of my beauty sleep to meet you, and then don't show up. You're a hot sketch!"

"Had an accident," he explained. "I'm awfully sorry. It couldn't be helped, you know. I was all ready to come up here when I had some bad luck with my car. I backed into a stove I'd just purchased and smashed the stove and stove in the gasoline tank."

Her gray eyes softened with quick sympathy. "I'm sorry. I knew it was something out of the ordinary."

Leith nodded mournfully.

"And now my plans are all upset, and I got fired from the only job I ever had."

The valet interrupted. "I've made a second batch of fresh coffee and toast, sir."

"Serve it," said Lester Leith. "I'm hungry as a bear, Scuttle, and Miss Bromley must be hungry, too."

They had their breakfast, and then Lester Leith called for the dice, the vise and the drill, also the emery wheel. "Now, Miss Bromley," he explained, "I shall want your help. I'll want you to help me grind the corners off these dice. Grind them into regular shapes, and I'll turn the emery wheel. Then we'll drill holes through the center."

The actress looked at him with calm, speculative eyes. The police spy interposed a comment.

"But, sir, you can't use them if they've got the corners all ground off that way."

"On the contrary, Scuttle, I can't use them unless they are ground, and in exactly that manner."

And Lester Leith started the operation of grinding off the corners of the dice, drilling holes through the center and, last of all, threading them in a string upon the silken cord. "Now, Scuttle," he said when he had finished. "There's not the slightest question but what I own this string of dice, is there?"

"No, sir. I bought them myself."

"Thank you, Scuttle. Kindly remember that. And now, Miss Bromley. I'll take you back to your apartment. You might remember, if you will, the words of my valet, also take a good look at this string of dice so you can identify them later if the occasion requires."

The puzzled gray eyes surveyed him with cool appraisal. "I do hope you know what you're doing," she said.

Leith bowed. "Perfectly. I am taking you home in a car I purchased only last night. Just a little flier in used automobiles.

"By the way, Scuttle, we were going to warm up the cold clews in that Riggers case over the cooking stove, and now our cooking stove is smashed. Do you suppose, Scuttle, it would be possible to warm up a cold clew on a broken stove?"

The valet drew himself up with dignity.

"One doesn't warm up a cold clew over a cooking stove, sir."

"No," commented Lester Leith, mournfully, "I suppose not. Come, Miss Bromley. I'll try and think up some other method of warming over clews."

And he escorted the actress from the apartment to the garage, introduced Bobo, the bull pup to her, and drove her to her apartment.

CHAPTER X

Lester Tries to Sell a Tank

That much was determined without question when Sergeant Ackley had occasion, somewhat later in the day, to examine the reports of the shadowers, in a puzzled perplexity of mental bewilderment.

From Miss Bromley's apartment, Lester Leith went upon many aimless expeditions. He seemed, as best could be determined by those who shadowed him, to be trying to sell the stove-in gasoline tank to various junk men and secondhand dealers.

Invariably, Lester Leith took out the broken tank, exhibited it, extolled its virtues, gave it to the junk dealer to handle, seemed always about to consummate a deal until the last minute, when there would be a dispute, and the tank would again change hands.

After the fifth occasion one of the detectives left the shadowing to the other, and dropped behind to interrogate the junk dealer who had been approached.

"What's the idea of the fellow with the tank?" asked the detective, nipping back his coat.

"I knew it! I knew it!" exclaimed the excited junk man.

"Knew what?"

"That he'd escaped from a nut house. Go after him. You can catch him. He's just down the street. Lock him up. He's nutty, cuckoo, goofy!"

"But," insisted the detective, "what did he say?"

"Say? He seemed all right at first. He showed me the gasoline tank and asked if I thought it could be repaired. When I seen the hole in it and told him he'd better throw it in the junk heap for metal, he seemed to agree with me. And then, right at the last, he wanted three dollars and a half for it. It ain't worth three and a half cents. I don't know as I'd even want to give it yard room."

The detective nodded, opened his notebook and laboriously noted the conversation. Then he reported to headquarters.

In the meantime, Lester Leith continued his round of the various junk men, nor did he cease his efforts until he had made the complete rounds.

Then he started in upon the metal works and obtained various estimates for the cost of rebuilding the tank. Men told him that it would cost more than a new tank, that there would have to be welding, patching, painting.

Lester Leith nodded patiently, got figures, had the tank examined and reexamined.

These facts were also duly reported to Sergeant Ackley. About the time these reports were coming in to headquarters, Scuttle was called to the telephone.

A very angry Mr. Garner, Cadillac dealer, was on the wire. He explained that Lester Leith had an appointment to exhibit a certain used Cadillac to a young lady who wanted to buy it at a fancy price. The young lady seemed inclined to feel the agency would be responsible if she lost the deal. It happened that Lester Leith, debonair, smiling, entered the apartment while Scuttle was floundering about for excuses.

The valet-spy explained the situation briefly, and Leith waved his hand.

"Tell her to come here," he said. "Explain to Mr. Garner that I have lost interest in automobile salesmanship."

Scuttle transmitted the message, then stepped back from the telephone, rubbing his left ear. "He hung up on me, sir."

"He would," said Lester Leith. "Trade, Scuttle, is very coarsening. I find that many business men are not gentlemen."

The valet looked at him dubiously.

Leith sank into his reclining chair, crossed silken ankles, lit a cigarette and smiled. "Do you know, Scuttle, if Sergeant Ackley tries to send me another case I think I shall turn it down."

The valet leaned forward, ears perked. "Yes, sir?"

"Yes, Scuttle. In detecting crime it is necessary for a man to play a part now and again, and I have been playing a part so much in this case that it seems a relief to be myself once more."

"Yes, sir—the stove, sir? Warming up the clews, sir? That was all a little joke of yours, sir?"

The wheedling voice of the spy was calculated to wring a confession from a graven image. But Lester Leith merely smiled.

"Surely, Scuttle, you didn't think I wanted the stove to warm up a clew?"

"No, sir."

"Yet," resumed Lester Leith, a twinkle in his eye, "that is exactly what I did want the stove for."

The valet flushed. "But it was broken, sir."

"Yes, Scuttle, and the breaking was exactly what I wanted. A three-hundred-pound stove, Scuttle, parked against a concrete wall, makes a very nice obstacle to back car into. It is almost certain to smash in an automobile's gasoline tank."

The valet thought that over with his little, protruding eyes glittering with suppressed excitement. "Then you had planned on—"

Lester Leith waved a nonchalant hand. "Hold it until a little later, Scuttle. I have some things to go over in my mind before the customer for the second-hand car arrives."

And Lester Leith closed his eyes and concentrated, his lips twitching, now and again, in a smile.

Had his eyes been open he would have seen the police spy's mouth sag in puzzled wonder, suddenly snap shut with a click, and the spy himself start for the telephone, pause, study Lester Leith, and then squirm about in an ecstasy of impatience.

But Lester Leith had his eyes closed, and could not have been expected to observe the panorama of expressions upon the face of his valet—unless he was actually holding his lids so that a narrow slit of vision permitted him to spy upon the spy.

Minutes passed. The valet fidgeted. "I should go out..." he began.

"Yes, Scuttle."

"Yes, sir. There is a certain—er—matter, a bill for repairs, sir. I should take it up with the landlord "

"Use the telephone, Scuttle."

"Yes, sir, but it happens I can do so much more good with this personally ..."

But at that moment the buzzer sounded its summons, and Scuttle went to the door to admit the anxious customer who wished to purchase the secondhand car.

"Miss Edna Morgan." he announced and stood to one side.

She was in the living room even before Lester Leith could formulate the words which bid the valet show her in.

One thing could be said about Miss Edna Morgan. She would arrest attention anywhere. Her clothes served to conceal sufficient to comply with current legislation, although twenty years ago she would have been promptly arrested. A hundred years ago she would have been hanged.

Her skirt struck her legs at about the top of the stockings. It had been cut in such a manner that it emphasized that which it concealed. Her cheeks were a vivid shade of orange. Her hair glinted in the light with synthetic golden shades. The lips were full, rich and crimson.

Lester Leith arose to greet her.

"Hello," she said.

Lester Leith bowed and smiled. "It is a pleasure, Miss Morgan."

She sat down, elevated one silken knee over the other. "What's the idea of parking the bulldog in the sedan?"

Lester Leith elevated his brows. "How did you know he was there?" he asked.

For the first time the girl showed some embarrassment. Her big eyes shifted momentarily. "Why, I took a look in the garage they said was yours to see if the car was okay, and the pup nearly ate me up."

"The dog," explained Lester Leith, "is a watch dog, and I keep him in the car to keep from having the car stolen. It has rather a long history of thefts back of it, you know."

"Yeah?" said the girl, and yawned. "How much?"

"You are familiar with the price quoted, I believe."

The girl's eyes blazed. "Too damn much!" she said.

Lester Leith bowed. "Very well, then, we will withdraw the car from the market. Mr. Booth Garner has some excellent new cars. If you will use my name, he will undoubtedly show you the very best bargains the place has to offer."

She sighed. "I don't want to use your name, and I don't want a new car. I want one that's limbered up. I'm taking a long trip. Here's your price. Let's deliver the car."

CHAPTER XI

Scuttle Sees Daylight

She flipped up a casual skirt, took a wallet from the top of her stocking. Her slender fingers, the nails manicured a bright red, started counting out bank notes of hundred-dollar denominations. When she had a considerable pile spread upon her lap she paused, glanced at Lester Leith and folded up the pile.

"I've gotta be sure the car's in good condition," she said.

"Condition guaranteed," remarked Lester Leith.

"Nope. I've gotta be certain it's okay. I want to look at it."

Lester Leith arose. "Scuttle, I am going down to my garage. Perhaps you had better come along."

The valet looked puzzled.

"Miss Morgan might feel better if she were chaperoned," added Lester Leith.

The girl looked at him with lips that were parted to show the sagging jaw. "Who, me?" demanded the girl.

Lester Leith closed one eye slightly. "Come, Scuttle," he said. And the police spy, sighing reluctantly, followed them to the hall, down the elevator and to the garage.

The method used by Miss Morgan for examining a car was highly original. She looked in the radiator, peered in the flap of the side pocket on the door, walked to the gasoline tank, took a coiled wire from her vanity case, unscrewed the cap, and started fishing around.

"Looking for leaks," she explained. "There's leaks in 'em so often."

The valet fairly danced from one foot to the other in his eager anxiety.

"All right," proclaimed the young woman, "sold! Get your dog out of there, and I'll drive the car out."

"First," said Lester Leith, "we have to make out the necessary papers of transfer."

"To heck with papers of transfer," promptly observed the young woman. "I want the car. You want the coin. We're both satisfied."

"No," commented Lester Leith, "the papers have to be in order. Scuttle, run up to the apartment and get the registration slips, and better bring a pen and ink."

The valet needed no second invitation. He oozed his bulk through the door of the garage with all the eager haste of a bowl of jelly sliding off a greased plate.

He rang frantically for the elevator, gained the apartment of Lester Leith and made a dive for the closet.

His finger frantically jiggled the receiver hook on the telephone. His eyes fairly glittered as he put through a call to Sergeant Ackley at police headquarters.

"Hello, hello, sergeant, this is Beaver talking. We've overlooked the bets on that Riggers's robbery case. Yes…yes…now get this.

"The string of diamonds was in the gasoline tank on the stolen car…Sure…It's a cinch. The thief was standing by the gasoline tank with the hose in his hand when the police car came up, see? And he thought it was a pinch with no get-away. So he slipped the sparklers into the gasoline tank figuring the police would never look there, and wouldn't find the ice on him, see?

"Well, he made a get-away, and wanted the stones back. He tried to steal the car; but Leith beat him to it. He's got a frail here now who's paying ten prices for the heap. She took a wire and fished around in the gasoline tank and something rattled in there.

"Get the sketch? He's busted the tank on the car after he bought it and taken out the diamonds. Then he's stuck the string of dice he'd been working on into the new gasoline tank to fool the people that were trying to get back the diamonds. He's got her to pay about three times what the car is worth, and she wouldn't do it until she fished around in the gasoline tank."

The undercover man stopped, breathing heavily, exhausted by the very vehemence of his harangue. There was a dead silence over the telephone while Sergeant Ackley digested the information he had received.

"Listen," said Sergeant Ackley, at length. "He's already pulled it too slick for us to nab him. He's taken that old gasoline tank to every crook junk dealer in town. If we should try to pinch him he could show a jury that twenty-live people had handled that tank. Any one of the twenty-five might have copped the sparklers.

"Now the only thing for us to do is to nab him with the goods, and I've got a scheme for doing that. Here's something you didn't know. Samuel Riggers has offered a reward of seven thousand dollars for the stones, and no questions asked. I have a hunch Leith may try to claim that reward. He rang up Riggers this afternoon and promised to have the stones delivered to him if Riggers would be ready to pay over the reward in cash.

"There are two men out front. Split 'em. Get one to tail Leith and turn the other on the broad. I'm rushing two more men out there. I guess you've got the right hunch on that gasoline tank-business. It explains a lot of things.

"Now get busy there and stall around until the extra men can get there."

And Edward H. Beaver, invariably called "Scuttle" by Lester Leith because of a fancied resemblance to a pirate, proceeded to get busy as instructed. He passed on Ackley's instructions to the shadows, carried a bottle of ink and a pen to Lester Leith in the garage, and managed to drop the ink just as he was setting the bottle on the running board of the car.

He went for another bottle of ink, returned with it, only to find that he had misplaced the pen. By one expedient after another, he managed to prolong the execution of the papers for some fifteen minutes.

At the end of that time the girl lost patience. The words that came from her lips were words that would have blistered asbestos eardrums, and they had the desired effect. Scuttle became a model of efficiency. The documents of transfer were signed.

"You'll have to take me to my other car. It's parked in front of the agency."

The girl made some pointed comments to the effect that Lester Leith had secured a sufficient profit on the deal to get himself a taxicab for his errands, but Leith was obdurate. He must be taken to the place where his roadster was parked, and the girl finally gave in with very poor grace.

That break gave Scuttle another opportunity to telephone Sergeant Ackley where the couple were going. Hence, by the time they arrived at the agency, the neighborhood fairly seethed with plain-clothes men.

Lester Leith transferred his dog to his roadster, raised his hat in polite token of farewell, and drove his roadster directly to his apartment.

His every move was observed by two shadows.

On the other hand, the red-striped car was followed by no less than three police cars, one of which contained Sergeant Ackley himself. For Sergeant Ackley had suddenly got an idea.

Lester Leith parked his roadster in his garage, took his dog out for a stroll, eventually sought his apartment. His manner was that of a man who is at utter peace with the world.

"Scuttle," he said, his eyes twinkling with lazy-lidded humor, "get Miss Bromley on the line and ask her if she can come over here right away. Tell her I feel certain the police are about to clear up the Riggers robbery. I think her brother will be exonerated."

The valet would have liked to discuss the matter, but Leith silenced him with a gesture, and smoked a cigarette, blowing a series of smoke rings, watching them drift toward the ceiling. From time to time he chuckled.

CHAPTER XII

Sergeant Ackley Arrives

Fifteen minutes passed and the buzzer sounded a swift summons, two long notes and two shorts. "Let her in, Scuttle," said Leith. And he took Bobo, the bulldog in his lap, soothed his ears, and admonished him against growling at the newcomer.

Rhoda Bromley was radiant. "Really, have you solved the case?"

Lester Leith shook his head.

"Remember, I am but an amateur. I think Sergeant Ackley is the one to solve the case. I have merely given him certain clews to work on."

Scuttle cleared his throat. "You mentioned, sir, I believe, sir, that the clews in the Riggers robbery were cold clews, did you not?"

Lester Leith nodded. "Permit me to remind you, Scuttle, that I also warmed them up."

"With a cooking stove, sir?"

"With a cooking stove, Scuttle."

The valet fidgeted. "But I don't see, sir—"

"You wouldn't," interrupted Lester Leith with a frown.

Rhoda Bromley squirmed into a comfortable position in her chair like a cat rolling into a ball before a friendly fire. "But *I* don't see!" she said, petulantly.

"You will," said Lester Leith. "Ah, I believe you are about to see now!"

As he spoke, there sounded authoritative steps outside the door. There was a rattling of the doorknob, the bang of the door being thrown open, and half a dozen men came trooping into the room, their faces scowling.

Lester Leith grabbed the collar of his dog, held him back in the chair, silenced his excited barking. "Do come in, sergeant! Do come in. Do you know I rather expected you. Please pardon my not getting up, but I have to hold the dog, you know."

Sergeant Ackley strode forward, and stopped. He had intended to grab Lester Leith by the shoulder in a dramatic and none too gentle gesture of arrest. But the presence of the dog made him suddenly decide it might be better to go about the affair in a little more orderly fashion.

"He's quite all right as long as I hold him and talk to him," said Lester Leith.

Sergeant Ackley glared at the dog, and the dog returned the glare. The canine lips curled back and the white fangs glinted. Sergeant Ackley turned toward the door. "Bring 'em in," he said.

There came two uniformed police officers. With them came three persons, Edna Morgan, the flashy girl who had purchased the car, a cringing youth with pale countenance and a trembling mouth that made him appear ready to cry, and a white-haired man who stooped forward slightly, and whose lined face was gray with despair.

"Know these people?" asked Sergeant Ackley.

Lester Leith smiled at them.

"Pardon my not arising, folks; but I must hold my dog…Yes, sergeant, I know some of them. Two of the men are shadows who have been dogging my footsteps for the last few days, and the girl is a Miss Edna Morgan to whom I have recently sold a car. Nothing wrong with the title, I hope?"

Sergeant Ackley grunted.

"This here," he said, jerking his thumb toward the white-haired man, "is Samuel Riggers, the jeweler. The other one is Harry Morley, his butler."

Lester Leith smiled.

"Scuttle, find chairs as best you can. You'll pardon me not getting up, folks. You can see for yourself how the dog is acting."

The white-haired jeweler dropped into a chair. "I'm ruined," he said, "a leak from my own house! I will never live it down. The profession will scorn me, laugh at me, refuse to deal with me. The big gem exporters will go elsewhere—"

His voice trailed off into a mournful silence, and that silence was punctuated by Sergeant Ackley who ripped a string of dice from his pocket, dice that had had the corners rubbed down on an emery wheel, had been drilled and joined with silken cord.

"Ever see these before?" he demanded of Lester Leith in his best third-degree manner.

And, as he spoke, one of the members of the party dropped into a chair, took out a notebook and began a series of pothooks and lines—a shorthand reporter, under oath to take down every word Lester Leith might say, that any damaging admissions might be used against that dapper suspect.

Lester Leith yawned.

"Of course," he admitted. "They're mine."

"They were in the gasoline tank of the automobile you sold Edna Morgan!" snapped Ackley.

Leith yawned again.

"They should have been," he said. "I put them there."

"You did? You admit it?"

"Yes, yes, sergeant. Of course I admit it."

"Why," demanded Sergeant Ackley, "did you put them there?"

"I was reconstructing the scene of a criminal about to be apprehended by the police," said Lester Leith, almost dreamily. "I pretended I was standing by the gasoline tank of my car, the hose in my hand, the cap unscrewed from the tank. And I pretended these dice were valuable diamonds, and that a police car was suddenly approaching; that the police didn't have anything definite on me, but that they would search me, and that I must not let the diamonds be found.

"Do you know, sergeant, my hand moved almost automatically and shot the dice into the open gasoline tank, and then I ran."

Sergeant Ackley gazed apprehensively at the shorthand reporter. "Get it?" he asked in a hoarse whisper. The man nodded his head.

Sergeant Ackley heaved a sigh of relief. "That admission," he said, "will send you to jail."

"Dear, dear," remarked Lester Leith in the tone of a woman who has just found that a quart of milk has turned sour.

Sergeant Ackley glared at him.

"But—" Miss Bromley started to protest.

"Shut up!" yelled Ackley. "I'm running this show."

He turned to Lester Leith again, his close-set eyes burning with emotion. "So then you knew the stolen diamonds were in the gasoline tank?"

Lester Leith shook his head vigorously, smiling. "No, no, sergeant. Of course not. I only made a little experiment to determine what *I* would have done had *I* been the thief and the police had been coming for me. I didn't say that was what the thief would have done. He probably would have done something entirely different.

"But I was interested in the case. You'll remember it was you, yourself, my dear sergeant, who got me interested. I merely mention the incident of the gasoline tank to account for the manner in which the string of dice happened to get in there.

"I made that string of dice, and said to myself that I would pretend they were the stolen gems. And, do you know, sergeant, I felt almost certain the thief was some member of Mr. Riggers's domestic staff?"

Sergeant Ackley's frown deepened. "Yes?" he said. "Tell us why."

It was a part of the policy of the police department to get a witness talking and to keep him talking. As long as Lester Leith chose to keep on with his talk, he was very likely to make admissions, and Sergeant Ackley felt that he needed but very, very few admissions to give him a perfect case.

Lester Leith beamed upon them. "You'll notice," he said, "that the thief was not known to any man in the store, yet he was well known to Mr. Riggers."

"How," demanded Sergeant Ackley, interested in spite of himself, "do you figure that out?"

"Simple," beamed Lester Leith, "very simple. The thief wasn't masked when he entered the store or when he left it. Yet he wasn't recognized by any of those who saw him. But he deemed it necessary to don a mask when he was holding up the two men. That meant he was known to at least one of those men. Now Señor Jose Camulos had arrived on a boat unmolested. He knew no one in the city. Had the thief been someone who had followed him from South America, there would have been countless better opportunities for robbery on the boat or while going from the boat to his destination than existed while the parties were negotiating in Mr. Riggers's private office.

"Therefore, the thief must have been well known to Mr. Riggers—so well known, in fact, that Riggers had discussed the prospective arrival of the gems in his presence, yet be unknown to every member of the store.

"That almost forces us to suspect the servants, doesn't it, sergeant? But, of course, the idea must have occurred to you much sooner than it did to me, since you are a professional investigator and I am merely an amateur."

CHAPTER XIII

"Lester Leith, I Arrest You!"

Sergeant Ackley flushed, and lost his temper.

"All right," he stormed. "Now I'll do some talking. You figured out where the stolen necklace was. You even had your valet telephone to Mr. Petterman to find out if someone had been hanging around his garage, or trying to get the car. You found out such was the case, and immediately bought the car.

"And you doped out what had happened. Harry Morley is an ex-con. He did a stretch for automobile stealing. He got out and went to work for Riggers. But he wanted to joy ride. He had Edna Morgan, the moll with the champagne appetite. So he started stealing, or rather borrowing, Petterman's car. He had been able to find the keys in the car one day, and had had duplicates made. Petterman lived within a few blocks of where Riggers lived, and it was all simple.

"Morley used the car a dozen times without Petterman even knowing the car had been taken and returned. Then, when he had to pull a theft and wanted a car, what more natural than that he steal the car again?

"He had heard Riggers discussing this necklace over the telephone, and thought how slick it would be to rush in, grab the stones, and rush out, jump in his stolen car, return it to where he had found it, lock it all up with his duplicate key, and duck into Riggers's house and go back to work, the same as though nothing had happened.

"But the police stumbled on him. He tossed the gems in the gasoline and escaped. Then he wanted the car. He tried to steal it again and couldn't.

"Then Lester Leith, the super crook enters the picture. He dopes out where the gems are, buys the car, gets a watchdog so no one can sneak up and empty the gasoline tank and fish out the sparklers without his being there.

"Then he gets a big stove, parks it where he can stave in the automobile tank on it, and goes ahead and does it, takes the old tank off and puts a new-one on. Then he works a little slick confidence game to make the thief loosen up with a fancy price for the car and get some more easy money. He drops the dice into the gas tank—the new one he's put on the car.

"Morley sends his frail to buy the car. She runs a wire around inside the gasoline tank, catches onto the dice and so thinks it's safe to pay a fancy price for the car. Leith sells it to her, has the diamonds, the big price for a used car, and thinks he's covered his tracks.

"But you can't fool the police department all of the time. The boys ain't so dumb as they're supposed to be. We got wise, trailed the Morgan woman until she contacted Morley. Then, when they fished the dice from the tank we swooped down on 'em, caught 'em red-handed, and got confessions from both of them.

"That's the case we've got against you, Leith. You can figure it out. It's circumstantial, of course, but you know what a jury will do.

"Have you got anything to say? If you don't make a statement, your silence will be taken as an admission. If you do say anything, it can be used against you!"

And Sergeant Ackley yanked a cigar from his pocket, ripped off the end with his fanglike teeth, spat it explosively and scraped a match across the sole of his shoe.

Sergeant Arthur Ackley was enjoying this moment very, very much indeed.

Lester Leith took one hand from the dog's collar, took a cigarette from the case on the table, smiled, lit the cigarette and sent twin streamers of smoke from his dilated nostrils.

The smile became a grin. The grin became a chuckle.

"Well!" yelled Sergeant Ackley.

"It's all very simple," said Lester Leith, suppressing his continued chuckles with difficulty. "I had no idea the necklace was in the gasoline tank. As proof of that fact, your own men will have to admit that I tried to sell that tank all over town for as much as three dollars.

"When I couldn't get a sale at that price I became disgusted. I had rather throw the thing away than sell it at an absurdly low price, and I drove out the river road until I came to a pile of old junk and threw the gasoline tank on the pile.

"Your own men were continually shadowing me, sergeant. They saw me do that."

Sergeant Ackley snorted, rolled his cigar in his puffy lips and finally clamped it at an aggressive angle with the yellow, horse-like teeth.

"Yes, after you'd emptied it of the gems. You had a six-inch hole in that tank. Simple for you to reach your hand in and pull out the jewels."

Lester Leith shrugged his shoulders.

"That, of course, is something for you to prove before a jury. You'll have to show it by some sort of evidence, not by mere conjecture. If my hand would have fitted into that hole in the gasoline tank and pulled out the diamonds, the hands of twenty-five junk dealers would have fitted through the same hole. And the twenty-five junk dealers had equal opportunity to do that very thing."

That was the weak point in Sergeant Ackley's case, and he knew it. But he wouldn't admit it. He reached in his holster, took out his ugly, blued steel revolver.

"Lester Leith, I arrest you in the name of the law. I am about to put handcuffs on you. If that dog shows any hostility, I shall shoot the dog. If you show any resistance or attempt to encourage the dog in any way, I shall shoot you!"

And Sergeant Ackley got up from his chair.

Lester Leith held up a hand.

"Just a minute, sergeant," he said, and then turned toward Samuel Riggers.

"Mr. Riggers, you offered a reward of seven thousand dollars for the return of those diamonds. Is that offer still open?"

For the first time since he had entered the room, a gleam of hope came into the gray eyes of the white-haired man.

"Make it eight thousand," he said. "The diamonds are worth a lot of money, but my reputation is at stake. If I can't recover those gems I am ruined. If I get them back I can still continue in business."

Lester Leith nodded.

"Will you promise in writing to pay me seven thousand dollars if I tell you exactly where those diamonds are, and you can recover them from that place?"

The man nodded his eager acquiescence.

Sergeant Ackley held back.

"Leith," he warned, "all I need to make a perfect case against you is to show that you have those diamonds in your possession. Perhaps, knowing everything is lost, you want to raise some money. If so, that's all right, but I've warned you what the effect of your admission will be."

Lester Leith sighed. "Yes, oh, yes," he said, almost casually, "but I want the reward. I'll tell—as soon as Mr. Riggers gets his offer in writing. Be sure, Mr. Riggers, to make it conditioned upon the fact that I furnish the information that will tell you where the gems are, and that you can go to that place and get them.

"I fancy Sergeant Ackley will deprive me of my liberty temporarily, so that I can't actually hand them to you."

Samuel Riggers was scribbling on the leaf of a notebook. He glanced sharply at Sergeant Ackley,

"You haven't any idea where they are, sergeant?"

Ackley shook his head in ponderous negation.

"I have reason to believe they're not on him or in the apartment. Our spy system tells us that. He's probably got 'em in some safe deposit box under an assumed name. He's clever as hell at ditching the swag, once he's copped it."

Riggers nodded, glanced at Morley, his disgraced butler. "Morley, you're sunk anyway. If you knew, I feel certain you'd tell me."

Morley sighed, a tremulous sigh. "Honest, Mr. Riggers, I thought they were in the gasoline tank where I slipped 'em. When we fished out that string of dice you could have knocked me over with a feather."

Samuel Riggers signed his name, passed over the sheet of paper. "Here you are, sir."

"Thanks," said Lester Leith, "the diamonds are in a wrecked gasoline-tank, and the gasoline tank lies on top of a pile of junk about two miles out on the river road, at the city dumping ground."

And he folded the paper and put it in his pocket.

The announcement was received in utter silence. Had Lester Leith suddenly vanished into thin air the consternation of his spectators could not have been more complete.

"Fat chance!" said Ackley, after he was able to get his breath. "You wouldn't have been dumb enough to carry around a string of diamonds in a gasoline tank and offer 'em to every junk dealer in town for three bucks. *You* wouldn't have been foolish enough to let a hundred-thousand-dollar string of diamonds slip through your fingers!"

But his tone failed to carry conviction. It was plain that Sergeant Ackley, himself, was dazed as he saw his carefully planned case going to pieces.

But Samuel Riggers, his mind trained in the ways of business, grasped the situation more quickly than the others.

"Not so dumb as you think, sergeant," he snapped. "You have sat by and let this man trap me into a promise by which I have to pay seven thousand dollars in return for information which you would already have had if you hadn't been so eager to suspect him of criminal intentions. The place he mentions is the one place where the diamonds could be and absolutely prove his innocence, the very place they would be in if your charges were false, and if he was telling the plain, unvarnished truth. And he capitalizes that fact to the tune of seven thousand dollars of legitimate money."

Sergeant Ackley abruptly sat down. "But—but—" he stammered. "You had the gasoline tank in your hands!"

Lester Leith smiled. One of the policemen actually snickered out loud.

"The fact that I carelessly threw the diamonds away without even knowing they were in the tank until I heard Morley's confession, is sufficient proof of my innocence. It absolutely proves *my* good faith."

Samuel Riggers got to his feet.

"Come on," he snapped at Sergeant Ackley. "Let's go get the diamonds before some more of your fool suspicions lets them slip through my fingers. This man has proved his good faith…also his diabolical cleverness.

"Mr. Leith, if you ever want to turn your intellectual talents to business pursuits, I shall deem it a pleasure to have you call upon me."

And Samuel Riggers stalked toward the door.

Sergeant Ackley was muttering to himself. Here and there a sentence was eligible to the cars of his audience. "… seven thousand dollars…proves we were mistaken about young Carl Bromley… leaves 'em in the one place on God's green earth where they could be found without convicting him of crime…*Damn!*"

Lester Leith called to him as he went through the door. "By the way, sergeant, this should be a good lesson to you not to browbeat witnesses into identifications. Unless the police had insisted and brought pressure to bear, none of the witnesses would have identified Carl Bromley as the man you wanted…and don't slam the door as you go out!"

Sergeant Ackley paused on the threshold. His hands were clenching and unclenching. His face was distorted with rage. He heard, as he-paused, the voice of Rhoda Bromley.

"Mr. Leith, you'd better take both hands to hold that bull-dog with, because I'm coming over there and kiss you!"

And then Sergeant Arthur Ackley banged the door with a terrific bang that threatened to crack the plaster.

Bibliography

All stories and books were written by Erie Stanley Gardner.

The Case of the Murderer's Bride and Other Stories, edited by Ellery Queen. New York: Davis (Ellery Queen Presents 1) 1969. Marked in the bibliography as MB.

The Case of the Crying Swallow, A Perry Mason Novelette and Other Stories. New York: William Morrow, n.d. [1971]. Marked in the bibliography as CS.

The Case of the Irate Witness, A Perry Mason Mystery and Other Stories. New York: William Morrow, n.d. [1972]. Marked in the bibliography as Irate.

The Amazing Adventures of Lester Leith, edited by Ellery Queen. New York: Davis (Ellery Queen Presents 1) 1980/1981. Marked in the bibliography as EQP.

The Bird in the Hand and Four Other Stories. Roslyn, NY: Published by the Ellery Queen's Mystery Club by Walter J. Black Inc., n.d. [1980]. Marked in the bibliography as EQMC.

Hot Cash, Cold Clews. Cincinnati, OH: Crippen & Landru Publishers, 2020. Marked in the bibliography as C&L.

Bibliography of Lester Leith Stories

"A Deal in Cement," *Detective Fiction Weekly*. July 30, 1932.

"A Hot Tip," *Detective Fiction Weekly*. May 11, 1929.

"A Peach of a Scheme," *Detective Fiction Weekly*. July 20, 1929.

"A Sock on the Jaw," *Detective Fiction Weekly*. ND. ***

"A Sugar Coating," *Detective Fiction Weekly*. November 29, 1941.

"A Thousand to One," *Detective Fiction Weekly*. October 28, 1939. EQ

"A Tip from Scuttle," *Detective Fiction Weekly*. March 2, 1929. C&L, EQMC

"Bald-Headed Row," *Detective Fiction Weekly*. March 21, 1936.

"Big Money," *Detective Fiction Weekly*. April 18, 1931.

"Both Ends Against the Middle," *Detective Fiction Weekly*. May 3, 1930.

"Caws and Effect," *Flynn's Detective Fiction Weekly*. July, 1943.

"Closer than a Brother," *Detective Fiction Weekly*. July 9, 1932.

"Cold Clews," *Detective Fiction Weekly*. January 24, 1931. C&L.

"Crocodile Tears," *Detective Fiction Weekly*. June 10, 1934.

"Crooks' Vacation," *Detective Fiction Weekly.* July 8, 1933.
"Dead to Rights," *Detective Fiction Weekly.* June 2, 1934.
"Double Shadows," *Detective Fiction Weekly.* September 21, 1929.
"Even Money," *Detective Fiction Weekly.* August 3, 1929.
"Fair Exchange," *Detective Fiction Weekly.* November 18, 1939.
"False Alarm," *Detective Fiction Weekly.* November 5, 1932.
"Faster than Forty," *Detective Fiction Weekly.* August 31, 1929.
"Hot Cash," *Detective Fiction Weekly.* May 23, 1931. C&L
"Hot Dollars!," *Detective Fiction Weekly.* July 26, 1930.
"In Round Figures," *Detective Fiction Weekly.* August 23, 1930.
    EQP, EQMC
"It's a Pipe!," *Detective Fiction Weekly.* August 10, 1929.
"Juggled Gems," *Detective Fiction Weekly.* December 24, 1932.
"Lester Frames a Fence," *Detective Fiction Weekly.* December 13,
    1930
"Lester Leith, Magician," *Detective Fiction Weekly.* September 16,
    1939. EQP
"Lester Takes the Cake," *Detective Fiction Weekly.* November 23,
    1929. C&L
"Lost, Strayed and Stolen," *Detective Fiction Weekly.* February 24,
    1934.
"Monkeyshine," *Detective Fiction Weekly.* March 16, 1940.
"Not So Dumb," *Detective Fiction Weekly.* June 27, 1931.
"One Jump Ahead," *Detective Fiction Weekly.* February 4, 1933.
"Planted Planets," *Detective Stories* December, 1938.
"Put it in Writing!," *Detective Fiction Weekly.* June 7, 1930. C&L
"Queens Wild," *Detective Fiction Weekly.* January 26, 1935.
"Red Herring," *Detective Fiction Weekly.* December 26, 1931.
"Rolling Stones," *Detective Fiction Weekly.* November 21, 1931.
"Screaming Sirens," *Detective Fiction Weekly.* November 2, 1935.
"Something Like a Pelican," *Flynn's.* January 1, 1943. Irate
"Sugar," *Detective Fiction Weekly.* January 20, 1940.
"The Artistic Touch," *Detective Fiction Weekly.* October 26, 1929.
"The Bird in the Hand," *Detective Fiction Weekly.* April 9, 1932.
    EQP, EQMC
"The Burden of Proof," *Detective Fiction Weekly.* December 2,
    1933.
"The Candy Kid," *Detective Fiction Weekly.* March 14, 1931. MB
"The Case of the Fugitive Corp," *Detective Fiction Weekly.* April 6,
    1929.
"The Crimson Mask," *Detective Fiction Weekly.* November 7, 1931.
"The Doubtful Egg," *Detective Fiction Weekly.* January 11, 1930.
"The Dummy Murder," *Detective Fiction Weekly.* March 23, 1929.
"The Exact Opposite," *Detective Fiction Weekly.* March 29, 1941.
    EQP, EQMC

"The Fourth Musketeer," *Detective Stories*. March 1, 1939.

"The Girl with the Diamond Legs," *Detective Fiction Weekly*. July 11, 1931. C&L

"The Gold Magnet," *Detective Fiction Weekly*. September 26, 1931.

"The Man on the End," *Detective Fiction Weekly*. September 27, 1930.

"The Monkey Murder," *Detective Stories*. January 1, 1939. EQMC

"The Painted Decoy," *Detective Fiction Weekly*. February 23, 1929.

"The Pay-off," *Detective Fiction Weekly*. April 27, 1929.

"The Play's the Thing," *Detective Fiction Weekly*. February 27, 1932.

"The Queen of Shanghai Night," *Detective Stories*. May 1939.

"The Radio Ruse," *Detective Fiction Weekly*. April 1, 1933.

"The Ring of Fiery Eyes," *Detective Stories*. August 1939.

"The Seven Sinister Sombreros," *Detective Stories*. February 1939.

"Thieves' Kitchen," *Detective Fiction Weekly*. June 4, 1932. C&L

"Thin Ice," *Detective Fiction Weekly*. June 10, 1933.

"With Rhyme and Reason," *Detective Stories*. April 1939.

*** This story was listed as published by Gardner's secretaries and was included in the Hughes' biography of Gardner, but insufficient publication information was provided to give a clear indication if this entry was correct.

HOT CASH, COLD CLEWS

Hot Cash, Cold Clews by Erle Stanley Gardner is printed on 60 pound paper, and is designed by Jeffrey Marks using InDesign. The type is Palatino Linotype, a old-style serif typeface designed by Hermann Zapf in 1949. The printing and binding is by Southern Ohio Printers and Cincinnati Bindery for the hard cover and the trade paperback version. The book was published in July 2020 by Crippen & Landru Publishers, Inc., Cincinnati, OH.